Praise for Chloe Neill's
Chicagoland Vampires Novels

Twice Bitten

"The pages turn fast enough to satisfy vampire and romance fans alike." —*Booklist*

"Neill's briskly paced third Chicagoland Vampires paranormal romance . . . will satisfy returning fans. Merit's frequently snarky voice and amusing observations about the occasional absurdities of her situation combine with the magic of Neill's world in a refreshing take on urban fantasy." —*Publishers Weekly*

"Neill continues to hit the sweet spot with her blend of high-stakes drama, romantic entanglements, and a touch of humor . . . certain to whet readers' appetites for more in this entertaining series!" —*Romantic Times* (4½ stars)

Friday Night Bites

"*Friday Night Bites* is wonderfully entertaining and impossible to set down." —Darque Reviews

"Proving that her debut was no fluke . . . this qualifies as first-rate fun!" —*Romantic Times*

Some Girls Bite

"Neill creates a strong-minded, sharp-witted heroine who will appeal to fans of Charlaine Harris's Sookie Stackhouse series and Laurell K. Hamilton's Anita Blake." —*Library Journal*

continued . . .

D0110107

"[With] the story's fast-paced plotline, entertaining characters, and lingering mysteries, I can just about guarantee that readers will want to read more of this series. *Some Girls Bite* is recommended reading for urban fantasy fans who shouldn't fail to be pleased with its vampire protagonist and the plethora of supernatural creatures that it introduces to modern day Chicago. Vampire fiction fans should be well served by this vamp-centric story too." —LoveVampires

"There's a fresh new voice in paranormal and that voice belongs to author Chloe Neill. . . . I was very happy to pick up a book that made me want to turn the pages. The author has created an interesting vampire mythology and a heroine who has spunk and daring; she's kick-ass without the hard edges." —Romance Novel TV

"Hands down, this is one of the best urban fantasy/paranormal romance novels that I've ever read. What makes this even more remarkable is that this is not only the first in a series, and therefore has to spend more time on laying the groundwork, but it's also a debut novel for author Neill. . . . She's created a unique vampire tale in a genre that's flush with look-alikes." —Undercover Book Lover (Not Really)

"This debut novel by Chloe Neill is not only action-packed—it's hilarious. I couldn't put it down; I finished it in hours and jumped online right away to see when book two was out. . . . [Merit is] extremely charming . . . a great read." —Wicked Little Pixie

"I didn't want to put it down . . . excellently written. . . . [*Some Girls Bite*] brings a fresh perspective on the vampire craze that is going around these days. The book has a little bit of Harry Potter in it, a little bit of the Southern Vampire Mysteries in it, but with a voice and perspective all its own. No offense to the *Twilight* fans out there, but the writing from Chloe Neill is IMMENSELY better than that from Stephenie Meyer. I just really enjoyed the book and I am very much looking forward to *Friday Night Bites*. If you are a fan of vampire novels, I think you should give this one a try. I loved it entirely and am now very anxious to read more from Ms. Neill." —Pink Is the New Blog

A CHICAGOLAND VAMPIRES NOVEL

DRINK DEEP

✦

CHLOE NEILL

NEW AMERICAN LIBRARY

NEW AMERICAN LIBRARY
Published by New American Library, a division of
Penguin Group (USA) Inc., 375 Hudson Street,
New York, New York 10014, USA
Penguin Group (Canada), 90 Eglinton Avenue East, Suite 700, Toronto,
Ontario M4P 2Y3, Canada (a division of Pearson Penguin Canada Inc.)
Penguin Books Ltd., 80 Strand, London WC2R 0RL, England
Penguin Ireland, 25 St. Stephen's Green, Dublin 2,
Ireland (a division of Penguin Books Ltd.)
Penguin Group (Australia), 250 Camberwell Road, Camberwell, Victoria 3124,
Australia (a division of Pearson Australia Group Pty. Ltd.)
Penguin Books India Pvt. Ltd., 11 Community Centre, Panchsheel Park,
New Delhi - 110 017, India
Penguin Group (NZ), 67 Apollo Drive, Rosedale, Auckland 0632,
New Zealand (a division of Pearson New Zealand Ltd.)
Penguin Books (South Africa) (Pty.) Ltd., 24 Sturdee Avenue,
Rosebank, Johannesburg 2196, South Africa

Penguin Books Ltd., Registered Offices:
80 Strand, London WC2R 0RL, England

First published by New American Library,
a division of Penguin Group (USA) Inc.

First Printing, November 2011
10 9 8 7 6 5 4 3 2 1

REGISTERED TRADEMARK—MARCA REGISTRADA

Library of Congress Cataloging-in-Publication Data:

Neill, Chloe.
Drink deep: a Chicagoland vampires novel/Chloe Neill.
p. cm.—Chicagoland vampires; 5
ISBN 978-0-451-23486-5 (pbk.)
1. Merit (Fictitious character: Neill)—Fiction. 2. Vampires—Fiction.
3. Chicago (Ill.)—Fiction. I. Title.
PS3614.E4432D75   2011
813'.6—dc22   2011026918

Set in Caslon 540

Printed in the United States of America

To Jeremy, with love.
(Now can I borrow twenty dollars?)

ACKNOWLEDGMENTS

I have a wonderful team of people who helped with the writing. Some suggested a phrase, some kept me sane when the writing got tough. Jessica, my editor, and Lucienne, my agent, provided invaluable advice. Marcel and Laurence (and undoubtedly others) translated Merit's adventures overseas. Sara kept the Meritverse consistent from novel to novel. Kevin, Brent, and Miah assisted with magical and military strategy. Krista and Lisa kept order in the Meritverse Forums (http://forums.chloeneill.com) so I could keep the word count flowing.

Thanks as always to Team Eel, the readers who encourage me with their kind notes and generosity, and keep reading Merit's adventures. Without you, there would be no Merit.

"A little learning is a dangerous thing;
drink deep, or taste not the Pierian spring. . . ."
—*Alexander Pope*

DRINK DEEP

❖❖❖

CHAPTER ONE

GRAVITATIONALLY CHALLENGED

Late November
Chicago, Illinois

The wind was cool, the fall night crisp. A waxing moon hung lazily in the sky, so low it seemed close enough to touch.

Or maybe it just seemed that way because I was perched nine stories in the air, atop a narrow metal grate that crowned Chicago's Harold Washington Library. One of the library's distinctive aluminum owls—either one of the best architectural features in the city or one of its worst, depending on who you asked—sat above me, staring down as I trespassed in his domain.

This was one of the few times I'd ventured outside my Hyde Park home in the last two months for a reason unrelated to food—it was Chicago, after all—or my best friend Mallory. As I glanced over the edge of the building, I began to seriously regret that decision. The library wasn't exactly a skyscraper, but it was tall enough that a fall would most certainly have killed a human.

My heart jumped into my throat, and every muscle in my body rang with the urge to kneel down, grasp the edges of the grate, and never let go.

"It's not as far as it looks, Merit."

I glanced over at the vampire who stood to my right. Jonah, the one who'd convince me to come out here, chuckled and brushed auburn hair back from his perfectly chiseled face.

"It's far enough," I said. "And this wasn't exactly what came to mind when you suggested I get some fresh air."

"Maybe not. But you can't deny the view is fabulous."

My white-knuckled fingers digging into the wall behind me, I looked out across the city. He was right—you couldn't fault the intimate view of downtown Chicago, of steel and glass and well-hewn stone.

But, "I could have looked out the window," I pointed out.

"Where's the challenge in that?" he asked, and then his voice softened. "You're a vampire," he reminded me. "Gravity affects you differently."

He was right. Gravity treated us a little more kindly. It helped us fight with more verve and, so I'd heard, fall from a height without killing ourselves. But that didn't mean I was eager to test the theory. Not when the result could be bone-crushingly bad.

"I swear," he said, "if you follow instructions, the fall won't hurt you."

Easy for him to say. Jonah had decades more vampiric experience under his belt; he had less to be nervous about. To me, immortality had never seemed so fragile.

I blew the dark bangs from my face and peeked over the edge one more time. State Street was far below us, mostly deserted at this time of night. At least I wouldn't crush someone if this didn't work.

"You have to learn to fall safely," he said.

"I know," I said. "Catcher trained me to spar. He was big on falling down correctly." Catcher was my former roommate and best friend Mallory's live-in beau. He was also an employee of my grandfather.

"Then you know being immortal doesn't mean being careless," Jonah added, extending a hand toward me, and my heart jumped, this time as much from the gesture as the height.

I'd put myself—and my heart—on a shelf for the last two months, my work as Sentinel of Chicago's Cadogan House mostly limited to patrolling the House's grounds. I could admit it—I was gun-shy. My newfound vampire bravery had mostly evaporated after the Master of my House, Ethan Sullivan, the vampire who'd made me, named me Sentinel, and been my partner, had been staked in the heart by my mortal enemy . . . right before I'd returned the favor to her.

As a former grad student in English literature, I could appreciate the perverse poetry of it.

Jonah, captain of the guards in Grey House, was my link to the Red Guard, a secret organization dedicated to providing oversight to the American vampire Houses and the Greenwich Presidium, the European council that ruled them from across the pond.

I'd been offered membership in the RG, and Jonah was the partner I'd been promised if I'd accepted. I hadn't, but he'd been nice enough to help me deal with problems GP politics made too sticky for Ethan.

Jonah had been more than happy to act as Ethan's replacement—professionally and otherwise. The messages we'd exchanged over the last few weeks—and the hope in his eyes tonight—said he was interested in something more than just supernatural problem-solving.

There was no denying Jonah was handsome. Or charming. Or brilliant in a weirdly quirky way. Honestly, he could have starred in his own romantic comedy. But I wasn't ready to even think about dating again. I didn't think I would be any time soon. My heart was otherwise engaged, and since Ethan's death, mostly broken.

Jonah must have seen the hesitation in my eyes. He smiled kindly, then pulled back his hand and pointed toward the edge.

"Remember what I told you about jumping? This is the same as taking a step."

He'd definitely said that. Two or three times now. I just wasn't buying. "It's a really, really long step."

"It is," Jonah agreed. "But it's only the first step that sucks. Being in the air is one of the greatest things you'll ever experience."

"Better than being safely on the ground?"

"Much. More like flying—except we don't do 'up' nearly as well as we do 'down.' This is your chance to be a superhero."

"They do call me the 'Ponytailed Avenger,'" I grumbled, flipping my long dark ponytail. The *Chicago Sun-Times* had deemed me a "Ponytailed Avenger" when I'd helped a shifter in a bar attack. Since I usually wore my hair in a ponytail to keep it away from the errant katana strike (my bangs not included), the name kind of stuck.

"Has anyone ever told you you're particularly sarcastic when you're scared?"

"You're not the first," I admitted. "I'm sorry. I'm just—this is freaking me out. There is nothing in my body or mind that thinks jumping off a building is a good idea."

"You'll be fine. The fact that it scares you is reason number one to do it."

Or reason number one to turn tail and run back to Hyde Park.

"Trust me," he said. "Besides, this is a skill you need to master," Jonah said. "Malik and Kelley need you."

Kelley was a former House guard now in charge of the House's entire guard corps. Unfortunately, since we were now down to three full-time guards (including Kelley) and a Sentinel, that wasn't exactly a coup for her.

Malik was Ethan's former second in command, Master of the House since Ethan's demise. He'd taken the Rights of Investiture, and the House had been given to his keeping.

Ethan's death had sparked a nasty case of vampire musical chairs.

As a Master, Malik Washington had gotten back his last name; Masters of the country's twelve vampire Houses were the only vamps allowed to use them. Unfortunately, Malik had also gotten the House's political drama, which had thickened since Ethan's death. Malik worked tirelessly, but had to spend most of his time dealing with the newest bane of our existence.

Said bane was Franklin Theodore Cabot, the appointed receiver of Cadogan House. When Darius West, head of the GP, had decided he didn't like the way the House was run, "Frank" had been sent to Chicago to inspect and evaluate the House. The GP said they were concerned Ethan hadn't effectively managed the House—but that was a total lie, and they'd wasted no time sending the receiver to check our rooms, our books, and our files. I wasn't exactly sure what data Frank was looking for—and why so much interest in a House an entire ocean away?

Whatever the reason, Frank wasn't a good houseguest. He was obnoxious, autocratic and a stickler for rules I hadn't even known existed to the exclusion of everything else. Of course, I was becoming pretty well acquainted with them; Frank had papered one wall of the House's first floor with the new House rules and the punishments that went along with breaking them. The system was necessary, he'd said, because House discipline had been lackadaisical.

Maybe not surprisingly, I had taken an immediate dislike to Frank, and not just because he was a blue-blooded Ivy League business school graduate with a penchant for phrases like "synergy" and "out of the box thinking." He'd salted his introductory comments to the House with those words, offering up the not-so-subtle threat that the House would be taken over by the GP on a permanent basis—or disbanded—if he wasn't satisfied with what he found.

I'd been fortunate enough to come from a family of means, and there were other vampires in the House who had old money backgrounds. But it was Frank's attitude of entitlement that really irked me. The man wore deck shoes, for God's sake. And he was most definitely *not* on a boat. In reality, despite the role he'd been given by the GP, he was actually a Novitiate vampire (if a wealthy one) from a House on the east coast. A House, granted, that had been founded by a Cabot ancestor, but which had long since been given over to another Master.

Worse, Frank spoke to us like he was a member of the House, as if his money and connections were a passport to status within Cadogan. Frank playing at House membership was even more ridiculous since his entire purpose was to itemize the ways we weren't following the party line. He was an outsider sent to label us as nonconforming and pound us, square pegs, back into round holes.

Out of concern for the House and respect for the chain of command, Malik had given him the run of the House. He figured Frank was a battle he couldn't win, so he was saving up his political capital for another round.

Whatever the drama, Frank was back in Hyde Park. I was here, in the Loop, with an ersatz vampire partner determined to teach me how to jump from a building without killing someone . . . or pushing myself beyond the limits of immortality.

I looked over the edge again, my stomach curdling with it. I was torn by dueling urges to drop to my knees and crawl back to the stairs and to hurl myself over the edge.

But then he spoke the words most likely to get me moving.

"Dawn will be here eventually, Merit."

The myth about vampires and sunlight was true—if I was still on this roof when the sun rose, I'd burn up into a pile of ash.

"You have two options," Jonah said. "You can trust me and try this, or you can climb back through the roof, go home, and never know what you might be capable of."

He held out his hand. "Trust me," he said. "And keep your knees soft when you land."

It was the certainty in his eyes that did it—the confidence that I could achieve the goal. Once upon a time, I'd have seen suspicion in his gaze. Jonah hadn't been a fan when we'd first met. But circumstances had forced us together, and whatever his initial doubts, he'd apparently learned to trust me.

Now was a good time to make good on that trust.

I held out my hand and death-gripped his fingers in mine. "Soft knees," I repeated.

"You only have to take a step," he said.

I looked over at him, ready to "Roger" my agreement. But before I could open my mouth, he winked and took a step, pulling me along with him. Before I could protest, we were airborne.

The first step was bone-chillingly awful—the sudden sensation of the ground—and our security—disappearing beneath us, a sickening lurch that flipped my stomach and shuddered through my entire body. My heart jumped into my throat, although that at least kept me from screaming out a bubble of fear.

But that's when it got good.

After the nasty initial drop (*really* nasty—I can't stress that enough), the rest of the journey wasn't much like falling at all. It felt more like hopping down a staircase—if the distance between each tread was a lot longer. I couldn't have been in the air for more than three or four seconds, but time actually seemed to slow down, the city decelerating around me as I took a step to the ground. I hit the ground in a crouch, one hand on the sidewalk, with no more impact than if I'd simply jumped up.

My transition to vampire had been scattershot, and my abilities had come "online" slowly enough that it still surprised me when I was able to do something the first time around. This move would have killed me a year ago, but now it left me feeling kind of invigorated. Jumping nine stories to the ground without a broken bone or bruise? That was a home run in my book.

"You've got hops," Jonah said.

I glanced over at him through my bangs. "That was phenomenal."

"I told you it would be."

I stood up and straightened the hem of my leather jacket. "You did tell me. But the next time you throw me off a building, I will bring the pain."

He smiled teasingly, which made my heart flutter uncomfortably. "In that case, I *think* we have a deal."

"You 'think'? You couldn't just agree not to throw me off a building?"

"What fun would that be?" Jonah asked, then turned and headed down the street. I let him get a few paces ahead before following behind, that teasing look he'd given me still in mind.

And I'd thought the first step off the roof had been nerve-wracking.

Cadogan House was located in Hyde Park, a subdivision south of downtown Chicago. It was also home to the University of Chicago, whose grad school I'd been attending when I'd been made a vampire. Ethan had changed me, beginning my transformation only seconds after I'd been attacked by a rogue vamp—one not tied to a particular House—sent by Celina Desaulniers. She was the narcissistic vamp I'd staked just moments after Ethan had been killed; she'd sent the rogue to kill me to piss off my father. As I'd later discovered, my real estate–peddling father had offered Ethan money to make me a vampire. Ethan declined the offer, and Celina had been miffed by my father's refusal to make the same offer to her.

The girl was a piece of work.

Anywho, Ethan named me Sentinel of the House. To help protect the House, and to avoid listening to Mallory's midnight (and noon . . . and six a.m. . . . and six p.m.) romantic escapades with Catcher, I moved into Cadogan.

The House had all the basics—kitchen, workout room, an Operations Room where guards kept an eye on the House, and dormlike rooms for about ninety of the three hundred Cadogan vampires. My room was on the second floor. It wasn't huge and it wasn't lush, but it was a respite from the drama of being a vampire in Chicago. It had a bed, bookcase, closet, and small bathroom. Plus, it was just down the hall from a kitchen loaded with junk food and bagged blood provided by our awfully named delivery service, Blood4You.

I parked my orange Volvo a few blocks up, then hiked back to the House. It glowed in the darkness of Hyde Park, new security floodlights—installed when the House was renovated after an attack by growly shape-shifters—pouring across the grounds. The neighbors groused about the floodlights until they considered the consequences of *not* having them—the protection darkness would afford supernatural trespassers.

The House was relatively quiet tonight, a band of protesters snuggled into blankets on the grass between the sidewalk and the wrought iron gate that surrounded the House. Their numbers were down from the masses that had swarmed the grass before Mayor Tate had been stripped of his office, arraigned, and imprisoned in an undisclosed location. The change in leadership had calmed down the city's voters.

Unfortunately, it hadn't calmed down the politicians. Diane Kowalczyk, the woman who'd replaced Tate, had her eye on the oval office, and she was using Chicago's supernaturals to prop up her future campaign. She was a big supporter of the proposed supernatural registration law, which would require all sups to register our powers and carry identification papers. We'd also have to check in every time we entered or left the state.

Most sups hated the idea. It was antithetical to being American, and it sang of discrimination. Sure, some of us were dangerous, but that was true of humans, as well. Would human Chicagoans have supported a law that required them to prove their identity to anyone who asked? I doubted it.

The humans who'd decided we were all untrustworthy dedicated their evenings to letting us know just how much they hated us. Sadly, some of the protestors were beginning to look familiar. In particular, I recognized a young couple—a boy and girl who couldn't have been more than sixteen, and who'd once chanted hateful words at me and Ethan.

Yes, I had fangs. Daylight was lethal, as were aspen stakes and beheadings. Blood was a necessity, but so were chocolate and diet soda. I wasn't undead; I just wasn't human. So I'd decided that if I acted normal and was polite, I could slowly challenge their preconceptions about vampires.

Chicago's Houses also were getting better about challenging misinformation. There was even a bulletin board in Wrigleyville with a picture of four diverse, smiling vampires beneath the words COME ON OVER! The billboard was supposed to be an invitation to get to know Chicago's Houses. Tonight, it was a reason for forlorn-looking teenagers to wield hand-painted COME ON OVER—AND DIE! posters.

I smiled politely as I passed them, then held up the two gingham bags of burgers and crinkle-cut fries. "Dinnertime!" I cheerfully announced.

I was greeted at the gate by two of the mercenary fairies who controlled access to the Cadogan House grounds. They offered the merest of nods as I passed, then turned their attention back to the street. Fairies were notoriously antivampire, but they were even more antihuman. Cash payments from the House for their security services kept that balance.

I hopped the steps to the portico and headed inside, where I was greeted by a knot of vampires staring at the wall where Frank had been hanging his declarations.

"Welcome to the jungle," said a voice behind me.

I turned to find Juliet, one of the remaining Cadogan guards, watching the vamps with a forlorn look. She was slender and redheaded, and had an elfish look about her.

"What's going on?" I asked.

"More rules," she said, gesturing to the wall. "Three new additions to the wall of shame. Frank has decided vampires are not to congregate together in groups larger than ten other than in officially sanctioned gatherings."

"All the better to revolt against the GP?" I wondered.

"I guess. Apparently 'freedom of assembly' isn't one of the GP's favorite rights."

"How very colonial," I muttered. "What's the second?"

Her expression went flat. "He's rationing blood."

I was so stunned by the idea it took me a moment to gather my wits. "We're *vampires*. We need blood to survive."

She looked disdainfully at the paper-dotted wall. "Oh, I know. But Frank, in his infinite wisdom, decided Ethan spoiled us by having bagged blood too readily available. He's cutting the Blood4You deliveries."

Although we usually drank bagged blood, Cadogan was one of the few vampire Houses in the United States—and the only one in Chicago—that allowed its vampires to drink blood from humans or other vamps. The other Houses had abolished the practice to better assimilate with humans. Personally, I had taken blood from only one man—Ethan—but I could appreciate that the option was available.

"Better us than Grey House," I mused. "At least we have other sources."

"Not this time," Juliet said. "He's also banned drinking."

That idea was equally preposterous—but for a different reason. "Ethan made that rule," I protested. "And Malik confirmed it. Frank doesn't have the power—"

But Juliet cut me off with a shrug. "It's part of his evaluation, he says. A test to see how well we handle our hunger."

"He's setting us up for failure," I quietly said, looking over the crowd of vamps, now chattering nervously. "There's no way we'll make it through a receivership, two months after losing our Master and with protestors at the gates, without someone freaking out from lack of blood." I looked back at her. "He'll use that as an excuse to take over the House, or close it altogether."

"Quite possibly. Has he scheduled your interview yet?"

Not surprisingly, Frank had required each vamp to participate in a private interview. From what I'd heard, the interviews were fairly standard "justify your existence" deals. I was one of the few vamps he hadn't yet spoken to. Not that I was bummed, but each day that passed without an interview made me that much more suspicious.

"Still nothing," I told her.

"Maybe it's a show of respect or something. Trying to respect Ethan's memory by not interviewing you first?"

"I doubt our relationship would sway the GP's evaluation of the House. Maybe it's strategic—he's holding out so I anticipate the conversation, worry about it." I held up my dinner. "At least I have comfort food."

"And speaking of which, it's a good thing you brought that in."

"Why?"

"The third rule: Frank has banned convenience food in the kitchens."

Strike three for Frank. "What's his rationale for that one?"

"It's unhealthy, overly processed, and expensive, he says. It's all apples and cabbage and granola in there right now."

Because I'm a vampire with an appetite, that almost hurt more than anything else Frank had done.

Juliet checked her watch. "Well, I should get back to it. You heading upstairs to eat?"

"Luc and Malik wanted to talk, and I promised I'd bring grub. What are you up to?"

She gestured toward the stairs that led to the House's basement level, where the Ops Room was located. "Just finished a shift on the monitors." She meant the closed-caption televisions that captured security footage from the House grounds.

"Anything newsworthy?"

She rolled her eyes. "People hate us, blah blah blah, wish we'd go straight to hell, or maybe Wisconsin, since it's closer, blah blah blah."

"Same old, same old?"

"Pretty much. If Celina thought outing vampires was going to usher in a happy vampire fairy tale, she was sorely mistaken."

"Celina was mistaken on a number of fronts," I said.

"That is true," she softly said, and I caught the hint of pity in her voice. But pity was as exhausting to bear as grief, so I changed the subject.

"Any sign of McKetrick?" I asked. McKetrick, first name unknown, was a military type who'd decided vampires were the republic's new enemy. He had black gear, combat weapons, and a strong desire to clean us all out of the city. He'd harangued Ethan and me one evening and promised we'd be seeing more of him. There'd been a couple of sightings since then, and I'd gotten a few more details about his military background from Catcher—think questionable tactics and chain of command issues—but if he had a master plan for vampirocide, he hadn't yet made it clear.

I wasn't sure if that made me feel better, or worse.

"Not even a ruffle." She tilted her head to the side. "What were you up to outside?"

"Out. Working out, I mean." I stumbled a little on the explanation, as I hadn't yet confessed to the guards that I'd been working with Jonah. Our time together had been triggered by our Red Guard connection, and that secret wasn't mine to tell, so I'd avoided the subject of Jonah altogether.

One more lie woven into the already tangled web.

"It's always good to stay in shape," Juliet said with a wink.

A wink that suggested I hadn't been so sneaky after all.

"Well, it's been a long night," she said. "I'm going to head upstairs."

"Juliet," I called out, before she'd gotten too far. "Have you ever jumped?"

"Jumped?" she asked with a frown. "Like in the air?"

"Like off a building."

"I have." Understanding dawned in her eyes. "Why, Sentinel—did you make your first landing tonight?"

"I did, yeah."

"Congratulations," she said. "Just be careful that you don't go too far or fall too fast."

Words to live by.

Frank had co-opted Malik's office—the office that had once belonged to Ethan. Malik had barely had two weeks in the room before Frank arrived and announced he needed the space to evaluate the House.

Malik—tall, cocoa-skinned and green-eyed—was deliberative. He picked his battles carefully, so he'd deferred and moved back into his old office down the hall.

It wasn't large; the room was nearly filled by Malik's desk, shelves of books and personal mementos. But the small size didn't keep us from meeting there regularly. Bound together by our grief, we were more likely to be crammed into the office in our spare time than anywhere else in the House.

Tonight, Malik and Luc sat on opposite sides of a chess set atop Malik's desk, and Lindsey sat cross-legged on the floor a few feet away, magazine in hand.

Malik's wife, Aaliyah—petite, gorgeous, and as humble as they came—joined us on occasion, but she was absent tonight. Aaliyah was a writer who spent more time in their apartment than out of it.

I could completely understand the urge to hunker down and avoid vampire drama.

Luc, now House Second and former captain of the Cadogan guards, was blond, tousle-haired, and laid back. He'd been born and raised in the wild west, and I assumed he'd been made a vampire at the barrel of a gun. Luc had pined for Lindsey, my House BFF and a fellow guard who'd apparently stolen some time away from the Ops Room tonight.

Their relationship had been stop and go for a long time, albeit more "stop" than "go." She'd been afraid a relationship would lead to a breakup, and a breakup would destroy their friendship. Despite her initial commitment-phobia, craving comfort after Ethan's death, she'd finally agreed to give Luc a chance.

I'd spent the first week after his death in a haze in my room, Mallory at my side. When I'd finally emerged and Mal had gone home again, Lindsey showed up at my door in a total tizzy. She'd gone to Luc in her grief, and consolation had turned to affection—a supportive embrace to a passionate kiss that totally rocked her socks (or so she said). That kiss hadn't erased her doubts, but she'd belayed her fears enough to give him a chance.

Luc, of course, felt completely vindicated.

"Sentinel," Luc said, fingers hovering over one of the black knights, apparently debating his options. "I smell those burgers, and you'd better have brought enough for everyone."

Decision made, he plucked up the knight, set it down heavily in its new position, then raised his arms in the air triumphantly. "And so we advance!" he said, winging up his eyebrows at Malik. "You got a response to that?"

"I'm sure I'll figure something out," Malik said, his gaze now fixed on the board, scanning left to right as he calculated odds and evaluated his options. The chess game had become a weekly ritual, a way—or so I'd guessed—for Malik and Luc to exert some minimal control over their lives while the GP's talking head sat a few yards down the hallway, deciding their fate.

I put the bags of food onto the desk, pulled out bacon-laced burgers for me and Lindsey, and took a seat beside her on the floor.

"So," I said, folding down the burger's paper wrapping. "Blood rationing?"

Luc and Malik growled simultaneously.

"The man is a stone-cold idiot," Luc said, taking an impressive bite of his triple-layer burger.

"Unfortunately," Malik said, moving his chess piece and sitting back in his chair, "he is an idiot with the full authority of the GP."

"Which means we have to wait until he royally screws the pooch before we can act," Luc said, hunched over the board again. "All due respect, Liege, the guy is a douche."

"I have no official position with respect to his douchery," Malik said, pulling a box of fries out of the bag, applying a prodigious amount of ketchup, and digging in. I appreciated that Malik, unlike Ethan, didn't need to be schooled on Chicago's best and greasiest cuisine. He knew the difference between a red hot and a hot beef, had a favorite pizza joint, and had been known to take a late-night trip with Aaliyah to a roadside diner outside Milwaukee to get Wisconsin's "best cheese curds." More power to them.

"But we will allow him to hang himself with his own rope," Malik added. "And in the meantime, we will monitor the vampires and intervene when the time is appropriate."

The tone was all Master vampire, something Malik had gotten better at using over the last few weeks. I took the hint, dropped the subject and dug into my burger while Luc used a fry to point to various chess pieces he was again deciding between.

"Deliberative, isn't he?" I whispered to Lindsey.

She smiled too knowingly for comfort. "You have no idea how deliberative he can be. How . . . thorough." She leaned toward me, nibbling on a bit of bacon from her burger. "Have I ever waxed poetic about the glory that is the fuzzy-chested vampire wearing nothing but cowboy boots?"

Midbite, I squeezed my eyes closed, but it was too late to block the image of Luc wearing nothing but his birthday suit and sassy, red boots. "That's my former boss you're talking about," I whispered. "And I'm trying to eat."

"You're thinking about him naked, aren't you?"

"Unfortunately."

She patted my arm. "And to think—I was actually hesitant about dating him. Oh, and speaking of which. Chaps. Enough said."

"Enough most definitely said." Lindsey was becoming my new, in-House Mallory, complete with conquest details. Sigh.

"In that case, I'll leave you to your imagination. But I strongly recommend the therapeutic application of fuzzy-chested vampire to grief. It works miracles."

"I am sincerely glad to hear that. But if you keep talking, I will poke your eyes out with a toothpick." I shoved a handful of napkins in her general direction. "Shut up and eat your burger."

Sometimes a girl had to lay down the law.

CHAPTER TWO

BITTERSWEET DREAMS

I stood on a high plain in my modern-style black leather—my long hair whipping in the chilling wind that rolled past, swirling the mist that curled at my feet.

The clothing might have been modern, but the setting was ancient. The landscape was bleak and empty, and the air smelled of sulfur and dampness.

I felt the footsteps before I heard them, the ground rumbling just slightly beneath my feet.

And then he appeared.

Like a warrior returning from battle, Ethan emerged through the mist in garb out of time and place for twenty-first century Chicago. Knee-high leather boots, rough-hewn pants, and a long leather tunic belted at the waist. There was a rust-red gash in the middle of his chest. His hair was long and wavy and golden-blond, and his eyes were vibrantly green.

I walked toward him, fear circling my heart, making a vise around it, squeezing my lungs until I was barely able to sip at air. I was glad to see him alive—but I knew he was a harbinger of death.

When I reached him, he put his hands on my arms, leaned forward and pressed his lips to my forehead. Such a simple act, but so intimate. A precious affection that made my chest ache with sentiment. I closed my eyes and savored the moment as thunder rumbled across the plateau, shaking the ground again.

Suddenly, Ethan raised his head and glanced warily around. When he looked at me again, he began to speak, the words flowing in a lilting language that sounded like it came from a time and place far away.

I shook my head. "I can't understand you."

His expression tightened, a line of worry furrowing his forehead, the words coming more quickly as he tried to get his point across. But the speed didn't help.

"Ethan, I don't know what you're saying. Can you speak English?"

Panic in his eyes, he glanced back over his shoulder, then grabbed my arm and pointed behind him. A low, thick storm front was rolling toward us, the wind beginning to pick up as the temperature dropped.

"I see the storm," I told him over the rising wind. "But I can't stop it."

Ethan yelled something out, but the words were lost in the howling wind. He started walking toward the thundercloud, pulling my arm in an attempt to drag me with him.

But I resisted, pulling back. "That's the wrong way. We can't walk into the storm!"

He was insistent, but so was I. Positive we'd be swept off the plateau and into the sea if we didn't seek shelter, I began running away from the wall of clouds . . . and him. But I couldn't resist a final glance back. He stood frozen on the plain, his hair whipping in the gale.

Before I could reach out to him, the storm reached us and broke, the wind knocking me off my feet, the pressure sucking the air from my lungs. The rain came as I hit my knees, blowing sideways and turning the landscape gray, the wind howling in my ears. Ethan disappeared in the onslaught, leaving only the echo of his voice on the wind.

"*Merit!*"

I jolted awake, bathed in sweat, gasping for breath, the sound of his voice in my ears.

Tears slipped from my eyes as I pushed drenched bangs from my forehead, and scrubbed my hands across my face, trying to slow the feverish race of my heart.

My first dream of Ethan had been miraculous; we'd bathed in the sun—a taboo to vampires. I'd savored that last memory of him.

But this was the sixth nightmare in the two months since he'd been gone. Each was louder and more vivid than the last, and waking up was like emerging from a tunnel of panic, my chest squeezed into a knot. In each nightmare we were pushed to some crisis, but the end was always the same—he was always torn away from me. Each time I woke with his voice in my ears, screaming out my name in panic.

I dropped my forehead to my knees, grief pounding at my heart like a kettledrum. The helplessness of loss overwhelmed me. Not just from the loss of Ethan, but from the frustration—the exhaustion—of being visited again by a ghost who wouldn't let me go. Tears fell, and I let them, wishing the sting of salt would wash away the hurt.

I missed his voice. The sight of him. The smell of him.

And probably because of that, I was stuck in a cycle that kept me dreaming about Ethan—watching him die over and over again. My grief had become a hollow I couldn't climb out of.

When my heart slowed, I sat up again and wiped the tears from my face with a shirtsleeve. I grabbed the phone from the nightstand and dialed up the one person who could calm me down.

"Crap on toast," Mallory answered over the resounding bass of a man's voice. "I'm on a study break—Catcher's naked and Barry White's on the stereo. Do you know how rarely I get study breaks?"

Mallory was a belatedly identified sorceress in training. She had just finished her apprenticeship with a cute boy-next-door type named Simon and had been prepping for her "finals" for weeks. Simon had seemed okay in the five minutes I'd been in the same room with him, but Catcher was definitely not a fan. That probably had something to do with the fact that Simon was a member of the Union of Amalgamated Sorcerers and Spellcasters (euphemistically called "the Order"), an organization that had kicked Catcher off its rolls.

Her voice was testy, and I knew she was super stressed this week, but I needed her, so I pushed on. "I had another dream."

There was a moment of silence before she yelled out, "Five minutes, Catch."

I heard grumbling, and then the room went silent.

"How many is this?" she asked.

"Six. I've had two this week."

"What do you remember?"

Mal quizzed me every time I had a dream—her morbid curiosity and love of the occult combining into a post diem interrogation. I obliged and gave her the details.

"Mostly just the end, as per usual. Ethan was dressed like an old-school warrior. There was this storm moving in, and he was trying to warn me, but I think he was speaking Swedish."

"Swedish? Why in God's name would he be speaking Swedish? And how would you know what Swedish sounds like?"

"He was from Sweden. Originally, I mean. And I have no idea. Interwebs, probably. Anyway, he was trying to get me to move toward the storm. I was trying to run away from it."

"Sounds like the sensible thing to do. Then what?"

"The storm hit. I lost sight of him, and woke up when he was calling my name."

"Well, the symbolism's pretty obvious," she said. "You're with Ethan, and then you're separated by some sort of calamity. Pretty much the real life scenario."

I made a vague sound of agreement and pulled my legs under me. "That's true, I guess."

"Of course it is. On the other hand, dreaming is never just dreaming. There's always something more going on. The wanderings of the mind. The escapades of the soul. I've said it before and I'll say it again—you and Ethan had some kind of connection, Mer. Not exactly a healthy connection, but a connection nonetheless."

"So, what, I'm visiting his ghost in my dreams?"

She laughed mirthlessly. "Would you put it past Darth Sullivan to figure out a way to haunt you postmortem? He's probably holding staff meetings in the afterworld. Offering up performance evaluations. Issuing dictates."

"Those were the kinds of things he loved."

Mal got quiet for a second. "Look," she said. "Maybe we're thinking about this the wrong way. I mean—we're talking about what it means and how often it's happening. But you've called me, what, half a dozen times about these things? Maybe we should start talking about how to make them stop."

I wasn't sure from the tone of her voice whether she was expressing concern about my mental state—or irritation that I'd been sharing it with her. I gave her a pass on the snark since she was stressed, but promised myself a good debriefing when it was all over.

As for her plan, I wasn't exactly thrilled about it. Pathetic as it sounded, at least in my dreams Ethan was alive. He was *real*. I had no pictures of him, and few mementos. Even my waking memories of him were fuzzy—each recollection seemed to dull the lines of his face. It was as if he were a faint star on the horizon—attempting to focus on the image only blurred it further.

But in my dreams . . . he was always there, always clear.

"I don't think there's any reason to do that."

"There is if your dreams become a substitute for real life."

That stung, but I took her point. "They won't. These aren't those kind of dreams. It's just—they make me feel closer to him." At the cost, of course, of having sweaty night terrors.

"Well, if it happens again, you'll have to talk to Catcher instead. Exams are starting."

"Now?" I asked her. "I thought you still had a week to go."

"Simon wanted to add 'an element of the unexpected,'" Mallory said, and I could all but hear the air quotes in her voice. "The testing goes in phases. He'll put me out into some situation; I have to fix it. I'll go home and make something in my chemistry lab, and then I'm back on the streets for round two. He'll ask me questions about the Keys, and I use the Keys to fix the problem. Rinse. Repeat. It's gonna be a whole, big thing."

The Keys were the four divisions of magic, which sorcerers had visualized by cutting a circle into four quadrants. It was apparently so important to sorcerers that Catcher'd had the four Keys inked onto his stomach.

"Well, if you can't be available at my beck and call," I said, trying to lighten the mood, "do you think Catcher would wear a blue wig in the meantime?"

Mallory's previously blond hair was now a notoriously bright shade of blue. It was straight and reached a couple of inches below her shoulders.

"Probably not. But you could always threaten to have his cable disconnected. That's how I got the kitchen cabinets painted."

"How is Mr. Chick Flick?"

"Infinitely happier not knowing you referred to him as that."

Be that as it may, Catcher was addicted. If a made-for-television movie featured a once-downtrodden lady doin' it for herself, he was in. It was an odd fixation for a gruff, muscular sorcerer with a penchant for swordcraft and sarcasm, but Mallory tolerated it, and I suppose that was all that really mattered.

"I call 'em like I see 'em. Wanna schedule a dinner break? Maybe sushi?"

"Breaks aren't really on my agenda right now. I have a lot to focus on. But you might think about not hogging down snack cakes right before bedtime."

"I have no idea what you're talking about."

"Liar," she accused, but I was saved the necessity of lying any further. My Cadogan House beeper—a guard necessity—all but buzzed off my nightstand. I leaned over and snatched it up. OPS ROOM, it read. ASAP.

Unfortunately, "ASAP" translated only one way in Cadogan House these days: "It's time for another meeting." Once again, with feeling: *another* meeting. Kelley, our newly appointed guard captain, was a fan.

"Mal," I said, climbing off the bed, "I need to run. It's time to play Sentinel. Good luck with your exams."

Mallory made a huffy noise. "Luck doesn't figure into it. But sweet dreams to you."

I hung up the phone, not thrilled about our conversation, but well aware that I needed to pick my battles. I'd done a really crappy job of supporting Mallory when she'd discovered she was a sorceress, mostly because I'd been knee-deep in newbie vampire drama at the time. I needed to be supportive, even if it wasn't exactly the most comfortable place to be. This was not the time to lay into her about sarcasm. She'd given me slack when I'd needed it; it was time to repay the favor.

Besides—we both had other fights to wage.

Luc took his job seriously, but he also had a pretty good sense of humor. He brought a jokey camaraderie to the Ops Room, along with a taste for denim, swearing, and beef jerky. Luc was a great strategist and a big picture kind of guy. I was perfectly fine with all those qualities.

Kelley, his replacement, was smart, savvy, and skilled . . . but she was no Luc—cowboy boots or otherwise.

When she'd accepted the position, she'd chopped her silky dark hair into a short, sleek bob. Her hair became all business, and so did the Cadogan House guards. Our schedule became tighter, our meetings more formal. She scheduled daily workouts and required us to complete end-of-shift reports. Virtually everything in the Ops Room had become virtual, and the few bits of paper that remained were color-coded, tabbed, alphabetized, and collated. We had time cards and name tags, and we were required to wear the latter during our nightly patrols of the House grounds "for public relations."

"Part of keeping a safe House," Kelley had said, "is instilling a sense of trust in the neighborhood. If they know who we are, they'll be less inclined to violence."

It's not that I didn't agree. It's just—name tags? Really?

But while I thought the idea was corny, I didn't voice the objection. When Ethan had been Master, before they'd needed me back in the guard corps, I'd spent most of my time on special assignments with him. Now that he was gone, Kelley was my boss and my primary point of contact for the House.

She was my boss, so she'd get no name tag arguments from me. Besides, now was the time for solidarity, name tags or not. We'd had enough upheaval lately.

Surprisingly, the Ops Room was meeting-free when I arrived, post-shower and clothed in my Cadogan uniform—a black, slim-fit suit. Lindsey and Juliet sat at two of the room's computer stations, while Kelley stood beside the conference table, a cell phone in hand, her eyes on the screen.

"What's up?" I asked.

Without a word, Kelley turned her cell phone around and thrust it toward me. A picture filled the screen—or what I assumed was a picture, since the screen was pitch-black and I couldn't actually see anything.

"I don't get it."

"This is Lake Michigan."

I frowned, trying to figure out what I'd missed. Lake Michigan made up the eastern border of the city. Since we were awake only at night, the lake was always pitch-dark by the time we woke up. So I didn't understand the concern.

"I'm sorry," I told her apologetically, "but I still don't get it."

Kelley pulled back the phone, punched some buttons, and swiveled it again. This time, it displayed a photo of a drinking glass full of inky black water.

"That's water from Lake Michigan," she explained before I could ask. "The Internet is going crazy. About two hours ago, Lake Michigan turned completely black."

"And that's not all," Lindsey piped up, then swiveled in her chair to face us. "Same thing happened to the Chicago River, at least as far as the city limits. They've both gone black, and they've stopped moving."

I struggled to understand what they were telling me. I mean, I understood the literal meaning of the words, but they didn't make any sense. "How could they just stop moving?"

"We aren't certain," Kelley said, "but we have a sense this might be involved." She flipped the screen to a third image. It showed a petite but busty woman with long red hair and a very tiny green dress. She stood on a bridge over the river, arms outstretched, eyes closed.

I'd seen a girl like that before—a number of them, actually. She looked like one of the nymphs that ruled Chicago's waterways. I'd met them before when my grandfather, the city's supernatural mediator, had helped them resolve a dispute.

"A River nymph," I concluded, leaning in to peer closer at the screen. "But what's she doing to the water?"

"We aren't entirely sure," Kelley said. "This photo's making the Internet rounds just like the one of the water. Based on the picture's time stamp, the lake went dark a few minutes after she did that—whatever 'that' was."

I grimaced. "That's not a good coincidence."

"No, it's not," Kelley agreed. "Especially not with the mayor convinced we're the root of all evil."

Former Mayor Seth Tate had made his mark—at least pre-indictment—by staying on top of the supernatural situation in Chicago and supporting our integration into the human population. He set up my grandfather's office, and when vampires came out of the closet, he positioned Chicago as the frontier of supernatural relations in the U.S.

Mayor Kowalczyk was no Mayor Tate, and she certainly wasn't

interested in positioning herself as a friend to sups. The campaign for her special election had been short, but she'd made her position plenty clear. Chicago might have been built on patronage, but under the Kowalczyk administration, that patronage didn't extend to vampires or shifters. No "special treatment" for supernaturals.

"As if we weren't already popular enough," I mumbled. When she and Lindsey exchanged a glance, I knew I was in trouble. "What?"

"Here's my thought," Kelley said. "I know this water thing isn't exactly our problem, especially if nymphs are involved. I seriously doubt any vampire created the issue, and probably the Ombud's office will get people working on it, right?"

"It's a definite possibility."

"But we are the public face of supernaturals." Kelley said. "The public only knows about us and shifters, and Gabe's keeping them on the down low. If people start freaking out . . ."

"They're going to blame us," I finished for her. Suddenly nervous, I tugged at the hem of my jacket a bit. "What do you want me to do?"

"Make contact with your grandfather. Find out what he knows, then get downtown. Keep an eye on things, and do whatever you can to help the Ombud's office, preferably with as little public drama or political involvement as possible."

"What about you? The House? If I'm out, you're going to be even more shorthanded."

She shook her head. "There won't be a House if the mayor finds a reason to crucify us." Then her expression softened. "I didn't think to ask—will you be okay doing this? You haven't been out of the House much since . . . you know."

Since Ethan, she meant.

The last time I'd left the House on a real mission, two vampires had ended up dead, and only one had deserved it. I could admit I was gun-shy. The wound was still raw, the fear that I'd screw up and someone else would end up dead still sharp. The fact that I already had a demerit in my file for investigating Celina and pissing off the GP in the process also wasn't encouraging.

Luc had argued the point, reminding me that Ethan had been staked not because I was careless, but because he'd jumped in front of a drug-addled vampire—and a stake meant for me. Unfortunately, that reminder hadn't done much to assuage the guilt or to make me want to try again.

Kelley had been patient, letting me work around the House instead of playing Sentinel outside it. That arrangement had suited Malik's plan to keep us under the radar for a while. We'd had more than enough drama lately, receiver included.

On the other hand . . . I glanced over at the nearly empty Ops Room. Other than me, Juliet and Lindsey were the only two arrows left in Kelley's quiver. Someone needed to step up, and I was the only candidate left.

"I'll be fine," I agreed. "I'll give my grandfather a heads-up about the picture in case they don't already know, and I'll head out now."

There was clear relief in Kelley's expression, but it didn't last long. "I hate to send you out alone, and I know you're used to working with Eth—with a partner. Unfortunately, we can't spare anyone right now. You'll have to take this one by yourself."

I'd anticipated that, and had a strategy in my back pocket.

"Actually, I met Jonah, the Grey guard captain, the night of the Temple Bar fiasco." Long story short, drugged-out Cadogan vamps had caused a ruckus that created city-wide attention. Jonah had walked down from Grey House to check out the fight, our faux first meeting. "Since we're short-staffed, and this isn't a Cadogan-specific problem, I could see if he can spare a guard." Of course he'd spare a guard—himself.

"Oh," Kelley said. "That's a good idea. I hadn't considered it, but it definitely has merit. No pun intended."

I smiled politely, but caught Lindsey's expression of uncensored curiosity. She'd definitely have questions about Jonah later.

"Do it," Kelley said. "Get to the lake, and figure out what the hell is going on down there—and what we need to do about it."

I promised I would. Reticence notwithstanding, that's what Sentinels were for.

With a mission in mind, I hopped back upstairs to my second-floor room and changed into leather pants and jacket, a gray tank beneath, and then pulled on boots and clipped on my beeper. I'd already been wearing my gold House medal—the official membership card of most American vampire Houses.

I unsheathed my katana, the official weapon of GP vampires, and checked its edge. It was sharp and still immaculate from its last rice paper cleaning.

I opened the top drawer in my bureau, where a double-edged dagger lay nestled atop folded T-shirts too thin for autumn in Chicago. It wasn't exactly a glamorous place for a weapon, but it was an intimate one that seemed fitting under the circumstances. A dagger was traditionally presented to the House Sentinel by its Master; most American Houses hadn't had a Sentinel in a while, so Ethan's appointing me—and giving me the blade—was a revised tradition.

The blade gleamed like chrome; the handle was pearl and silky smooth to the touch. And on the end of the handle was a gold disk, a near match to my Cadogan medal, inscribed with my position.

I picked it up and ran my thumb across the ridges left by the engraved lettering. It was one of the few physical reminders I had of Ethan, along with the medal and a signed Cubs baseball he'd given me to replace one I'd lost. It was such a strange thing—to be in a House surrounded by vampires he'd made and décor he'd chosen, to have vibrant dreams and memories of him, to have been on the verge of a relationship when he'd been killed—but to have so few mementos of our time together.

I might have been immortal, my life theoretically eternal, but I had no more control over the passage of time than any mortal. I assumed my memories would eventually fade, so I savored the tangible reminders of who he'd been.

Kelley had given me time to grieve, but it was time to get back to work. I pressed my lips to the engraving, then slid the dagger inside its boot holster. I pulled my hair into a high ponytail and grabbed my cell phone, dialing up Jonah's number.

"Lake Michigan?" he answered.

"Yep. Do you mind playing Sentinel sidekick this evening?"

Jonah made a sarcastic noise. "I'm the older, wiser vamp. That makes you the sidekick."

"I'm better with a katana."

"That remains to be seen. And I've got more degrees."

He was right; he had me beat on that one. My change to vampire had interrupted my own doctoral studies; Jonah had managed four graduate degrees even with fangs. I was woman enough to admit to some academic envy.

"Fine," I said, rolling my eyes. "No one's the sidekick. Equal rights, et cetera. Where should we meet?"

"I've got a friend with a boat, but it's already in dry dock for the season. Navy Pier. Half an hour. Oh—and Sentinel?"

"Yes?"

"If the gate's locked, don't forget you're strong enough to scale it."

Excellent. I could now add "breaking and entering" to the skills section of my résumé.

Dagger in boot and in hand, I headed down the House's main staircase to the first floor—and a few feet closer to my chilly car.

I was in the lobby, keys in hand, when Luc and Lindsey came downstairs holding hands, both looking very much in love. Their blooming relationship didn't make my own grief any easier to bear, but if I was playing the dopey-eyed optimist, at least something good had come from Ethan's demise.

"Sentinel," Luc said. "You heading out to check out this water problem?"

"I am."

"First time on the streets in a while."

"First House-related mission in a while, certainly."

"You nervous?"

I thought about my answer for a few seconds. "Not nervous so much as uncomfortable. I know Ethan wasn't always easy to be around. He was a tough teacher, and there were days when I felt like a lump of clay he was trying to mold into something else."

"Like every trip was a teaching point?"

"Like that, yeah," I said with a nod. "But I think he was figuring me out. Learning who I was, and learning that I could be a help to the House on my own, without amendment." I smiled a little in spite of myself. "He was an imperialistic, self-righteous pain in the ass. But he was my pain in the ass, you know? And tonight, I won't be with him. That definitely feels strange."

Without warning, Luc reached out and gripped me in a chest-crushing bear hug. "You can do this, Sentinel."

I held my breath and patted him on the back until he released me. "Thank you, Luc. I appreciate that."

"You have backup?" Lindsey asked.

"Jonah—the Grey guard captain—volunteered to take point. He's going to meet me downtown. And I can call my grandfather, of course."

Luc put an arm around Lindsey's shoulder. "You know we're here for you, of course."

"I do. You're two of my favorite vampires."

"You barely tolerate most vampires," Lindsey said with a wink. "So I'm not sure that's saying a lot."

I stuck my tongue out at her, but gestured toward the door. "You wanna walk me outside?"

"Sure thing. I'm heading out for a walk around the grounds anyway." She leaned over and kissed Luc on the cheek. "I'll catch you after shift."

"You know it, Blondie," he said. He gave her butt a slap for good measure, and then offered me a salute. "*Bon chance*, Sentinel."

Lindsey took my hand and practically dragged me to the door. But she managed to wait until we were outside and on the sidewalk before the interrogation began.

"So, you're hanging out with Jonah again?"

"Again?" I wondered aloud, not willing to commit to an answer until I knew how much she knew.

"Hon, give me some credit. I've been alive a long time, and I'm one of the best guards this House has to offer."

"It's a small sample," I snarked, but she poked me in the shoulder.

"Focus. I'm pretty sure he's the reason you were glowing a little last night."

"I wasn't glowing." Had I been glowing? And how had she known I'd seen Jonah? When had I become a topic of House conversation?

"You were glowing." She put a hand on my arm. "And that's okay. It's okay for you to have a friend, or a lover . . . ?"

There was actually hope in her voice; I decided not to take that as a compliment.

"He's a friend. A colleague. Only a colleague."

"Does he know that?" At my raised eyebrows, she shook her head. "I mean, Merit, from what I hear the guy's spending time with you. Call it work or whatever, but guys don't invest time if they aren't interested."

"Trust me," I said. "This is business." Even if he was vaguely interested, Jonah was still my RG recruiter. He had an interest in keeping me safe.

"Is it going to stay that way?"

I looked away, embarrassed by the question. Ethan had been gone for only two months. I knew Lindsey wanted to see me come back to life, but the idea of dating anyone seemed rushed, disrespectful of Ethan's memory.

"You aren't ready to talk about it, are you?"

"What answer will you believe?"

Lindsey sighed and wrapped an arm around my shoulders. "You know what we need? We need to toughen you up a little. Rough up your edges. You'll find being a heartless vamp a helluva lot easier when the shine is gone."

"Yay," I said without enthusiasm, twirling my fingers like a party favor. "I am really looking forward to that."

"You should be. You'll get a membership card and a lifetime subscription to *Heartless Vampires Monthly*."

"Does that come with a free tote bag?"

"And a toaster." She gestured toward the back of the House. "I'm gonna get to work and take a look around the yard. Good luck tonight."

If only it were a matter of luck.

CHAPTER THREE

⋯⊱⋅⊰⋯

DEAD IN THE WATER

Some aspects of this city were spectacular. A river cruise at sunset. The Field Museum on a rainy day. Wrigley Field pretty much anytime. There was even thirty-course molecular gastronomy, if you were into that (no, thanks), or red hots, if they were your bag (yes, please!).

Other parts were less fabulous. Winters in Chicago had all the charm of a late sleeper at seven a.m. Politics were a combustible mess. And then there was perhaps the greatest irony of all: Despite the public transportation, despite the traffic, despite the construction, despite the fiasco that was on-street parking, most of us had cars. Even residential parking required a permit, and don't get me started on "dibs."

Because parking was usually a disaster, I'd been prepared to text Jonah and advise him it would take me an hour to meet him at Navy Pier—twenty minutes to get there and forty minutes to find a parking spot and make the hike.

Fortunately, although Chicago was a busy city at pretty much any time of day, it was a little less busy in the hours vampires roamed. Business in the Loop was winding down as I searched for a parking space, so I found an on-street spot and jogged back to the pier entrance, a hand on my sword to keep it from bouncing at my side.

I'd avoided Lake Shore Drive, thinking it would be swamped with gawkers. Consequently, I didn't get a look at the water until I neared Navy Pier. My first look might have been delayed, but that didn't dampen the shock. Sure, the lake at night had always been dark. Sometimes it was so dark it seemed the lakefront was the edge of the world, Chicago the final outpost before oblivion. But you might spy the break of a white wave or a glint of moonlight on the water, and you knew the sun would rise and the lake would appear again.

But this dark was something altogether different. There was no movement, no life, no reflection. There were no breaking waves, and the moon reflected off the slick, black surface like it was a lacquered void in the earth.

And it didn't just look strange—it *felt* wrong.

Vampires weren't magical creatures per se. We were the result of a genetic mutation that made us a little more powerful than humans, but with profound weaknesses—including aspen stakes and sunlight. But we could sense magic around us, usually a mild, peppery, caffeinated buzz in the air.

Tonight there wasn't just an absence of magic—the lake actually felt like a magical vacuum, sucking what magic there might have been into its maw. I could feel the magic being leached past me, like a freezing winter wind wicking away moisture. The sensation was uncomfortable, an irritating breeze beneath my skin, and it was all the weirder since the air was perfectly still.

"Who could turn Lake Michigan into some kind of magic sink?" I quietly wondered.

"That would appear to be the principal question."

I jumped at the words, then glanced behind me. Jonah wore jeans, boots and a long-sleeved gray T-shirt with MIDNIGHT HIGH SCHOOL across the front. The school was fake, a cover used by RG members to signal their membership in case things went awry.

It probably didn't bode well that he was wearing one now.

"You can feel it, too?" I asked.

"I can now. I couldn't at the House. I don't like it," he added, scanning the lake. "But let's walk the pier. I want to get closer to the water."

I nodded and followed him, only just realizing that throngs of people were moving toward the lake. I guess everyone wanted a glimpse. Unfortunately, lines of bundled-up Chicagoans moving en masse through the dark looked uncomfortably zombie-esque. I shivered involuntarily, and followed Jonah.

He was right about the pier. The ten-foot gate was locked. After waiting to avoid a couple of passing guards, he vaulted over the fence with minimal effort. He glanced back at me, then motioned me over with a hand.

I'd mounted a fence before, but wasn't thrilled to try again in front of this particular audience. My nerves ramped up, I blew out a breath, backed up a few feet, and jumped. I made it a few feet up, and scrambled to reach the top. But just as I swung my legs over the side, I got caught in a tangle of fence posts and jacket pockets. Arms and legs twisted, I hit the ground butt-first, bruising both my derriere and my ego.

"So much for falling gracefully," Jonah snickered, offering me a hand. I growled out a few choice comments, but took his hand and let him pull me up.

I stood up and dusted off my bottom. "I can scale a fence. I've done it before."

"Then what's the problem?"

The audience, I thought, but kept the thought to myself. "Nerves, I guess."

Jonah nodded. "To truly utilize your skills, you'll have to let go of your human preconceptions and trust your body."

Before I could make a snappy response, Jonah grabbed my hand and pulled me around the corner of a building just before the guard walked by, his walkie-talkie buzzing with chatter about the lake.

When he'd passed, Jonah peeked around the corner. "He's gone. Let's go."

We headed around the pier in the opposite direction. It was deserted, the ticket booths, restaurants, and snack vendors closed up for the night, the tour boats in dry dock for the winter. We skirted the edge of the buildings to keep a low profile and jogged the length of the pier—nearly a mile—to the end.

There was an open area at the end of the pier, so we checked for guards and then hustled past the stand of flags that dotted the concrete to the edge. I kneeled down and gazed into the water. Just as we'd seen earlier, the lake was pitch-black and absolutely still. The water looked like a black sheet of ice, perfectly frozen and flat. It carried no scent, and it was completely silent. There was no sign of life, and no sound of it, either. No crashing waves. No seagull *caws*. The lake was eerily still and eerily silent.

It was also eerily antimagical. The vacuum was stronger here, as was the sensation that magic was being pulled toward the lake.

Chicagoans had always had a love-hate relationship with the lake. We flocked to it in the summertime, and bemoaned the freezing winds that rolled off it in the winter. But humans' reactions to this were going to be different by magnitude. Before, humans feared supernaturals because of who we were. Now, they were going to fear what we could do.

It wasn't the first time I wished Ethan was here, if only to brainstorm with. He'd already be deep in strategy territory, figuring out how to avoid the possibility humans would blame vampires for whatever was going on.

I glanced behind me and up at Jonah. "This is going to be bad."

"That's my thinking. And I am at a complete loss. Four graduate degrees," he added, with a mischievous grin, "and still at a complete loss."

Predictably, I rolled my eyes. "Well, let's do what we can with what we have. Maybe we can find some clue as to the origin."

The first step in that task, I figured, was getting down there and getting a feel for the water. I glanced around and spied an access ladder that led down to lake, then searched the pier for something to prod it with. After all, there was no way I was dipping toe one into a magical black hole.

After a few seconds of fruitless searching, Jonah handed me what looked like a used-up sparkler stick.

"Tourists," he blandly suggested when I glanced at it curiously.

"Probably," I agreed. "But it'll work." I unbelted my katana and handed it to him, then climbed down the ladder. When I was close enough to the water, I dipped the sparkler into it.

The water was so opaque I'd half expected the stick to bounce off the top. Instead, it offered no resistance at all. When I lifted the sparkler from the water, there were no ripples—the few errant, inky drops simply dropped back into the water with no effect.

"Are you seeing this?" I asked, looking up at the pier.

"Yes, although I still have no idea what it is." He reached out a hand. "Come on up. You're making me nervous."

With a nod, I sacrificed the sparkler to the lake and climbed back up again. Jonah handed back my katana and I rebelted it, and we stood there for a moment silently regarding the water.

"So, to review," I said, "we have a lake and apparently a river that have turned black, absorb magic, and no longer obey the laws of physics. And that's only what we can see. There could be more turmoil under the surface."

"The questions now are 'why' and 'how.'"

"Did you see the photo of the River nymph on the bridge? It looked like she was casting some kind of spell."

"I did," he said, "but this can't be the work of nymphs. Even if they were fighting each other, they love the water. They wouldn't do anything to destroy the lake or the river."

"Not on purpose," I suggested. "But as we know, there are ways for supernatural populations to be controlled." After all, Tate had manufactured V, a drug that made vamps more aggressive and bloodthirsty than usual. He'd used it to control Celina. Maybe he hadn't been the only one in the city with supernatural control in mind.

"That's true," Jonah said. "But if you wanted to control a population, why the nymphs? They manage lake and river resources. That's not exactly big magic. And even if they were being targeted, why kill the lake? What's the point?"

"Maybe the goal was knocking the city off-kilter," I suggested. "Some of the city's water comes from the lake, so maybe they wanted to futz about the water supply?"

"To dehydrate us to death?"

"Or incite riots."

We were quiet for a moment.

"So we have two theories," he said. "This has something to do with the nymphs, which would explain the picture, or this has something to do with the lake. Unfortunately, neither one of those theories really tells us anything."

"Actually, it gives us at least a place to start." I pulled out my cell phone. I'd met nymphs before, and I knew two people who had a way with them. My grandfather and Jeff Christopher, my grandfather's employee. The boy had a touch.

Handily, Jeff answered the call. "Talk to me, Merit."

"We're at the lake. Have you seen it yet?"

"Yeah. We're at DuSable Harbor. We wanted to see it for ourselves. And now that we're here . . ." He paused. "Crazy, isn't it?"

"Very much so. Any thoughts on how it happened?"

"We've been talking it through, but this is completely unprecedented. Even Catcher's shocked, and Catcher's not shocked by a lot." I could hear the thread of concern in his voice, like a child who has, for the first time, seen his parents at a loss. I didn't envy the feeling.

"Jeff, there's an image floating around the Internet of a nymph standing over the river, and it looks like she's casting a spell or something. Is it possible they'd be involved—or that someone would want us to think they're involved?"

"Nymphs don't cast spells, so whatever she was doing, that wasn't it."

"So maybe she was framed?"

"Or a tourist caught the wrong shot at the wrong time."

"That's a possibility," I allowed. "But either way, it would probably pay to talk to the nymphs and get their perspective. We're over at Navy Pier. Can we meet you somewhere?"

There was a pause, probably while he discussed logistics with Catcher or my grandfather.

"We'll meet you in front of the pier," he said. "Ten minutes."

That was just long enough for Jonah and me to walk back the

length of the pier ... and hopefully not get called out by a security guard.

"We'll be there," I promised him, and we set out for land again.

We walked quietly back to the rendezvous point. There was no sight of the guards, who'd probably abandoned their routes to stare at the lake. Trouble emerged only after Jonah had leapt the gate. I was a few feet behind him, preparing myself mentally to make the hop again. Much to my surprise, I performed the vault much more gracefully and was on my way down again when the screaming began. The noise was just enough to jar my concentration. I lost my form midair, and hit the ground in an ungainly stumble. It took a few steps, but I finally ended up on my feet and began scanning the grounds for the source of the screams.

Easier said than done. The noise echoed weirdly off the buildings on the pier and Lake Pointe Tower, the clover-shaped tower that sat between Navy Pier and the rest of Streeterville.

Jonah homed in on the drama first, pointing toward a patch of green space in front of the pier. A tangle of people—maybe a dozen—were yelling and screaming into the otherwise quiet night air. From the tingle in the air—a tingle that was being sucked back into the vacuum behind us—it was clear the scuffle was magical.

We jogged over, and I nearly ran into Jonah when he stopped short, eyes wide on the scene in front of him. He barely managed to stutter out a response. "I've seen pictures, but never in person. They are— *Wow*. There's so many of them. And they're so—with the dresses and the hair—"

Jonah was right. There were so many of them, and the dresses and hair definitely made them noticeable. They were petite and curvy, all with long hair, all with short dresses. Each dress was a different color, corresponding to the chunk of the Chicago River for which they were responsible.

A single nymph—the redhead from the picture Kelley had shown me—was surrounded by ten or twelve others. They were currently only yelling obscenities, but they looked more than eager to start rumbling.

I'd seen River nymphs fight before, and I didn't want any part of it. They used nails and pulled hair. I preferred a crescent kick to the head any day.

"Those are the River nymphs," I told Jonah, then nudged him forward. "Come on."

We reached the circle of nymphs within seconds, but they couldn't have cared less. They were too busy berating the red-headed nymph in the middle of their circle. And while they may have been cute and petite and all things womanly and manicured, they had vicious little potty mouths. Even Jonah cringed when a blond nymph made a rather unflattering comparison between the redhead's mother and a female dog.

"That is not ladylike," he muttered.

"Welcome to the world of the nymphs," I said, and stepped forward, just as I'd seen Jeff do once before. "Ladies, maybe we could calm down a bit and cool off?"

Whether too fired up to notice the suggestion of détente or too unmoved to care, they ignored me. During an effort to punctuate her insult with a physical threat, a brunette's stiletto caught in the grass. She stumbled forward, but the rest of the nymphs thought the move was a threat. With dolphin-pitched squeals and the sounds of tearing fabric and stomping heels, the entire circle erupted into violence.

Unfortunately, I'd edged too close to them and got sucked into the tangle.

I covered my head with an arm and pushed my way into the middle of the circle, trying to reach the redhead and pull her out of the scrum. I squinted against flying nails and winced at the force of small, pointy elbows. I'd stepped into their fight, so knocking them out wasn't a politically viable move. But neither was I going to lose an eye to a nymph catfight.

I'd just managed to get a hand on the redhead's dress when a stiletto caught me on the temple. I threw out a curse, dropping to my knees in the middle of the fight as pain sang through my head. I gingerly touched the spot and pulled back fingertips coated in blood.

Unfortunately, I wasn't the only one bleeding. The nymphs were slicing one another with French-manicured nails and expensive heels, and each cut put nymph blood—astringent and cinnamony and full of magic—into the air. Like I had only the control of a still-pink vampire, I felt my fangs descend, and guessed my eyes—normally blue—had silvered from bloodlust.

I was debating whether to crawl out to safety or stand up again and make another attempt at separating the cloud of bodies when a shrill whistle split the air.

All fighting stopped. The nymphs dropped their holds on one another and turned toward the noise.

Jeff Christopher walked into the fracas like James Bond, all cool swagger and unfailing confidence, and he had the attention of every last one of them.

I wasn't sure if it was because he was a shifter, or because he was Jeff, but this was the second time I'd seen him play the nymphs like a Stradivarius, and it wasn't any less impressive the second time around. Jeff spent a lot of his time playing Catcher's young, skinny, geeky sidekick, but there was no mistaking the man he was becoming.

Jeff reached out a hand and helped pull me to my feet, wincing at what felt like a pretty good gash. "Are you okay?" he asked.

"I'll be fine," I confirmed, swiping the back of my hand at the trickle of blood. "They were ganging up on the redhead. I stepped in to get her out, and that was the end of that. I'm tapping out. You're in."

"You go take care of yourself," he said, his voice an octave deeper than usual as he played macho peacemaker. "I'll take this one."

Perfectly content to let him do that, I moved out of the way and stood still while Jonah pressed a cotton handkerchief to my forehead. But I kept my eyes trained on Jeff and the nymphs, as there was no way I was going to miss watching him work his mojo.

I wasn't the only one interested in the floor show. Catcher walked across the grass with my grandfather in tow. Catcher, by all accounts, had been born with a gruff attitude, although the muscles and green eyes—and the fact that he loved and respected my best friend in the world—usually made up for it. In his usual style, Catcher wore a snug T-shirt with LAMESAUCE written across it in capital letters, and dark jeans over boots. The thick, black Buddy Holly–style glasses he'd paired with them were a relatively new twist, but he pulled them off.

My grandfather was dressed in typically grandfatherly attire— cotton trousers and a button-up plaid shirt under a comfy-looking jacket with elastic at the sleeves and waist. His face scrunched in concern when he saw me, but I waved it off.

"Are you all right?" he asked.

"I am now that the uncaped crusader has arrived." I gestured at Jeff, who had crossed his arms over his chest and was staring down each of the nymphs in turn. They looked rumpled and cha-grined—as if embarrassed both because he'd seen them fight and because they didn't look their best. A few of them fluffed their hair and straightened their hems, apparently unaware that Jeff was thoroughly taken by Fallon, a female shifter with an attitude and the skills to back it up.

"How many times do I have to tell you not to get too close?"

I glanced over at Catcher, who was regarding me with a typical mix of amusement and irritation, and stuck my tongue out at him. "I tried to help. They were ganging up on one of the girls. I got hit in the head."

"With a stiletto," Jonah helpfully threw in. "She got hit in the head with a stiletto."

I smiled tightly. "Oh, and this is Jonah," I told my grandfather. "Captain of Grey House's guards. Since we're short-staffed, he volunteered for a ride-along. Jonah, my grandfather and the Ombudsman, Chuck Merit, and Catcher Bell." They knew of each other, but I made the formal introductions just in case.

Jonah and Catcher shared one of those manly, "It's nice to meet you, but I'm going to barely acknowledge your existence with a small nod because that's the manly thing to do" gestures.

My grandfather, on the other hand, looked at me quizzically. "Merit, I know Jonah, obviously."

"Obviously?" I asked, looking between the two.

My grandfather and Jonah exchanged a glance that suggested Jonah hadn't been entirely forthright about his history—or I'd forgotten something substantial.

My chest fluttered a bit at the possibility that struck me, and I pointed at Jonah. "You're the vampire source! My grandfather's secret vampire employee."

"I don't recall being a secret vampire employee," Jonah slowly said, "and I feel like I would have remembered that. Surely I'd have at least seen a tax form or something." He looked at my grandfather. "Are you hiring?"

"Not currently," he answered. "And while it's an interesting guess, it's a wrong one. Don't you remember him?"

I frowned. "Remember him? From what?"

But before that mystery could be solved, events unfolded in nymph town.

"What, in God's name," Jeff forced out, "would make you think fighting in the middle of Navy Pier Park was a good idea? It's a public place! The city is barely holding itself together right now, and you're squabbling like children. Do you think this is going to help your cause?"

The nymphs looked appropriately shamed. I looked around, wondering what people were thinking. Jonah and I had heard the yelling from yards away, and given the state of the river, we weren't the only people out and about.

Jeff stared them down like a general displeased with his troops. "All right," he said. "Lay it out for me."

"Alanna jinxed us," proclaimed a nymph named Melaina, whom I'd met the last time the nymphs had been fighting. She pointed to the redhead. "Have you seen the picture of her? We've been jinxed!"

"So it was magic?" I asked aloud. "Did Alanna do some kind of charm?" While I wasn't thrilled by the possibility that River nymphs were playing abracadabra with the city, at least it gave us an answer. I liked answers.

Alanna jumped forward, her green dress barely containing her assets as she moved. "I did no such thing!"

Jeff looked back at me. "Melaina means 'jinxed' metaphorically."

Jonah leaned over. "Told you," he whispered.

I held up a hand, then pointed at Alanna. "What were you doing to the river?"

Alanna closed her eyes, now streaming with tears. "I was embracing it. I could feel it changing, dying. It needed me."

As if saddened by the reminder, the nymphs began to keen in low, sad voices, singing a dirge for the magic-sick water.

Their grief notwithstanding, they weren't ready to forgive Alanna. "She made us look bad," pouted a brunette nymph. "She made it look like we did bad magic. And now the city blames us for what happened."

"Who took the picture?" I asked Alanna.

She shrugged. "I don't know. There were human boys on the next bridge over." She smiled a little. "They said I was pretty."

And they have the photograph to prove it, I thought.

"It hurts now," cried a red-dressed pinup-type with a perfect red manicure.

"It hurts?" Jeff asked.

"We can feel the magic leaving us," she said, rubbing her arms as if against a sudden chill. "Something is pulling away the magic, and it makes us feel . . . empty."

Now that she mentioned it, the nymphs did look a little more tired than usual. It was dark in the park, but I could see the faint shadows of circles under their eyes and gauntness in their expressions.

"Can you do anything about this?" I asked Catcher. He shook his head.

"There's magic at work here. It's not the kind of thing I can control. I can work the universe," he added at my confused expression. "This isn't the universe. It's magic—someone else's magic—and that's outside my wheelhouse."

"Is it magic you recognize?" I asked, grasping at straws. "Is there any signature in it? Maybe a spell you've seen before or a familiar buzz? Anything?"

"It's not familiar to me. I've seen the occasional borrowing spell. That's basically just a way to 'borrow' someone else's magic. But in that spell, the vacuum flows from the one who cast the spell. Here, the lake is the vacuum. And it's not like the lake could cast its own spell."

We both looked at the lake in silence.

"I can feel my strength diminishing as I stand here," he quietly added. "I'd guess it's down to eighty percent? But damned if I know what to do about it."

"And if we don't fix this?" I asked him.

The look he gave back didn't offer much hope. "I suppose it's possible," he quietly said, "that the nymphs' magic would dissipate completely and they'd lose their connection to the water altogether. I assume I'll get stronger the farther I get, but they can only go so far from the water for so long."

Catcher had spoken quietly, but the nymphs must have heard him. There was more crying, and their grief was telling: Whatever had happened to the water, these girls weren't responsible.

"Is this the complete universe of nymphs?" I asked Catcher, who did a quick visual count, then nodded.

"They're all here."

"None of these girls spelled the lake," I said. "Not with this kind of sadness. I really think we can rule out the nymphs' involvement."

"I agree. Unfortunately, that also makes this lead a dead end," Jonah said.

"Maybe not," I suggested, then stepped forward. "Ladies, it's clear you wouldn't hurt the river or the lake."

The singing stopped, replaced by a soft, satisfied humming.

"But something is going on out there. Someone has turned the lake into a magic vacuum. Maybe to hurt the lake. Maybe to hurt the city. Maybe to hurt you. If the River nymphs weren't involved, do you know who might be?"

To a one, the nymphs stopped and looked at me, their eyes narrowed with malice.

"Lorelei," said a blond nymph with serious self-assurance. "The siren."

——— ❈❖❈ ———

CHAPTER FOUR

CHICAGO GIVETH; CHICAGO TAKETH AWAY

S o, it turns out each body of water had its own protector. There were spring nymphs and fountain nymphs, ocean nymphs and waterfall nymphs. And sirens, not nymphs, controlled the Great Lakes.

In Chicago, the River nymphs had control of the river and its boundaries. Lorelei, the Lake Michigan siren, controlled the ebb and flow of the lake. She was the only inhabitant of an otherwise deserted, woody, three-square-mile island in the middle of the water.

Most important, the nymphs *hated* her. They treated us to a screechy, twenty-minute-long lecture on her faults, an antiperformance evaluation. I reduced the list to her biggest faults:

1. Lorelei made a pact with the devil (who lived on the island with her);
2. Lorelei was a purveyor of black magic, including made-to-order hexes and jinxes;
3. Lorelei ate babies (human and otherwise); and

4. Lorelei was an all-around, black-wearing, Goth-leaning, antisocial freak (frankly, just the kind of girl a bunch of cute, pretty, busty nymphs would hate).

I had a pretty clear mental image of Lorelei—helped along by having read way too many fairy tales and horror novels as a teenager—as a hunchbacked crone draped in shabby black fabric, standing above the lake in a position not unlike Alanna's had been. Arms outstretched, craggy nose poised over cruelly twisted lips, offering up incantations to kill the lake for some reason we hadn't yet determined.

But planting that image in my brain seemed to soothe the pretty girls, who were now hugging and adjusting their slips and wiping their tears away in a giant nymphy hug-fest.

Frankly, it was hard to keep the boys' attention. A little throat-clearing did the trick.

"We could pay her a visit," Jonah suggested.

To be honest, that idea didn't thrill me. Unfortunately, this problem was bigger than my discomfort. The nymphs were getting weaker, and God only knew how the other sups were faring.

"It's probably a good idea," my grandfather said, "if there's even a small chance it would make a difference. And I don't recall there being any means of communication out there, so it's not as if we could simply call her." He looked at me, a question in his eyes.

I sighed. "Why me?"

"Because you're a girl," Catcher said.

It took me a moment to fathom a response. "Excuse me?"

"She's a siren," Catcher said. "Luring sailors to their deaths? Singing songs beautiful enough to make them weep? Trapping them in eternal ecstasy?"

Jonah's eyes went big as saucers, which made me roll mine. "And that makes my visiting her a bad idea because . . . ?"

"Because you wouldn't come back," Catcher dryly said. "She'd be magically bound to seduce you, to entrance you, and you'd be stuck in siren limbo for the rest of your immortal days."

"Again, I'm not really feeling dissuaded."

"You'd feel dissuaded when you'd forgotten to eat or drink because you couldn't stand to be out of her presence. Dying of starvation ain't a pretty way to go."

"Okay," Jonah said with a grimace. "That's a better argument."

"And that's why we're sending Boobs McGee."

I slowly swiveled my head to glare at Catcher. "Seriously. You're, what, twelve now?"

"The point is, men don't visit a siren on purpose. She'd have no choice but to seduce them, and that's not really going to help us drill down into the magic problems."

"Then I guess that settles that," I agreed. "My boobs and I will go. But I'm not crazy about the idea of getting in a boat in that water. Transportation ideas, anyone?"

"I'll take that one," my grandfather said. "I'll make some calls and see if I can find a helicopter pilot willing to visit an isolated island over a lake tainted with magic. Of course, there'll be paperwork, so it will be tomorrow before we can take any action."

"And in the meantime?" I asked, looking at the group. "What do we do about the lake?"

The question set off the nymphs again. When Jeff knelt down to pat the closest nymph on the back, she turned, wrapped her arms around him, and began to sob with impressive dramatic flair.

"Well done, vampire," Catcher muttered.

"It was a legitimate question," I said. "We still have a crisis— and since we can't travel at night, an entire day will go by before we're talking to the siren about it."

"First step is move the nymphs inland," Jeff said over the shoulder of his embracing nymph. "Farther from the water and whatever is going on out there. Maybe that will help them retain some strength in the meantime."

Cue the crying.

"I know, honey," he said, patting her back with brotherly affection. "But we need to let the lake heal, don't we?"

She bobbed her head while sniffing, but maintained her vice-like grip on Jeff.

"I'll coordinate the move," Catcher said. "Maybe the fairies will host some of them overnight."

"The Breckenridges have a huge house in Naperville, but putting shifters and nymphs together probably isn't a good idea." As if on cue, I watched the nymph's hand sneak down Jeff's butt and get in a good squeeze. He yelped and politely pushed her away, but she smiled unapologetically. I wasn't sure if she didn't know Jeff had a girlfriend—or just didn't care.

"That would be a 'no' on the Brecks," Catcher grumbled.

"What do we do about the humans?" Jonah said, watching as more lines of people moved toward the lake to get a look. "They are going to freak out."

I couldn't blame them. As paranormal events went, this one was very disconcerting, and it hit something close to our hearts. Chicago curled around the lake, and the river ran through the heart of the city. They were bound together, and humans would inevitably see this as a paranormal violation of that connection. I didn't look forward to the outcry.

"I'll work up some talking points for Mayor Kowalczyk," my grandfather said, "although God knows how we'll explain it."

"Focus on the part about how this isn't the apocalypse," I suggested, but a frisson of fear still tightened my chest. "And try to make sure they don't automatically blame it on vampires. We have enough to deal with right now."

He patted my back. "We'll work the problem, do a little research.

You kids get home. I know you're short-staffed at the House. I'll give you a call when we've got the transportation lined up."

I nodded, although I hated bailing on a project. Sitting around and anticipating things to come wasn't exactly a favorite pastime. To keep busy, I made a mental note to check out the House's world-class library; if there was information to be found about our reclusive siren, the library would have it.

I made my good-byes to Jeff (still entangled in nymph), but pulled Catcher aside for an update. "How goes the studying?"

Catcher rolled his eyes. "I'm told her stress level has only been historically exceeded by the 'Meisner-Moxner Presentation,' whatever that was."

I grimaced. Meisner-Moxner was a household products company for which Mallory, a former ad exec, spent two straight weeks preparing a kick-ass branding campaign, only to be told three days before the presentation that her boss "just wasn't feeling it."

The next seventy-two hours involved a caffeine-induced and sleep-deprived haze of massive proportions. Mal chained herself to her desk, surviving on diet soda, energy drinks, and a creative euphoria she later described as "epic." When all was said and done, the agency bagged the deal and she slept for two straight days.

The Meisner-Moxner campaign went down in advertising history as one of the most successful household product rollouts of the century. Unfortunately, Junior Moxner spent the company's newfound money on call girls and cocaine, and Meisner-Moxner Home Brands, Inc., went bankrupt soon after that. Mallory slept for another two straight days after learning about that.

So if her exam prep was even close to Meisner-Moxner, I felt for Mallory . . . and Catcher.

"God bless you, man. But at least Simon has to take the brunt of the stress. Since he's seeing her during the testing part, I mean."

Catcher's expression went flat. "I'm sure he's seeing plenty of her."

The squint in his eyes had all the hallmarks of a jealous boyfriend. But how was that possible? This was *Catcher*. Six-pack-abs-and-ridiculous-body-and-brilliant-wielder-of-magic Catcher. He who took gruff from no one. Maybe I misread him. Maybe he just didn't like Simon. I'd had a sense of that before, but curiosity killed the cat, not the vampire, so I pushed ahead.

"Bad blood between you and Simon?" I wondered.

"I don't trust him."

When he didn't elaborate, I almost asked if he meant he didn't trust Simon with Mallory, but thought better of it. Catcher was a man's man, and suggesting he was jealous would not go over well.

Instead, I gave him a supportive pat on the back. "When this is all over, I'll buy drinks for you and your newly minted official sorceress."

Catcher grumbled something I didn't catch, but I assumed it was related to his hatred for the Order. He'd been excommunicated, and it couldn't have been easy for him to watch Mallory struggle so hard to gain membership. What Chicago giveth, Chicago taketh away.

We made our good-byes to Catcher, and Jonah and I headed back toward our cars.

"I know you're bummed you won't be able to visit the siren tomorrow," I offered.

"Clinically depressed," he agreed. "Do you think her skirt will be shorter than the nymphs', or maybe a bit longer?"

I rolled my eyes, but couldn't keep from smiling. He was funny. But I wasn't going to contribute to what I'm sure was already a healthy ego.

"Since we're effectively done for the night, you wanna grab a bite?"

He probably meant the question in a purely platonic way, but it still triggered fluttery panic in my chest. On the other hand, dinner would give me opportunity to quiz Jonah about his relationship with my grandfather. Having learned my father had tried to bribe Ethan to make me a vampire, I was understandably suspicious about vampires' relationships with members of my family.

"Will you tell me how you know my grandfather?"

"Possibly. How do you feel about spicy?"

"Nuclear-explosion spicy or supermarket-salsa spicy?"

"Whichever you prefer. The world is your oyster."

"I should probably say no. You totally sold me out."

"How so?"

"You told them I got hit with a stiletto." Getting sliced up by a Jimmy Choo knockoff hadn't exactly been my finest moment as Cadogan Sentinel. I saw no need to spread the news around.

He faked shock. "Merit, would you have me lie to your grandfather?"

"That depends on how long you've known him."

Unfortunately, he didn't take the bait. "Quid pro quo. Dinner first, then details."

I sighed, knowing I'd been beaten. "Fine. But I want the truth."

"Oh, you'll get the truth, Merit. You'll get the truth."

Somehow, that didn't make me feel any better.

The Thai Mansion was stuck in the middle of a squatty strip mall, a dry cleaner on one side and take-out pizza chain on the other.

A bell on the door rang when we walked in. "El Paso" by Marty

Robbins played on a small radio perched on the glass counter beside a golden Buddha, an ancient cash register and a plastic bucket of peppermints.

The interior of the restaurant wasn't much to look at. The walls were painted concrete blocks and bore a random mix of 1970s B-movie posters. These were mingled with handwritten signs warning patrons not to park in the spaces owned by the dry cleaner or attempt to pay with anything but cash. Plastic was not the new black at the Thai Mansion.

"This is the best Thai food in Chicago?" I wondered.

"Trust me," Jonah said, then nodded to a petite, dark-haired waitress who smiled back pleasantly, then nodded when he pointed to an empty table.

We took seats, and I scanned the plastic-covered, handwritten menu. There were a few sloppy translations, but most of the words weren't in English, which I figured was a good thing in a Thai restaurant. "You come here a lot?"

"More than I should admit," he said. "I'm not knocking the Grey House cafeteria, but Scott's big on convenience foods. We've had entire meals that were beige."

I imagined a plate of bread, mashed potatoes, tater tots, stuffing, and pound cake. "Not that there's anything wrong with that."

"On occasion, no. But a vamp with a taste for life likes a little more variety."

"And you're a vamp with a taste for life?"

He shrugged modestly. "The world has a lot to offer. There's a lot to explore. I like to take advantage of that."

"So immortality's come in handy, then?"

"You might say that."

A waitress with long, dark hair scuffled over the restaurant's green carpet in white sneakers. "You ready?"

Jonah glanced at me, and when I nodded, offered his order. "Pad thai with shrimp."

"How spicy tonight?"

"Nine," he said, then handed over his menu. Their transaction complete, she looked at me.

I assumed that nine was on a scale of one to ten. I liked spicy food, but I wasn't about to order a nine at a restaurant I'd never vetted. God only knew how hot their nine might be.

"Same for me. How about a seven?" I requested, but the waitress looked dully at me.

"You been here before?"

I glanced between her and Jonah. "Um, no."

Shaking her head, she plucked away my menu. "No seven. You can have two."

With that pronouncement, she turned and disappeared through the curtain into the backroom.

"A two? I'm not sure how not to be insulted by that."

He chuckled low in his throat. "That's only because you haven't had a two yet."

I was doubtful, but didn't have much evidence to go on. And speaking of missing evidence . . .

"All right, quid pro quo time. How do you know my grandfather? I know you were friends with Charlotte. You told me that before. Is that the connection?" Charlotte is my older sister. I also have a brother, Robert, who was following in my father's property-grubbing footsteps.

"I did and do know Charlotte," Jonah said. "I knew you, too."

I was drawing a complete blank. "How did you know me?"

"I took Charlotte to prom."

I froze in my seat. "You did what now?"

"I took Charlotte to her senior college formal."

I closed my eyes, trying to remember. I'd been home for spring break and had been witness to Charlotte's meltdown when she'd had a fight with her then-boyfriend and now-husband, Major Corkburger (yes, seriously). She'd gone with a guy named Joe to the formal instead.

The lightbulb lit.

"Oh, my God," I exclaimed, pointing at him. "You were 'Joe'! I didn't even recognize you."

Joe had been a very short-lived rebellious phase. I saw him only a couple of times after prom. A month later, Charlotte and Major were back together, and Joe had disappeared.

"You had a perm," I reminded him. "And you took her to the formal in one of those hoodies made of rugs."

"I'd just gotten here from Kansas City." He'd said it like that explained his ensemble, like Kansas City was a foreign country with a completely different culture. "The pace was different down there, even for vampires. A little slower."

"And Charlotte introduced you to my grandfather?"

I could see Jonah's blush even in the dark. "Yeah. To piss off Major, I think. I was finishing up one of my degrees. This gorgeous girl approached me on campus one day and asked me out." He shrugged. "It's not like I was going to say no. And when we met with Noah, you had no idea who I was."

That explained why Jonah had copped such an attitude the first night we'd met near the lake. "That's why you were irritated with me," I said. "Not because you thought I was like Charlotte, but because you thought I'd forgotten you."

"You *had* forgotten me, and you aren't as unlike Charlotte as you'd like to believe."

I started to protest, thinking he meant to tease me about society soirees or luxury brands or winters in Palm Beach, none of which I was interested in. But instead of assuming, I gave him the benefit of the doubt and asked the question. "Why am I like Charlotte?"

He smiled. "Because you're loyal. Because you both value your families, even if you define them differently. Her children and Major are hers. Your House is yours."

It hadn't always been that way, but I couldn't disagree with him. "I see."

A few minutes later, our waitress returned with two steaming piles of noodles.

"Nine," she said, placing a plate in front of Jonah. "And two," she said, dropping an identical plate in front of me.

I removed the wrapper from a pair of chopsticks and glanced up at Jonah in anticipation. "You ready?"

"Are you?" he asked with amusement.

"I'll be fine," I assured him, plucking up a tangle of noodles and bean sprouts. My first bite was huge . . . and I regretted it immediately.

"Two" was apparently a euphemism for "Flaming Inferno." My eyes watered, the heat building from a slow burn at the back of my throat to a firestorm along the tip of my tongue. I would have sworn flames were actually shooting from my ears.

"Oh, God. Oh, God. Oh, God. *Hot*," I got out before grabbing my glass of water and finishing half of it in a single gulp. "That's a two?" I hoarsely asked. "That is insane."

"And you wanted a seven," Jonah nonchalantly said, eating his plate of noodles like it had been doused in nothing more than soy sauce.

"How can you possibly eat that?"

"I'm used to it."

I took another bite and chewed quickly, barely enjoying the flavor, mostly trying to choke it down before the spice caught up with me.

The waitress approached again, a carafe of water in hand. She refilled Jonah's glass, then glanced at me. "Two?"

"Still too hot," I admitted, chugging down another half glass of water. "What's in it? Thai peppers?"

Shrugging, the waitress refilled my glass again. "Cook grows them in her yard. Very hot."

"Very, very hot," I agreed. "Do people actually order the ten?"

"Longtime customers," she said. "Or on dare."

With that pronouncement, she toddled away with her now-empty carafe.

I looked at Jonah with spice-spawned tears in my eyes. "Thank you for not daring me to eat the ten."

"It wouldn't have been right," Jonah said, shoveling noodles into his mouth. A thin line of sweat appeared on his forehead, and he'd begun to sniff.

"I thought the heat didn't get to you?" I asked with a self-satisfied smile.

He wiped at his brow with the back of a hand, then grinned up at me. "I didn't say it wasn't hot. I just said I was used to it. Immortality's hardly worth the trouble if there's no challenge."

I wasn't positive, but I had a sinking suspicion he wasn't talking about the food. I took another bite, and focused on the burning sting.

"Tell me about Ethan."

Startled, I looked over at Jonah. "Excuse me?"

Nonchalantly, he shrugged and swallowed another knot of noodles. "You told me you weren't together. That may be true, but I don't get the sense it's the entire story."

I watched him for a moment, smiling as he chewed, as I decided what to tell him. My time with Ethan had been tempestuous. More stops than starts, and those stops had been traumatic.

Ethan was gone before the relationship had had a chance to blossom, but that didn't make the grief any easier to bear—or explain.

"We had moments together," I said. "We weren't quite a couple—although I think we might have been if he hadn't . . ." I couldn't make myself finish the sentence.

"If Celina hadn't done what she'd done," Jonah finished kindly.

I nodded.

"He meant a lot to you."

I nodded again. "He did."

"Thank you for telling me," he said.

He let the subject drop, but I still had the sense he was asking something more. And his subtlety didn't make the rest of our dinner any less awkward. I kept the conversation moving (and light) until we paid and headed back to our cars. That's when he got to the heart of it.

"You had feelings for Ethan," he said. "You were close and that affected your perception of the Red Guard. But you know now the GP isn't always on the side of the good and the just. Grey House knows who's in the wrong about Celina, and about Ethan's death. The GP should have supported what you were doing in Chicago, and instead of offering help when V surfaced, they ignored it and blamed you for the aftermath. The RG's argument isn't with the Houses; it's with the GP."

"I swore an oath."

"Working with us to ensure the GP doesn't tear your House apart supports that oath."

I considered the argument in silence. He had a point; the GP was no friend to Cadogan House. On the other hand, wasn't joining the Red Guard still a slap in Malik's face? An agreement to work behind his back even if supposedly for the "greater good."

"Why?" I wondered.

He frowned. "What do you mean, why?"

"Why do you want me to join the RG? What's the benefit? We already know the GP is self-centered and more focused on perception than real work. They leave the hard stuff to us and still blame us after the fact, so what's the point? Membership doesn't change anything, except risking that we'll be nailed to the wall if they find out."

"We?"

I looked back at him, and wasn't thrilled by the self-satisfied grin that was overtaking his expression.

"You said 'we,'" he pointed out.

"It was a turn of phrase. You know what I meant." I tried to keep my tone nonchalant, but he had a point. Jonah and I were working together—had been working together—to keep the Houses safe. Was I already implicitly a member?

"No, Merit, I don't know that," he countered. "I know you just confessed you already consider yourself to be doing the work of the RG." He stepped in front of me and looked down. "You want to know why you should join? Because for the first time in your life, you'd have a partner. You'd have someone on your side, at your beck and call, ready to serve and assist you in whatever the assignment might be."

He was wrong about that. When Ethan was alive, I'd had a partner.

"I'm already working with you," I pointed out.

"You have me because you don't have a better option. If Ethan was still here, or if there was an extra guard in your House, you'd go that route."

I couldn't disagree with him there.

"But here's the real kicker," he said. "For the first time in your life, you'd be offered the choice. You were dragged unconscious into Cadogan House. You were appointed Sentinel with no say in the matter."

He tipped his head down, his lips nearly brushing my ear. The move was intimate, but it didn't feel sexual. Jonah wasn't attempting to break through my defenses—he was demonstrating how close we'd already become. "You'd be making the *choice* to serve."

He was right. I hadn't had the choice then, but he was giving me the choice now. I could admit it was a powerful argument.

He apparently knew that, too, because without another word, he stood straight again and walked away.

"That's it?"

He glanced back. "That's it. This call, Merit, is all yours."

As he got into his car and drove away, I blew out a breath. To RG or not to RG, that was the question.

Since the lake was still dark and unmoving, I wasn't excited about the report I'd have to give Kelley back at the House. But at least we had a plan, and if anyone in Chicago could corral a helicopter, my grandfather could.

When I pulled up to the House, the protestors were louder and larger in number, their signs promising even more hellfire and damnation than usual. "Apocalypse" and "Armageddon" were sprinkled among the hand-painted posters, just as we'd feared. And to be frank, I couldn't completely blame them. Even I wasn't sure why the lake had turned black and started leeching magic, so I guess the end of the world was on the list of possibilities. It was at the bottom of the list, but it was still on the list.

The protestors weren't the only ones out in force. We'd been the subject of picture- (and money-) hungry paparazzi for a while now; a corps of photographers was usually camped out on a corner near the House. Tonight, though, news trucks lined the street, reporters waiting to see vampire shenanigans. Anything that went wrong in this city and was remotely paranormal in nature led them straight to our door. It was an argument for outing the rest of Chicago's sups, if only to take some of the heat off us.

The reporters, familiar with me through the Ponytailed Avenger story and my patrols of the Cadogan grounds, called me to a stop.

I didn't want to support their efforts at sensational journalism, but I figured their theories would only get worse if I ignored them. So I walked over to a knot of reporters and offered a muted acknowledgment.

"Tough night out there, isn't it?"

Some chuckled; others began shouting out questions.

"Did vampires poison the lake?"

"Is this the beginning of the end for the city of Chicago?"

"Is this the first plague?"

I had to work to keep my expression neutral and not roll my eyes at the questions. That I had no idea made that a little easier.

"I was hoping you'd tell me!" I said, offering a light smile. "We're trying to figure that out ourselves."

"This wasn't something created by vampires? A magic spell?"

"Vampires don't do spells." I scanned the media badge of the man in front of me. "Maybe it was Matthew here who turned the water black."

The crowd laughed but the questions kept coming. "Believe me," I said, raising my hands, "we want the lake back to normal as quickly as you do, and we're trying to figure it out just like everyone else in Chicago. Problem is, we didn't do it, so we're having trouble figuring out where to start."

"Merit, is this the start of the apocalypse?" piped up a reporter in the back.

"I certainly hope not. But if I'm going down, let it be in Chicago with a red hot in hand. Am I right?"

Sure, it was sycophantic, and I'm sure some of the press guys picked up on that. But what else could I do? If I didn't keep the focus off vampires, things were going to get very nasty very quickly. With questions peppering the air behind me, I waved good-bye and walked into the House, sharing a sympathetic eye roll with the fairies at the gate when I passed them.

I felt a pang as I wondered what Ethan, a PR master strategist if there ever was one, would have said to them. I wasn't him, but I hoped I'd done enough to keep things calm for a little while longer.

I headed immediately to the Ops Room; Kelley and Juliet were the only guards there. Both looked up when I entered, but their expressions fell after seeing my face.

"No luck?" Kelley asked.

"Not much," I said, taking a seat at the conference table beside Kelley. "The River nymphs are grieving, and by all accounts had nothing to do with the water. They've pointed their little manicured fingers at Lorelei, the lake siren. She lives on an island in the middle of the lake. The Ombud's office is arranging for transportation, but not until tomorrow. I hope it's a solid lead."

Kelley frowned and nodded. In the way of all managers, I imagine she wanted a crisis addressed and solved so she could move on to the next matter at hand—whether dealing with a shortage of guards or a receiver in the House.

"If that's the best we can do, that's the best we can do," Kelley said. "It doesn't exactly take pressure off the House, but I wouldn't condone sending you into the middle of the lake a few hours before sunrise, either."

I told Kelley about my grandfather's plans and my discussion with the paparazzi outside.

Kelley looked suddenly tired, and I wondered if she was tired of the drama, or if Frank's blood restrictions were beginning to take their toll. The Thai food had quenched one appetite, but I could feel the hunger for blood slinking around in my mind, waiting for a time to strike. I made a note to check the kitchen upstairs for a bag of Blood4You.

"We do what we can," Kelley said. "That's all we can do. We work the problem and pray we can get out in front of it before the next crisis hits."

"Second that," Juliet said from her computer station.

Kelley sighed. "And speaking of unpleasantries, I'm advised you're next on Frank's interview list."

"Yay," I said with zero enthusiasm. "I'm totally looking forward to that."

"I could assign you to spend the rest of your evening in the library, researching the lake siren to get a feel for her strengths and weaknesses. After all, it would be a dereliction of my duty to send you out to an island without being prepared. And if you were in the library stacks, Frank may not be able to find you . . ."

I grinned in appreciation. "Sneaky. I appreciate that."

"Not sneaky. Just willing to use the tools at my disposal. And right now, you're my tool. I need you investigating this problem and keeping humans off our back. Being interrogated by a GP pencil pusher is not going to assist in that process." She stood up and walked to her desk, then sat down behind her computer. "Learn what you can, and fill me in on what you find out."

I gave her a salute and headed upstairs again.

CHAPTER FIVE

PAPER TOWERS

The library was on the second floor of the House, not far from my room. It had two floors—the first held the majority of the books and a balcony wrapped in a wrought-iron railing held another set. It was a cavalcade of tomes, all in immaculate rows, and with study carrels and tables thrown in for good measure. It was my home away from home (away from home).

I walked inside and paused for a moment to breathe in the scent of paper and dust—the perfumes of knowledge. The library was empty of patrons as far as I could tell, but I could hear the rhythmic squeal of a library cart somewhere in the rows. I followed them down until I found the dark-haired vampire shelving books with mechanical precision. I knew him only as "the librarian." He was a fount of information, and he had a penchant for leaving books outside my door.

I cleared my throat to get his attention. He looked up, eyes narrowed, probably prepared to give me a lecture about making noise in the library. (A set of rules inside the door warned, among other things, that cough drops were required for patrons with scratchy throats. The librarian wanted no aural interruptions within his domain.)

But when he realized it was me, he held up a hand and ducked down to the bottom shelf of his cart. He popped up again with a bundle of books, which he hefted toward me.

"For you," he said. I scanned the titles; they were, unfortunately, more books of vampire politics. He'd already given me lots of books on vampire politics, which seemed to barely scratch the surface of the number of books actually *written* on vampire politics. We were a political bunch, and we apparently liked to ruminate on that particular obsession.

But he was a man who could help me with my current problem, so I didn't look a gift horse in the mouth.

"Thank you," I said, and took the books from him. "A question—what can you tell me about the lake siren?"

The librarian made a disdainful sound, then abandoned his cart to head down the aisle.

I stuck the books into an empty spot on a shelf and trailed him down the aisle and across the room to the staircase that led up to the balcony.

I followed him up, the staircase so narrow and steep my nose was practically in the back of his knees. When we reached the second floor, he passed a few rows before stopping at a shelf of oversized books and sliding one out.

Thankfully, this wasn't a treatise on politics. It was a book of art, a catalog of paintings of lovely, russet-haired maidens near streams and pools of water.

"These are nymphs and sirens," the librarian explained, flipping through some of the paintings. "Nymphs reside in the rivers. Sirens reside in the lakes. They're the governing supernaturals for those areas. They are embodiments of the essences of the bodies of water. Intimately connected to them, part of them."

"And River trolls do the enforcing for the nymphs?"

"Very good, Sentinel," he said, then frowned absently. "No known enforcers for the sirens. Both tend to keep to themselves—except for their odd relationships with shifters."

"Powder keg," I suggested.

"A chemical reaction of some kind, certainly. In any event, while the nymphs and shifters have a connection, the nymphs and sirens most definitely do not. Call it a matter of competition. Nymphs believe rivers are better than lakes: the water's constantly flowing, they move commerce, et cetera. Sirens believe lakes are better than rivers. They hold more volume. They're better for recreation; they support more fishing."

"Lakes versus rivers seems like a minor issue. The nymphs acted like they hated Lorelei."

"It isn't a minor issue when you're a supernatural being tied to the body of water. The nature of that body of water matters."

"And if that water is currently sucking away the city's magic?"

"Then you've got a problem that threatens to destabilize supernatural relations in the city even more."

That wasn't exactly news. "I'm supposed to go visit Lorelei tomorrow. What should I expect?"

The librarian closed the art book again and slid it back onto the shelf, then walked a few feet ahead and slid out a wide, flat drawer that held large sheets of paper. He flipped through them, then beckoned me forward. He'd selected a map of the Great Lakes region, but unlike normal maps, only the bodies of water were labeled.

"The island's rumored to be woody," he said, pointing to a

green dot in the middle of Lake Michigan, "but the house will have to have some kind of water feature. A pool, a waterfall, et cetera. Water isn't just important to a siren—it's a necessity."

"Aquariums?" I wondered. I imagined a wall-sized aquarium filled with a rainbow of tropical fish, or maybe a koi pond in the backyard.

The librarian shook his head. "Never aquariums. Water spirits are strong believers that animals should be left in their natural habitats."

"What about strengths? Weaknesses?"

"Both water related. Both nymphs and sirens need to stay in relatively close contact with water, either geographically or chronologically."

"You mean, they can go for a little while without touching water, or they can go a little bit away from the water, but not for very long."

He nodded. "Exactly. As for powers, they are regulators of the water, which means they can feel it. They understand its health, its problems."

"So if the river's polluted, it affects the nymphs?"

"Exactly. I assume this water sickness is affecting them keenly."

I nodded. "They're very upset. They're also getting weaker, and proximity to the water seems to make it worse."

"That's bad news."

I agreed, but didn't yet have a solution. "Anything else?"

"Sirens also have the typical power of water women." He lifted his eyebrows suggestively.

"Seducing and capturing men? Yeah, I feel like I'm pretty safe on that one. That's why I'm flying solo on this one."

With a matter-of-fact nod, he slid the map drawer closed, then pointed back to the shelf of art books. "Grab a few of those and flip through them. Pay attention to the characteristics of the women in the paintings. Their expressions. Their clothing. Are they holding weapons?"

"But these are art books. Are they reliable?"

The librarian snorted. "All artists have models, Merit. If you're a water spirit, to whom else would you rather reveal yourself than an artist who will make you immortal? Just keep one thing in mind."

"What's that?"

"If it takes too long to turn the waters back, you may not be able to bring any of them back from the brink."

Not that there was any pressure.

I spent the next few hours doing what any mature adult would do—hiding out in the library so I didn't have to face down the receiver. It's not just that I didn't want to play justify-your-existence with Frank—I didn't want to play justify-your-existence with a man charged with cataloging Ethan's failures.

That was a threshold I didn't want to cross—a bridge between my life with Ethan and my life without him. Not just emotionally, but because Ethan had initiated me into his House and taught me to stand Sentinel.

Frank, on the other hand, was an interloper, an interruption. When I met with him, I'd no longer be able to deny how different things in the House had become. That wasn't an admission I was ready to make.

I also wasn't ready to talk about the night Celina and Ethan had been killed. I didn't think it possible that Frank, a GP representative, wouldn't mention my role in the death of two Master vampires. I'd been waiting for the day the GP laid their deaths at my doorstep, blaming me for what had happened even though

Tate had been controlling Celina, and Celina had killed Ethan. I wasn't looking forward to debriefing him on those events.

So I was seated at a desk in a perfect hiding place, a carrel tucked back in the stacks at the end of a row—almost completely hidden from view.

I was scanning a book of Waterhouse paintings and scribbling notes about the spirits' characteristics when I heard the efficient *clip-clap* of plastic-soled shoes heading in my direction.

I glanced up.

Helen, the House liaison for new vampires and a den mother for the House, came into view. She was a taskmaster, and she was dressed for the part tonight in a boxy gray suit paired with sensible heels and classic X-shaped earrings that probably cost a fortune. Since she was staring down at me, I assumed she was here on a mission.

"Yes?" I prompted.

"Mr. Cabot is ready to speak with you. Please join him in the office." She didn't wait for a reply, but turned and walked back toward the door.

Ugh. Busted.

Helen was the type who ran only hot or cold, and offered no warning about which temperature might be in the pipes on any given day. She could fawn over a new pair of shoes one day and treat you like a stranger the next, barely acknowledging your existence. She was an odd duck, but since I didn't usually interact with her, I didn't worry too much about it.

Frank, on the other hand, apparently used her as an errand girl.

I dropped my forehead to the library table, gearing myself up for a meeting I knew I wasn't going to enjoy. After a moment, I shut the book, then rose and scooted my chair beneath the table. I offered the librarian a nod as I passed him, then headed back to the stairs and Frank's first-floor abode.

Why did I do all those things? Because sometimes, especially for vampires, drama was unavoidable. And on those days, a girl just had to suck it up.

For some reason, my favorite game as a child had been playing school. Except that I didn't pretend to teach a class or be a student. I played class administrator. I put GREAT JOB! stickers on fake homework. I penned students' names and attendance records in old-fashioned class roll books. I organized papers into piles, including ticket stubs and hotel letterhead from my father's business trips.

I'm not sure why, but I loved paper and pens, markers and stamps, all manner of ephemera. As an adult, that translated into an appreciation for fancy pens and slick-papered notebooks. But as vast as my love of paper was, it was nothing compared to Frank's.

He'd filled Ethan's office with piles of paper. Trees would have wept from the sight. The sheer abundance made me wonder if Frank imagined the reams to be the source of some secret power—as if his ability to push paper (and stack it into tidy columns) were the keys to the Cadogan kingdom.

I was standing at the threshold, staring at the forest of white, when Frank waved me in from the conference table that filled the back half of the office.

He wasn't unattractive, but his features were aristocratically pinched, like being born into wealth had sharpened them. His brown hair was short and carefully combed. He wore khakis and a tucked-in white dress shirt. An expensive gold watch was wrapped around his right wrist. I guessed if I peeked under the table I'd find brown loafers with tassels on the top.

"Come in," Frank said. "Have a seat."

I did as I was told, taking the chair across from him. He didn't waste any time.

"You left the House this evening under order of the Captain of the Guards to investigate the"—he paused to look down at a sheet of paper on the table—"incident of Lake Michigan turning black?"

"Yes," I said. "Out of concern humans would automatically blame the city's supernatural populations."

He just made a vague sound that indicated he found the notion ridiculous. "I understand Darius previously ordered you not to involve yourself in city affairs."

"It's not just a city affair if vampires are blamed," I pointed out. "And that dictate was issued before we lost another guard. The guard corps is short-staffed, and I'm next in line to help out."

He made that sound again. "Merit, as you know, I've been tasked by the GP to evaluate the stability and sanctity of the House, both in terms of its financial accounting and its staff. In doing so, I'm interviewing every member of the House to better understand their roles." He shuffled through a few papers, then pulled out a document to which a picture of me had been clipped.

He scanned it for a moment, then placed it back on the table and linked his fingers together on the tabletop.

"You stand Sentinel," he said. His voice carried the distinct impression of disapproval.

"I do."

"And you became a vampire in April of this year?"

"Yes." I saw no reason to elaborate.

"Mmm," he said. "And you were appointed Sentinel at your Commendation, after you'd been a vampire for a matter of, what, essentially a week?"

"Approximately."

"Were you in the armed services before you became Sentinel?"

He was asking questions to which he undoubtedly knew the answer. He wasn't confused about what I'd done prior to becoming Sentinel; he was gathering evidence of Ethan's mismanagement. Unfortunately, I couldn't figure out a way around the game.

"I was not," I answered. "I was a graduate student working on my doctoral degree in English literature."

He frowned, feigning confusion. "But you serve as Sentinel—a warrior for the House. A protector. Surely Ethan would have filled the position with someone trained and ready to take on the challenge?" Frank tilted his head, his brow still furrowed, but a gleam of "Gotcha!" in his eyes.

And now it was time to elaborate . . . and throw back this farce he was perpetrating.

"I'm sure you've seen my file. I'm sure you know I'm rated a Very Strong Phys, a Strong Strat, and a Strong Psych because I can resist glamour. I was strong on the day I was made a vampire, and I've only become stronger since then. I've been trained with a katana, I have political and financial connections throughout this city, and I'm strong enough to have bested Ethan in training. I'm well educated and take seriously the oaths I gave to this House. What else would you have me do?"

"You aren't an infantryman. You aren't trained in combat."

"I'm the Sentinel of the House, charged with protecting the House as an entity. I am not captain of the House guards, and it's not my job to create military strategy. I fight only as a last resort, when all other options have failed. I find that people too willing to jump into the fray usually have an ulterior motive for doing so."

Frank sat back in Ethan's chair, brow pinched as he considered his next tack. "Your ties to Mayor Tate did nothing to help this House."

"Mayor Tate was intent on using vampires for his own purposes. He created an empire of illegal drugs using the imprimatur of his office. There was nothing I could have done to stop that. But I discovered it, and I put an end to it. And because of my work, he's no longer manufacturing drugs or using those drugs to control vampires."

"Your involvement led to the deaths of two Master vampires."

I considered a variety of responses—throwing a fit; offering back evidence of my innocence, that I'd done all I could; complaining about the GP's lack of support when things were going bad in Chicago. But I disregarded all those options.

I knew what had gone down in that room, and I had a fairly good sense the GP did, as well. They may have supported Celina, and they may have hoped for quiet assimilation in Chicago, but they weren't stupid. I wasn't going to play their game, and I wasn't going to give them the aspen to stake me with.

"I am sure you've been well briefed on what occurred at the mayor's house," I politely said. "Is there any specific information you need me to provide?"

Frank looked at me for a long moment. No, not looked at— regarded. He considered me, evaluated me, estimated who I was and what I might be capable of.

He wasn't just an accountant of Houses. He was an accountant of vampires.

"Merit, I'm going to be frank."

I had to bite my lips to keep from making an inappropriately snarky comment about his name.

"The GP exists to ensure no individual vampire or House tips the balance against the rest of us. Cadogan House, however, is a problem child. You already have a demerit in your file, which means you know full well the GP's feelings about the chaos this House has wreaked."

I'd "earned" that demerit because I'd intervened in a drug-induced fight that put Cadogan House on the front page. It was coincidence that I'd been there, but the GP had been looking for someone to blame. And wasn't that what all this was about?

"I imagine the GP is not pleased with the fact that vampires are now out of the closet," I allowed. "But that was Celina's doing. Neither Ethan nor Cadogan House had anything to do with that. If you want to blame someone, pay a visit to Navarre House."

"Ah, but it's not as if I can speak with Celina, can I?"

My chest tightened, and I threw back some vitriol. "Since I staked her after she killed my Master, no. You can't speak with her."

"That's your side of the story, of course."

The hair on the back of my neck stood up. "That's my *side* of the story? That's what happened."

Frowning, Frank shuffled in his chair. "We've received other information."

"From who? There were only five of us in the room, and two of them are dead."

He looked at me for a moment, just long enough for the light-bulb to pop on.

"You spoke with Tate."

"We did. And he tells an interesting tale about your barging into his office and threatening him and his associate. According to Tate, all the drama that occurred was your doing, the deaths your responsibility."

I borrowed an Ethanism and arched a sardonic eyebrow at Frank. "I interrupted Tate harboring a fugitive and controlling Celina with drugs and magic. Celina tried to kill me." The next part was hard to say and harder to admit. "Ethan jumped in front of the stake to save me, but Celina kept coming, and I killed her in self-defense."

"That sounds terribly convenient to me. I don't suppose you have any notion to move up in the chain of command in the House?"

I took a moment to collect myself, and then looked up at Frank again. "I have no interest in being Master of Cadogan House."

"That's not what Tate suggested. He suggested, in fact, that you had a specific plan to deal with the rest of the House hierarchy."

My blood boiled. Seth Tate and I were definitely going to have words. "Tate lied, and I have nothing but respect for Malik. Tate is the one with the secret agenda. And with all due respect, Ethan's death happened two months ago. If you had any legitimate doubts about the events of that night, the GP would have staked or excommunicated me by now."

Frank's expression steeled, his eyes flattening in disgust. I'd called his bluff, daring him to show his cards. He was a GP representative, but maybe he had even less evidence against me, Ethan, and the House than I thought.

"The GP will act as it deems appropriate."

Like never before, I had a sudden empathy for Jonah, Noah, and everyone else involved in the Red Guard. That was precisely the attitude they were battling against—the GP's sense that it was infallible, and the very real fact that there was no other check on its power.

"I'm sure it will," I told him.

Frank clenched his jaw for a moment before returning his attention to the pile of papers in front of him. He gathered them up and tapped them together, then slid them aside, another tower of paper.

"The GP is very disturbed by the actions of this House. Under my authority, it will operate as it was meant to—as one House of twelve. It will not make a spectacle of itself. Is that understood?"

"Perfectly."

"We'll speak again," he assured me, and waved a dismissive hand.

I took that as my cue to exit; I rose, pushed back my chair, and headed for the door.

"Merit."

As I had on so many other occasions, I glanced back from the doorway of the office that had once been Ethan's. But the room, with its towers of paper and ignorant interloper, was different now.

"One way or the other," Frank said, "the truth will come out."

"I hope so," I told him. "I really do."

Dawn was on its way, but the sun hadn't risen yet. I found the books I'd left in the library outside my door, so I carried them into my room. Hunger gnawed at me, the pad thai having left me with the munchies, so I wandered to the kitchen to take stock of whatever free-range, shade-grown munchables Frank had allowed.

Out of curiosity, I also checked the refrigerator, which was usually fully stocked with blood. This time, there were only three sad-looking Blood4You pint bags on the top shelf. The fact that Frank thought it was just to deprive vampires of blood—making them aware with every breath how beholden they were to him—filled me with a surge of anger. It was downright sadistic.

Gnawing my lips, I contemplated diving into one of the bags. My hunger hadn't yet fully arisen, but it was beginning to gnaw in my chest. I was also going to have to face down the lake siren tomorrow, and God only knew what that might involve. I needed the blood—but I hated to take a pint away from someone else. On the other hand, a blood-crazy Sentinel wasn't going to help anyone.

I grabbed a pint from the fridge and set about sating my other hunger. I pulled open a random cabinet and grimaced at the sight.

Just as Lindsey had predicted, the munchables were all free-range and shade-grown, full of organic goodness and without a single saturated or hydrogenated whatnot in sight.

"Miserable, isn't it?"

I glanced behind me. Margot, the House's head chef, stood in the doorway with a dour expression. She wore her chef's whites and rubber clogs, her sleek bob of dark hair gleaming, the pointed bangs resting just between her catlike amber eyes. Her eyes, though, looked a little watery, and they were marked beneath by dark circles.

Was that an effect of blood rationing?

"It is miserable," I agreed.

Margot pulled a small cart into the kitchen, its top and bottom shelves laden with healthy snacks and the crunchy sorts of vegetables that only tasted good when drowned in creamy dill dressing.

I know I wasn't a model for healthy eating. But I'd been careful about my weight my entire life. Now, because of my vampire metabolism, I couldn't gain a pound. I considered that a challenge.

"I like to bake," she said, opening a cabinet and stocking the shelves, "and I enjoy my fruits and veggies, but that doesn't mean I don't enjoy plastic-wrapped carbs now and again."

"I'm sure he thinks he's doing the right thing."

Margot paused, hand on a bag of all-natural dried fruit snacks that probably tasted like Styrofoam, and looked over at me. "Do you really believe that?"

"Unfortunately, yes. I think he truly believes he's doing the right thing for the GP."

She lowered her voice. "Then maybe it's the GP we should be arguing with."

I made a sound of agreement.

Margot stocked the cabinet, then opened the refrigerator door.

"Not much blood," she said, frowning as she looked over the bags that were left.

"Rationing, I assume."

"You'd be right. He's reduced our Blood4You delivery by forty percent."

"I think he's hoping someone loses it," I quietly predicted. "That someone goes after a human, or goes crazy from hunger in front of a camera."

"So he can prove to the GP how flawed the House is. Convince them to turn it over to him for good."

I nodded. Margot and I shared a worried look, before she suddenly brightened.

"I might have a little something that will cheer you up, actually," she said, kneeling down to dig around the bottom shelf of the cart. When she stood up again, she had a gleaming box in her hands.

"Mallocakes!" I whispered, my eyes probably lighting up like roman candles. It wouldn't have surprised me if my fangs had descended out of sheer excitement. Mallocakes were my favorite snack-cake delight, chocolate bars of spongey goodness stuffed with marshmallow crème.

"Contraband," she corrected, then pulled the paper strip off the box and pulled out a Mallocake. With much reverence, she handed it to me. "I'm only brave enough to sneak these in one box at a time," she quietly said, hiding the box again in the jumble on the bottom shelf. "But we all need a little something to get through the day. And if this is what it takes, so be it. You find me when you need a fix."

And so it began, I thought, *the first wave of a revolution against oppression, fought with corn syrup and chocolate.*

"I appreciate it," I said. "And your secret is safe with me."

Margot rolled her cart back down the hallway. I headed back to my room and downed the blood immediately. I stared at the Mallocake in my hand for a moment, but ultimately stuffed it into a drawer. There would undoubtedly be a moment when I needed it even more than now.

Chicago—especially with vampires—just seemed to work that way.

CHAPTER SIX

NO MAN (OR WOMAN) IS AN ISLAND

The message from my grandfather came sometime during the day when I was fast asleep and, thankfully, nightmare free. I snapped up the phone as soon as the sun fell again and read the message: STREETERVILLE HELIPORT. 21:00 CST.

As expected, my grandfather had managed to find a helicopter, and also had developed a taste for using military time.

Being late fall, the sun set earlier and stayed down longer. That gave us a little more time to be awake and about, and it meant I had time to get dressed and take care of secondary business in the few hours before my trip to the island. First item on the list—talking to the people who could make it happen.

I dialed the Ombud's office. Jeff answered the phone on the first ring.

"Merit!"

"Hey, Jeff. I don't suppose the lake magically fixed itself?"

"Not so much, as it looks exactly the same and is still pulling in magic like a Hoover."

"Awesome." If we weren't careful, and fast, there wouldn't be any magic left in Chicago.

"How are the nymphs doing?"

"Not great, but could be worse. We moved them around until we found a place with a relative equilibrium—couldn't move them too far from the lake, or they got weaker because of the distance. Move them too close to the lake, and they get weaker from the vacuum. We eventually hooked them into a couple of condos your father is managing; your grandfather made the arrangements."

That was awfully nice of my father, but undoubtedly a ploy of some kind—either to gain the favor of a supernatural group that was new to him . . . or to gain favor with me. I still hadn't forgiven him for bribing Ethan to make me a vampire; Ethan hadn't taken the bribe, but that didn't lessen the sting of the betrayal.

"Did you find anything in your research?"

Jeff yawned. "We did not. Stayed up most of the day looking, too. Our best theory is this is some new kind of spell."

"We know Catcher's not involved, and Mallory's freaked out about her exams. Simon's the only other sorcerer in town. You think he could have something to do with it?"

"Simon? I don't know. He doesn't seem the type. Catcher looked into his background when he started tutoring Mal. From what I've heard, he had a rough start as a kid, cleaned up when he apprenticed with the Order. I don't think he found anything suspicious, but that didn't really help. Catcher does not like Simon."

"I noticed," I said.

"So, anyway, long story short, we're at a dead end. Maybe your talk with Lorelei will clear things up. You psyched for the trip?"

"I'd be more psyched if this was a casual visit, and not a trip to an isolated island to solve a magical problem she might have caused."

"Eh, piece of cake," Jeff said.

"We'll see about that. But that's not actually why I'm calling. I need a favor."

"In addition to the helicopter ride?"

"In addition to that. I need to talk to Tate."

Silence.

"Are you sure that's a good idea?"

I could hear the question he wasn't asking—are you sure it's a good idea to visit the man responsible for the death of your lover? But I'd already thought that one through.

"Of course it's not a good idea," I said. "But he's talked to the GP, and he's spreading rumors about what went down that night. He's not the type to waste energy unless there's something in it for him, and I want to know what that is."

"He could just be baiting you into visiting him."

"He probably is. But that doesn't make the trip any less necessary."

"Okay. I'll talk to Catcher and Chuck. There are protocols, I imagine."

"Understood. But he's making trouble for the House, so I can't just let this go. Do the best you can."

We said our good-byes, and I hung up with Jeff, but the call left me with a lingering worry. I wasn't crazy about the idea of visiting Tate. I was pretty sure he wasn't human, and I was already facing down one unknown magical creature tonight. Two was really pushing it.

"Big girl panties," I quietly reminded myself. "Big girl panties."

And since I was playing grown-up, I dialed Mallory's number.

She'd been a little growly when we'd talked before, but as BFF it was my job to check in. Since I didn't claim my own money-grubbing family (aside from borrowing the family name, which I actually liked), Mallory has been my primary family. Hell, we'd been *each other's* family. And losing Ethan had reminded me how much I needed her.

Of course, I wasn't exactly surprised when the phone flipped to voice mail almost immediately.

"Hey, it's me," I told her. "I just wanted to give you a call and wish you luck on your exams. Kick ass, and impress Simon, and become a real, live sorceress, and all that other inspirational crap. Go, Mallory! And now that I sound like a perky teenager, which I am most definitely not, I'm going to hang up now. Call me when you can."

I flipped the phone closed and silently wished her luck. I'd seen Mallory stressed to the gills a few weeks ago, crying from the stress of the work she was doing—and the physical pain. Apparently, funneling the power of the universe through your body was a tough job. It certainly wasn't anything I wanted a part of. Dealing with vampires was more than enough work for me.

My chores done, I showered and dressed. I wasn't exactly sure what to wear to accuse a siren of ruining Chicago's water, but I decided the full leather ensemble was a little aggressive. I stuck with the leather jacket, but paired it with jeans and a thin, long-sleeved T-shirt. My Cadogan medal and boots were my accessories, as was my dagger. I figured dropping out of a helicopter with a thirty-two-inch sword probably wasn't the most diplomatic of entrances.

When I was dressed, I headed to the Ops Room to update Kelley. She sat at the conference table, reviewing information on a tablet computer. Lindsey sat at one of the computer stations on the wall; Juliet was nowhere in sight.

"What's up, ladies?"

Kelley glanced up from her toy. "Good evening, Merit. Did Frank find you?"

"Unfortunately, yes," I said, checking my wall file for information. We usually received "Dailies," updates about House visitors, news and happenings. Since we were short-staffed, they were closer to "Weeklies," and Kelley paged us if anything needed to be relayed immediately.

"He questioned my ability to serve, Ethan's decision to appoint me, and every other decision he made while in charge of the House."

"Oh," she said with a fake smile. "So the usual stuff."

"Pretty much." I took a seat at the table. "He also asked me about the night Ethan was killed."

I saw, out of the corner of my eye, Lindsey's shoulders stiffen. She glanced back at me, concern in her expression, and I nodded in thanks.

"As it turns out," I said, "Tate gave the GP a different version of events."

"Why, in God's name, would the GP talk to Tate about that night? I mean, there were tapes of Tate's involvement in the drugs. Why would they take his word over yours?"

"Because he's not me. And for whatever reason, they don't trust me."

"Jerks," Lindsey muttered.

"Agreed. But we've heard from Darius, Charlie, and now Frank that the GP really does think we're creating problems for ourselves. They have this idea we're cowboys in the American wilderness, randomly stirring up trouble with humans."

"Instead of laying the blame for that at Celina's door?" Kelley wondered.

"My thoughts exactly. Silent assimilation is only a viable strategy when you haven't been dragged kicking and screaming out of the closet."

Kelley sighed and tapped her crimson nails on the tabletop. "And yet, what can we do about it? Whenever the GP gets information in front of them, they ignore it."

"We defect," Lindsey said.

Kelley's gaze snapped to Lindsey. "Don't say that out loud," she warned. "God only knows how secure the House is with him here."

"Is that even an option?" I quietly wondered. I had a short version of the *Canon*—the laws that bound North American vampires—but I didn't recall having seen anything about defection. Not that the GP would advertise that kind of thing.

"Only twice in the GP's history," Kelley said, "and never by an American House."

"Never say never," Lindsey muttered.

"Lindsey," Kelley warned again, this time with a tone of authority in her voice.

Lindsey glanced back from her computer, brows lifted. "What? I'm not afraid to say it aloud. This House is governed by the GP. The GP is supposed to keep things stable and protect the House. Is that happening now? Hells to the no. Instead, they're criticizing and investigating *our* vampires when they should be working to keep these crazy-ass humans away from us."

She pointed to one of the monitors in front of her, and both Kelley and I moved closer for a better look. The screen showed the sidewalk outside the House, where the number of protestors seemed to have tripled since dawn. They were marching up and down with signs that blamed the still-dark waters of the lake on Cadogan House. As if we'd created the problem, instead of trying to stop it.

"They blame us," I concluded. "They have no evidence we have anything to do with the lake; they just don't know anyone else to blame. That's the only reason they're here."

"Oh, no," Kelley said. "That's not the only reason." She walked back to the table, tapped a bit on the tablet, and handed it over to me.

The screen displayed a video of Mayor Kowalczyk, wearing a sensible red power suit and a bouffant of brown hair, and standing in front of a podium.

"Press conference?" I asked.

"Oh, yeah," Kelley said, then swiped the screen to start the video.

"You know what?" the mayor asked, leaning over the podium. "I don't care. You did not elect me to this office so I could spend my time in office kowtowing to special interest groups. And rest assured, my fellow Chicagoans, that these vampires are a special interest group. They want to be treated differently. They want the rules that apply to us to not apply to them."

"Was that even English?" I quietly wondered. Her linguistic skills notwithstanding, she kept going.

"There's more to this city than a handful of fanged rabble-rousers—good, old-fashioned, hardworking folks who know that everything isn't about vampires. *This* is one of those things. The lake is ours. The river is ours. They are about tourism, about fishing. I won't allow this city to be co-opted. And I will tell you one thing—the registration law is the best thing that will ever happen to this city."

"Blah blah blah," Lindsey muttered. "Blame the vampires instead of actually working to fix the problem."

Kelley paused the video. "Mayor Kowalczyk has a different constituency," she said. "And a very different outlook on things."

Lindsey humphed. "A naïve outlook."

"Be that as it may," I said, "it's the outlook she's providing the city. And they'll believe her, which is why we need to get in front of this." But as I stared daggers at the image of our new political foe, I saw something even more disturbing. "Kelley, increase the image."

There was confusion in her expression, but she did it. And there behind Diane Kowalczyk, in all his black-fatigued glory, stood McKetrick.

"That's McKetrick," I said, pointing him out.

"Are you sure?" Kelley asked, tilting her head at the picture.

"Positive. It's hard to forget a man who's stuffed a gun in your face. Well, who's ordered his goon to stuff a gun in your face, anyway."

"Shit," Kelley uncharacteristically said. "So our paramilitary foe has made friends with a politician."

"That might explain where some of her worst ideas come from," I suggested, my stomach curdling at the thought, McKetrick and his hatred would have political legitimacy in Chicago.

"Add that to his info sheet," Kelley told Lindsey. "Kowalczyk's a political ally, and he's got enough sway to stand on a podium beside her."

"This night keeps getting better," I said, then glanced at Kelley. "And speaking of horrible ideas, I'm going to see Tate, and we're going to have a little chat about the GP and what went down in Creeley Creek."

"There's a possibility that's part of his plan—that he's lying to the GP to get you out there."

That echoed Jeff's concern, and I'd decided they were both right. "I'm counting on it," I said. "But I figure the faster I make an appearance, the faster we figure out what he's up to."

"Not that he'd give up his plan willingly," Lindsey said.

"There is that," I allowed. "After that, and assuming he doesn't use his power to turn me into a mindless zombie, I'm going to see the siren."

Kelley nodded. "Godspeed, Sentinel."

I wasn't sure if God, however he or she might exist, had any eyes on the drama in Chicago. But just in case, I said a little prayer. Couldn't hurt.

I found a voice mail awaiting me when I headed up the stairs and to my car.

It was Jeff, with instructions. I'd been directed to meet Catcher and my grandfather at a CPD facility near the lake, in an industrial part of town full of rusty towers and crumbling brick factories. It wasn't exactly a cozy setting for a chat with Tate, but it undoubtedly posed less of a public threat than if he'd been incarcerated downtown. I'd warned the CPD officers who'd picked him up to be careful as they'd taken him in for questioning. I hadn't heard any stories about cops or guards being tricked into doing his bidding; maybe that was why.

Tate was definitely not human; he'd all but confessed as much. Although he'd partially drugged Celina Desaulniers into submission, he'd also used some power of his own to accomplish that task. But what powers? And how much of it did he wield?

Frankly, we had no idea. That wasn't exactly comforting, but what could we do?

As I stepped into the cool fall night, I was assaulted by the sounds of protestors. There were tons of them outside, shouldering signs promising my eternal damnation and shouting out epithets. What was it about humans that made such behaviors acceptable?

But I wasn't human anymore, so vampire etiquette won out. Even as they screamed at me, I managed not to offer them an obscene gesture on the way to the car. The self-satisfaction didn't quite lessen the sting.

I drove southeast, the address Jeff had given me leading me to a gravel road that dead-ended in a ten-foot-high chain-link fence.

Warily, I got out of the car and walked toward the fence.

A warning blast suddenly filled the air, and a portion of the fence began to slide open.

Pushing down fear, and wishing Ethan had been at my side, I walked inside.

The fence surrounded a series of brick buildings—six in varying sizes laid out in no apparent pattern. I guessed they comprised an old manufacturing plant. Whatever their purpose, they'd clearly stood empty for some time.

I'd previously visited the Loop office of the Chicago Police Department. The perps who were booked there might have been down on their luck, but the facility was pretty nice. It was new, clean, and efficient in the way a police department had to be.

This place, on the other hand, had an air of hopelessness about it. It reminded me of a photo I'd seen of an abandoned building in Russia, a structure designed and built for a different kind of regime, left to rot alone when the philosophy was abandoned.

I couldn't imagine Tate—used to all things luxurious and gourmet—was thrilled about being here.

I turned at the *scritch* of rocks on my left. Catcher and my grandfather rolled up in a golf cart. Catcher, as fit his aggressive personality, was driving, although he looked like he hadn't gotten any sleep since last night. My grandfather was holding on, white-knuckled, to the bar above his head. I guess he wasn't impressed by Catcher's driving.

"This is where you're holding Tate?" I asked, climbing on to the backward-facing backseat. Catcher pulled away almost immediately, turning in a circle tight enough that I nearly fell off. Lesson learned, I grabbed the bar, as well.

"Until we know more about what or who he is," my grandfather said above the sound of whirring toy-car motor and gravel, "we take all precautions."

I surveyed the landscape as we passed, from bits of trash and debris to piles of fallen bricks and rusting carcasses of metal that might once have been factory equipment. "You couldn't find a place more out of the way than this?"

"Third-biggest city in the country," Catcher said. "We took what we could get."

"Which is?"

"A bit of land the city took over when the former tenants vacated. It's a former ceramics factory," my grandfather said. "They used to form and fire bricks and tile out here."

"Which means lots of thick, fireproof, and insulated buildings," I guessed.

"Precisely," my grandfather said.

We drove (twice as fast as probably recommended) around the compound, circling around until we came to a very bumpy, quick stop at a building with a long bank of yellow doors bearing sizable black numbers.

"These were the wood-fired kilns," my grandfather explained as we climbed from the cart.

"Interesting," I said. "Creepy" was what I thought.

Silently, I followed them down a narrow path beside the kiln building, stopping in front of a small but pretty brick building that stood alone in the center of the circle made by the rest of the buildings.

The small one couldn't have been more than forty feet square. Fairy guards stood at the door and each corner, leaving little doubt about its purpose.

My stomach began to churn as the anticipation built. I looked at my grandfather. "He's in there?"

"He is. This used to be the factory's main office. It's divided into two rooms. He's in a room by himself."

Catcher's phone beeped, and he pulled it out, glanced at it, and smiled.

"Kind of bad timing for sexy messages, isn't it?"

He rolled his eyes and showed me the screen of his phone. It bore a picture of a brick room, empty but for a cot on the floor and small sink on one side.

"Tate's cell," he explained. "Since he's out of the room, I had it searched."

"Clever," my grandfather said.

"It might have been if there was anything in it," Catcher said, tucking the phone away again. "Room's empty. He may not have a shiv, but that's not to say he doesn't have power. You'll want to hand over any weapons. We don't want them to fall into the wrong hands," he explained. "And if you need help, we'll be right outside."

I hesitated, but lifted my pant leg and pulled the dagger from my boot. The thought of playing supernatural cat-and-mouse with Tate without weapons didn't thrill me, but I took Catcher's point. If Tate managed to best me and take a dagger, he'd be a much bigger threat against me, the fairies, or anyone else he managed to pass.

Catcher took the dagger with a nod, his gaze skating across the engraving on the end.

"Are you going to be okay in there, babygirl? You sure you need to do this?" my grandfather asked. There was concern in his voice, but I didn't think he was worried about me. I think he was worried about Tate. After all, if it hadn't been for Tate's machinations, Ethan would still be alive.

I took a moment to actually consider his question. Honestly, I didn't know if I was going to be okay. I knew I needed to talk to him. I also knew he was dangerous. While he'd been masquerading as a politician with Chicago's best interests in mind, he'd been a drug kingpin and a manipulator. And he'd practically scripted the drama that had taken place in his office two months ago.

Fear and anger battled. I was smart enough to be afraid of who Tate was and what he might do. His motivations were opaque but surely self-interested, and I had no doubt he'd take me out for fun if the mood struck him. That thought put a knot of tension in my gut.

But beneath the fear was a core of molten fury.

Fury that Ethan had been taken from me because of Tate's need to play out some childish game. Fury that Ethan was gone and Tate was still alive, if stuck in his anachronistic prison. Fury that I hadn't been able to stop Tate's game before he'd played the final piece, and that even now he was trying to undermine my position in the House.

But I wasn't a child, and I wasn't Celina. I wasn't going to kill him for revenge, or to avenge Ethan's death, or because I was pissed that he'd taken something from me. What good would violence do other than putting me and mine in hot water?

No. Tate had caused enough drama, and I wasn't going to give him the satisfaction of baiting me to violence. Tonight, we were talking about the GP, and the grift he was currently running. God willing, when I walked through the door and looked into his eyes again—the first time I'd seen him since the night of Ethan's death—I'd keep that nice, tidy, logical conclusion in mind.

"Yes, I need to do this," I told my grandfather. "Tate wouldn't lie to the GP without a plan, and I want to know what it is. The last time we were too late. I won't be fooled by him again. I'll be fine," I added, crossing my fingers that I wasn't lying to him—or myself.

With an apologetic smile, he pulled a packet of indigo-blue silk from his vest pocket. "This might help a bit," he said, holding it in the palm of one hand and unwrapping the silk with the other.

With that much buildup—careful disrobing, silk lining—I'd imagined a much fancier trinket than the one he showed me. Upon the cushion of silk sat a three-inch-long rectangle of heavily grained wood, the finish so smooth it gleamed. Half the wood was a darker shade than the other, as if two pieces had been fused together and the edges carefully rounded into a fluid, organic form.

"What is it?" I asked.

"We call it 'worry wood,'" my grandfather said. "It's a kind of magic blocker. We aren't entirely sure what magic Tate might be working. But added to your immunity to glamour, this should keep you safe from whatever tricks he might try to pull."

"The fairies carry them, as well," Catcher said.

My grandfather extended his hand, and I plucked the worry wood from the silk. It was warmer than I expected it to be, and softer to the touch. The wood had been carefully sanded, leaving the grain only just rough enough that it still felt like wood—not plastic. It fit perfectly in the palm of my hand, the curves situated so they left a soothing depression for my thumb.

In a strange way, it was reassuring, tangibly comforting in the same way prayer beads might be. I slid the wood into my pocket, thinking it might behoove me to keep Tate unaware of it for as long as possible.

My grandfather nodded at the gesture, then refolded and repocketed the square of silk. With a hand at my back, he escorted me to the door, where the fairy looked me over.

"We'll be right outside if you need us," my grandfather reminded me.

"Okay," I said, blowing out a breath. "I'm ready."

Only the first step will suck, I reminded myself, and headed inside.

There were plenty of beautiful people who'd been successful—actors, rock stars, models. But there were probably just as many who'd squandered their genetic gifts on drugs, crime, lust, greed, and various other deadly sins.

Tate, unfortunately, fell into the latter category.

He'd been swiftly climbing the political ladder, his brooding good looks helping him woo Chicago voters. But he hadn't been satisfied with a meteoric political career. He'd traded it all in for the chance to control the city's vampires, and he'd wound up in an orange jumpsuit that wasn't nearly as flattering as his Armani had been.

But for all that, Seth Tate still looked good.

He sat at an aluminum table, one leg crossed over the other, one elbow back on the chair, his eyes alert and scanning the room . . . and me when I walked in.

He looked a bit leaner than he had when I'd last seen him, his cheekbones a bit more hewn. But his hair was still dark and perfectly arranged, his eyes still piercingly blue, his body still lean and mean. Seth Tate was the kind of handsome that packed a punch, and it was a shame all that pretty was going to waste in a lonely part of town.

Except for the part about him being a murderous bastard.

There was also a faint scent of lemon and sugar in the air, which always seemed to be the case around Tate. It wasn't unpleasant—quite the contrary. It just wasn't the kind of scent you expected from a man as cold-blooded as Tate.

The prickle of magic in the air, however, seemed very appropriate. This was only the second time I'd been able to detect Tate's magic; he'd done a bang-up job of hiding it before. I hated the feel of it: oily, heavy, and old, like the incense you'd find in the sanctuary of a Gothic church.

"Ballerina," Tate said.

I'd danced when I was younger, and Tate had seen me in toe shoes and tutus. He'd decided on "Ballerina" as a nickname. Of course, since he was the man responsible for the death of my lover and Master, I wasn't keen on his use of the familiar.

"I prefer Merit," I said, taking the seat across from him. The aluminum chair was cold, and I crossed my arms over my chest, as much from the chill as protection against the magic in the air.

As I took a seat, the room's steel door closed with a resounding *thunk* that shook the room a bit. My stomach jumped with nerves.

We sat quietly for a moment, Tate gazing at me with concentration.

The pressure in the room suddenly thickened, and the smell became stronger, both cloyingly sweet and sour enough to make my mouth water. The room seemed to sway back and forth. It wasn't like any other magic I'd felt. This was magic of a different caliber. Of a different age, maybe. Like magic that had been born in a different time. In an ancient era.

I put one hand on the chair beneath me to keep from falling over and another on the bit of worry wood in my pocket. I kept my gaze trained on Tate, like a ballerina spotting during a pirouette to keep from getting dizzy, and squeezed the wood so hard I feared it would splinter beneath my fingers.

After a few seconds, the swaying stopped and the room stilled again.

Tate sat heavily back in his chair again and frowned at me. That's when I realized what he'd been trying to do. "Did you just try to glamour me?"

"Ineffectively, it seems. Worry wood?"

I smiled demurely and focused on keeping my cool. I wasn't sure if it was the wood or my natural resistance to glamour, but I wasn't about to give that away to him. I slid my hand from my pocket again. "A lady never reveals her secrets."

"Hmph," he said, shuffling in his seat. He crossed his arms over his chest and looked back at me, head tilted, studying me. Each time he moved, a bit of magic sifted through the air. However he'd hidden it before, he didn't seem to be bothering now. I wasn't sure if that made me feel better or worse.

"I wondered when you'd pay me a visit."

"I'm sure you did. But to be honest, I've had a difficult time deciding what to do with you." I leaned forward and crossed my hands on the table. "Should I start by blaming you for Ethan's death? Or for your blaming Ethan's death on me and telling the GP I was aiming to become head of Cadogan House? Or maybe for lying to me about my father? You told me he paid Ethan to make me a vampire."

"I had that on very good authority."

I lifted my brows in question.

"Granted," he allowed, "she was under the influence at the time . . ."

"Celina was hardly a source of reliable information. Especially when you were manipulating her with magic."

Tate rolled his eyes. "Did we have to jump into this? How about asking how I've been? Or what life is like on the inside? Are we so common we don't bother with the polite formalities?"

"You manufactured drugs, hooked vamps on them, and facilitated the deaths of two vampires. Not to mention blaming me for all the above. Why should I be polite to you?"

"That was a very bad week," was all he said.

The remark was callous, but the tone was sincere. I had a sense he wasn't kidding. Maybe he had magical drama of his own.

"You told the GP I orchestrated Celina's and Ethan's deaths so I could take over the House," I said. "They're looking for an excuse to kick me out, and you're giving them the ammunition."

"Haven't you ever wondered what Cadogan House might be like if you were in charge? And I didn't say you orchestrated their deaths," Tate matter-of-factly said. "I said you were responsible for them. And you were. If Celina hadn't hated you, she wouldn't have thrown the stake. If Ethan hadn't tried to save you, he'd still be alive. And if you hadn't thrown the stake, Celina would still be alive. Ergo, you are responsible for their deaths."

His voice was so matter-of-fact, it was difficult to tell if he believed what he was saying or was trying to bait me to anger. But I forced myself to stay calm.

"That analysis ignores your role, of course. If it hadn't been for your machinations, none of it would have happened."

He lifted a shoulder. "You have your truth; I have mine."

"There's only one truth."

"That's naïve, isn't it? Merit, there's no harm to me in insinuating you were involved in their deaths. And if it creates reasonable doubt supporting my release, so be it." Tate leaned forward. "The real question, of course, is why you're here. Because I can't imagine you traveled to this part of town in the middle of the night just to vent in my general direction or complain that I'd tattletaled."

He had a point. It wasn't as if I could convince him to call the

GP and recant his story; he wouldn't do it, and they wouldn't believe him anyway. So why was I here? What had I hoped to accomplish? Did I want to confront him about that night?

Maybe this had nothing to do with the GP. Maybe this was about me. Maybe I feared Tate was right, that the blame for their deaths hadn't all been attributable to him.

"I can hear you thinking from across the table," Tate said. "If silent mea culpas are the best you can do, then you aren't nearly as interesting as I'd imagined."

"Two vampires are dead."

"Do you know how many beings have lived and died since the origins of this world, Merit? Billions. Many billions. And yet, you give little regard to the preciousness of their lives, only because you happened not to know them. But two vampires who've lived more than their share of years die, and you mourn them into the ground, so to speak?" He clucked his tongue. "Who's being illogical now?"

I stood up and pushed back my chair. "You're right," I said. "Maybe it's selfish to grieve. But I'm not going to apologize for it."

"Big words," he said.

I walked to the door, then turned back and looked at him, the playboy in convict orange. "Maybe, deep down, I wanted you to admit to me what you'd done and that you'd lied to the GP. Maybe I wanted you to take responsibility for their deaths."

"You cannot obtain absolution from me."

"I know." And I did. I knew that railing at Tate wasn't going to change anything, and it wasn't going to assuage my secret fear that I'd been the cause of Ethan's death. After all, if it hadn't been for me . . .

There were many truths about the events of that night, and Tate couldn't relieve me of the burden of my own guilt. But I knew—as sure as I knew anything else—that I'd gone into his office to stop the spread of drugs, to help the Houses, and to help the city's vampires. Whatever the GP may ultimately decide, I knew what had gone down in that room, and I wasn't going to stand trial for a crime I hadn't committed.

I looked back at Tate, and felt a little of the weight in my chest ease.

He beamed. "There we are," he said, his voice a bit deeper, his cold blue eyes gleaming with pleasure. "Now we're back to interesting again. You came because you aren't afraid to. Because as much as you believe you relied on Sullivan, you are your own person. I've always known that about you. For better or worse, your father made you the woman you are today. Maybe he was cold. But you are self-reliant because of it."

A wave of magic thickened the air again as he spoke the words, sounding a lot like a mentor imparting wisdom to a student. That only confused me more.

"What do you want from me?"

His eyes gleamed. "Nothing at all, Merit, except for you to be who you are."

"Which is?"

"A fitting adversary." Perhaps at the chilled expression on my face, he sat back in his chair, a smug expression on his. "And I do think I'll enjoy this particular round."

I had the distinct impression I wouldn't.

"I'm not engaging in games with you, Tate."

He clucked his tongue. "Don't you see, Merit? The games have already begun. And I believe it's my move."

There was something comforting about the scratchy gravel beneath my feet and the cool fall air. The air in the room had been heavy, Tate's magic unnerving. I sucked in a few deep breaths and tried to slow my racing heart again.

Catcher and my grandfather stood a few feet away from the building and walked toward me as I exited.

"You're all right?" my grandfather asked.

We stopped together thirty or so feet from the building. I glanced back at it. From the distance, it looked so completely innocuous—just a small brick building that had once upon a time housed time cards and invoices. And now—it held a supernatural being of unknown origin.

"I'm fine," I told him. "Glad to be outside again. There was a lot of magic in there."

"Insidious magic," Catcher explained. "You rarely feel it until it's too late. Did you learn anything helpful?"

"No. He played coy, although he seems to truly believe I was responsible for what happened that night."

That seemed to be enough to satisfy the both of them. Silently, we climbed back into the golf cart and made our way back to the gate. A breeze was picking up. I huddled into my jacket, not sure if it was the looming winter, or the experience, that had chilled me to the bone.

As it happened, I'd previously been to the heliport where my grandfather directed me to meet the helicopter for the flight to Lorelei's island.

My father, a member of the Chicago Growth Council, had fought for two years to get a heliport installed in Streeterville, an area north of downtown Chicago along the lakefront, despite concerns that that part of the city was too thick with skyscrapers to safely provide helicopter service. That heliport was breaking news for the four months it took politicians to decide whether it was electorally riskier to veto the heliport or allow it. As was often the case when money was involved, the CGC won out, and the heliport was installed.

I parked on the street in front of the sleek, silver building that housed the landing pad and walked inside. A security guard took my name and then sent me to the elevator.

The doors opened at the building's top floor, a giant asphalt circle with an "H" marking the center. The pilot met me with a wave—the only way she could communicate given the vicious wind and noise from the smallish helicopter, whose rotors were already spinning.

She motioned me toward the door, indicating I'd get headphones when I got inside. I nodded and made a run for it, ducking farther than I probably needed to avoid the rotors, but why take a chance? When I was buckled in, headphones installed, we lifted off, and the city disappeared beneath us.

Forty-two roaring minutes later, we approached the island. I hadn't expected it to be visible until we touched down, but the helicopter's lights bounced off a breaker of white—the bony hulls of ships that had been dashed upon the edges of the siren's island.

Thank God we hadn't come in a boat.

The island was covered in trees but for two small clearings—one that held a structure, probably Lorelei's home, and a smaller area closer to shore. We touched down there. The pilot switched off the rotors, and pulled off her headphones.

"This is spooky," she said, peering out into the darkness, then looked at me. "I've got to make another flight in a couple of hours. You think that's enough time for you to do whatever you need to do?"

"I certainly hope so," I said, then climbed out of the copter. I glanced back at her. "If I'm not back by the time you need to leave, call my grandfather and bring out the troops."

She laughed like I was kidding.

Unfortunately, I wasn't.

A path led into the woods, and I couldn't help thinking about Dorothy and Little Red Riding Hood and all the others who had dreaded that walk. But the pilot had a schedule to keep, so I needed to get the show on the road.

I took one step, and then another, until the clearing disappeared behind me and I was ensconced in a forest alive with noise. All manner of animals not yet bedded down for the coming winter shuffled through the underbrush, and the canopy of trees above the path created a fretwork of moonlight on the ground.

Recalling I was a vampire—and a sharp-sensed predator myself—I let my senses off the leash. My night vision sharpened. I could smell damp soil and the faint musk of animals in the trees. Acrid smoke and the greenish smell of fresh resin drifted down the path from what I assumed was Lorelei's house. Someone had been chopping wood, maybe.

The night was alive with things most humans would rarely see or consider, an entire world that turned while they were unconscious. Would it frighten them, I wondered, to imagine how much went on while they were oblivious?

I walked for a little less than ten minutes. The path moved gently uphill, and I emerged onto a plateau that, during the day, probably would have afforded a beautiful view of the lake. I considered it a good thing my father didn't know the property existed; he'd have razed Lorelei's house to make way for a luxury lodge.

The house glowed in the middle of the clearing. It was low, with walls that alternated between curvy glass and long swaths of wood. The house spread low across the earth like it might simply have grown there, like it might melt back into the ground if you turned your back long enough. A tamped dirt path led across the grass to a giant wooden door I assumed was the main entrance.

I stood at the edge of the woods for a moment and savored the irony. A few minutes ago, I'd been afraid to enter them. Now, I was dreading the exit. Sure, I was supposedly immune to Lorelei's siren call, but that didn't exactly calm my nerves. I'd seen the boats at the shoreline. What had happened to their captains?

In the silence while I waited, I heard the singing for the first time. It sounded like a low dirge of mourning, sung by a woman with perfect pitch and a sensual tone.

The siren.

I closed my eyes and waited for a moment . . . but nothing happened. I didn't feel compelled to stalk her, or live out the rest of my immortal nights on her island. Other than feeling a little light-headed from relative lack of blood—horrible timing on Frank's part—all was well.

I blew out a breath, walked toward the door, and knocked on it.

No more than a second later, a heavyset woman in her fifties or sixties opened the door, her eyes narrowed. "What?"

Surely this woman, who wore a T-shirt and cut-off stretch pants and held a feather duster in one hand, wasn't the siren of the lake. But the singing continued from somewhere in the house, so this couldn't have been her.

"I'm Merit. I'm here to see Lorelei."

She seemed unmoved by my interest and stared blankly back at me.

"I'm a vampire from Chicago," I told her. "I need to talk to Lorelei about the lake."

Without a word, she shut the door in my face. I blinked back shock, then gnawed my lip for a second, considering my choices.

I could barge into the house, but it was a rule of etiquette that vamps had to wait for an invitation before entering someone's home. It wasn't going to do much good if I pissed off the lake spirit by breaching protocol.

Alternatively, I could pout my way back to the helicopter and advise the pilot she'd have plenty of time to get to her next appointment.

Since neither of those options would solve my current problem, I decided to go for option three—stalling while gathering a little intel. Quietly, I tiptoed across the small portico and peeked into a window.

I got only a small peek at wood and stone before I heard a voice behind me.

"Ahem."

I jumped and turned to find the woman who'd opened the door standing behind me with a suspicious expression and a menacingly wielded feather duster.

"Lovely home," I told her, standing up straight again. "I was just curious about the interior design. With the wood. And furnishings." I cleared my throat guiltily. "And such."

The woman rolled her eyes, then flipped her feather duster out like a composer directing an orchestra. "I have been authorized to invite you into the abode of Lorelei, the lake siren. Welcome to her home."

Her delivery was desert dry, but it got the point across. I followed her inside.

The interior of the house was as organically designed as the outside. The window looked onto a two-story living room. One wall was made of rounded river stone, and a trickle of water spilled down the rocks and into a narrow channel that ran through the middle of the room, where it disappeared into an infinity-edged trough on the other side.

A curvy woman sat on the floor beside the channel of water, trickling her fingers into it. Her hair was dark and pulled into a topknot, and she was dressed simply in a shimmery gray T-shirt and jeans, her toes bare. Her eyes were closed, and she sang out low and clear.

I looked back toward the woman with the feather duster, but having done her duty, she was gone.

"Are you Lorelei?" I quietly asked.

She stopped singing, opened her eyes, and looked up at me with eyes the color of chocolate. "Honey, if you're on my island, you know there's only one person I could be. Of course I'm Lorelei." Her voice carried a hint of a Spanish accent, and a lot of sarcasm.

I bit back a smile. "Hi, Lorelei. I'm Merit."

"Hi, yourself. What brings you here?"

"I need to ask you some questions."

"About?"

"The lake."

Her eyes narrowed. "You think I had something to do with the water?"

"I don't know whether you did or not," I admitted, kneeling beside the channel so we could speak at eye level. "I'm trying to figure out what happened, and you seemed like a good place to start. It's not just the lake, you know. It's the river, as well."

Her head shot up. "The river? It's dead, too?"

Neither the question nor the look of defeat in her eyes comforted me.

"It is," I said. "And the river and the lake are bleeding all the power out of Chicago. The nymphs are growing weaker."

Wincing as if in pain, Lorelei pressed her fingers to her temples. "They aren't the only ones. I feel like I finished up a four-day shift and a two-day bender. Weak. Exhausted. Dizzy." She looked up at me. "I didn't cause this. I'd hoped the nymphs might have the answer, that they'd become too involved in some kind of unfamiliar magic, but that the magic could be reversed."

"They thought the same thing about you."

"That's no surprise," she dryly said.

"You don't get along?"

She barked out a laugh. "I grew up near Paseo Boricua. Born and raised in Chicago by parents from Puerto Rico. The nymphs aren't exactly a diverse crew. They see me as the odd one out. An interloper in their pretty little world of magic."

"How so?"

She looked up at me curiously. "You really don't know, do you?"

I shook my head, and she muttered something in Spanish. "The lake turns black and I get the vampire right off the assembly line," she said, then cast her own apologetic glance. "No offense."

"None taken."

Lorelei sighed and dipped a hand back into the water. Her features relaxed a bit, as if touching the water soothed her.

"Being a siren isn't like being a nymph," she said. "They are born into their roles; their mothers are nymphs, as well. A siren's power doesn't work that way."

She pointed to a table across the room. Propped upon it was a dark, iron disk about six inches across. There was writing on it, but it was too far away to read.

"*Piedra de Agua*," she said. "The water stone. The siren's magic is carried within it."

I frowned back at her. "I don't understand."

"To own the stone is to *become* the lake siren," she said. "To trigger its magic, you must request the stone, but it only accepts certain owners. Once it's yours, it's yours until the next owner comes around."

"So you chose to be a siren?"

Lorelei looked away, staring down at the water. "Technically, I had a choice to accept the stone and its burdens, although my options were limited."

"And the boats at the shoreline?"

She looked back with pride in her eyes. "I chose to accept the stone, but I work things a little differently. I'm the siren of the lake, and I have to sing, but I picked the most isolated spot I could find. Rosa and Ian, my husband—they help steer the sailors back to the mainland. The damage to the boats I can't do much about." She smiled a little. "But everybody's got insurance."

I couldn't fault that logic. "How long do you have to serve as siren?"

"The Lorelei before me—we all take the name to keep the myth alive—lived here for ninety-six years. Of course," she said with a burgeoning smile, "she was forty-two when she became siren, so that's not a bad perk."

Because I had a sense it might help, I offered up my own story. "I was made a vampire without my consent. To save my life, but it wasn't something I'd planned. That came as a surprise."

She regarded me with interest. "So you know what it's like to rewrite your life. To weigh who you were against who you must become."

I thought of all the things I'd done and seen over the last year— the death, the pain, the joy. The beginnings . . . and the endings.

"Yes," I quietly agreed. "I know what that's like." That thought reminded me of my purpose. "Lorelei, if you didn't cause this, do you know who might have?"

"If the nymphs aren't involved—if this wasn't caused by a water spirit—then I think you need to look more broadly."

"Such as?"

She looked away, guilt in her expression.

"Lorelei, I need to know. This isn't just about the nymphs. Our Houses are at stake. Humans are already blaming vampires, and if it goes any further, I can guarantee the registration law will pass."

"There's only one group as tied to the natural world as we are," she finally said. "We find our solace and our awe in the water. In the flow of it, the power of it, its ability to cleanse and destroy." She closed her eyes. "They find their power in the earth. They treasure it—the woods, the wilds."

My stomach sank. "You're talking about shifters?"

"The Pack is in Chicago, isn't it?"

"Because we asked them to stay. They wouldn't do this."

"Did you think they'd attack your House?"

Technically, only a handful of vengeful shifters had attacked the House, but I took her point. "Of course not."

"You can't turn a blind eye to who they are or what they're capable of. You are aware of the chemistry between nymphs and shifters?"

"It's hard to miss."

"It's because of the chemistry between earth and water," she said. "A kind of elemental union. Maybe the water's sickness is because there are too many shifters and nymphs in one city."

Not that I had any better theory, but it seemed too convenient to blame shifters, a group with whom nymphs and sirens clearly had a tempestuous relationship.

A man suddenly walked through the front door, a handful of cut logs in his hands.

Despite the chill in the air, he wore grubby jeans but was naked from the waist up, his torso soaked with sweat. He smiled and kept walking through the living room to the other side of the house.

Grubby clothes or not, he was undeniably gorgeous. He was tall and well-built, with short wavy hair and a day's worth of stubble along his square jaw. He had long, dark brows and deep-set eyes, and curvy lips above a dimpled chin.

When he disappeared through a door on the opposite side of the room, I looked back at Lorelei. She smiled knowingly.

"That, of course, is Ian. We've been married for four years. He knew me before I became siren, so he's immune to the songs. He was thoughtful enough to follow me out here to the middle of godforsaken nowhere. I try to accept my lot gracefully."

As soon as she'd gotten the words out, she put her hands on her forehead and bent over, clearly in pain. The woman who'd answered the door hustled into the room, muttering words in Spanish. She leaned beside Lorelei and wrapped an arm around her shoulders.

"Be well, *niña*," she said, and then whispered more words I couldn't understand.

I stood up, taking the hint. "Thank you for your time. I don't want to bother you anymore."

"Merit." I glanced back. Lorelei had lifted her head again, tear tracks visible on her cheeks. "If this doesn't get fixed soon, it will be too late."

I promised her I'd do my best . . . and then I hoped I'd made a promise I could keep.

I let myself out and walked back around the house to the path. Ian was outside again as well, and the air was thick with the scent of fresh resin.

Axe in hand, he stood in front of an upturned log. A second log stood vertically atop it. He pulled the axe over his head, muscles rippling, then heaved the axe down. The log split cleanly, its twin halves falling to the ground. Ian put another log onto the stump, then glanced up. His breath was foggy in the chill.

"You're here about the lake?" he asked, wiping sweat from his brow.

"I am."

"This isn't her fault, you know. None of it. She carries the burden for someone else, and now she's sick—or worse—because of that burden."

He swung his axe up again, then cleaved the second log in two.

"I didn't accuse her of anything," I said. "I'm just trying to figure out what happened."

He stood up another log. "Then figure it out. And if you don't, we'll be here when the world ends."

With no good response to that, I made my way back to the helicopter.

CHAPTER SEVEN

PARADIGM SHIFT(ER)

The ride back was miserable. The wind had picked up, and we were tossed around with enough force that the pilot's hands were white-knuckled around her controls. She spent half the trip praying under her breath.

I'm pretty sure I was green when we reached the helipad again. I made it to my car without incident, but sat in the driver's seat for a few minutes, unwilling to brave the drive home until I was sure I wasn't going to ruin the upholstery. The last thing a boxy, twenty-year-old Volvo needed was the stench of airsickness.

While I had a moment, I checked my phone. I'd missed a call from Jonah, and Kelley had left a voice mail checking in. I did my duty and called her back first.

She answered the phone with a squeal. "You are amazing!"

"I'm—what now?"

"You! The lake! I don't know how you did it, but you are a miracle worker!"

I had to shake my head to catch up. "Kelley, I just got back to the city, and I have no idea what you're talking about."

"Merit, you did it! The lake's back to normal. Just all of a sudden, boom, and the water's clear again and the waves are flowing, just like nothing happened. I don't know what you told Lorelei, but it totally worked. It mattered, Merit. *You* mattered. Do you know how much this helps the House? The protestors have actually gone home tonight. This might get the GP off our back completely."

I'd only been out of the helicopter for fifteen or twenty minutes, tops, and the lake hadn't looked any different from the sky or when we landed. As much as I appreciated the praise and the possibility that I was giving the House room to breathe, I was skeptical. I'd believed Lorelei, and there was nothing on that island that made me think she had anything to do with what had happened to the lake, much less that she could stop it an hour or so after my visit. Something else had to be going on.

"Kel, I'm not sure it's that simple. I mean, I'm glad the lake is back, but I didn't do anything, and I don't think she did either. In fact, I don't think Lorelei had anything to do with the lake at all. She's weak like the nymphs are."

"Occam's Razor, Merit. The simplest solution is usually the true one. The lake went bad, you talked to Lorelei, the lake is back again. Maybe you scared her straight. Let's not look a gift horse in the mouth, right?"

I frowned. That those things happened in order didn't mean they were related to each other. Lorelei certainly hadn't worked any magic while I'd been there. Would she have had time to do anything after I'd left?

This wasn't the first time I'd been presented with an answer that seemed too easy. Celina had confessed her involvement in the V trade while standing in the middle of a public festival. That had briefly seemed like a miraculous end to our drug-related drama, at least until we discovered she'd been under Tate's magical thumb.

Nothing was that easy. But maybe, for now, Kelley needed to believe we were making a difference, that we'd actually managed to solve a problem. The entire House probably needed to believe it. Maybe forgoing the truth was occasionally the right thing to do, so I gave her what she needed to hear.

"You're probably right," I said. "It would have been a pretty big coincidence otherwise."

"Right? Anyway, go play! Take the night off. I'm just thrilled. Excellent job, Sentinel. And I'll make sure Cabot knows it."

The phone went dead, but that didn't do anything to quell my anxiety. If I couldn't discuss my findings in Cadogan House, I'd find a more receptive audience. Problem was, my best audience—the Ombud's office—might not be all that receptive, either. I wasn't thrilled about the idea of telling Jeff that Lorelei blamed the Packs for the lake, and decided that confession needed to be made in person. Telling him shifters were my new suspects wasn't going to go over well.

On my way to the Ombud's office, I called Jonah to check in. He answered on the first ring.

"Well done on the lake," he said.

"Thanks for the performance eval. But it wasn't me. Any word on the nymphs?"

"I've heard they're getting more healthy and hale by the minute and are big fans of yours right now."

"Crap."

"That wasn't the reaction I expected."

"I'm ruining the punch line here, but I didn't actually do anything at the lake. Lorelei and I just talked."

"You just talked?"

"That's it. She was also weak and getting weaker, and she denies having done anything to the lake. I tend to believe her."

"And I'm guessing you aren't going to be content with the fact that the lake's back to normal?"

I wasn't sure if I should be flattered or insulted by the sentiment. But either way, he was right. "You would be correct. I'm gonna visit my grandfather and pick his brain. You wanna join me?"

"No can do. I'm in the middle of something. You want to meet later to debrief?"

"We can do that. I'll call you when I'm done."

"I'll bring popcorn," he promised, then hung up.

I gnawed my lip all the way to my grandfather's south side office, hard enough that I eventually tasted the metallic bite of blood. The lake's time as a giant magic vacuum might have ended, but I was convinced this wasn't the end of the story. And if I was right and the fix was a coincidence, we had another force working major magic in the Windy City. I had a sinking fear we were going to find out soon what Tate's "next move" would be.

Traffic was light, so the drive to the south side didn't take long. The office of the Ombudsman was located in a low brick building in a working-class, residential neighborhood. I parked on the street and headed to the door, hitting the buzzer to signal Jeff, Catcher, my grandfather, or Marjorie, my grandfather's admin, that I was there.

Marjorie was an efficient woman, and she answered the door the same way she answered the phone—handing me off to someone else as quickly as possible.

"Good evening," I told her after she uncoded the door and held it open for me, but by the time I got out the words, she'd relocked the door and was headed back to her office. Maybe supernatural diplomacy buried her in paperwork.

The building sported some serious 1970s décor, and Catcher and Jeff shared an equally ugly office down the hall. Metal desks probably grabbed from a city surplus auction filled their small room, and posters of River nymphs lined the walls.

I found Jeff and Catcher at their desks, but they were so heavily immersed in conversation they hadn't even heard me enter.

"Her hair's a lot darker," Jeff was saying, while simultaneously typing on one of the rainbow of keyboards that covered his desk. "So I'm pretty sure our kids would have darker hair, too."

"That's not necessarily the case," Catcher disagreed. He was folding a sticky note into a tiny, origami something-or-other. "I mean, they could get your genes. And your hair is lighter. You're taller than Fallon, too."

"True. True," Jeff said.

Was this for real? Were these two magically oriented, problem-fixing, ass-kicking guys talking about what their kids would look like?

Jeff leaned over and offered a bag of pistachios to Catcher. Catcher smiled genially—and without even a bit of snark—dropped the origami and plucked a few from the bag. Jeff split the hull on one and chewed it.

"You ever think about coaching baseball, that kinda thing, when you and Mallory have kids? You know, doing the whole soccer dad routine?"

Catcher threw a pistachio in the air and caught it in his mouth. "While hoping they don't fry the universe from day one? Yeah, that thought has occurred to me." He sat up straight and looked at Jeff. "Can you imagine some little girl with Mallory's hair? The blond, I mean."

"Heart. Breaker," Jeff said. "You'll have to keep a shotgun by the front door just to ward off the players. Or, I guess, you could have Mallory do it for you."

"I could," Catcher allowed, then—realizing I was in the room—

looked up and glared right at me. "I'll do that right after I have her kick Merit's ass for spying."

I grinned and stepped inside, offering each a wave. "Hello, proud papas of children not yet conceived."

Jeff's cheeks blossomed crimson. "You could have given us a heads-up."

"And miss the parental discussion? No thank you. It was adorable. You two kids, being all chummy and paternal."

"I guess the siren didn't drown you?" Catcher dryly asked, getting me back to the point.

"Not even close. She was pretty nice, actually."

"She must have been," Jeff said with a grin. "I mean, you convinced her to do the right thing. The lake is back to normal."

"Thank Christ," Catcher said. "Did she make the trip worthwhile and confess to fucking up our lake?"

"As a matter of fact, she didn't," I said, pulling out a chair of my own. "Let's call in my grandfather. He'll want to hear this, too."

I didn't mean to set a dramatic scene, but I wanted them all in the room at the same time when I laid down the facts about our lake siren.

After a few minutes, my grandfather walked in, offered me a hug and a smile. But then his eyes changed, the joy flattening as he prepared to get down to business.

"Lorelei has been the lake siren since she took possession of the *Piedra de Agua*, the water stone, which somehow imparts its power to the holder. She's weak—looked pretty awful, actually—and seems to be in pain. She'd actually hoped the nymphs had been responsible. We flew back to Chicago, totally uneventful, and I'm told when we arrive the lake is suddenly back to normal. *Magically* back to normal."

There was silence in the room.

"It wasn't her," my grandfather concluded.

"Not unless she was lying and worked some really fast magic."

Catcher frowned and began to rock in his ancient metal office chair, which squeaked in time to his movements. "So we're dealing with something unknown."

"She did have a theory," I began, and offered Jeff an apologetic glance. "She thinks it's the combination of shifters and nymphs in town that made the magic. Their elemental magics working together or against each other, and the result of all that power in one place, she thought."

Jeff looked taken aback. "That's a new one."

"Is that even possible?" my grandfather asked. "That the number of sups would create spontaneous magic?"

Jeff frowned and scratched absently at his head. "I guess it's theoretically possible there'd be some lambent magic spillage, but you'd expect to see a positive increase in magic—not something that's sucking the magic out of the city."

"Unless it's like the effect of a tsunami," Catcher suggested. "Is it possible the shifters being together in one place pulled out so much magic the lake began to pull it back in?"

Jeff shook his head. "If that were true, we'd shift ocean currents every time we met in Aurora or anywhere else." He glanced at me. "I'm not aware of any instance of a magical vacuum being created because too many shifters got together. This would be a first."

His tone was polite, but his expression made clear he didn't buy Lorelei's theory.

"I didn't really buy it either," I said. "Although I like even less the fact that we have no explanation for something this powerful."

"We may not have an explanation," my grandfather said, "but

at least we have a reprieve. I know times are not easy at the House. Let us do the heavy lifting on the rest of the investigation."

My lip curled at the implicit mention of Frank. "I can't schedule my work based on what the GP might say. They're going to criticize me regardless, so I have to do the right thing by the House and by the city. And if worse comes to worst . . ."

"Merit," Jeff quietly said, "you don't want to be cast out of the House."

"No, I don't," I agreed. "But I'm not going to act like there's nothing going on when, clearly, something is brewing. I can't let the city go to hell because the receiver has his head up his ass. Sorry, Grandpa," I added about the language.

He patted my back. "We'll carry the burden," he said. "You keep your head down and do your job. I know how hard it's been for you lately. How hard it must be without Ethan. He was a good man—a good Master for his people. But tough times don't last forever, and Malik will need you when he's free and clear of the receiver."

It was great advice; it was just going to be hard to follow. Ethan hadn't exactly trained me to sit on the sidelines and watch a problem unfold. He'd taught me to strategize and investigate. To soldier. And what soldier bowed out because the pressure was too high? Sure, following orders was important, but a soldier still had to rely on her own conscience, right?

Marjorie peeked into the office and knocked on the open door, worry in her expression. "Chuck," she said. "I think you'd better come out here."

Frowning, my grandfather stood up and walked to the door. After exchanging a glance, Catcher, Jeff, and I followed. We stood at the door, each of our heads poking around the door frame at various heights, like kids in a slapstick comedy.

My grandfather stood in the hallway, Marjorie beside him, their gazes on the front door. A nondescript black SUV was parked outside. It was the kind of SUV that moved in the dark of night, that you didn't know was coming until the passengers were already out of the car with guns . . . or worse.

"McKetrick?" I wondered.

"I wish," Marjorie spit out. "At least then I'd see some action." We all stared at her.

"Sorry, sorry," she said with a thick Chicagoan accent, the word sounding more like "sarry" than "sorry."

"Pushing paper on sups just gets a little dull around here sometimes, ya know? But, no. It's not McKetrick, who I understand is a very bad person. Horrible." She crossed herself. "God bless us all. It's the mayor."

"Turn off the alarm," my grandfather said, and Catcher stepped into the hallway, moved to the keypad and uncoded the lock.

"Did you know she was coming?" I quietly asked.

My grandfather shook his head. "It's a surprise to me."

We waited for her arrival in a heavy, worrisome silence. The mayor showing up unannounced at the Ombudsman's office probably didn't portend anything good.

She was preceded to the door by two beefy security guards. When they opened it, she walked inside and peered around. She wore a burgundy pantsuit, her hair flipped at the bottom into an odd curl, her expression disdainful. Chunky costume jewelry was draped around her neck and wrists, and there were chunky rings on her fingers.

After a moment of disdainful review of the office, she made eye contact with my grandfather. "Mr. Merit."

"Madame Mayor," he said in greeting.

"I hear you and your . . . *staff* . . . have been using the city's resources for private helicopter rides."

He blinked back surprise. "Ma'am, if you have budgetary concerns, we can move to my office and discuss them."

"I'm on a bit of a schedule, Mr. Merit. I'd prefer an answer now."

My grandfather wet his lips, then continued. "As detailed in my requisition report, we needed a ride to Bear Island. We believed its resident might have been involved with the lake."

"And was she?"

Choose your words carefully, I thought. *You don't want to give her the ammunition and the gun, too.*

"As I'm sure you've seen, the lake is back to normal."

She frowned, and it wasn't an attractive look on her. Diane Kowalczyk was the kind of person who looked good—and even then, not great—only when she was smiling with political vigor.

"Mr. Merit," she finally said, "my job is not to waste taxpayer dollars kowtowing to supernatural boogeymen. My job is to ensure the resources of this city are used wisely."

"My apologies, Madame Mayor," my grandfather diplomatically said. "If you'd prefer, the cost of using the helicopter can be doubly removed from our budget for the year. As always, we'll have a surplus, and we'll return that money to the city."

The mayor smiled thinly—and meanly. "That won't be necessary. You see, Mr. Merit, effective today, you have no more budget."

My jaw dropped, as did Catcher's, Jeff's, and Marjorie's. The hallway filled with uncomfortable magic. The mayor and her guards seemed oblivious to it, and she stared us down with an evil glint of triumph in her eye.

To his credit, my grandfather's expression stayed neutral. "And what does that mean, Madame Mayor?"

"It means the position of Ombudsman is hereby suspended.

Your employees are on administrative leave, and your office will be closed until further notice."

"You can't just—" Jeff started, but my grandfather held up a hand, and then he made me proud.

"I have held my tongue," he said. "Many times, over many issues, I have held my tongue. I walked the streets of this city for a long time—before you were even born into it, I'd imagine. Every man and woman who walks this earth must make his or her own way. And I see you're trying to do what you believe is correct. But you couldn't possibly be more wrong. The supernatural populations of this city need a friend now more than ever. Now is the time to foster mutual understanding, not leave supernatural populations adrift in a sea of hostility."

"That hostility is their fault and their burden," she retorted. "They made their bed."

"Mayor Tate made their bed," he corrected.

The mayor rolled her eyes. "This city no longer tolerates favoritism, whatever label you might put on it, and however well you sell that favoritism to the special interests that support it."

The demagoguery in her tone and the gleam in her eyes had Future Presidential Candidate written all over them.

"And if humans attack us?" I asked her. "If they gather up their stakes and pitchforks—or their guns—and rise against the Houses, will that be tolerated? Will they be treated with impunity?"

She shifted her gaze to me, the peon who'd bothered her with a practical question. "That is the kind of exaggeration that has turned our city into a national laughingstock. This is the real world, and we have more important concerns than whether vampires deserve special treatment."

"We'll appeal this to the city council," Jeff said. "We'll talk to our alderman."

"And they'll tell you the same thing that I have. It's time we prioritize, Mr. Merit. This is how I'm starting that process. You have twenty-four hours to clean out your offices—and you might recommend your constituents plan on getting their registration papers in order. Good night."

With that, she turned on her heel and walked outside again, her bodyguards behind her.

"I don't use this word lightly," Marjorie said, "but that woman is a stone-cold bitch."

My grandfather wouldn't be outdone by Marjorie's swear. He let loose a string of curses the likes of which I'd never heard before. There were words in there I couldn't believe *he'd* ever heard before.

"If she thinks," he finally said through gritted teeth, "I'm going to take this lying down, she has another think coming. I am not going to destroy all the forward progress we've made for the sups of this city for the sake of her presidential campaign."

"She can't do this," Jeff said. "Not unilaterally. It's not right."

"That woman couldn't differentiate 'right' from a hole in the ground," my grandfather said. "But I will be damned if that's the end of us."

The five of us stood in silence in the hallway.

"You know," Catcher finally said, "there may be a bright side to this."

"What's that?" my grandfather asked.

Catcher looked at my grandfather with a gleam in his eyes. "Every decision you've made in the last four years you've made with the mayor in mind. We were beholden to the position, which means anyone who relied on the office was beholden. We may not have governmental sponsorship anymore—but we also don't have government repression," Catcher said. "We've started from less.

Four years ago, we had no contacts, no friends, and no legitimacy. Sups were afraid of us. She might be able to take away our funding, but she can't turn back time."

My grandfather smiled, just a little. "Mr. Bell, you may have a point there."

I walked back to my car, leaving Jeff, Catcher, Marjorie, and my grandfather to pack their boxes and consider their options. Given the gleam in my grandfather's eye, I had no doubt he'd find another solution. The four of them—and their secret vampire employee—would probably have a new office set up before the sun rose again. I wondered if Grandpa would make them meatloaf to celebrate? He made a fantastic meatloaf.

Meatloaf on my mind, I pulled out my phone. I called Kelley and advised her my grandfather was going to look further into the lake's darkening. I had also promised Jonah a debriefing. And yes, I'd let my grandfather do the heavy lifting about the lake problem, but I wasn't going to ignore the situation, especially now.

"Are you done with your project?" I asked when Jonah answered my call.

"I am. Let's get together and debrief. Where are you?"

"South side. Just leaving my grandfather's office. Where are you?"

"Grey House. I don't want to meet here, obviously, and I'm not going anywhere near Cadogan. Too many protestors." He was quiet for a moment. "How about the Midway? We'll have some privacy there."

Midway Plaisance Park was a mile-long strip of green space that ran east-west across the city near the U of C campus. It had been carved out for the 1893 Columbian Exposition, the World's Fair that made Chicago the "White City."

"Sure," I said. "I'll be there in fifteen."

"See you then."

I hung up the phone and tossed it into the passenger seat, then stared at it for a moment. It was times like these I'd normally have called Ethan to debrief. Even if he didn't know precisely what to do, he'd have some kind of suggestion. He had hundreds of years of experience as a vampire and a ridiculously keen grasp of politics and strategy—even if that got him into trouble sometimes.

I'm sure Jonah would have valuable advice, as well; I wouldn't have agreed to the meeting otherwise. But Ethan and I had a camaraderie. A style. We'd learned how to work together. Ethan and I had an intimacy born of shared experiences; Jonah and I simply didn't. Maybe, if in some strange new world I accepted the RG's offer and he became my partner, it would develop. But tonight . . .

Tonight, I missed Ethan.

Seeking oblivion, I pulled my gaze from the phone and flipped on the radio. Snow Patrol blasted through the speakers, and although I turned it down to a slightly less eardrum-shattering volume, I left it loud enough to wipe unpleasant thoughts from my mind. The band sang about bravery and taking difficult steps, even if you were afraid to do so. I pretended the universe was daring me to be brave, to step into this new life as I'd done once before. The last time—from graduate student to warrior for Cadogan House. This time—from constant companion of the Master of that House to . . .

To what?

As I drove in the dark, the song rose to a crescendo, and I concluded that was the crucial question. What would I be without Ethan? *Who* would I be without Ethan?

It was probably time to find out.

The Midway linked Washington Park to the west and Jackson Park to the east. It was bounded by art, including the Masaryk memorial, a statue of a mounted soldier, on the east end. The horse and soldier sat atop a rectangular plinth above a set of raised concrete steps. Jonah stood in front of the plinth, arms crossed, looking up at it.

"You rang?" I asked him, hopping up the steps.

He turned around. "Do you ever wonder if we'll get to the point where we're considered part of Chicago?" He gestured toward the statue. "I mean, enough that they'd consider memorializing one of us? That they'd actually be proud of what we've done?"

I sat down on one of the steps, and he moved over and sat beside me.

"This city has been through a lot of phases since Celina's press conference," I said. "Denial. Hatred. Celebrity."

"And now back to hatred?"

I made a sound of agreement. "Something pretty profound would have to change before they'd consider us equal to humans. And speaking of equality," I said, and filled him in on the mayor's visit.

His eyes went wide. "The Ombud's office—they can't close it. The city needs it. The sups need it. They trust your grandfather. They think he gives them a voice. Without him, people only know about troublemakers, about Celina and Adam Keene."

"I agree, but don't fret. When I left, they were already brainstorming a plan to help out. They'll do what they have to do; taxpayers just won't be paying for it."

We sat quietly for a moment, the cool air raising goose bumps along my arms.

"I'm guessing you think something else is going on with the water," he said. "Something beyond the siren?"

"I do. It's too convenient otherwise. I was there with her, Jonah. And she wasn't working any magic."

"So we should keep looking."

"Quietly," I said. "Let my grandfather do the heavy lifting, as he put it. There's just too much pressure on me to be more active. Frank's not thrilled I'm standing Sentinel. It wouldn't surprise me if he tried to push me out of the position."

"He doesn't have the power to do that."

I gave him a dry look. "There may not be a rule in the *Canon* that says he can, but who's going to stop him? He's got the House over a barrel, and if it came down to me and the House, Malik has to pick the House. How could he not pick the House?"

My stomach sank at the thought—and not just from the possibility I'd no longer be Sentinel, but because I'd chided Ethan about having to choose between me and the House. I'd suggested it was wrong of him to even consider picking the House over me. Maybe I hadn't given him enough credit—not because I would have agreed with the decision, but because the decision had been harder than I'd thought.

"Where are you right now?"

I looked over at Jonah. "Just thinking."

"About?"

I looked away again, and he must have understood the embarrassment in my expression.

"Ah," he said.

"Ah," I repeated with a nod.

"Can I tell you something?"

"Sure."

Whatever he was going to say, it took a few seconds for him to work up to it. "I know we didn't exactly hit it off in the beginning, mostly because of my admittedly preconceived notions about who you were."

"And because I'd forgotten you'd masqueraded as a human to date my twenty-two-year-old sister."

"Also that," he quickly agreed. "But that doesn't change the obvious."

"Which is?"

"Which is, you're rather intriguing, Merit, Sentinel of Cadogan House."

"Thanks," I said, but couldn't manage to make eye contact.

Jonah put a finger beneath my chin, turning my head so I had to face him. The touch of his finger sent a warming *zing* of power straight down my spine.

"What the hell was that?"

Surprise in his eyes, he pulled back his fingers and stared down at them before lifting his gaze to mine. "Complementary magic," he whispered. "I've heard it was possible, but I've never actually seen it. Vamps aren't magical per se, you know. We feel it. We sense it. We know it's around us. We disrupt the balance of it when we're upset."

That wasn't exactly how I'd learned it. "I thought we leaked magic when we were upset?"

Jonah shook his head. "The magic doesn't come *from* us. It flows *around* us. Strong emotions—fear, anger, lust—change the way we interact with it, sending ripples through it. We aren't making the magic or leaking it. We're altering the currents."

"I see," I said.

"But this," he began, picking up my hand and tracing a finger across my palm—and sending frissons of magic down my body. "This is unexpected. The theory is that some vampires affect magic in complementary ways—as if on the same frequency. It looks like we might have some of that."

Magical novelty or not, this sounded like a complication I didn't need. And yet, every movement of his fingers sent shivers down my spine and shut off the part of my brain that should have been thinking better.

"All right," he suddenly said, jumping up from his seat. "Let's get back to work."

The abrupt change in conversation surprised me again.

He must have caught the shock in my face, as he smiled. "This city is bigger than a magical novelty. Bigger than three Houses or two vampires or a pain in the ass council. I'm not going to sweat the small stuff."

Relief at his casual tone coursed through me. "I'm now 'small stuff'?"

He grinned. "And you've got yourself a nickname. I'm thinking 'Shorty.'"

"I'm five eight without heels."

"It's not a description. It's a nickname. Get used to it, Shorty."

We stood there for a moment, waiting for the tension to evaporate. When it did, we smiled at each other. "Don't call me Shorty," I told him.

"Okay, Shorty."

"Seriously. That's very immature."

"Whatever you say, Shorty. Let's call it a night."

"Fine by me."

I'd worry about the humiliation in the morning.

—◆≡◆—

CHAPTER EIGHT

LITTLE MISS SUNSHINE

I dreamed in darkness. I stood atop Chicago's John Hancock Center, the wind swirling around me. A yellow moon hung low in the sky, huge as it balanced just above the horizon, as if too heavy to make its way higher.

Ethan stood beside me in his black Armani, his golden hair tied at the nape of his neck, his green eyes glowing. "Look," he said. "It's disappearing."

I followed the line of his outstretched hand and looked into the sky. The moon was higher now—small and white in the midsky—and a fingernail crescent of it had turned dark.

"A lunar eclipse," I said, watching the earth's shadow crawl across the face of the moon. "What does it mean?"

"Darkness," Ethan said. "Chaos. Destruction." He looked back at me and squeezed my hand until it ached. "The world is changing. I don't know how. I don't know why. I'm still . . . stretched thin. You have to find the cause."

I blew him off, offering him a smile. "It's nothing. Just an eclipse. They happen all the time." But when I looked again, the moon was no longer disappearing behind a round disk of shadow. The circle had morphed, the edges blurring into shapes that more closely resembled tentacles than the smooth curve of the earth. They undulated across the moon like a ravenous monster intent on devouring it.

My chest clenched with panic, and I squeezed Ethan's hand as tightly as he'd squeezed mine. "Is this the end of the world?" I asked him, unable to look away from the dancing shadows.

That he didn't answer didn't comfort me at all.

Together, fingers tangled, we watched the moon disappear behind the monster's shadow. And as it happened, a cold wind began to blow, the temperature dropping precipitously.

"You have to stop this," he said into the silence.

"I don't know how."

"Then you must find someone who does."

I looked over at him, there beside me, hair whipping in the wind. And as the wind rose, each gust stronger than the last, I watched him disappear behind the monster's shadow, until there was nothing left of him.

Until I stood alone in the chilling wind beneath an empty sky.

There was no sound except the howling of the wind in my ears, and his screaming of my name.

"*Merit!*"

My eyes flashed open. I was still in bed, warm beneath the blankets in my chilly room.

I pulled a pillow over my face and screamed into it, frustration pulling my nerves so taut I felt ready to snap. These dreams were killing me.

I'd always been a fan of ripping off the bandage—dealing with the pain all at once rather than suffering death by a thousand stings. These dreams were torture by a thousand memories: Seeing his green eyes, his face, all the while knowing the Ethan in my dreams was a weak facsimile of the man I'd known.

Maybe I needed more sleep. More vegetables. More exercise. Maybe I needed more Mallory and less vampire, more Wicker Park and less Hyde Park.

Whatever the reason, I needed a change. I threw off the blankets and hopped out of bed, then pulled on a long-sleeved T-shirt and yoga pants. My hair went up, and I headed downstairs for a workout session as long and brutal as I could make it. For a workout, I hoped, that would push the grief right out of me.

Vampires had a long history of martial arts work in a style that mixed swordcraft, defensive postures, and offensive attacks. We practiced those efforts in the House's sparring room, a giant space in the basement that was prepped for combat. The walls were lined with wooden paneling and antique weapons, and tatami mats were spread across the floor.

I kicked off the flip-flops I'd donned for the trip downstairs and stepped onto the mat. The room was big and silent, and it felt strange to stand in the middle of it alone. I'd lost a workout partner in Ethan, and I hadn't trained with Catcher since Ethan had taken over the job earlier in the year. I worked out with the House guards on occasion, but we were so short-staffed opportunities for long workouts and training sessions didn't arise very often.

Silence, I quickly decided, wasn't going to work tonight. There was a sound system in one corner of the room, and I flipped through the channels until I found an angry alternative song (courtesy of Rage Against the Machine) and turned up the volume. And then I returned to the middle of the mat, shook out my shoulders, closed my eyes, and got to work.

Katas were the building blocks of our martial arts work, short

combinations of punches, strikes, kicks, and the like. Put them together, and you had a pretty fierce looking demonstration of our
skills. With the music pounding behind me, I used strikes, spins,
and flips to push out the grief.

Workouts were tricky. Some days it was easier than others.
Some days you felt light as air; some days you felt heavy as lead.
Tonight was somewhere in between. It felt good to move, but I
could feel the gnawing thirst itching beneath my skin.

I pushed through it. An out-of-shape Sentinel wasn't going to
do anyone any good. Given the trouble I often managed to get
into, I needed to make sure my muscles were honed and my skills
were fine-tuned.

After twenty minutes or so, the door opened, and Luc stepped
inside. I pushed sweaty bangs from my face.

"I heard the music down the hall," he said. "Getting in some
exercise?"

When I nodded, Luc walked to the edge of the mat and looked
down at the tatami. "There are nights when he seems more absent
than others."

The grief in his voice brought immediate tears to my eyes. I
looked away to keep them from falling, but didn't disagree with
the heart-clenching sentiment.

"There are nights when the world is completely askew because he's gone," I agreed.

Luc crossed his arms over his chest and glanced around the
room at the objects displayed on the walls. He nodded toward a
shield that bore images of acorns.

"That was Ethan's when he was in Sweden."

More than four hundred years ago, Ethan had been a Swedish
soldier, changed into a vampire during a vicious battle.

"Family crest?"

Luc nodded. "I believe so. He'd been a helluva soldier, at least until the reaper got him. Two lives instead of nine, I suppose." He laughed mirthlessly, then looked down at the floor, as if ashamed he'd made a joke. "Well, I'll leave you to it."

"We all miss him," I assured him.

He looked at me again. "I know, Sentinel." He turned and walked out again, and I stood in the middle of the tatami mats, closed my eyes, and let the music wash over me. So much for escaping the grief.

One workout, one hot shower, and one much-too-small drink box of Type A later, I decided another way to get out of my rut was to focus on something other than myself. In this case, Mallory—who was now in the middle of her apprenticeship exams—seemed like a pretty good option.

When I was dressed, I drove to a funky little gourmet store in a commercial district of Hyde Park and loaded up a handled, brown paper bag with treats. A nice candle. A cup with an "M" inscribed on it. Some mixed nuts and dried fruit. A bottle of water and some chocolate bars.

Granted, the chocolate itself was unnecessary; I'd left an entire kitchen drawer of chocolate goodies at her brownstone when I'd moved out. It seemed unlikely that she'd cleaned it out already. But these had bacon in them. *Bacon*, people.

All the goodies for a study break box in hand, I put my purchases on the counter.

When the cashier began to ring me up, I decided to poll the public. "So, you're pretty close to Cadogan House. Do you get vampires in here often?"

The register beeped as he ran the chocolate bars across the scanner. "Occasionally, yeah."

"Are they as bad as everybody says?"

"The vamps? Nah. They ain't bad. Pretty nice. Some of the girls ain't bad to look at, you know what I mean?" He smiled grandly.

"Thank you," I said, handing over cash and picking up my bag. "I'll tell the rest of my friends at Cadogan House you said that."

I gave him a wink, and left him in the store with cheeks blushing crimson.

I made it to Mallory's house just in time to see her tutor, Simon, walking out the front door. He moved down the sidewalk with a perky kick in his step, which matched pretty well his boy-next-door good looks. His dark blond hair was closely cropped, his eyes bright blue. He wasn't overly tall, but he looked like the friendly, gregarious type who might have been senior class president.

"Hi," he said, squinting a little. "Merit, right? You're a friend of Mallory's?"

"Yep." I lifted up the care package. "Just bringing her a little something. Is she in the middle of a test?"

"Oh, no. Not tonight. Just studying. I came over to help her with a tricky spot."

"I see." Mallory had thought Simon had a weird vibe, and Catcher clearly wasn't a fan. I didn't get a bad sense, but it did seem odd to me that his focus was Mallory's exams, not the water. After all, he was the Order's official representative in Chicago.

"How is the Order feeling about the issues with the lake and the river? Did they have any thoughts?"

He blinked, like the question didn't make sense to him. "The lake and the water? They're fixed now, aren't they?"

"They are, but it's still weird, don't you think?"

He looked nervously down at his watch. "I'm sorry to be rude,

but I need to go. I've got an appointment. Good seeing you again."
He hustled down the sidewalk toward a German sports car parked
on the street.

I watched until the car disappeared down the block, wondering at his reaction, at his lack of concern because the problem
had been "fixed." He was a *sorcerer*, and by all accounts this was a
magical problem. Did he have no curiosity about why it had happened?

Maybe he was just happy it was fixed, and was focused enough
on getting Mal through testing.

Or maybe he knew exactly what was going on, and was keeping it close to his vest.

Either way, I found the reaction suspicious, so I filed it away,
popped onto the porch and knocked on the door. Catcher opened
it with brown slippers on his feet, glasses on his nose, and a *TV
Guide* in his hand. Maybe he was taking his sudden retirement seriously.

"Big night?"

"I've spent the last forty-eight tripping through books trying to
find an explanation for the water. I've searched every online forum
I could think of for references to spells or creatures or prophecies
that might explain what's going on. And to show for it, I have nothing. I haven't slept. I've hardly eaten. Mallory is in a tizzy, and
Simon is calling my house every five goddamned minutes. I need
a break or I am going to lose my shit."

There was no mistaking the defensiveness in his voice or the
dark circles under his eyes.

I tried to lighten the mood, and pointed at the house shoes—
the last things I'd have expected to see Catcher Bell wearing. "And
the shoes?" I asked with a grin.

"My house, my rules. These shoes happen to be comfortable,"

he said. "If you two roamed around the house naked and carrying bows and arrows before I moved in, it's none of my business."

The snark notwithstanding, he moved aside to let me in.

"How's life in the post-Ombudsman era?" I asked as he closed the door behind me.

He smiled thinly. "Like I said, exhausting, but surprisingly well organized. You know that room in the back of Chuck's house he uses for storage?"

I did. That had been my grandmother's treasure room. She loved garage sales, and she inevitably found something she thought one of us needed. A wooden pull toy for Charlotte's daughter, Olivia. An antique desk blotter for Robert. A book of poetry for me. She kept them in boxes or paper bags in tidy stacks and passed them out during visits like Santa Claus. When my grandmother died, my grandfather left the room and its treasure trove intact. At least, he had before . . .

"Well," Catcher continued, "it's been reorganized. It's now home of the Chuck Merit School of Supernatural Diplomacy."

"Tell me you aren't really calling it that."

"It's only a temporary name," he assured. "The point is, we're still on the map for folks who need help."

"And the folks who need your help probably don't care if you're working out of a fancy office or a back bedroom."

"Precisely." Catcher assumed his position on the couch—ankles crossed on the coffee table, *TV Guide* in one hand, remote in the other, his gaze on the television over the top of his glasses. A lemon-lime soda and a bowl of gummy orange slices sat on the coffee table in front of him. This was a man ready for a break, uninterrupted by trips to the kitchen for nosh.

I assumed that was my cue. "I assume Mallory's home?"

"She's in the basement."

That was a surprise. It was an Amityville spider trap down there. I couldn't imagine she'd be down there on purpose, much less studying.

"Seriously?"

"It's chemistry night. She needed quiet and room to make messes. I wasn't willing to give up the kitchen."

"Basement it is," I said, and walked to the back of the house. The door to the grungy cellar was in the kitchen, which also housed the ice-cold diet sodas Mallory usually kept on hand. I grabbed two from the fridge and opened the basement door.

The smell of vinegar that poured up the stairs made my eyes water instantly.

"Mal?" I called out. The basement stairs were dark, but some light crept around the corner from the main part of the basement. "Is everything okay down there?"

I heard the clunking of what sounded like pots and pans—and then she began to belt out the lyrics of a hip-hop song with much gusto.

I considered that the all clear and began to pick my way down the basement stairs.

I'd never been a fan of basements. Before my parents moved into their modern, concrete box of a house in Oak Park, we lived in a Gothic house in Elgin, Illinois. The house had been a century old, and looked—and felt—like the setting for a horror movie. It was beautiful but haunting. Luxurious, as was their way, but lonely.

The house had a basement in which my mother had stored the pottery kiln she'd purchased when ceramics had become her temporary obsession. She kept the kiln immaculately clean, but it was the only clean item in the basement; the rest had been dark, cold, damp, and spidery.

"Not unlike this one," I muttered, finally reaching the concrete floor and peeking around the corner.

A single, white-hot bulb hung down into the room. There was no sign of the source of the vinegary smell, but the scent was definitely stronger down here. Mallory sat at a giant worktable made from sawhorses and sheets of plywood. Books and bowls of unidentifiable bits were stacked feet high upon it, as were a variety of potted plants. Some looked like regular houseplants; others had viciously pointy leaves with crimson-red tips or thick, luscious leaves that looked like they were full to bursting with water.

Mallory's ice-blue hair—now showing a little blond at the roots—was pulled into a ponytail, and black headphones covered her ears. There were dark circles under her eyes, and her cheeks looked a little more gaunt than usual. The exams must have been taking their toll.

She spit out lyrics with nimble speed while she perused a hefty book that sat open on the tabletop before her. She was oblivious while I picked through the maze of cardboard boxes, unused furniture, and waiting bags of ice melt that covered the basement floor . . . and she jumped when I put a can of soda on the table.

"Jesus H. Roosevelt, Merit!" she exclaimed, ripping off the headphones. "What are you doing here? I nearly zapped you into next month."

"Sorry. You were busy communing with Kanye. What's with the smell?"

Mallory pointed to a series of homemade wooden shelves tucked into a nook across from the table. It was probably eight feet tall, and each of the shelves was lined with rows of home-canned fruits and vegetables. I could identify pickles, apples, and tomato sauce. The rest of the jars were a mystery. But the vinegar smell wasn't—there was an empty slot on the pickle row.

"Missing a jar?"

"I blasted one of Aunt Rose's pickle jars," Mallory said, looking down at her book again. She'd inherited the town house, and its contents, when her aunt died a few years ago. Since the jars had been sitting in the same spot unused, Mal apparently wasn't a fan of her aunt's canned goods.

"I didn't even know this stuff was down here."

"I didn't bring any jars upstairs," she flatly said. "They didn't taste very good. They were garlic-spiced apples."

I wrinkled my lip. "Foul."

"Hella foul. After that, I didn't open another jar. Until last night. And that wasn't on purpose."

"Funny the pickles didn't make it smell like dill."

"No dill," Mallory said. "Just vinegar. I think Aunt Rose's sense of taste was a little off. Too bad she hadn't at least thrown some garlic into it. And it wouldn't have even bothered you, since you aren't that kind of vampire."

She was right that garlic wasn't the vamp repellent of myth; on the other hand, the thought of a basement sprayed down with garlic and vinegar didn't exactly make me eager for a visit, either.

"That is true." I plopped the care package onto a clean strip of table. "And speaking of snacks, this is for you."

Without a word, she closed her book, then looked inside the bag and pulled out the bag of nuts and fruit, which she pulled open with her teeth. After pouring some into her hand—which was seriously chapped, like it had been one of the last times I'd seen her—she extended it to me, and I rooted around until I found a couple of whole cashews.

"Thanks," I said, enjoying the satisfying snap when I broke them in half with my teeth. "How are exams?"

"Complicated. Lots of math. It's not like the exams Catcher

took," she said, with a little feistiness. "He's been out of the Order for years more. He's not exactly up to speed on sorceress testing procedures."

I guessed she and Catcher had exchanged some words about the tests. "I see," I said neutrally.

A low cry suddenly lit through the air. I heard shuffling across the floor, and nearly jumped onto the table, imagining it was a spider the size of a football.

But a small, black cat with a pink rhinestone collar padded into view from beneath the table. It sat down on its haunches on the floor beside Mallory and looked up at me, its eyes chartreuse.

"Your familiar?" I wondered, and Mallory nodded. At Simon's suggestion, she'd adopted a black kitten to help her perform her sorcery duties.

"That would be Wayne Newton, yes."

"You named your familiar 'Wayne Newton'?"

"They have the same haircut," she dryly said. I moved my hand. Sure enough, the small cat had a bouffant of dark hair between its ears.

"Huh. It does seem a lot calmer than the last time you mentioned it," I said. I reached down to scratch Wayne Newton between his ears. He nuzzled against my hand, but swayed a little as he did it, as if he was drunk.

I glanced back at Mallory. "What's wrong with him?"

She glanced down, then frowned at the kitten. "Her, not him. And it's the fermented pickle juice. I didn't quite get there in time, and she was lapping it up."

"Poor kid."

"I know. And it's another strike against Aunt Rose. I don't even think she liked pickles, anyway."

Apparently equally bored of me and Mal, the cat wandered off. But there was an odd, dizzying sway to its gait.

"Are you feeling better about the kinds of things you're doing?"

Mallory had previously expressed concern about Simon introducing her to black magic. Although a spell prevented her from spilling all the details, she'd clearly had some ethical qualms about it. I'd encouraged her to talk to Catcher. I knew they'd talked, but maybe the conversation—or its follow-ups—hadn't gone well.

She tapped a finger against the red leather cover of the book she'd been reading, which was inscribed with gold text. Frankly, it looked exactly like the kind of book a sorceress would read.

"The world is what it is," she said. "Just because something makes me uncomfortable doesn't mean it's bad, you know? Sometimes it just takes a little exposure to really understand it. I was just a little paranoid before."

I waited for more elaboration, but that's all she said. To be honest, that answer didn't thrill me. Coming to terms with something unpleasant was one thing. But deciding it wasn't so unpleasant after all was entirely different.

"Just a little paranoid?" Her hands—chapped and raw—were a side effect of the magic she'd been practicing. That didn't seem like paranoia to me; it seemed like cause and effect.

"It's fine," she said, putting a hand down on the table hard enough to make it shake. I jumped a little at the sound, but if she was trying to shut me up, she succeeded. "I needed the cat to help me funnel the magic. And what I still need are three more of them to help me get all this done. There's too much to do, too much to learn, for one person."

This wasn't Mallory—not the attitude. I laid responsibility for that at Simon's feet; she'd seen him more often lately than anyone else. But here it was just her and me, and I wasn't about to lead our friendship to the precipice over some temporary stress.

"Okay," I allowed. "You know if you need to talk you can call me anytime. Day or night."

"You'll answer your phone in daylight?" she snarked.

Not if you don't lose the attitude, I thought, but kept that thought to myself. *She's been there for me*, I mentally repeated, and kept repeating it until my anger calmed.

"Whatever you need," I told her.

She humphed and flipped a page in the book. "I should get back to work. Thanks for the food."

I frowned, unsuccessfully fighting the feeling that I'd been summarily dismissed. "You're welcome. Take care of yourself, okay?"

"I'm fine. Even if I get sick, I could just will myself back to health."

When it was clear I'd lost her attention, I left her with her books and plants and care package and a secret prayer that she'd weather this particular storm.

I didn't like the sense she was hiding things, but I understood the single-minded focus. I'd had dozens of exams in college and grad school, and preparing took that kind of focus. I'd had to remember characters, plots, and details, as well as trends, metaphors, and similarities. You had to dive into the books completely to have enough familiarity to spend hours answering essay questions. I assumed, given her attitude today, that magic exams required a similar immersion.

On the way back up, I made a quick pit stop in the brownstone's kitchen, pulling open the long, flat drawer that housed my chocolate collection. I was a little saddened to discover the bulk of it—if not all of it—was still in there. I wanted to know Mallory still snuck chocolate after a return from the bar or a gym session, or had used the high-cocoa bars to make her famous truffle cupcakes. Instead, the drawer was frozen in time, a bit of me she and Catcher hadn't yet managed to assimilate into their lives.

Well, if they weren't going to eat it, I would. I rummaged through to find a few special treats—famous brownies special-ordered from a New York bakery, a favorite mini dark chocolate bar, and a novelty bar filled with one of my favorite cereals—and stuffed them into the pockets of my jacket. Given Frank's House ban on all things delicious, I was going to need them.

My pockets full, I closed the drawer again and walked back to the front door. Catcher was still on the couch, frowning at what looked to be another Lifetime movie.

"What's the appeal?" I wondered aloud, watching a montage of a woman getting a makeover with girlfriends, probably after some ridiculously bad breakup.

"Normalcy," he said. "The stories are melodramatic, sure, but the problems are profane. They're about love and illness and money and nasty neighbors and creepy ex-boyfriends."

"They aren't about magic and irritating vampires and awful politicians?"

"Precisely."

I nodded in understanding. "I pulled some stuff from the chocolate drawer. But I don't think you'll miss it. Hey, have you noticed anything weird about Mallory? She seems, I don't know, really focused. And not really in a good way."

"She's fine," was all he said. I waited for more, but got nothing but thick tension and a little peppery magic. He may have verbally disagreed with me, but there was nothing in his body language that said he was okay with her behavior.

"You sure about that? Have you talked to Mallory about Simon? About what he's having her do? I get the sense she's doing things she's not comfortable with."

"This isn't exactly your area of expertise."

There was a sharpness in his voice I hadn't expected to hear.

Catcher may have been gruff, but he was also usually patient about supernatural issues.

"True," I allowed. "But I do know Mallory. And I know when she's avoiding something."

"You think I don't know her?"

"Of course you know her. I just know her in a different way than you do."

Ever so slowly, he slid me a skewering glance. "What goes on in this house between us isn't exactly your business, is it?"

I blinked from the sting, but decided to give him the benefit of the doubt. After all, he'd just lost his job and his girlfriend was a giant stressball.

"Okay," I said, hand on the doorknob. "Fine. You guys have a good night."

"Merit."

I looked back.

"Before you go . . ." He began, then wet his lips and looked away. It wasn't often that I'd seen him uncomfortable about voicing an opinion, and that made me nervous. "I've heard you've been spending time with Jonah lately. I have to admit: I'm not thrilled about it."

How did word travel so fast? This was like being in high school all over again. "We're working together," I said. "He's my backup."

"Is that all?"

I gave back the same doubtful expression he'd offered me. "Is that all?"

"I know it wasn't always obvious, but Ethan and I were close."

"I could say the same thing."

"And are you respecting his memory?"

The question was as brutal as a slap, and as surprising as it was harsh. "Not that it's any of your business, but yes, I am. And regardless, I have a right to live my life even if he's not here."

My heart pounded with adrenaline and irritation and . . . hurt. This was Catcher, my best friend's boyfriend. He was basically a brother-in-law, and he was accusing me of disrespecting Ethan's memory?

"That was a really shitty thing to say," I added, as the irritation grew.

Silence.

"He was a pain in the ass," Catcher said. "But I'd gotten used to him, you know?"

The hurt softened a bit. "I know."

It was another minute before he spoke again. "Have I ever told you how Sullivan and I met?"

I shook my head.

"The Order was convinced there shouldn't be sorcerers in Chicago. But I knew—we all knew—that supernatural issues were going to come to a head here before anywhere else. I'd always thought the Order just didn't want to get their hands dirty. Now I think they were afraid. At any rate, I'd had a prophecy, and I'd told them about it. I told them we needed sorcerers here. That it was imperative that we have sorcerers here."

"They didn't believe you?"

"Or were in denial. And when I came to Chicago anyway, they saw that as a breach of the chain of command and they kicked me out. They left me without a sponsor, and they accused me of being arrogant, of trying to usurp the authority of the union. As an act of courtesy, I called the Houses and let them know I was coming. I didn't want my arrival to ruffle any feathers. Scott wouldn't talk to me; he didn't want to get involved in Order issues. Celina offered me a meeting, but that was largely an exercise in self-absorption."

"Not entirely surprising."

He made a sound of agreement. "I called Ethan, gave him a

heads-up. He invited me over. We talked about Chicago, the Order, the Houses. We talked for hours. And at the end of that conversation, he offered to let me stay in Cadogan House until I got situated in Chicago."

Catcher was silent for a moment, maybe letting that sink in. Except that it didn't really surprise me. Ethan was strategic, and he was also loyal. He'd have rewarded Catcher for following the etiquette, and he'd have had the grace to offer him the House afterward.

"That was years ago," he finally said. "Years before you became a vampire, years before you met Mallory. Years before you moved back to Chicago. Years before the city turned against its own."

"Years before we lost Ethan. But we did lose him."

"I know," Catcher said. "I know he's gone, and I know your relationship was rocky right up to the end. But deep down, he was good people."

"I know he was."

Catcher nodded, and silence reigned for a moment.

But before I could speak, my cell phone rang. I pulled it from my pocket and checked the screen. It was Jonah.

"Hello?"

"Have you looked outside recently?"

"Not in a couple of hours. Why?"

"Go and look."

"Is this a joke?" I asked him. "I'm kind of in the middle of something."

"It's aspen serious. Go look outside. Check the sky and the moon."

"I'll call you back," I told him. I tucked the phone away and glanced back at Catcher. "Excuse me for a moment," I said, opening the door and peering outside.

I froze. "Oh, my God," I muttered, and heard Catcher rustling behind me.

The sky was ruby red. Not sunrise or sunset pink, but *red*. A dark, rich red of cherry cola or well-worn mahogany. A glowing bloodred moon hung low in the sky, and brilliant white forks of lightning crossed it with alarming frequency.

Mallory had made a prophecy about a red moon once, something about the fall of "White City kings." Once upon a time, parts of Chicago had been called the "White City." Was this the moon she meant? If so, who were the "kings" that were supposed to fall?

My stomach churned in warning. I'd dreamed about a moon, but that had to be coincidence. Because if it wasn't, and the rest of the dream hadn't been coincidence either . . .

I shook my head. That was grief-driven wishful thinking and a ridiculous waste of time that was only going to make me feel worse—or stupid—in the long run.

"Jesus Christ," Catcher muttered, stepping beside me at the door. "What in God's name happened?"

"I'll tell you what happened," I said, pulling out my phone to call Jonah back. "Our second crisis for the week."

Dead lake. Red sky.

At least there was only one crisis at a time.

CHAPTER NINE

THE FAIRY TALE

Except there wasn't only one crisis at a time. I reached Jonah on my way to the House—the river and lake were back to black and still sucking magic from the city like it was going out of style. Which meant not only had that problem *not* been solved—the entire situation was escalating. I felt a real jolt of fear. I had no idea where this was headed.

When he met me at Cadogan, we joined the dozens of other vampires who stood on the lawn behind the House, staring up at the sky. And we weren't the only ones. I hardly passed a single house between Wicker Park and Hyde Park where folks weren't standing outside, fingers pointing upward or hands over their mouths in shock.

White lightning flashed across the sky, and claps of thunder drowned out the sounds of the city. There wasn't a thunderhead in sight, and I could all but hear Chicagoans' silent accusations: *These things didn't happen before vampires.*

What they weren't considering, of course, was that vampires and other sups had been in Chicago at least as long as humans, and this didn't have anything to do with us. Unfortunately, I didn't know how to prove that to them.

I'd texted Malik to give him a heads-up that I was bringing a Grey House vamp onto Cadogan soil, and he offered Jonah a handshake when we joined him and Luc in the backyard.

"I don't suppose there are Moon nymphs out there who could be responsible for this?" I asked. "Or maybe Wind witches? Atmospheric gremlins?"

"Not that I'm aware of," Malik said.

"Me, either," Jonah said. "But we clearly can't deny there's something larger at work here."

"The question now is what to do about it," Luc said. "Especially within our current operating limitations."

He'd only just spoken the words when a bolt of lightning shot across the sky. We instantaneously hit the ground, just in time to watch the blaze of plasma strike the weathervane on the roof of the House accompanied by the loudest bang I'd ever heard.

The block went dark. The lights in the House flickered and went off, and then came back on in a sickly shade of orange—security lights I'd only seen during previous emergency drills. We had a couple of emergency generators in the basement to keep the emergency lights, security systems, and blood refrigeration on during power outages.

The following silence was filled with the shouts of humans down the block and the sound of sirens already heading down the road.

Beside me, Malik sighed. "We do not need this. Neither the drama nor the danger."

When another bolt of lightning lit the backyard, Malik cast a wary glance across the lawn. The crowd of vampires was splitting as someone walked through them. After a moment, Frank pressed through the final knot to step in front of us. He surveyed the sky suspiciously, then looked at Malik with obvious disdain. His thoughts were easy to read: *Goddamn Chicago vampires. Incapable of managing their affairs.*

"What is this?" he imperiously asked when he reached us. I didn't bother introducing him to Jonah. He didn't seem the type to be interested in others, and there was no point in dragging Jonah into our problems.

"This is not the work of vampires," Malik assured him. "We have no information beyond that."

"This isn't going to help the reputation of the Houses overmuch," Frank said.

"No, it is not," Malik agreed. "Which is why we will investigate the cause in order to limit the effect."

You could all but see the wheels turning in Frank's mind. But at least the wheels were turning. This was usually the point at which the GP henchman blamed us for whatever was happening, regardless of our role, and made us swear we wouldn't leave the House to fix it.

There was no way to win.

But Frank actually seemed to be considering the problem and our options. Maybe he was capable of independent thought, instead of just blaming Cadogan for the ills of the world.

"There is a group you could contact," Frank said.

We all looked at him expectantly.

"The sky masters."

Malik immediately shook his head. "No."

"Who are the sky masters?" I whispered.

"The fairies," Jonah whispered back. "The mercenary fairies."

"There's a reason they're referred to as mercenary fairies," Malik pointed out. "Our relationship with them is tense, at best, and it's only that good because they are well paid for their efforts."

"Be that as it may, this is clearly a matter within their purview. There is no better group to ask. There is no other group to ask. I suggest you select an away party and send it. Now."

Frankly, I thought it was a stupid idea. We'd already talked with two supernatural representatives—nymphs and the siren—and neither had anything to do with the problems the city was facing. Would visiting a group that already hated us accomplish anything other than raising their ire?

Malik, ever the diplomat, managed a respectful nod for Frank before looking at us. "Tread carefully into the world of fairy. They are a different breed of supernaturals, no pun intended. Different expectations, different formalities. But they know things. He's right; it's worth the trip. Find the queen. Pay her a visit and discover who's doing this."

"And make them stop," Franklin said. "Anything less is unacceptable."

The away party arranged and orders issued, Malik looked at Luc. "Get everyone back into the House. It's not safe to be outside."

Jonah and I shared a nod and began to walk back toward the House. Anticipation began to flutter in my stomach, but it was Malik's parting words that triggered the full-out panic.

"And may God help us all."

The emergency lights didn't provide much ambience, but they provided enough illumination for me to find my way upstairs and grab my sword and dagger.

Jonah trailed me all the way to my room, which surprised me. I hadn't expected him to follow, and I certainly hadn't invited him. But by the time I realized he was traipsing up the stairs behind me, telling him to stay put would have been that much more awkward.

He stood in the threshold of my door as I sent Catcher a message. I wasn't exactly thrilled with Catcher right now, but I wanted a non-vamp to know I was heading into fairy territory. His response was nearly immediate: YOUR FUNERAL.

Charming.

I pulled out my dagger and slipped it into my boot, then took my sheathed katana from its horizontal wall mount. That had been a gift from Luc; he'd installed one for Lindsey one rainy Saturday, and she'd decided it was fabulous enough that I'd needed one, too. I couldn't disagree—it was a gorgeous way to display the sword. Even in its scabbard it was a beautiful weapon, sleek and gleaming, the blade inside equally sleek but deadly and curving just so.

"Your rooms aren't quite as lush as ours are," Jonah said.

"You have more room and fewer vampires," I pointed out, gathering up my belt. He stepped aside as I closed the door behind us.

"True."

He followed me back downstairs, but pulled me to a stop before we went outside. "I don't actually know where the queen lives—it's a secret the fairies guard with their lives. In order to get that information, we'll have to offer them something in return."

So much for Chicago's sups being in this together. "What will they want?"

"Precious metals or stones." He grinned. "They're still on the gold standard. I don't suppose you have any sitting around?"

"Gold? No. No, I don't. I left all my bullion in my room."

"Smart-ass," he said, but he was smiling when he said it.

As I considered our options, I absently touched the Cadogan medal around my neck . . . and got an idea.

"Follow me," I told him, and walked down the House's main hallway, where the administrative offices were located. Vampires were funneling back into the House now, and we found Helen in her office. Her Barbie-pink office.

The room lit by candles, she sat behind her desk in a pink tracksuit, every hair in her steel gray bob in place. She was making notes on a pad with an old-fashioned dip calligraphy pen. She glanced up when we entered and dipped her pen back into a small glass jar of black ink.

"Yes, Sentinel?"

"I don't suppose you have any extra Cadogan medals in hand?"

Alarm flashed through her eyes; that wasn't entirely unexpected. We'd already lost one blank Cadogan medal; it had been stolen and used by a former Cadogan vampire to try to frame the House in a series of murders. It stood to reason she'd be hesitant about throwing them around now.

"We've been directed by the GP and Malik to visit the fairies," I explained. "In order to ascertain how and where to do that, we need to talk to the fairies at the gate."

She nodded in understanding. "And they require payment for information." She stood up and walked to a file cabinet, then unlocked the top drawer. But before she opened it, she looked suspiciously at Jonah.

"He's the captain of the Grey House guards," I informed her. "He's been instrumental in helping us deal with these issues. You know, inter-House cooperation and all that."

She nodded, unlocked the door, and pulled out two blank Cadogan medals, which she handed to me. "Do everything you can," she said, a tremor in her voice. "It's hard to know how to react or what I should do . . . I don't know what's happening."

"I don't think anyone does," I said, and assured her we'd do our best. But that didn't make me any less nervous at the weight being placed on our shoulders. Not that I'd let that deter me.

Cadogan, at least, was short on guards and barely had enough to keep watch outside. Who else could do it?

Medals in hand, we walked back to the front door and stood on the small stone porch for a moment, watching the fairies at the gate . . . and trying very hard to focus on the task at hand and not the chaos around us.

"I'm guessing you have more information about the fairies than I do," I told Jonah. "Would you like to handle this one?"

He nodded. "I can take it. Although I've never met Claudia before."

"Claudia?"

He smiled. "The fairy queen. The one they would die to protect."

"Of course they would," I muttered, then handed over the gold and followed him down the sidewalk.

Two male fairies stood point at the gate, their gaunt features exaggerated by their long, dark, straight hair, pulled back tightly at the temples. They were tall and slender and they both wore black, and when they realized we were approaching them, they shared a none too flattering glance.

Jonah cut to the chase. "We need information, and we have treasure to offer."

The interest in their eyes was unmistakable; it might have been fair to call it "lust." They had the same expressions of yearning you might have seen on an inveterate gambler offered a seat at a lucky table.

"What kind of treasure?" asked one of the fairies.

"Gold," Jonah told them. He rattled the medals together in his pocket, and their heads twitched a bit at the sound.

"What information?" the fairy asked.

"We need to speak with the queen."

Silence.

"And if the queen does not wish to speak with you?"

Jonah slowly lifted his gaze to the brilliantly red sky.

"The sky is on fire," he said. "You are the masters of the sky; it is your realm. If you've done this . . ." Jonah began, but a look of menace from one of the fairies made him pause. The look in their eyes left little doubt they'd be willing to go the distance to protect their honor.

But Jonah was undeterred. "If you've done this," Jonah repeated again, "your queen must have a reason. In order to assuage the humans, we need to advise them of it. And if your queen is not involved, then she will undoubtedly be concerned. We seek knowledge. That is all."

The fairies exchanged a glance. "Let us see the gold," said the chatty one.

Slowly, as if letting the excitement build, Jonah slipped the medals from his pocket. They dangled from their chains and spun slowly, and the fairies' eyes went wild.

"You will find her in fortune's tower," said the fairy, reaching out his hand. Jonah dangled the medals above it.

"More," Jonah said. "This is a big city."

"It is the only remaining spire of what once stood strong." He made a play for the medals again, but Jonah pulled them out of reach.

"There are hundreds of skyscrapers in the Loop," he said. "A standing tower could be anywhere. That's insufficient information for this amount of gold."

The fairies were becoming tenser; I could feel the rise of magical angst in the air.

"There is water," he said. "Earth, and sky."

"Again," Jonah firmly said after waiting for a moment, "that could be anywhere in the city. That doesn't mean anything to us."

But I touched Jonah's arm. "It's okay. I think I know where that is."

"You're sure?"

I looked at the fairy. "It was the home of the city's human king?"

When the fairy nodded back, I pulled the medals from Jonah's hand and placed them into his. "Thank you for your business," I told him, then pulled Jonah away. "Let's go."

Without objection from Jonah, we walked to our cars, climbed inside and were on our way.

We drove separately and parked on the edge of the street. We got out, suspiciously eying the trails of lightning that were creating a strobe light effect across the park.

There were a number of mansions in Chicago that had once been home to famous families. During the city's golden age, entrepreneurs built homes along Lake Shore Drive in the Gold Coast neighborhood (now home, not coincidentally, to Navarre House), affording the fashionable a view of the lake and access to the rest of the city's wealthy.

Some of the mansions were still standing; some had been razed. One of the most famous—the Potter Mansion, built by ancestors of the city's former mayor—had been demolished when the mayor moved to Creeley Creek.

Well, *mostly* demolished.

The Potter family donated the grounds to the city, which was turned into the aptly named Potter Park. The only remaining bit of the mansion—a four-story brick turret—punctuated the middle of the park like a spear.

"This is it?" Jonah asked.

I filled him in on the history. "The tower was built by a family with a manufacturing fortune, and is all that's left of the house. It reaches into the sky, it's surrounded by green, and it's two hundred yards from the lake."

"Well done, Nancy Drew."

"I try. The more interesting question is how the parks district doesn't know there's a fairy queen living in their tower?"

"Magic, I'd imagine. Although I'm surprised they'd allow their queen to live in a house built by human hands."

"I had heard they hate humans."

"And for good reason," Jonah said. "You know of the changeling myth?"

I did. It was a prominent story in medieval literature, and warned that fairies occasionally stole healthy human children, replacing them with sickly fairy children. Thus, as the story went, any humans born with unusual features were actually fairy children who'd been switched at birth. Humans called the sickly children changelings, and would leave them in the woods in a ploy to win back their human children.

"I do," I said.

Jonah nodded. "Thing is, it's not myth. The stories are real— fairy tales in the truest sense of the word. They just got the protagonists wrong. Fairy children were stolen by humans, not the other way around. Sometimes their children were replaced with sickly human children; sometimes they were taken by parents desperate for a child."

"And because fairies were, at best, myths or, at most, real-life monsters, no one considered such things a kidnapping."

Jonah nodded. "You got it. Unequal treatment of supernaturals is centuries old. In any event, they probably won't be glad we're here. Keep your sword in hand, a finger on the steel at all times. Steel and iron solve the same problem—keeping fairies at bay."

"I thought the point of this exercise was asking them for help."

"The point of this exercise is finding out if they're to blame. And from Frank's perspective, it was also probably to get us to piss off the fairies so we incite a war."

"How is our starting a war with the fairies going to help him?"

"Chicago is the only American city with three vampire Houses. Even New York and L.A. can't claim that. We are the locus of vampire power in the United States, and Cabot knows it. Cabot House is small. Elitist, and necessarily small. If he minimizes Chicago's importance—"

"He increases Cabot House's power proportionally," I finished. I knew I'd given the little weasel too much credit.

"Precisely. I'd say it's part of a long-term plan to wrest control of Cabot House for himself. Victor Garcia is the current Master. He's a good man, a solid leader. He was Cornelius Cabot's right-hand man, which irked Franklin to no end. Franklin was just a cousin from some far-off branch of the family tree, but he thought he had a right to the House. That it was his birthright."

"And Cornelius disagreed?"

"I've heard the old man thought Franklin was too caught up in human affairs to effectively manage the House. Too concerned with prestige and fast cars and human girls, which didn't exactly fly for an old school, under the radar, east coast House."

"Let me guess," I said. "The GP figures he's ambitious and is willing to play ball, even against another House, so they appointed him receiver for Cadogan House. He figures he comes down here, screws over the Chicago Houses and wins the support of the GP, and that positions him perfectly for a spot at the top."

"That's how it plays for me."

I blew out a breath. So much drama, so little of it actually originating in Cadogan House. Whatever the original goal of the GP and the House system might have been, they were now tools for the narcissistic and the manipulative. Maybe Jonah was right about the Red Guard.

"Won't they take it as a threat if we come in bearing weapons?"

"Only if we're lucky," he said. "Let's go."

Lightning flashing around us, we ran toward the tower. The exterior was narrow and crumbling. An open doorway led to a spiral of old stone steps that weren't in much better shape than the exterior. I took the first step, pausing on the tread to make sure the staircase didn't crumble beneath us.

"All the way up?"

"Yep. I assume they prefer to live above the human plane."

He began to pick his way up and around the spiral. I gripped the handrail and started the slow climb behind him. After a few thigh-burning minutes of climbing, we reached the landing at the top of the stairs.

A door led into the tower room. It was huge, made up of long, horizontal strips of wood. Two giant, circular, filigreed hinges connected it to the wall.

"Lovely door," I said.

"They're known for their love of beauty," he said, then glanced at me. "Are you ready for this?"

"I'm working from the assumption it's going to go horribly wrong. If we get out of here with limbs intact and no aspen slivers in uncomfortable places, we're calling it a win."

"Well put." After a heartening breath, he pulled his hand into a fist and rapped on the door.

After a moment, it opened with a grating, metallic sound. A man in black—a fairy of the same dress and build as the ones who guarded the House, stood in the doorway. He asked a question in a quick, guttural language I didn't understand, but thought might be Gaelic.

"We ask if the queen would deign to see us," Jonah said.

With a jaundiced eye, the fairy looked us over. "Bloodletters," he said, the word obviously a slur.

"We are what we are," Jonah advised. "We make no attempts to hide it. We are here as emissaries of vampires."

The fairy's lip curled at the mention of vampires. "Wait," he said, then closed the door in our faces.

"As if we could do anything else," Jonah muttered.

"Not up to pushing your way into a fairy enclave tonight?"

"It's not high on my agenda," he said. "Not that you couldn't take them, of course."

"Of course," I allowed. Before we could continue the back-and-forth, the door opened again, and the fairy stared out with raven-dark eyes.

Before a second had passed, his katana was at my throat, and a second guard—this one female—was positioned behind Jonah, her katana pointing into his back.

"You are invited into her abode," the fairy said. "And it would be rude to decline the offer."

✦ ❊ ✦

CHAPTER TEN

THE MAD HATTER'S TEA PARTY

We lifted our hands into the air.

"We can hardly say no to such a sweet invitation," Jonah dryly said.

The fairy dropped his sword just enough to allow us to pass, while the one behind us poked us in the back like cattle until we maneuvered in the door. Once in the tower, they shut and bolted the door again and took point beside us, katanas at the ready.

I'm not sure what I should have expected to see in a fairy queen's abode in the top of a tower. Ancient, dreary furnishings encased in a thick carpet of dust and spider silk? A broken mirror? A spinning wheel?

The round room was larger than it should have been given the narrowness of the tower, but it was tidy and decorated with simple hewn wooden furnishings. A canopy bed sat across the room, its round, fluted columns wrapped in flowering vines that perfumed the air with the scents of gardenias and roses. A giant table of rough-hewn, sun-bleached wood sat nearby. There were draperies of cornflower blue silk along the walls, but not a window to be seen.

What I thought was a delicate chandelier hung from the ceiling; on closer reflection, I realized it was a cloud of monarch butterflies. There were no bulbs in the chandelier, but it glowed with a golden, ethereal light.

And katanas weren't the only weapons in play. As I suddenly heard the echoing sound of a lullaby played on an antique child's instrument, the pressure in the room changed. A panel of wispy fabric was moved aside on the canopy bed . . . and she emerged.

The fairy queen was pale and voluptuous, with wavy strawberry blond hair that fell past her shoulders. Her eyes were dusky blue, and she was barefoot, dressed in a gauzy, white gown that left nothing of her curvy form to the imagination. A crown of laurel leaves crossed her forehead, and a long, ornate locket of gold rested between her breasts.

She walked toward us with shoulders back and an unmistakably regal bearing. I had the urge to genuflect, but wasn't sure of the etiquette. Was it appropriate for an enemy of the fairies, for a bloodletter, to bow to their queen?

She stopped a few feet away and I felt the rush of dizziness again. I pushed it back and focused my attention on her face.

She looked us over, and after a moment, raised her hand, palm out. That being their cue, the guards lifted their swords.

"And you are?" she asked, a soft Irish lilt in her voice.

"Jonah," he said, "of House Grey. And Merit of House Cadogan."

She linked her hands together in front of her. "It has been many years since we allowed bloodletters to cross our threshold. Perhaps the riddles are not as strong as they once were. The magic not as concealing. The guardians not as careful." Her eyes darkened dangerously, and I decided I had no interest in crossing Claudia.

"We have need to speak to you, my lady," Jonah said. "And those who offered the riddle of your location were well rewarded for it."

For a moment I saw the same avarice, the same lust for gold, in her eyes that I'd seen in the guards.

"Very well, then," she said. "You are here to discuss contracts? It seems money is all vampires and fae have to speak about these years."

"We are not," he said. "We're here to discuss events of late in the city."

"Ah, yes," she said with slow deliberation. She moved across the room to the table, then glanced back over her shoulder at me and Jonah.

She was quite a sight to behold, like a character stripped from a fairy tale painting: the hidden fairy queen, equally ethereal and earthy, gazing back at the mortal with innocent invitation, beckoning him into her woods.

I'd known women who used their sexuality to advantage. Celina, for one, was the type to entice men to do her bidding with overt sensuality. But Claudia ensnared men differently. The sensuality wasn't a tool; it was a *fact*. She had no reason to *try* to entice you. *You would be enticed*. And if you were, God help you. I couldn't imagine succumbing to the seductions of the Queen of the Fae, accidentally or not, was a safe course of action.

I looked at Jonah, wondering if he felt the pull. There was general appreciation in his eyes, but when he looked at me, it was clear the gears were still turning. He gave me a nod.

"I have means at my disposal other than seduction, child," she said in a chiding tone, then took a seat in one of the tall, weathered chairs at the table. "We will speak of many things. But first, you will sit. You will join me for tea."

I had a moment of panic. Didn't the myth say you were supposed to avoid any food or drink given to you by a fairy?

"My lady," Jonah carefully said. "We have need of—"

"*Silence,*" she ordered, the single word carrying enough power to lift the hair at the back of my neck. "We will speak of those things in due time. If you ask a boon, you shall give a boon. Sit at my table, bloodletters. Sit, and let us speak of pleasantries. It has been many moons since I have shared my hospitality with your kind."

I wasn't thrilled about the delay, but I didn't think the two mean-looking mercenaries at the door would allow a slight.

"We would be honored to join you," I told her, and her laugh tinkled through the air.

"So she speaks," Claudia cannily said. "I am glad to know you are more than his guard and protector, child."

"As am I," I responded.

As we walked to the table and took seats of our own, a silver platter full of food—crusty loaves of bread, piles of grapes, decanters of wine—appeared in the middle of it. The platter sat on a bed of tossed rose petals in the palest shades of pink and yellow, the colors barely discernable but undeniably there.

I surveyed it suspiciously, and not just because she wanted a snack while the sky was burning around us.

Claudia poured a silver goblet of wine for herself, then did the same for us. "Drink deep," she said, "for there is no enchantment in my hospitality. Had I permanent need of your company I could most certainly assure it without such lures."

She raised her dusky eyes to me, and opened the door on the power she'd been holding in. There was a lot of it, and it wasn't nice. Claudia may have projected elfish sensuality, but the magic beneath the shell was cold, dark, primal, and greedy. Crossing her, I decided, was not a good strategy.

"You are wise," she said into the silence. I blushed at the intrusion into my thoughts, but held my peace. I was freaked out, however, that she could read minds. That was a trick no one had warned me about—and it certainly hadn't been mentioned in the *Canon*. There was a siren in Lake Michigan, Tate had some sort of ancient power, and fairies could read minds. Maybe it was the English lit geek in me, but I was reminded of a line from *Hamlet*: "There are more things in heaven and earth, Horatio, than are dreamt of in your philosophy."

Jonah reached forward and plucked a small plum from the platter. I opted for a grape nearly as big as the plum had been; smaller fruit, less enchantment by volume, I figured. And credit where credit was due—it was the best grape I'd ever eaten. As sweet as a grape could be, with a flavor that sang of springtime and sunshine and sun-kissed skin. If this was enchantment, sign me up.

Claudia glanced between me and Jonah. "You are lovers, I think."

"We are friends," Jonah said, shifting a bit in his seat, unhappy with the admission.

"But you desire more," she countered.

Awkwardness descended, and Jonah and I avoided eye contact.

Claudia took a long drink of wine, then looked at me. "You are hesitant, for you have lost your king."

I caught Jonah's rueful expression out of the corner of my eye. The grape turned bitter in my mouth. "The Master of my House," I corrected. "He was killed."

"I knew the true Master of your House. Peter of Cadogan. He did a service for my folk, and he was rewarded in the manner of our people. He was given a jewel of great repute and fortune. It was nestled in the eye of a dragon."

I'd seen that reward in Ethan's apartment. It was an enamel egg around which was curled a sleeping dragon. The dragon's eye was a great, shining ruby. Ethan had kept the treasure in a glass case.

"The dragon's egg came to Ethan after Peter died. He treasured it." The memory tightened my gut, and I forced myself to keep talking, to keep the tears walled away. "But I was told the egg was a gift to Peter Cadogan from Russian royalty."

Claudia smiled faintly. "The worlds of the fae are not limited by human boundaries. We are royalty regardless of our environs, King or Tsar, Queen or Tsarina. I have known many in my time."

"That must have been fascinating," Jonah said, but Claudia was unmoved.

"We care little for politics, for shifting of alliances and changing of guards. They do no service to longevity, to loyalty, to honor." She looked away, staring blankly across the room.

As she did, the food on the table disappeared again, leaving only the scattering of rose petals behind. I reached out and traced my finger across one; I wasn't sure about the food, but the petal was definitely real.

"The lives of humans are transient," she said. "You connect yourselves to them, and you can only expect the same of your own lives."

"That's why we're here," Jonah reminded her. "I assume you know about the sky?" I noticed he kept his tone light, carefully not mentioning the fact that my de facto master had sent us here to accuse Claudia of being behind the transformations.

"The sky is no concern of yours."

"It is when the sky is burning and humans believe vampires are responsible. And now the water has darkened for the second time."

She arched a delicate eyebrow. "The problems of humans have nothing to do with the sky. Nor are they reflected there."

Jonah and I shared a glance. Was she unaware? Had she not looked outside? Although now that I thought of it, I couldn't hear the crash of lightning in the tower. That was odd.

I stole a glance at the guards and checked their expressions. A bit of guilt, I thought, and maybe a little malice. Maybe they'd dissuaded her from opening the door. Shielded her from the happenings outside, not unlike Rapunzel in her tower.

"My lady," Jonah said, "with all due respect, you may wish to look outside and see the world for yourself. The sky isn't normal, and we don't know why."

There was indecision in her eyes—only for a second, but still there. The debate whether to acknowledge a vampire and look foolish, or refuse Jonah's request and risk discovering the same information later.

"It is not so easy as that," she said. "I cannot look outside. The rules of your world do not apply here, not to me."

"What rules?" I wondered.

She slid me a disdainful glance. "I am an ancient one, child. I have lived more lifetimes than you can even conceive. But we are not an immortal race. I survive in my tower because I am protected here."

Not unlike the portrait of Dorian Gray, I thought. That explained why she didn't know about the sky.

"Nevertheless," she said, "I have companions to advise me of matters of which I should be aware." She offered a nasty look to the guards, then strode across the room to a table.

She picked up a clear glass orb the size of a grapefruit and held it in front of her at chest height. She closed her eyes and began to murmur words beneath her breath. The language wasn't one I'd heard before, but the room filled again with dusty magic, the magic of ancient books and antique tapestries.

Slowly, she released her hands, and the sphere floated in the air in front of her, spinning slowly on an invisible axis. She opened her eyes again and watched it spin. Whatever she saw there, she didn't like it.

Her eyes widened, and she let out a banshee-esque scream. The spell broken, the globe hit the floor and shattered into a spill of glass.

"The sky is bleeding!" she said, then flipped her head around, strawberry locks framing her face, to glare at her guards. They cowered at her murderous expression.

"I have seen it," she said. "I have seen the bleeding sky, the dark water. The city drips of elemental magic, and you thought not to tell me?"

The guards looked at each other. "My lady," one quietly began, "we only just learned, and we didn't want to concern you."

"You didn't want to *concern* me? We are the sky folk. We master the moon and sun. You didn't think I should be called upon?"

My stomach fell—and not just from the burgeoning magic in the room. This was our third attempt to connect the supernatural dots, and we still hadn't managed to do it. Not only had the fairies not caused the sky to change, the queen hadn't even known about it.

"My lady," began the other guard, but Claudia held up a hand. She closed her eyes, her expression pained.

"Is she unspelling it?" I whispered, hope rising in my chest.

Jonah shook his head. "I don't think so."

After a moment, she opened her eyes.

"There was a time when the fae were free to roam," Claudia said. "Before magic was forbidden. When the world was green. The world is no longer green, and I am relegated to my tower. Those years have passed, and the fae hardly remember the shape of the green world. They become entangled in human drama just as you do. They believe they know how to survive. Am I no less to blame? The world moves slowly here, and on occasion I forget the meadow and the field."

Without ceremony, she strode across the room to the guards, the gauzy fabric *shushing* against the stone with each step. She reached the first guard, the man, took his katana in hand, and before I could even grip the handle of my sword, she whipped it through the air.

A long red line of crimson appeared at the guard's cheek.

"You have *failed* me," she hoarsely said.

The scent of fae blood flowed across the room, and my eyes rolled back at the temptation of it. However much I might have enjoyed blood of the bagged and vampire varieties, the hunger they inspired was nothing compared to the scent—from across the room—of a few droplets of fairy blood.

My fangs descended. I struggled to retain control over my hunger, to avoid leaping across the room and jumping on the bleeding fairy for a snack. Thanks to Frank's restrictions, I'd had barely any blood in the last few days, and my hunger roared back to life.

I squeezed my fingers around the hilt of my katana until my nails began to bite into my palm, confident that if I lost control, we'd lose the fairies . . . and possibly our lives.

"You defy your queen," Claudia told him, "and you will bear the scar of it."

She dropped the sword to the floor, where it bounced and clanked, steel against stone, and finally came to rest, a drop of crimson hanging from the finely honed edge.

Claudia moved to the female guard, pulled away her sword, and repeated the act, the air now doubly permeated with blood and magic.

I shivered in anticipation. "Jonah."

"Merit," he gritted out. "Hold it in." But his voice was hoarse, and when I looked, I saw that his eyes were silver, as well.

Had no one known about this reaction? Had no one thought to warn us that if mercenary fairies bled—when violence was in their names—we'd be in trouble?

The second sword hit the ground, and both fairies stood bleeding, their queen before them, the instruments of her wrath on the ground.

"You, too, will bear the scar," she said. "For refusing to remember that I and I alone am your queen, to whom you owe all fealty. You do not make decisions for the fae!"

Her words rose to a crescendo. The guards dropped to the floor as the power in the room rose.

I fought back the urge to cower, the hunger for blood too strong.

I took a step. That first step taken, the second, third, and fourth were easier, and I was nearly to the fairies and the scent was delectable . . .

"Merit! No!" Jonah called out my name, but I crossed the room so quickly the fairy had no time to react, only to struggle in my arms as I moved in for a bite.

I was there and at his throat, my teeth bared and ready to strike. And it wasn't an insult or a threat or a risk to his life. It was flattery. A compliment to the blood that coursed through his veins, liquid gold in its worth . . . But Claudia would have none of it.

"Bloodletter!" she cried, and without warning, I was in the air and flying across the room. I hit the stone wall behind me with energy enough to force the air from my lungs—and the bloodlust from my body.

My head rung, my body aching, chest heaving with the effort of pulling in air. I put a hand on the floor and just managed to raise my head enough to see her striding toward me.

"You dare to seek the blood of the fae in my home? In my tower?"

Claudia was furious, her eyes black with it, and she strode toward me with such anger there was little doubt about what she'd do when she reached me.

But then she was blocked from view. Jonah stepped between us, his katana outstretched.

"You touch her, and I will strike you down, the repercussions be damned."

If I hadn't already been on the ground, you could have knocked me over with a feather.

"You defy me, bloodletter?"

"I defy anyone who would seek to harm her. We have advised you of things no one else would, and you have had your fun with us. We leave here with the scales balanced. And besides, she is a bloodletter, and that makes her kith and kin to me. You would do the same—have done the same—to protect your own."

My head was reeling with the truth of that one.

"She attacked my guard," Claudia persisted.

"Because you baited her with blood and violence, and you attacked her in kind. We are even. As master of the sky, you will see it is just."

Silence, and then a nod. "I will spare your life on this day because you speak the truth. Let it be recorded that I have no quarrel with you or yours."

The deal struck, Jonah reached out a hand to me, and when I took it, he pulled me to my feet. Every bone and muscle ached, and the room was still spinning, although I wasn't sure if that was an aftershock of the bloodlust, the throw, or the magic that still peppered the room.

He scanned my face for injuries. "You're okay?"

"I'm fine."

"Heed this, bloodletters," Claudia said. "There was no enchantment. The sky was not turned because someone wished it. Because someone spelled it for revenge or love or power. If you look to the sky, you see the symptom, not the effect."

"Then what caused this symptom?" Jonah asked.

"That would be a question for those who did it, aye?"

As I'd seen with the guards, Jonah was kind, but not especially patient, so I stepped in. "Do you have any idea who that might have been? The humans are growing restless, and the mayor seeks to punish us for transgressions that aren't our own."

"The punishment of bloodletters is no interest of mine."

"More than vampires are affected," Jonah persisted. "The lake pulled magic from others in the city. From the nymphs. From the sorcerers. It was dangerous and created trouble for everyone."

"I am Queen of the Fae, bloodletter, not a waif who seeks the blood of others to survive. I have knowledge of sky and mastery over it. I have legions of fae at my command and Valkyrie to ride with them. Do not dare to tell me what is and is not dangerous."

She sighed and strolled back to the table, where she took a seat. "The sky has not been burned by me or mine. There is magic on the wind. Old magic. Ancient magic. And we will not stand aside while that magic destroys the world."

My heart began to beat again; that was a clue I could work with.

"Meaning?" Jonah asked.

Claudia smiled grimly. "Meaning we would destroy meadow and field ourselves before allowing for its piecemeal destruction."

"You can't destroy the city because you don't like the direction it's taking."

"If we destroy the city, it is only because that destruction is inevitable and we seek a merciful inferno over a moldering decay.

Leave now," she said, rising from the table and walking back to her bed and sitting upon it. "I have tired of you."

The guards moved toward us, malice in their eyes. I had offended their queen, and it was time to pay up. But Claudia spoke again before we could move.

"Vampires."

We looked back.

"The city is unbalanced," she said. "Water and sky reveal that imbalance. If you are to save it, you must do this. Find the illness, and return the balance." Her eyes turned cold and dark again. "For if you do not, then we must. And I submit you will not like our cure."

I had no doubt she was right.

⊷ ⊷ ⊷

CHAPTER ELEVEN

DEAR JOHN

We made it out the door and down the steps, my head pounding, but the body ache nearly gone. Some nights it did pay to be a quickly healing vampire, fairy angst notwithstanding.

The bloodred sky was now dotted with angry storm clouds, and lightning still flashed in great, glowing arcs. Not thrilled about being its target, we decided to debrief in my car.

We walked through chill air and damp grass and back to my Volvo. We moved silently, the air between us charged by what he'd done, and my mixed feelings about it. It was definitely good to be alive, but I had a bad track record with self-sacrifice. Ethan had stepped in front of a stake meant for me because he'd had feelings for me; had Jonah done the same?

I decided to focus on my dangerous actions instead of his heroic ones.

"I am so sorry," I told him when we climbed inside. "Frank's rationing blood. But even beyond that, the hunger was overpowering. I've never felt anything that strong." Even my First Hunger, during which I'd launched myself at Ethan, hadn't been that bad. The guard had come a lot closer to being fang-marked.

"The receiver cut back on your blood supplies? Is he trying to incite riots?"

"Or make us go crazy and attack the first supernaturals in sight."

"Mission accomplished," Jonah said.

"If vampires have always reacted that way to fairy blood, it explains why fairies don't like us any more than humans."

"It does," he agreed. "And it explains why they keep their distance and why we have to pay them so much to guard the House. That kind of power is dangerous. Unfortunately, it doesn't really help us with the bigger issue."

"Figuring out what the hell's going on?"

"That's the one. Claudia mentioned a couple of times that she didn't think this was about the sky or water per se, but that they were symptoms of a larger problem."

I nodded. "And I think she had something there. She accused the guards of not telling her about elemental magic. What if she meant it literally?"

"What do you mean?"

"So far, we've seen water and sky affected. Water and *air*," I repeated, and watched understanding dawn in his expression.

"Water. Air. Earth. Fire," he said. "The four elements."

"Exactly. We've seen two so far. If she was right about these things being symptoms—"

"Then someone is working magic with elemental effects," Jonah finished.

I wasn't entirely sure what that meant or who might be doing it, but my gut told me we were on the right track. And after the week we'd had, I'd take any victory I could get.

"She also blamed ancient magic," Jonah said. "Old magic. Any theories on who that might be?"

"Actually, yeah. What do you know about Tate?"

"Seth Tate?" He shrugged. "I know it's believed he has magic—that you've felt it before—but that no one knows what magic it is. Why?"

"Because when I visited him, I had a sense of something old. A different kind of magic. Closer to what I felt from Claudia than what I've seen of vampires."

"Okay, but this is the third time we've approached a supernatural group thinking they might have initiated the problem. We've been wrong all three times."

"I know. Our batting average sucks. But like she said, we've been looking at the symptoms, not the cause. Besides, we have to try something. If we can't tie this to a supernatural working magic, then what else would there be?"

"Radiation? A new kind of weapon? Global warming? Or if no sups are doing this on purpose, is it accidental magic of some kind?"

I thought about Lorelei's prediction that too many shifters in town were doing just that—accidentally throwing off the world's balance. On the other hand, she'd blamed shifters when the water had been the only problem. This time we had water *and* air.

"If Claudia's right," he said, "and this is about some deeper imbalance in the city, maybe the key isn't the *who*. It's the *what*. What kind of magic would be powerful enough to screw up both water and air? Sorcerers?"

"I can vouch for Catcher and Mallory. He's exhausted from working on this problem, and she's wrapped up in her exams. Besides, even asking them about it would make them both go ballistic." And I did not need any more ballistic right now.

"I was actually thinking about the only Order-sanctioned sorcerer in town."

"You're talking about Simon?" I asked. "To tell you the truth, when I asked him about the water, he seemed to be in denial about the whole thing. A little shady, yeah, but largely in denial. This could be a cover for some kind of secret magic he's working, but I didn't have the sense of it. And if you're the only sanctioned sorcerer in town, you're already the big man on campus. Why risk that? What's the benefit? The prize?"

"Be that as it may, we don't have much else to go on. It might pay at least to sit him down and talk to him about it. See what information he, or the Order, can provide."

"Good point. I'll see if Catcher can set it up."

A bolt of lightning crashed nearby, shaking the car. We both looked out the windows and up at the sky, clouds whirling across it.

"If this is a symptom," I said, "a side effect, maybe we can find its heart?"

He looked over at me. "What do you mean?"

"The effect on the river stopped at the city limits, right? So it's unlikely the sky is red *everywhere*. And if there are boundaries, maybe there's also a center. An origin point."

"Like a giant sucking tornado in the middle of the Loop?"

"Hopefully not that, but that's the idea, yeah. If we can't find the people responsible for this, maybe we can find their location. We can drive through different neighborhoods to see if there's a focus, and we'll cover more territory if we split up. If we find something, we can rally at that place?"

"That sounds like a decent plan," Jonah said, but he made no move to get out of the car. Was he waiting on me to say something about what had happened in the tower? To offer thanks . . . or maybe vitriol?

I silently swore, and reminded myself that the point was what he'd done—not why he'd done it. "And thanks, by the way, for defending me."

"You're welcome," he said. "It's part and parcel of being some-one's partner."

"We aren't partners yet," I reminded him, thinking of the Red Guard.

"Aren't we?" He gazed back at me, and it was clear he wasn't thinking of the RG, but had something much more fundamental in mind. His eyes changed, and then his hand was behind my head and he was leaning toward me, pulling me toward him, and before I could stop him his lips were on mine, his mouth insistent.

Jonah kissed me with the intimacy of a lover and the confidence of a challenger to the throne, daring me to think outside the box I'd walled around me.

And for a moment, I let him.

It felt so good to be wanted, to be needed, to be desired by someone again. It hadn't been that long since Ethan had been gone, but Ethan and I hadn't been together long, if at all.

And the kiss was just . . . toe curling. Jonah wasn't a novice, and he used every part of his body to his advantage, his fingers at my jaw, his tongue teasing mine, his body moving closer and closer, a suggestion of things he could offer: warmth; the solace of touch; another kind of intimacy.

But a shock of guilt turned my stomach. I wasn't ready.

I pulled back and turned away, covering my mouth with a hand. It had been only a kiss, not initiated by me, and certainly no viola-tion of any promise I'd made. But my lips were swollen, and my skin was flushed, and there was a ball of heat in the pit of my stomach. However unexpected it may have been, and however long Ethan may have been gone, my reaction felt like a betrayal to his memory.

"You're not ready," he quietly said.

"I'm not. I'm sorry—but I'm not."

His next words surprised me nearly as much as the kiss had. "No, I'm sorry," he said. "I shouldn't have pushed. It's just—I didn't expect this. I didn't expect to find a connection."

I looked back at him again, my heart racing at the desire in his eyes and the sudden sense of panic that tightened my chest. "I am flattered, really, but—"

He held up a hand and smiled gently. "You don't have to apologize. I took a chance, and the timing isn't right. No harm, no foul." He cleared his throat, then nodded confidently. "Let's just forget the temporary humiliation and get back to work."

"You're sure?"

"I'm sure," he said with a nod, and pulled out his phone, a shiny gold wafer, to check in with Scott Grey. I did the same and sent a message to Kelley, advising her that we hadn't discovered anything helpful, and that Claudia apparently hadn't even known about the sky.

Her response chilled me: "PROTESTORS DOUBLED B/C OF SKY. ALL VAMPS ON GUARD. EXTRA FAIRIES AT GATE. NATIONAL GUARD CALLED. HUMANS BELIEVE APOCALYPSE IMMINENT," was the immediate follow-up.

I muttered a curse.

"What?" Jonah quietly asked, but I held up a hand while I typed out a response to Kelley.

"RETURN HOME?" I asked her, "OR KEEP LOOKING?"

"CRISIS BEING MANAGED," she responded. "KEEP LOOKING."

I could definitely keep looking. It was the "finding" that was proving difficult. The message sent, I tucked the phone away again and updated Jonah.

"Humans think the end is nigh," I told him. "The protestors at Cadogan House have doubled again."

Alarm flashed in his eyes. "Do we need to get back?"

"Kelley says she's on it and wants us to keep looking. Do you think you could have Scott make a call, maybe send some guards over?"

He answered without hesitation, sending an immediate message on his phone.

"Done," he said after a moment, pushing the phone away again. "Scott is advised. Grey House is quiet, and he'll contact Kelley and offer up some friends."

Cadogan House didn't have any alliances with other Houses in Chicago; maybe we could make an ally of Grey House, even if the circumstances weren't ideal.

"I'll go back to the Loop. I'll search there for something that looks like a focus, and I'll stick close to the water in case there's some link we don't know about between the water and sky. Why don't you drive around this part of town? Hit the rest of the Gold Coast and Jackson Park. Call me if you find anything."

He nodded. "Sure," he said, then climbed out of my car and into his. I felt awkward leaving him after the kiss, but what else could I do?

There was only so much a girl could accomplish in a night.

Once I was on my way to the Loop, I turned the heat to maximum. Even though I'd felt a little claustrophobic in the tower, there was something weirdly soothing about cranking the heat on a cold night. There had been cold nights during grad school—nights when Mallory had been late at work or on a date with some law firm or financial services cutie—when I'd taken a study break by climbing into my car and driving across the city. I knew which roads had less traffic and relatively few lights, and I'd use the drive to zone out, to forget myself, to forget everything except the road in front of me.

Occasionally, I'd bring along an audiobook, the twelfth or thir-teenth installment in some long-running mystery or action series I couldn't seem to stop buying, even as the books became formulaic copies of the ones that came before. I'd crank up the sound just as I had the heat, and I'd drive across Chicago—sometimes into Indi-ana, sometimes into Wisconsin, sometimes into the Illinois coun-tryside—to have a little time away.

This, of course, wasn't one of those times. I didn't have time for a joyride, and the trip wasn't relaxing. The city was still filled with groups of people huddled on sidewalks or porches, staring tenta-tively up at the sky, taking pictures with cell phones and cameras.

There was no way "Crisis in Chicago!" wasn't the lead story on every news station in the country, especially if the National Guard was involved. They'd all be looking for some reason for the sky and water, and I had absolutely nothing to offer them. I wish I had the answers they were looking for.

I crossed the river, the gleaming, inky black slice of it, and drove back into the Loop. The buildings were tighter here, but the sky seemed as red as it had at Potter Park, the lightning strikes just as frequent. No more, no less.

"Damn," I quietly muttered. It was probably one of the few times anyone other than a meteorologist or storm chaser had rued the absence of a giant sucking tornado, as Jonah had put it, in a populated area. But it would have given me an answer. And those were few and far between these days.

Instead . . . there were questions. Questions about me. Ques-tions about sorcerers. Questions about the House and its staff. Questions about the city and whether they trusted us to live our own lives without our constant reassurances that we meant them no harm.

After what I'd seen tonight—a fairy queen willingly scarring those who worked for her because they hadn't brought issues to her attention fast enough maybe they were right. Maybe we shouldn't be trusted.

God, I was beginning to depress myself.

Without any better option, I pulled over into a parking space and turned off the car. The city was relatively quiet, but the night still carried a quiet *buzz*. There was an energy in Chicago. Even if we weren't the city that didn't sleep, we certainly were the city that never rested.

Thinking a katana was a little too lightning rod for my taste, I unbuckled the sword and left it in the car. Humans were already afraid of us; there was no point in riling them up when we had other problems to address.

I was a block from State Street, so I walked over to it, sticking close to the edge of the buildings while looking for anything that might be amiss. The streets were relatively empty except for bar-hoppers and folks scanning the sky for meteors or aliens or some other explanation for its color.

I followed State to the river, noting the strange tingle of its increasingly powerful magical vacuum, and walked across the bridge, stopping in the middle to take a look. The river stretched out in front and behind me—a frozen, black artery through downtown. The sky was uniformly red above, heavy clouds also tinted red by . . . whatever. The side effect of some curse, some ancient charm, some bitter hex?

Unfortunately, I had no clue. If there was a focus, I hadn't found it. Nothing seemed any different out here. There were no sorcerers casting spells upon the sky. No fire-breathing dragons. Tate, as far as I was aware, hadn't escaped into the Loop to transfix us all with his strange magic.

While none of those developments would have been exactly welcome, at least they would have been *developments*. Hints of answers.

I walked back toward my car, pausing at a bus stop and sitting down on the empty bench. The city was undergoing natural disasters with no obvious cause, and apparently these were only the symptoms of some larger issue. How was I supposed to figure this out? Vampires could sense magic, but only if it was really close by. This was way beyond my expertise. I needed a diviner—the witches who walked around with forked branches and searched out hidden springs—except I needed one for magic.

I sat up straight and pulled out my phone. And since he was the closest thing to a water witch I had, I dialed up Catcher.

"You're still alive."

"Last time I checked. And here's a fact to add to your database—fairy blood turns vampires batshit crazy."

I heard the creak of his chair as he sat up. "You shed fairy blood?"

"Actually, no. Claudia, the queen, got irritated with her guards. They hadn't filled her in on the sky yet."

He made a low whistle. "Since the sky is still red, I assume the fairies weren't the problem."

"They were not. That's three strikes. The water sups didn't mess with the water; the sky sups didn't mess with the sky. Claudia thinks we're seeing the effects of a larger magical problem with elemental magic as the visible symptoms."

I heard his sigh through the phone. "Elemental magic," he said. "I should have put two and two together. I should have thought about that."

My heart raced—were we getting somewhere? Did he have an answer? "Does that mean something to you?"

"It gives the magic context. It shows the pattern."

"Is there a group, a species, a person who uses that pattern?"

"Not specifically. But it proves that magic is involved."

I rolled my eyes. Hadn't we already figured magic was involved? Jonah's suggestions notwithstanding, it seemed unlikely humans had simply flipped a switch that had turned the sky red and sent lightning crashing across it.

As if irritated by the thought, a bolt of lightning suddenly struck a car three blocks down the street. Its car alarm began to chirp in warning. I huddled back into the bus stop, wishing I was already back in my car. I *hated* lightning.

"I don't suppose you have any better sense of what Tate might be? Claudia kept mentioning old magic, and that's the sense I get from him."

"Old magic wouldn't surprise me," Catcher said, "although that's not a magical classification per se. That his magic feels 'old' doesn't signal what he is or who he might be."

Of course it didn't. That would be too easy. "Then we need to work that angle and figure it out. Can you get me in to see him again?"

Catcher whistled. "Since our office has been officially disbanded, we aren't exactly on the approved visitors list for the secret facility holding our ex-mayor. We may be able to pull some strings, but that'll take time."

"Do what you can. I'm getting nowhere fast." Although there was one group I could look into. "I know this question is going to hurt, but I need an answer regardless. What about the Order?" I gnawed my lip in anticipation of a snarky response. But that's not what I got back. Catcher had changed his tune.

"I've been racking my brain," he said, and I could hear that in the hoarse exhaustion in his voice. "But I can't come up with any way they're involved. I just don't know what advantage they'd see in doing this. They may be naïve, but they aren't evil."

"What about Simon?"

"I don't know how Simon spends his days, Merit, other than monopolizing almost all of Mallory's time and every ounce of her mental energy. She seems to be the number one focus of his attention. Besides, he's king of the city right now. Why cause trouble?"

"I had the same thought."

"Keep your people calm and off Simon's radar. He may seem mild-mannered, but he's still a fully trained member of the Order, and vampire interference will only piss him off. Let me look into it."

"I'll stall," I warned, "but Frank's antsy, and you know the kind of pressure he's putting on Malik. Humans are freaking out, and the National Guard is on its way to Cadogan House. Whoever is involved in this, we need evidence, and we need it fast."

"I'll handle it. Where are you anyway?"

I decided not to tell him I was hunched in a bus stop on State Street because I didn't have any better ideas. "I'm playing Sentinel," I told him. "Give me a call as soon as you have something."

Catcher grunted his agreement, and the phone went dead. I tucked it away again and looked out into the night. Noise began to roll down the street as a parade of humans dressed in white clothes walked toward me. They carried white poster board signs announcing the apocalypse and recommending Bible passages for immediate consideration. The warnings were scrawled in bloodred paint, drips marking the edges of the letters. They'd painted the signs in a hurry, frantic to make a difference before it was too late.

"Before vampires destroy the world," I quietly muttered.

The humans might be right about the end of the world; that wasn't exactly information I was privy to. But I was pretty confident they'd have more than words for me if they caught me out here alone, so I hunkered back into the corner and watched as they passed, a Greek chorus warning of the coming tragedy.

A few minutes later they disappeared from view and the street was quiet again. I stood up and stretched my legs, but just as I prepared to leave the bus stop, a streak of white lightning shot across the sky and rain began to pour down in heavy sheets.

"Of course it would rain," I muttered.

I stood in the doorway of the bus stop for another few moments, rain splashing onto my boots, waiting for a break in the downpour and wishing, once again, that Ethan had been here with me. He'd know what to do, have some plan of attack in mind.

I knew this burden was mine to bear; I just hoped I had the brawn to carry it and the brains to figure it out.

As quickly as it had begun, the rain slowed and stopped. As I stepped onto the street, I caught scents of water and city and sulfur, but there was something else: the smells of lemon and sugar, the same scents I'd caught around Tate.

Claudia thought the magic was old, and now the rain smelled like Tate? That couldn't just be coincidence.

Dawn was approaching, but I knew exactly where I needed to go tomorrow night. Hopefully my grandfather's name still carried some cachet, and they'd be able to get me in to see Tate again.

Still afraid of the lightning, I sprinted back to my car, my skin buzzing from the ozone in the air. I'd only managed to put the key in the lock when the barrel of a gun was pushed against my cheek.

"Hello, Merit," McKetrick said pleasantly. "Long time, no see."

* ✠ ✠ ✠ *

CHAPTER TWELVE

HAPPINESS IS A WARM GUN

I looked down at the dark, cold steel now pointed at my chest. The weapon was longer and stockier than a handgun, closer in shape to a sawed-off shotgun with a single, wide barrel.

I glanced up. McKetrick smiled smugly. He was a handsome man, with short dark hair, sculpted cheekbones, and a body that wouldn't quit. His eyes were wide and exotic-looking, but his mouth was twisted with cruelty—and there was a new scar across his upper lip that hadn't been there the last time I'd seen him.

"Hands in the air, please," he pleasantly said.

For the second time in a night, I lifted my hands into the air. Ironic, wasn't it, that I'd left my sword in the car so I wouldn't scare off any humans? And here he was, pointing a gun at my chest.

"McKetrick," I said by way of greeting. "Could you move that gun, please?"

"When it's so effective at getting your attention? I don't think so. And in case you have any thought of taking a shot for the good of the cause, we're using a new variety of bullet. Something a little less iron-and-steel. Something a bit woodier. A new process that combines the shock of a bullet with the chemical reaction of aspen. It's proven very effective."

A chill ran through me. If he'd managed to turn aspen wood—the one thing that, shot through the heart of a vampire, would turn us to dust—into bullets, and he knew it was "effective," how many vampires had died in the testing?

"Is that how you got the scar?" I wondered aloud.

His upper lip curled. "I am none of your concern."

"You are when you've got a gun pointed at me," I said, and mulled my options. Trying to knock the gun from his hand with a well-timed kick might be successful, but he was former military and undoubtedly skilled at hand-to-hand. Besides, the "might" carried a pretty high risk—that I'd take a sliver of aspen to the heart and end up a cone of ashes. There was also a pretty solid chance he had minions waiting in the wings with similar weapons.

There'd been too much death lately, so I quickly decided playing martyr wasn't an option. Instead, I opted to gather what information I could.

"I'm surprised you're out tonight," I told him. "Shouldn't you be warning folks about the apocalypse? Or maybe hanging out with the mayor? We saw you at the press conference."

"She's a woman with a plan for the city."

"She's a moron who's easily manipulated."

He smiled. "Your words, not mine. Although she has certainly proved receptive to my position on vampires."

"So I've seen. I assume you're one of the brains behind the registration law?"

"I'm not a fan," he said.

"Really? It seemed like keeping close tabs on our activities would be right up your alley."

"That's only short-term thinking, Merit. If you allow supernat-

ural aberrations to register themselves, you condone their existence." He shook his head like a lecturing pastor. "No, thank you.
That's a step in the wrong direction."

I wasn't really eager to hear what McKetrick thought the "right
direction" for the city might be, but he didn't afford me the luxury
of his silence.

"There's only one solution for the city—cleaning it out. Rid-
ding it of vampires. That solves the apocalypse problem. In order
to clean up the city, we need a catalyst. If we rid the city of a vampire who's known to the public, we might be able to make some
headway."

My stomach sank. McKetrick wasn't just looking to kick vamps
out of the city.

He wanted to exterminate them, starting with me.

With the gun pointed at me, I didn't have a lot of options. I
couldn't grab my cell phone, and calling out for humans within
hearing range would only put them in the line of fire. I couldn't
take that risk. With my increased vampire strength, I might be
able to best McKetrick in hand-to-hand combat, but he rarely traveled alone. He usually came with a pack of equally brawny guys in
unrelieved black, and although I hadn't seen them yet, I couldn't
imagine they weren't out there waiting for me.

So I opted to use one of my best talents—stubbornness.

"What exactly do you think taking me out is going to accomplish? You're only going to piss off vampires and incite humans
who don't want murder in their city."

McKetrick looked hurt by the accusation. "That's incredibly
naïve. Sure, there may be a few in Chicago who don't realize the
breadth of the vampire problem. But that's what this is all about.
People need something to rally around, Merit. You're the rallying
point."

"You mean the ashes I'll become? You know that's all that will be left, right? A cone of ashes, there on the sidewalk." I gestured down to the concrete below us. "It's not as if you'll be standing over the dead body of a fallen vampire. Believe me—I've seen it."

I said a silent prayer of apology to Ethan's memory for my callousness, but given the twitch in McKetrick's jaw, I kept going. "It'll look more like you emptied a vacuum cleaner than staked a vampire, and that's not exactly going to make great television. You aren't even at the front lines."

"What is that supposed to mean?"

"It means there's a mess of humans outside Cadogan House right now protesting our existence, and the National Guard is on its way. Why aren't you out there with them? Getting to know them? Recruiting like-minded souls? Oh," I said, nodding my head. "I get it. You don't really like people any more than you like vampires. You just like playing the hero. Or what you imagine to be a hero. I personally don't think genocide is terribly heroic."

He slapped me across the cheek hard enough to make my head ring, and I immediately tasted blood.

"I will not," he menacingly said, stepping even closer to me, "let some little fanged bitch turn me from my mission."

My anger—aided by my knife-edge hunger—began to spread through my limbs in a gloriously warm rush that pushed the chill from my bones.

"Your mission? Your mission is murder, McKetrick, plain and simple. Let's not forget that. And I'd reckon that what you know about me—or vampires—would fit on the head of a pin."

"Check the sky," he said, pushing the barrel of the gun into my chest. "You think that doesn't have something to do with you?"

"Actually, it has nothing to do with us," I told him, but spared him the details about the other groups it might have had something to do with. There was no point in putting them on McKetrick's radar, too.

"How could it not have something to do with you? What else could be responsible for this?"

"Global warming?" I suggested. "Have you recycled today?"

That earned me a punch in the stomach that put me on the wet ground on my knees. I coughed a little, exaggerating the injury. It had definitely hurt—but not that bad. I think he'd pulled his punch a little at the end. Maybe punching a "fanged bitch" was harder than giving her a good slap across the face. His thinking I was more delicate than I actually was only worked to my advantage.

"You're a sadist," I spat out.

"No," he patiently said, "I'm a realist. You make me violent. You make me fight a war I shouldn't have to fight."

"Blaming the victim is so last year," I told him. I braced for a kick, but nothing came. Instead, he crouched down on his knees, his brows furrowed in concern.

"You don't understand."

"I do. You're an egoist, and you think you know more than anyone else in Chicago. But really, McKetrick, you're an ignorant coward. You're fighting to take away our rights, and we're the ones trying to solve the problem. Your ego has blinded you. I feel sorry for you, actually."

That was apparently the end of his patience. He stood up again, stuck two fingers in his mouth and whistled. Two men in black fatigues ran toward us. One pointed another wide-barreled gun at me, while the other wrenched me to my feet and pulled my arms behind my back.

I cursed him—loudly—and stomped on his foot, but McKetrick's barrel at my chin was a pretty good deterrent for more violence.

"Put her in the vehicle," McKetrick said. "We'll take her back to the facility."

Seeing "the facility" would definitely help me close McKetrick's operations, but it seemed unlikely I'd ultimately survive the visit. Getting into that car was a death sentence, so I fought with all my might. I squirmed in the goon's arms, and as he struggled to keep me upright, shifted my weight and kicked out at McKetrick's gun. It flew from his hand. He immediately went after it.

The goon's grip loosened in the chaos, and with a quick back kick to the jewels and a low roundhouse that connected squarely, I put him flat on his back.

"That's one of my favorite moves," I told him, thinking of a conversation Ethan and I'd had. Too bad I was fighting this one solo.

"Get her," McKetrick said, having plucked up the gun a few feet away and begun walking back to me, arms outstretched.

I turned to run and ran squarely into goon number two. I looked up at him, smiled a little, and offered another below-the-belt kick. This one was smart enough to anticipate the move. He blocked it, but he wasn't the first man who'd blocked one of my kicks. I ducked a punch, and while I was down pounded a fist into his shin. When he hopped in pain, I jumped up and executed a picture-perfect crescent kick that put him on the ground.

That was two goons on the ground with well-executed kicks, but I didn't even have time to enjoy the victory before a jab to my kidney put me on the ground again.

I looked behind me.

McKetrick stood there, gun outstretched, arm shaking with obvious fury.

"I have *had* it with you," he said, trigger finger shaking.

After being beaten down by Celina on another rainy night, I'd made a promise to myself. So I stood up and gazed back at him, forcing myself to look calm—and locking my legs so they didn't tremble.

"If you're going to stake me," I told him, "you'll do it while looking me in the eye." I prepared myself for the shock: to feel the sharp sting of splinters if he happened to miss my heart, or to lose myself completely if his aim was true. I was brave enough to admit that either end was a possibility.

He extended the gun toward my chest, just above my heart.

I tried one final ploy. "I appreciate this, you know."

I watched him fight the urge, but he still asked the question. "Appreciate what?"

"What you're doing." I took a miniscule step forward, pushing my chest into the muzzle of the gun. "Making me a martyr. I mean, I get that you'll have to make up some tale about how I tried to hurt you and you saved the city of Chicago from me." I lowered my voice a bit. "But the supernaturals will know, McKetrick. The vampires. The shifters. They like me. And they won't believe you."

I stood up on tiptoes and looked him in the eye. "They'll *find* you."

Funny thing about anger—it could help you, or it could hurt you. It could ruin your composure, and make you blink.

McKetrick blinked.

"You bitch," he said, teeth gritted. "I will not let you ruin this city." The gun wavered, shaking in his hand just a bit. I took the opportunity, striking up beneath the gun and pushing it out of his hand. It flew through the air and skittered across the concrete.

He dived for it.

I could give credit where credit was due: McKetrick was bigger and brawnier than me. But I was faster.

I got there before he did, scraped fingers against asphalt to ensure the gun was safely in hand, and by the time he reached me, turned it on him.

His eyes widened. "You are ruining this city."

"Yeah, you said that. I'd like to point out, though, that vamps aren't pulling over civilians and threatening them, nor are we pointing guns in their faces."

He growled, spit out a few more curses, and moved to his knees. "Does this make you feel powerful? With me down on my knees before you like some sycophantic human?"

"No. And you know why not?" I gave him a pistol-whipping to the temple that put him on the ground and knocked him out cold. "Because I'm not you."

I closed my eyes just for a moment—just for a moment to breathe—and then opened them again at the sound of squealing tires.

I looked back. The two goons had disappeared, and the black SUV was peeling down the street.

"So much for loyalty," I muttered, then looked down at McKetrick and around the neighborhood. The bus stop was a few yards away, but the eastern sky was beginning to lighten. I didn't have much time, so I was going to need backup.

Lightning still flashing around us, I dragged McKetrick into the bus stop and propped him up against the bench. I pulled out my phone.

Catcher answered with a question. "What do you want, Merit?"

That entire house was testy this week, and I was beginning to reach the end of my patience with the Bell/Carmichael clan. Still, I had work to do.

I gave him my address. "If you can get here fast enough, you'll find McKetrick in the bus stop, out cold."

"McKetrick?" he asked, his voice suddenly suffused with a lot less snark. "What happened?"

"He and two of his goons surprised me in the Loop. Same song and dance about hating vampires and wanting them out of Chicago. But with a really bad twist. He has, or at least claims to have, aspen bullets. I managed to grab one of his guns, but not his goons, who took off. He also mentioned he has some kind of facility. I'm hoping he'll give you some details."

"That would be helpful. You interested in pressing charges against him for assault and battery?"

"Only if it's necessary to keep him locked up."

"Shouldn't be," Catcher said. "If you'll recall, we're no longer affiliated with the city. This is just a couple of guys having a friendly conversation off the record. Funny how the Constitution is no longer an issue."

Maybe not, but that didn't mean my grandfather couldn't still end up in hot water for kidnapping. "That's your call. But I don't know how long he's going to be out, and since the city's going to start stirring pretty soon, you might want to give Detective Jacobs a heads-up. You don't want a random CPD uniform finding him before you get here."

Jacobs knew my grandfather, and had interrogated me after a dose of V, the drug Tate manufactured for vampires, had turned the Cadogan House bar into a deadly mosh pit. Jacobs was cautious and detail oriented, and he was honestly on the side of truth and justice. There weren't a lot of people like that around anymore, so I'll deemed him an ally.

"I'll float the idea to Chuck, see which direction he wants to take. I know he wants to stay on the good side of the CPD, but there's something to be said for testing this newfound freedom the mayor has given us."

I heard the sounds of shuffling. "We're leaving now," he added. "Should be there in twenty."

"It's nearly dawn, so I'm heading back to the House. And

speaking of your newfound freedom, any luck arranging a second meeting with Tate?"

"I'm working on it. I'm cashing in the political capital we've got, but the bureaucrats are greedy. Kowalczyk's made them nervous. I'll let you know tomorrow night."

"I would appreciate it. Hey—while I've got you on the phone, have you ever smelled anything weird around Tate?"

"I make it a habit not to smell politicians or convicts."

"I'm serious. Whenever I'm around him, I smell lemon and sugar. And a little while ago, after the downpour, I smelled it again—like there was some sort of similar magic flowing from the rain. Like he'd been involved in it somehow."

"We got a little rain out here, but I didn't smell anything. I wouldn't put a lot of stock in smells. Besides, Tate's locked up. What could he do?"

So he said. I knew there was something in it, but I let it go. "Take care. Be gentle with our soldier."

"Not that he deserves it," Catcher said, and he hung up the call.

The edge of the sky now searing yellow, I put the phone away again and left McKetrick in his bus stop, looking like a partygoer who'd had a little too much fun.

Lucky him.

—●—≡×≡—●—

CHAPTER THIRTEEN

THE BEST PART OF WAKING UP . . .
IS TYPE A IN YOUR CUP

I called Kelley on the way to give her an update about McKetrick and reached the House a bit too close to dawn for comfort. I ran from my car into the House, only barely realizing in my sun-fed exhaustion that the protestors had quieted, no doubt thanks to the two dozen camouflaged members of the National Guard who stood at equal points around the fence.

I immediately headed upstairs to fall into bed, but stopped at the second floor landing, and cast a glance at the third floor above me. Before my better judgment kicked in, I was drowsily climbing the stairs to the third floor, then tiptoeing down the hallway to the wing that held the consort's suite . . . and Ethan's rooms.

I stood in front the double doors to his apartment for just a moment, before pressing my palm to the door and my forehead to the cool wood.

God, I missed him. Jonah's kiss might have been glorious for that one moment of oblivion, but its wake was so much worse, miring me in thoughts of Ethan.

Without warning, the door slipped open.

I stood up again, heart pounding. I hadn't been in his rooms since the night he'd been killed. Some of his personal effects had been boxed up, but the rooms had otherwise been closed off. Frank had chosen other quarters and Malik and his wife had remained in their own. I'd avoided Ethan's apartment altogether, thinking it was better to go cold turkey than become a phantom, haunting his rooms to foster the memories.

But tonight, after lightning and fairy queens and kisses and guns, I needed a different kind of oblivion.

I pushed the door open farther, and walked inside.

For a moment, I just stood in the doorway, eyes closed, drinking in the familiar scent. His sharp, clean cologne was giving way to the scents of cleaning polish and dust, but it still lingered there, faint and fresh, like the whispers of a ghost.

I opened my eyes, closed the door behind me, and surveyed the room. It was nicely decorated, with expensive European furniture and furnishings, more like a boutique hotel than the rooms of a Master vampire.

I walked across the sitting room to the second set of double doors. These led into Ethan's bedroom. The sun now above the horizon, I walked inside and caught the lingering scent of him again. Before I could think better of it, my shoes and jacket were on the floor and I was crawling into his bed, tears spilling from the familiar sensation of the linens and the scent of him that filled them.

I thought of the few times we'd made love, the tenuousness and joy of it, and the quirky, teasing smile he'd given me when he'd been pleased with something I'd done—or something he'd done to me. His eyes were so brilliantly green, his mouth perfection, his body as finely hewn as any marble statue.

Wrapped in the scent of him, I smiled and savored the memories. There, in his bed in his darkened rooms, I fell asleep.

We were in a casino, surrounded by a cacophony of electronic chirps and flashing lights, jostled by a parade of smiling waitresses with trays of drinks in short glasses. I sat in front of a slot machine with dials that spun in random increments, occasionally slowing to showcase a single image. A stake. A raindrop. A curl of fire.

Ethan stood beside me, a gold coin between his thumb and index finger. It spun slowly on its axis, the light catching each rotation like a gold-edged strobe light.

"Two sides of the coin," he said. "Heads and tails. Wrong and right. Good and evil." He lifted his gaze to me. "We all have choices, don't we?"

"Choices?"

"Between bravery or cowardice," he suggested. "Ambition or contentment."

"I guess so."

"Which choice will you make, Merit?"

I knew he meant something important, something heavy, but I couldn't tell what it was. "What choice do I have to make?"

With a flick of his thumb, he popped the coin into the air. The ceiling seemed to rise as the coin flew upward, so that if gravity hadn't worked its peculiar magic, the coin might have lifted forever, never touching the ceiling. Over and over it flipped, heads and tails and heads again, catching the light with each rotation.

"Disappearing," Ethan said.

I watched the coin grow smaller in the distance, rising to infinity. "It isn't disappearing," I told him. "It's still there. It's still turning."

"Not the coin. Me."

The soft fear in his voice drew my eyes back to him. He was staring at his hands, now palm up in front of him. Having thrown the coin in the air, Ethan was beginning to fade, the tips of his fingers dissolving into ash that fell onto the psychotically patterned carpet below us.

"What's happening to you?" I couldn't do anything but stare as his fingers disappeared one millimeter at a time. Instead of screaming in horror or trying to stop it, I just gazed with clinical fascination, watching my lover being slowly erased into nothingness.

"I made my choice. I chose you."

Frantically, fear rising in my gut, I shook my head. "How do I stop it?"

"I don't think you can. It's natural, isn't it? That we all devolve to ashes. To dust. And we're put away again." His attention was suddenly drawn away. He looked up and away at something across the room, his gaze widening farther.

"Ethan?"

His eyes snapped back to mine. "It's too dangerous. Don't let them do it, Merit."

"Do what?"

"They'll take advantage. I think they're trying now." He looked down at his hands, now halfway turned to ash. "I think that's where I'm going."

"Ethan? I don't understand."

"I'm only ashes," he said. He looked at me again, and I felt my own panic finally rising at the fear—the honest-to-God fear—in his eyes.

"Ethan—"

Without warning, the disintegration accelerated, and he began to slip completely away, his last move the screaming of my name.

"*Merit!*"

I jolted awake in a cold sweat and a tangle of Ethan's blankets, dread sitting low in my stomach. It took a few moments to adjust to being awake again, to remember that it had been only a dream. That the horror wasn't real, but that he was still gone.

The nightmares were coming faster now, no doubt the result of the stress I was feeling. I hadn't solved the problem yet, and there were potentially two more elemental dangers—perhaps the biggest dangers—lurking out there. Earth and fire.

God forbid, I could figure something out before the city burned.

When my heart slowed again, I untangled myself from the blankets and walked to the bedroom window. The automatic shutters that covered it during the day had already lifted, revealing a gloriously dark sky, a couple of stars peeking through.

I closed my eyes in relief. The sky was back to normal, and that probably meant the lake and river were, as well.

If Claudia and Catcher had been right—that the magic was elemental and following a kind of pattern—the reprieve would be only temporary. We'd seen air and water. Earth and fire couldn't be far behind. But even a temporary reprieve would take some of the heat off us.

I returned to my room. With Tate on my agenda, and a message from Catcher confirming our second meeting, I showered and dressed in my leathers. I wasn't trying to impress Tate with my business acumen tonight; this was about fixing supernatural problems. The bit of worry wood, of course, was back in my pocket.

Jonah, on the other hand, hadn't called. That bothered me a little. I hoped he wasn't going to avoid me because I'd rebuffed him. We were a green team, but a good one. And while I was beginning to learn that I could stand Sentinel on my own, I'd have much rather done it with a partner.

Thinking misery loved company, I dialed up Mallory. It took five rings before she answered, and even then she wasn't thrilled about it.

"Kind of in the middle of something."

"Then don't answer the phone next time," I joked, but the comment still stung.

"Sorry," she said, and it sounded like she meant it. "I'm just—every exam gets a little worse, you know? And then I'm crazy tired, and I'm nearing the end of my rope. I just want this entire process to be over. I don't even care if I pass. I just want it done."

I could hear the exhaustion in her voice, and in the speed of her words. It wouldn't surprise me to learn she'd been downing energy drinks.

"I hear you," I said. "I've got an errand to run, but would you be up for a breather afterward?"

"I start my next exam in a few minutes."

"That sucks."

"Tell me about it. And to add insult to injury, Catcher's being a gigantic pain in the ass right now. I don't think he has any idea of the stress I'm going through."

Her voice was testy, and I wondered if any of us knew the stress she was going through. Other than Simon, who seemed to be directing it.

And while I had her on the phone . . . "Hey, I know you're in a hurry, but is there anything you can tell me about what's going on in the city right now with the lake and sky? I understand it's magic tied to the four elements—water, air, earth, and fire. Is that anything you've learned about?"

Her response was fast and furious. "Jesus, Merit. How many times now have you wondered if the city's problems come back to sorcerers? You did it with the drugs, as well."

"I wonder about a lot of things," I said, reminding myself of the stress she was under. "It's my job to wonder about the possibilities, and then to figure out the truth."

"Oh, so we're possibilities?"

I had no idea why we were arguing. I certainly hadn't accused her of anything. Was she lashing out at me because she'd thought the same thing, or because she was stressed?

"It's not like I'm out there just randomly making mischief," she said, before I could respond. "Or researching random pieces of magic. I'm taking exams, Merit."

Since when was city trauma a random piece of magic? The comment was irritating, but I stayed calm. "I know you are. I'm not accusing you of anything. But there's some kind of magic at work here that I don't understand. I just thought maybe you would."

"You know what I know about, Merit? I know about sigils and callefixes and magical algorithms and seeding auras. That's what I know about."

"You know what?" I told her, forcing myself to remain calm. "I'm going to let you go so you can get back to studying. Okay?"

"Maybe that's a good idea. And maybe you should hold off on the phone calls and the accusations until my exams are done."

The phone went dead, leaving me wild-eyed and flustered and completely at a loss for words.

Lindsey picked that moment to pop her head into my room. "Breakfast?"

I held up the phone. "Mallory just hung up on me!"

Lindsey frowned, stepped inside, and shut the door behind her. "What did you do?"

"Nothing. I mean, I did ask her if she knew anything about the lake and the sky, but nothing other than that."

Lindsey whistled. "Way to play it smooth."

"It was a legitimate question. And she's one of only three people in town who would know."

"True. I really don't have a dog in this fight. I just like not being the one getting into relationship trouble for once."

That comment suggested it was going to be followed by details I didn't want to hear, but it also sounded like a cry for help. "What did you do?"

She didn't waste any time. "Long story short: relationships are hard, I don't fight fair, and I am the messiest person he knows."

I grimaced—and agreed with him about the first and last things. Her room was a riot of stuff, and not in a stuff-tidily-arranged-in-those-identical-wicker-baskets-people-put-on-bookshelves way. "You don't fight fair?"

Her shoulders slumped. "I might make references to breaking up when we fight?"

"Yikes."

"Yeah. It's just—I've never really done this for real, you know? Not a relationship this serious. Sometimes I just feel like there's all this fear bottled up, and it has to go somewhere. I convince myself this isn't going to last."

"He loves you."

"I know. But he might stop someday. And someday, he might be gone, and then where am I? I'm all wrapped up in a boy, and I can't untangle myself."

She fell back on the bed. "I'm tired, I'm overworked, I'm being forcibly underfed, I'm stressed, and I have a boyfriend—a *boyfriend*, Merit—with his own issues, and the only thing I want to do is gorge on ice cream. And let's face it—the only problem that's going to solve is the 'hey, my pants are too loose!' problem. And that's not a problem I have right now."

She stood up and pooched out her belly. Her tiny it's-really-just-skin belly.

"Really?" I asked her, my voice dry as toast.

"It's just—I never used to be this girl. I was Lindsey, Cadogan House guard and all-around hot shit. I was on the cover of the *Chicago Voice Weekly* for Christ's sake. I *knew* I looked good. And now I'm worrying about how my hair looks? And whether these jeans look fan-fucking-tastic."

"They really do."

"They should. They cost two hundred bucks."

"For *jeans?*"

"They're butt-lifting." To prove the point, she turned and gave me a pinup-worthy pose.

But I wasn't impressed. "They're *jeans*. They're made of the same butt-lifting denim as the rest of the jeans in the world."

"If they were Pumas, you wouldn't be complaining about the price."

She had a point. "Continue," I magnanimously offered.

"The point is, I didn't used to worry about this stuff. I cared, but I didn't worry about it. I didn't worry about what this boy would think of me because I didn't care what this boy thought of me, you know? And now . . ." She shook her head as if disgusted with herself.

"Now you think about other people instead of yourself?"

The narrowing of her eyes was the last thing I saw before the pillow smacked me in the face.

"Ow," I instinctively said, putting a hand on my cheek. "Even if I did deserve that, *ow*."

"You take my point?"

"I take your point. But maybe it's not a bad thing. I mean, it's not so much that you're becoming über-neurotic or anything. You like Luc, and you want him to like you back. You want to be validated."

"I guess."

"So focus on the Luc part, instead of the Lindsey part. I mean, he's probably doing the same thing. Wondering if his boots are shined up enough or whatever cowboy-vampire types worry about."

"Chaps. As we have discussed, they frequently worry about chaps."

I pressed my fingers over my eyes. "You know, I moved out of Mallory's house just so I could avoid conversations like this."

"No, you moved out of Mallory's house so you could avoid seeing Catcher in boxer briefs. Which, frankly, is crazy. That boy is hella delicious."

"I saw him naked more than I saw him in boxer briefs. And pretty or not, sometimes I just want to sit down with my leftover Chinese without his naked ass strolling through my kitchen."

Lindsey chortled and sat down again. "So really it's a hygiene issue."

"It really is."

We were quiet for a moment.

"Is he worth it?" I finally asked.

"What do you mean?"

I remembered the night I'd gone to Ethan, finally sure he was willing to accept me for who I was and that I could do the same for him. There'd been no doubt then, no fear. Just acceptance of the risk that I was taking and the confidence that he was worth it.

That *we* would have been worth it.

It had taken time for me to get there, and for Ethan to be ready for a relationship. Maybe if we'd gotten there earlier we'd have had more time together—but there was no point in ruing that now. He was gone except in my dreams, and those were becoming too traumatic to want to relive.

"I think," I finally said, "you reach a point where you're willing to take that chance. Where you know you might still get hurt in the long run, but you decide it's worth it."

"And if I never get there?"

"Then you're honest with him. But don't let fear make the decision. Make the decision based on who he is and who you are when you're with him. On who he helps you to be."

She nodded, a tear slipping from her eye. I had the sudden sense the decision would come easier—and faster—than she might have imagined.

"You'll be fine," I pronounced, then gave her a sideways hug. "He loves you, and you love him, and someday, if we're lucky, things will get back to normal around here."

She crossed one leg over another. "What would that be like, even?"

"You tell me. I assume it's what life was like before Celina outed the Houses."

"Ah, yes. The halcyon days of . . . God, those days were pretty dull, now that I think of it."

"Damned if you do, damned if you don't."

"Grass is greener," she agreed, then slid me a glance. "Now that we've worked through my relationship issues, are you ready to talk about Jonah?"

What I wanted to do was nip that conversation in the bud. "There's nothing to talk about."

"Look," she said, her tone softening. "I'm not saying now is the time for you to find an eternity partner. But maybe it's time for you to consider considering someone. A friend. A lover. A friend with benefits." She bumped my shoulder playfully. "Jonah is like—I mean, Jesus, Merit. He's crazy beautiful, smart, he's got the trust of his entire House, and he appreciates you."

"He's not Ethan."

"That's not fair. There was no Ethan before him, and there will be no Ethan after him. But Ethan's gone. I'm not saying you forget he existed. I'm just saying eternity is a long time. And maybe you could consider the possibility that there are other people who could become a part of your life if you let them."

We sat there quietly for a moment.

"He kissed me."

Lindsey offered up a dolphin-worthy squeal. "I knew he would. How was it?"

"The kiss? Great. My regret after the fact? Less enjoyable."

"Eek," she said. "What did you do?"

"I kind of bailed on him?" I thought putting it into the form of a question would make it sound a little less bad. Maybe not surprisingly, it didn't.

"Bad form, Sentinel. Bad form. You still on speaking terms?"

"Possibly not, but that'll change. It has to, since he's the only partner I've got at the moment."

"True dat. Times are tough, guards and partners are in short supply, and humans are whiny little babies. I mean, we've been here as long as they have. You wanna bet the murder rate among humans is a lot higher than it is among vampires? We are not the ones causing this city's issues."

She stood up and moved her hands down in front of her body, blowing out a breath as she did it. "I'm calm. I'm calm. I'm also really hungry. You ready for breakfast?"

I shook my head. "I don't have time. I'm visiting the mayor."

She whistled low. "Again? Are you that hard up for a date?"

"Har har. I think he might have information about what's going on." I filled her in on my lemon and sugar theory. Unlike Catcher, she thought there was merit to the idea. But that didn't deter her from her goal.

"Mayor or not, even vampires have to eat." She tapped a finger against her head. "Empathic, remember? I can feel how hungry you are. And if you're going to figure out what the hell is going on here, you need to be ready for it. You can't put off food just because you're tired. It will only make you tireder."

I didn't disagree that she had a point, but I wanted this matter done sooner rather than later. On the other hand, I did have a tendency to run myself until I was quite literally sick of it, until I was in bed for a week with a virus that knocked me completely on my ass. A week of no sleep, slamming down junk food, and stress tended to do that to a girl.

I wasn't sure if vamps could get colds, but it probably wouldn't be very responsible of me to test that theory now.

We walked downstairs and moved into the cafeteria line. Unfortunately, Juliet and Margot had been right about Frank's new nutritional choices: free-range eggs; turkey bacon; organic fruit salad; and a grain-heavy gruel that looked like it would have been served in Little Orphan Annie's orphanage.

"Ugh," I remarked, but scooped up eggs and fruit and grabbed a drink box of blood.

We took our food to a table and were quickly joined by Margot and Katherine, another Novitiate with a wicked sense of humor and a fabulous singing voice.

"So it's been a really freaky week. How's it going out there?" Margot asked, picking through her bowl of fruit.

"I've been beating the streets. But I'm not sure I'm making progress."

"That's all you can do," Margot said, pointing at me with a cantaloupe-laden fork. "Besides, things are back to normal for now. Maybe they'll stay that way."

I wouldn't bet on it, but I nodded my agreement.

Margot gave me a sly look. "I hear you're working with Jonah—the captain of the Grey House guards. Any details you want to pass along?"

I felt my cheeks warm. "Not really," I said, hoping Lindsey wasn't going to spill the beans about the kiss. I was proud; she chewed her muffin with obvious deliberation, and kept quiet. "We're just working together."

"And what's on your agenda for the day?" Katherine asked.

"I'm meeting with the mayor, actually. Well, the former mayor."

"You think he turned the sky and river?" Margot wondered.

"I think information keeps pointing in his direction."

"Have you talked to Cabot lately?" Lindsey asked.

I shook my head, my stomach grumbling sympathetically at the mention of his name. "Not since he sent us to talk to the fairies."

"Probably figured fairy-cide was an easier way to get rid of you," Katherine grumbled.

"Wouldn't surprise me," I agreed. "What's he done now?"

"Now he's got a wild hair about our skills. Strat, phys, psych. Says he's reviewing our files to ensure we've been appropriately categorized."

"He's assessing whether or not we're threats," I muttered. "And it's probably my fault. When we met, I told him I was a Strong Phys. He probably didn't like the reminder that we're actually competent out here in Cadogan House."

"He is a piece of work," Margot agreed. "And we want to escape him for a few hours." She pointed at me with her fork. "What's your schedule tonight? We're thinking about an *Evil Dead* and *Army of Darkness* marathon."

I blinked. "Like, the Bruce Campbell movies?"

The table went silent.

"Show a little respect, Merit," Lindsey said with more than a little offense. "Have you ever been overtaken by a Candarian demon?"

I glanced among them all, trying to ferret out whether they were joking or I had stepped into some kind of Bruce Campbell cult. "Not in the last few hours."

"Yeah, well, it's not really funny, is it? With the crazy eyes and uncontrollable limbs." She shivered, and I honestly couldn't tell if she was serious.

"You're joking, right?" I quietly asked. "I mean, I thought you were joking, but some pretty weird stuff goes on in Chicago, and I haven't read the entire *Canon* yet, so maybe I just missed the Candarian demon chapter?"

She managed a good fifteen seconds more before she couldn't hold in the snort. "Oh, my God, totally. But I almost didn't make it. Seriously, though, I love the flicks. You in?"

I reached out and punched her a few times in the arm while the rest of the table chortled. "I'll let you know," I said.

"You do that. Oh," she exclaimed, "I just felt a pretty solid hint of Cabot irritation." She tapped her forehead again, which was apparently international code for "I've got empathic powers and I know how to use them."

"In case he's looking for an outlet for his obsessions," she said, "you might want to take that breakfast to go. I hear he made three Novitiates cry yesterday."

She didn't have to tell me twice. I nodded and grabbed my drink box, then hopped up. "If he calls an assembly to announce he's leaving Chicago, save me a seat."

"You'll be the first we call," Lindsey promised, and I took her at her word.

＊＊＊

CHAPTER FOURTEEN

MAYORAL PRIVILEGE

When I was dressed, fed, and katana'd, I walked back to the front of the House. I was on my way to Malik's office—I thought I'd give him a direct report—when I heard shouting.

I didn't like the idea of shouting in the vicinity of my Master, so I put a hand on my katana to keep it balanced and ran down the hall. I found Luc and Malik in his office. The door was open, and they stood in the middle of the room, both with arms crossed. Their expressions were blank as they listened to a news report from a very expensive stereo. Both looked over and offered a nod of acknowledgment.

"And this man," said the woman on the radio, whom I guessed was the mayor, "this colleague of mine, was *accosted* by vampires on the *street*. And then he was questioned by the police as if *he* was to blame for it. What is this city coming to if these are the kinds of shenanigans playing out on our streets right now?"

McKetrick. I closed my eyes ruefully. Not just because he had been released—and so much for that plan—but because I'd played right into his hand. Granted, I was guilty only of walking down the street and defending myself, but he had friends in high places, and his version made a much more interesting headline.

Kowalczyk started up again. "I am, however, very happy to announce that by the end of the evening, supernatural registration will be *law*. By the end of the night, we'll have the authority to track the location of supernaturals across the city, and they will no longer be able to surprise citizens on the street."

With a sickened expression, Malik reached over and flipped off the radio.

"That woman is a piece of goddamned work," Luc spat out. "Who does she think she is, and how stupid is she that she believes McKetrick?" He blew out a breath and linked his hands atop his head. "She's a fascist with an ache to be president, and she isn't going to stop."

"Not while there are headlines to be made," Malik agreed. He looked at me. "Kelley told me what actually went down, that you arranged for Catcher to pick him up. I'm hopeful he at least got some useful information before the release?"

"I'm going back to visit Tate. Catcher should be there, and I'll ask for the details."

"You're thinking Tate is in play?" Luc asked.

"I think, at a minimum, he knows what's going on." I told them about the old magic Claudia had mentioned and the scents of lemon and sugar that Catcher hadn't been convinced were meaningful.

But that didn't seem to faze Malik. "You stand Sentinel of this House for a reason, Merit. He trusted you. I trust you. Luc trusts you. Your instincts are good. Follow them where they lead, and we will support you whatever the result."

He may have taken the reigns of the House in regrettable circumstances, but there was no doubt he was a Master.

———

The second verse of getting to Tate was pretty much the same as the first, except for the part about carefully skirting the men with large guns who stood in front of the House. The members of the National Guard looked more than capable of keeping the screaming protestors at bay. Problem was, if McKetrick had convinced the mayor of the third biggest city in the country that vampires were evil, could they be convinced, as well?

I drove toward the lake and met Catcher at the factory gate. He looked exhausted, and I wasn't sure if the problems in the city or his sorceress were responsible for the bloodshot eyes.

"I hear McKetrick's back on the street."

"I heard the broadcast," he grumbled. "We didn't have a secure facility for interrogation. We called Jacobs, who hauled him in. He questioned him through the night, let us sit in." That explained the exhaustion, I thought. "At least until the mayor called and Jacobs had to let him go. I assume he trotted down to her office and they concocted the story."

"Did you get anything out of him?"

"Not much—but I'm not sure he has much to hide. McKetrick's pretty clear about his position on vampires. Genocide's a harsh word, but I wouldn't put it past him."

"Let's hope Kowalczyk is smart enough not to buy in. I don't suppose he gave up the location of his facility?"

"He did not. But he did give up his fingerprints and a little DNA, and we got another set from the gun you brought in. That gives us something to work with if he starts making trouble."

"I suppose that's something," I conceded, but wondered if that data had been worth the risk. McKetrick was going to be *pissed*, and the episode was only going to tie McKetrick and Kowalczyk closer together. She'd rescued him, and that wasn't going to be something either one of them forgot.

He pulled to a stop in front of the building, and I realized uniformed CPD guards, not fairies, were guarding it.

"This is a bad idea," I quietly said, surveying the officers, who all looked like rookies just out of training—and undoubtedly had no defenses against whatever magic Tate wielded.

"They're the reason we were able to get in at all," Catcher said. "Chuck served with one of their grandfathers, and he called in a favor. The boys in blue are loyal to each other."

"Maybe so," I said. "But these kids are no match for Tate. He was able to manipulate Celina, and she's as stubborn and resilient as they come."

"There's no other choice," he said. "Chuck had to fight to keep Tate separated from the rest of the prison population. To tell you the truth, I'm not sure if it's better or worse that Tate's no longer mayor. He started off strong enough—opened the Ombud's office. He was a real supporter of Chuck."

"Until he started manufacturing drugs and attempting to control vampires?"

"There is that," Catcher agreed. "I'm not saying those were good deeds. I just think they're anomalies in the bigger scheme of Tate."

I didn't disagree the change was odd, but I thought it revealed true colors Tate hadn't been able to hide any longer. "Scheme," I thought, was the key word.

I hopped out of the cart, offered up my weapons, then glanced back at Catcher. "You're staying here?"

He'd already pulled out a book and was flipping through the pages. "Right here waiting, just like the song. I'm scanning the Order's annals for any evidence of whether anything like this happened before—including whether Tate might be involved." With a frown, he absently scratched the back of his head. "I'm hoping if

I can find that kind of entry, I can backtrack and figure out what kind of magic was behind it."

Given his obvious exhaustion and tireless efforts, I managed not to make a juvenile joke about the "annals" of an organization with the acronym U-ASS.

"That sounds perfectly reasonable."

"We'll see," he grumbled in response, but he was already scanning the pages.

I headed for the door. The kid in uniform offered me a salute, then opened the door to the building. A second uniform stood point at the steel door that led into the office.

"Ma'am. Be careful in there," he said, and when I assured him I would, opened the door and let me inside.

It immediately slammed shut behind me.

I jumped a little, which wasn't exactly the brave facade I'd hoped to put on for this meeting.

"I don't bite, Ballerina," Tate cannily said. In his orange jumpsuit, he was seated at the aluminum table again. Since he clearly wasn't going to use my name, I didn't bother to correct him. I'd also already decided it was useless to play games with a liar, so I sat down across from him and got down to business.

"Are you the one manipulating the city right now?"

He looked back at me, head slightly tilted, his expression inscrutable. "I don't know what you're talking about."

His tone was equally opaque. I couldn't tell if he was being sarcastic or if he was truly surprised by the question.

I decided there was no point in not putting all my cards on the table—not when the city was at stake.

"The lake went dead. The sky turned red. I understand we're seeing elemental magic, symptoms that are popping up because the city is unbalanced. We've seen water and air so far. Fire and earth could be next."

"And?"

I paused, picking a tone to offer up my theory. I opted for Ethan's "Slyer Than Thou" voice. "It's the strangest thing, Tate. Whenever I'm in your presence, I smell lemon and sugar—like cookies baking."

His expression stayed flat, but his pupils had narrowed just a smidge. I was on to something.

"Yesterday, while the sky was red, it rained. And I smelled the same thing." I linked my hands together on the table, and leaned forward. "I know you're doing this. And you're going to tell me how to stop it, or we're going to go a round. Right here. Right now."

Okay, I might have gone a bit overboard on the last bit, and not just because I had no weapons and wasn't entirely sure what he could do. But Tate ignored the bravado.

"If I am the maker of these events, how, exactly did I arrange them from my humble abode?"

"I hadn't exactly gotten to that part."

He made a sound of disdain. "You hadn't gotten to *any* part. You could hardly be more wrong, and that bodes as poorly for the city as anything else. It is not in my nature to produce that kind of magic."

"What are you?" I asked him.

"If this magic isn't mine, why does it matter?"

"How could it possibly *not* matter?"

Tate frowned and shuffled in his chair. "Humans have an irritating desire to group their fellow men and women into categories. To give them a type, and to give the type a name, so that by definition 'they' are otherwise. 'They' are not who 'we' are. Frankly, I find the endeavor exhausting. I am what I am, just as you are what you are."

A confession from Tate—of his magical identity and his responsibility for the water and sky—would have been nice. But I knew when to push and when to listen. And even if he wasn't going to confess, he seemed to honestly believe he understood what was happening. That was definitely worth my time.

"If you didn't have anything to do with this, then tell me who did. Explain to me what's happening."

Slowly, a smile curved his lips. "Now this is interesting. You asking me for information. For a favor, as it were."

"It's not a favor if I'm helping save the city you swore an oath to protect."

"Oaths are overrated. You've sworn them as well, did you not? To protect your House?"

"I did, and I have," I growled out. He hadn't expressly suggested that I'd broken my oaths—presumably by failing to protect Ethan—but it rode beneath his words.

"Hmm," he noncommittally said. "And if I was to give you this information, what's my incentive? My payment? My boon?"

"The public good?"

He laughed heartily. "You amuse me greatly, Ballerina. You really do. And while I enjoy Chicago, there are plenty of cities in the world. Saving this one is hardly incentive enough for the kind of information you're talking about."

It wasn't surprising that he wanted payment for the information. But I didn't want to offer up a prize without a little negotiation.

"I owe you nothing," I told him. "If anything, you owe me. You're responsible for my Master's death."

"And the death of your enemy," he pointed out. He leaned forward over the table, hands flat on the tabletop, and stared at me like I was the subject of his psychological experiment. Which I probably was. "Does it bother you that you've killed? That a life was extinguished by your hand?"

Don't take the bait, I reminded myself. "Does it bother you that you were the true cause of her death?"

"Let's not get into a philosophical discussion about causation."

"Then let's agree that you owe me one, and you can tell me what you know."

"Interesting tactic, but no."

Probably not surprising that his questionable ethics didn't prompt him to help me out of his own accord. "What do you want?"

"What do you have?"

I thought about the question. Honestly, I didn't have much. My dagger and sword were outside with Catcher. I didn't have much else of value beyond the family pearls in my room and the signed baseball Ethan had given me, and I wasn't giving those up.

While I considered the question, I absently touched the Cadogan medal around my neck. Tate's eyes widened at the move.

"That would be an interesting prize."

Instinctively, I cupped my fingers around it. His expression was guarded, but clearly sincere. I wasn't sure about his motivation, but unlike the fairies, I didn't think his interest was in the gold. Did the medal have magical properties? I'd never thought to ask. Regardless, it was precious to me.

"There's no way in hell you're getting this."

"Then we have nothing to talk about."

I recalled the first time I'd made a bargain with a supernatural creature. "How about I owe you a favor? A boon of some kind?" That offer had worked with Morgan Greer, now Master of Navarre House, but Tate didn't seem impressed with it.

"You're a vampire. You could renege on your offer."

"I would never," I said, but since there's no telling the kind of favor Tate would extract, I silently admitted there was a possibility I wouldn't go through with it.

Tate sat back. "We're done here. You can solve this problem on your own. Perhaps one of your friends could help you. They're sorcerers, no? They should be able to explain things to you."

Should be able, but were at a loss, I thought.

I touched the pendant again, running my fingertip across the engraved letters. The medal had been mine since I was Commended into the House—promoted from Initiate to Novitiate vampire and given the position of Sentinel.

Ethan had clasped the medal around my neck. Since his death, I'd rarely removed it. But the problems facing Chicago and its supernaturals were bigger than me or Ethan or a small bit of gold, so I relented.

Without a word to Tate—although I could feel his smug satisfaction from across the table—I unclasped the medal and let it fall into my hand.

Tate held out his hand to receive it, but I shook my head.

"Information first," I told him. "Prize later."

"I had no idea you were so . . . *tenacious.*"

"I learned from the best," I said, smiling sweetly. "Get on with it."

Tate considered the bargain for a moment, and finally nodded.

"Fine. The deal is struck. But as you might imagine, I don't get visitors often. I'm taking the long road. Besides, you are clearly woefully undereducated about the supernatural world."

I couldn't fight back a sigh. Getting a lengthy history lecture from Tate wasn't high on my list of things to accomplish tonight. ("Saving the city" was actually number one on that list.) On the other hand, he was probably right. I was undereducated.

While he may have planned to take the long road, he didn't waste a moment getting comfortable in his chair and imparting his wisdom.

"Magic wasn't born on the eve of vampires' creation," he lectured. "It existed for millennia on this plane and others. Good and evil lived together in relationship slightly more, shall we say, symbiotic than this one. They were partners, neither better than the other, coexisting in peace. There was a certain justice in the world. Magic was unified—dark and light. Good and evil. The distinctions didn't exist. Magic only *was*. Neither moral or immoral, but amoral, as it was meant to be. And then one red-letter day, humans decided evil wasn't merely the other side of the coin—it was *wrong*. Bad. Not the other half of good, but its opposite. Its apotheosis."

Tate drew a square on the tabletop with a finger. "The evil was deemed a contamination. It was drawn from good, separated."

Mallory had once told me that black magic was like a second four-quadrant grid that lay above the four Keys. It sounded like her explanation had been pretty accurate.

"How was the magic separated?" I wondered.

"Carefully," he said. "There were a number of iterations. Gods were divided into two halves; one moral, one immoral. Sides were taken, and angels were deemed true or fallen. Most important, some would say, evil was placed into a vessel that would contain it. It was parceled out only to a few who would seek to wield it."

"What was the vessel?"

"It's called the *Maleficium*."

"So what does this have to do with the city? I've been told we're seeing effects in the lake and sky because the four elements—earth, air, fire, and water—are unbalanced."

"Like I mentioned, that's a typical human instinct—to create categories to explain the world and blame the unfamiliar on a disruption in the categories. But categories don't explain things; they describe them. You've heard the myth of the four Keys?"

"The four divisions of magic? Yeah, but I've never heard them referred to as a 'myth.'"

Tate rolled his eyes. "That's because sorcerers aren't honest with themselves. Every categorization of magic—by Keys, by elements, by astrological signs, whatever—is just a way of ordering the universe for purposes of their practice. Each sect creates its own divisions and distributes magical properties into those divisions. But the divisions don't matter."

I found that revelation to be surprisingly disappointing—that the philosophy of magic Catcher had imparted to me those months ago wasn't quite accurate, or at least it was only one of many half-accurate ideas.

"The point, Merit, is not that the magical systems are incorrect—but that they simply aren't important."

"Then what is?"

"The distinction between dark and light." He placed a hand flat on the table. "Assume this hand is the entire world of magic." He spread his fingers. "Call each finger a Key, an element, a drawer, what have you. The name doesn't matter. The point is, however you describe the categories, the categories are all part of a single system."

"Sure," I said with a nod.

"Now, imagine the system is ripped in two by those who decided good and evil were anathema to each other." His left hand flat on the table, he placed his right hand palm down a few inches above it. "Each hand is now half of the magic in the world. The world continues to function as we know it only while those two layers remain in balance."

My thoughts stopped whirling chaotically and fell into order. "Which is why the lake stopped moving and the sky turned red—because the natural laws are askew."

"I wouldn't say 'askew.' I would say 'undergoing reorganization.'"

"So the nymphs, the siren, the fairies. They truly have nothing to do with it?"

"Bit players at best."

I sighed, regrouped, and kept going. "Why would things become unbalanced?"

"Because light and dark magic are being blended together. Because the separations between them have been violated. There are a variety of reasons, I suppose, to employ dark magic. Murder. Binding someone to service. The creation of a familiar. Prophecy, for those who don't have the gift. Conjuring demons. Communing with otherworldly creatures."

"Then who's doing it? And how do I fix it?"

"How do you fix it?" He barked out a laugh. "You don't *fix* it. It's not a screw that needs tightening. It simply *is*. Some would say it's a return to the original world. The First World. That Which Existed and Should Exist Again."

There was a self-satisfied gleam in his eyes that suggested he was looking forward to that day. It seemed clear he thought the world was ready for change.

"Wouldn't it be a return to war?" I wondered. "To Armageddon?"

He clucked his tongue. "That's such a naïve view. Good and evil existed together for eons before humans—or vampires, for that matter—came into being. Don't knock what you don't understand."

I ignored the sass. "And the *Maleficium*. Where can I find it?"

He sat back in his chair and threw an arm over the back. "Now, now, Ballerina. I can't give away all my secrets, can I?"

"Are you using the *Maleficium* to make magic of your own? To bring about that new world order?"

He smiled at me through half-lidded eyes. "Would I do such a thing?"

"Yes. And you'd lie about it."

He tilted his head to the side in obvious interest. "After all I've just given you, you accuse me of dishonesty?"

"You've lied your entire life. That you had the city's welfare at heart. That you were trying to help vampires. That you were human."

"Yes, well. Amorality was easier before evil intent was ascribed to it."

I rolled my eyes. "If you didn't have anything to do with it, why do the fairies think old magic is involved? And why did the city smell like lemon and sugar after it rained?"

"Just because I didn't make the magic doesn't mean I can't enjoy it. The *Maleficium* is old magic. The recombination of good and evil leaves its mark on the natural world—the water and sky. It also leaves its mark on the wind. In the latent magic in the air. I can't be faulted for wanting to sample it, can I?"

"How can you sample airborne magic from across town?"

"There is more to the universe, Horatio, than what you can see or believe to be true."

"I'm aware," I dryly said.

"The point is, magic doesn't need a freeway."

"If you don't have the *Maleficium*, who does?"

"The Order maintains possession of it. Guards it, if you will."

My stomach churned with butterflies. I was going to have to go back to Catcher and accuse a sorcerer of screwing with the *Maleficium*. Yeah—maybe Mallory was distorting the natural world in her fifteen minutes of free time each day.

Well, regardless of whether I liked his answer, I couldn't fault him for not sticking to his word. I placed the medal on the table and slid it toward Tate. Without looking back, I rose from my chair and walked toward the door.

"Thank you for the prize," Tate said. "And don't be a stranger."

Frankly, I'd be fine if I never had to see him again. But I doubted I'd be that lucky.

CHAPTER FIFTEEN

BLACK BIRD

Catcher met me in the golf cart just outside the door. I climbed in, and he took off for the gate.

"What happened to your medal?"

"I traded it for some magic beans," I grouchily said.

He gave a low whistle. "Those better have been good beans."

"Jury's still out. Tate agrees the sky and earth issues are caused by a magical imbalance—basically someone mixing good and evil a little too liberally. He's not convinced the change wouldn't be a good idea. He mentioned the *Maleficium*. Do you know anything about it? Is there any chance he could have gotten it?"

Catcher's brow furrowed, but he shook his head. "The Order has the *Maleficium*. It's in Nebraska in the silo under thirty feet of farmland and Order lock and key."

"I'm sorry," I interrupted. "The silo?"

"Abandoned missile silo. Nebraska's in the middle of the country, so it's full of Cold War strategic defense munitions. You know—far enough away from the coasts that you could keep the important stuff there."

"If you say so. Is it secure?"

"Whatever else I might say about the Order—and believe me, I have many choice words in mind—they would not allow the *Maleficium* to leave the silo. Tate just likes watching you squirm. The man is a total sadist."

"He succeeded," I said. "I'm squirming. If he doesn't have the *Maleficium*, maybe he's working through someone else. Has he had any visitors?"

"You're the only one we've allowed in."

So much for that theory. "Then by my estimation, here's what we're left with: He says he's not involved, and I tend to believe him. And last we talked, you did, too." I braced myself. "If it's not Tate, and if the *Maleficium*'s involved, and if the Order has the *Maleficium* . . ." I let him fill in the blank.

"It's not me or Mallory."

"I know. But that only leaves one person. Simon is the only person in Chicago who's officially associated with the Order. Wouldn't that also make him the only person in Chicago who has access to the *Maleficium*?"

Catcher didn't respond.

"What's the history with you and Simon?" I asked.

Catcher squealed the golf cart to a stop in front of the gate in a flurry of rocks and gravel. "The problem," he said, "isn't historical."

"We're past personal vendettas at this point."

"It's not a goddamned personal vendetta!" Catcher yelled, slamming his fist into the cart's plastic dashboard. "I wanted to protect her from this. I didn't want her dealing with Order bullshit, dealing with Order politics, dealing with Order flunkies. She is freaking out, and we are both exhausted, and he is in there with her—down there with her—every single day. God only knows what he's putting into her brain."

"Mallory would never be unfaithful," I quietly said.

"Unfaithful to our relationship? No, she wouldn't," he agreed. "But there are lots of ways to be turned against someone, Merit. If someone you loved was being brainwashed, what would you do about it?"

"Brainwashed? That's putting it a little strongly, isn't it?"

"Does she seem like the same person to you?"

She hadn't, actually, since she met Simon, which supported my theory that Simon was involved.

"One way or the other, Simon is the linchpin in this thing. If you can't stand to talk to him, then set up a meeting with me."

"Simon won't meet with a member of the House. The Order won't allow it. There's a formal process that has to be followed just to make the request, which they won't grant."

"I've talked to him before."

"Casually. You're talking about making him answer to vampires about his actions. That's different."

My patience with sorcerers—Catcher included—was growing thin. I climbed out of the cart, then looked back at him. "If I can't meet with him, then you do it."

Catcher's jaw tightened. He tapped his fingers on the steering wheel, apparently ready for me to leave.

At least I could do someone a favor.

With another break in the action—since I was surely not going to interrogate Simon without Catcher as backup—I called Kelley and offered an update. I advised her about the *Maleficium* and our new theory that reunification of good and evil was causing the city's problems.

I also called Lindsey, who confirmed the Bruce Campbell movie-thon was under way. I didn't exactly have time for a movie, but I was stressed and tired and I needed real food. If a movie was playing during the meal, so be it. With dinner in mind, I pulled over at a taco truck on the way back to Hyde Park and ordered as much as I could stuff into a single bag, which I thought was less likely to raise Frank's ire if I was caught sneaking junk food into the House.

I drove back and slid into a parking spot, then walked back into the House past rhythmically chanting protestors and stoic men and women in uniform. The House was quiet when I walked in, only a few vampires milling about in the front rooms. There was a kind of solemnity in the House under Malik's rule, and I wasn't sure if that was because the House reflected his generally solemn personality, because vampires were still grieving, or because we were still under GP occupation.

A mix of all three, maybe.

Without my medal but with contraband, I hustled upstairs to Lindsey's third-floor room. I didn't bother knocking, but carefully opened the door—there were usually vamps spread out in every spare nook and cranny, and if you weren't careful, you inevitably banged someone on the head.

The dark room was, as per usual, full of noise from Lindsey's wee television and full of vampires. Lindsey, Margot, and Katherine had spots on the bed, and a slew of vamps I'd seen only in passing were packed onto the floor, maybe fifteen in all? That was certainly a violation of Tate's rule against assembling in groups larger than ten.

Long live the revolution!

I picked my way across the Novitiates, distributing paper-wrapped tacos like a culinary Santa Claus, and eventually stopping in a small empty spot in a far corner of the room. The vamp beside me smiled and offered one of her pillows, which I took with a whispered "thanks."

One campy horror movie later, I reached two conclusions:

One: I loved my friends.

Two: I still didn't get it.

We'd just cleared the room of taco wrappings and vampires when my and Lindsey's beepers simultaneously erupted.

I pulled mine off and checked the screen. "TRAINING ROOM," it read, with a "DRESS FOR TRAINING" follow-up.

I looked up at Lindsey. "What's this about?"

"I'm sure Frankfurter has some vital lesson he wants to teach us."

"Sadly, Frankfurter does not ask us for advice," I said. "And I totally support the use of 'Frankfurter.'"

"I knew you would," she said, heading for her bathroom door, probably to go change into our required yoga pants. "He could learn a lot from two hip, big city vamps."

"Did you just cast your own sitcom?"

"I believe I did, yeah. I'm some witty dialogue and an afterschool special away from an Emmy. You know, in case this vampire guard thing doesn't work out."

I offered a sound of agreement and walked to the door so I could change clothes. "Frank's still here," I pointed out. "There's probably a good chance this guard thing won't work out for either of us."

It said a lot that she didn't disagree with me.

Once clothed in a black sports bra and yoga pants, I gathered together with Lindsey, Juliet, and Kelley in the sparring room.

We stood barefoot at the edges of the mats, waiting for our call to arms—or whatever Frank had in store. He stood in the middle of the room—in the middle of the *mats*—still in a suit and fancy shoes.

Lindsey quietly clucked her tongue. "Luc is not going to be thrilled Frankfurter's wearing shoes on his tatami mats."

"No," I whispered in agreement. "That is not going to go over well. Not that he can do anything about it."

Malik and Luc stood together on the other side of the room, irritated magic seeping from their corner. The balcony that ringed the room was filling with House vampires, their expressions ranging from curious to concerned. They clearly didn't trust Frank any more than we did.

When the balcony was full, Frank loudly cleared his throat and stared daggers at the vampires until everyone was seated. Then he lowered his gaze to the four of us.

"I have determined it is in the best interests of the House that your semiannual physical testing be held tonight."

Stunned silence descended over the room, at least until the whispering started. The Novitiates' quiet comments echoed my own: This wasn't the time to take the House guards out of commission for a test. And even if we failed, who was going to replace us?

This had all the markings of an attempt to charge us as incompetent—or make me look worse than Frank already imagined I was.

Luc was the first to speak aloud. "You want to give them a test? That's ridiculous. They need to be outside defending the House, not dealing with bureaucratic nonsense."

"Fortunately," Frank said, "I did not ask for, nor do I require, your opinion. As the GP has repeatedly attempted to drill into this House, this House and its operation is your primary—and only—concern. The complications of human existence are not."

"As you and the GP are well aware," Luc spat back, "the city is falling apart, one piece of real estate at a time, and you don't think we need to be worried about that? You don't think we need to be out there on the streets dealing with it?"

"Luc," Malik said, putting a hand on Luc's arm. "Not now."

His words suggested Luc show respect for Frank, but his own emotions were clearly roiling. It was evident in the furrow of his brow, the tenseness in his posture and the vibration of tense magic from his corner.

The conflict Malik faced was obvious—to stand up for your guards and your second in command, or to obey the council responsible for your House's existence and the protection of your vampires.

Sometimes, you had to lose the battle to win the campaign.

"Mr. Cabot," Malik said into the tense silence. "Continue."

Frank nodded pompously, but the rest of the vampires took Malik at his word, and immediately quieted. "As I was saying, you will be tested and evaluated in various forms of physical fitness and endurance. If you refuse to participate, you will be stripped of your position in the House. If you fail, you will be stripped of your position in the House."

The room went deathly silent, all of us shocked. He looked up and looked right at me.

"You're all rated Very Strong Phys. Let's see if those classifications hold true." Frank looked down at his watch. "You will begin . . ."

"This can't be for real—" Kelley pleaded, but she was silenced by a withering glance from the narc.

"You will begin," Frank said again, "now."

Testing a vampire's strength and endurance was tricky, especially if the vampires were guards of one of the nation's oldest vampire Houses. We were obviously strong, fast, and flexible. We'd been trained in combat, both with and without swords, and we'd run our fair share of miles. We'd done thousands upon thousands of sit-ups and squats, push-ups, and chin-ups. The four of us probably could have exercised into infinity. But Frank wasn't interested in infinity.

Frank was interested in what we could do right now on half rations of blood, measured by a testing regimen probably created in the 1950s. Our strength was tested by throwing giant iron balls and weights across the Cadogan grounds. One smashed window notwithstanding—they were *really* hard to aim—we managed to surpass his arbitrary milestones.

Our flexibility and speed were tested with jump ropes that we were expected to use with ever-faster repetitions. We belly-crawled across the backyard, flipped gigantic truck tires he'd hauled in for the task, and ran back-and-forth sprints until our legs felt like dead weight. He ordered us into the pool, freezing in the November chill, and made us swim laps until our skin was milky white and our teeth chattered from the cold.

We climbed out of the pool with soaked clothes and hair, steam rising from our bodies, and hatred of Frank growing in our hearts.

Frank carried around a clipboard and made notes as we worked through his drills, his gaze disdainful, as if we were failing in every respect to meet whatever mental criteria he'd established.

Not that that was surprising. He couldn't have honestly thought this was a good time to test the only remaining three-and-a-half guards in Cadogan House. The House was peaceful only because we'd paid Claudia's minions to protect us, and it was a waste of time trying to prove a point he was never going to accept. Whether we passed or we failed . . . we still failed.

But while the workout was exhausting, it was still just a work-out. Painful, sure. Tiring, yes. But just as in a normal workout, you reached a point where you zoned into the rhythm. We were vampires, and strong ones, and that meant something. We were strong, fast and flexible, whatever Frank's criticisms.

And we weren't the only ones who thought so. Word of the test spread through the House. Slowly but surely, a trickle of Cadogan vampires began to spill into the yard. They formed a protective circle around us as we worked, occasionally handing over blood boxes and bottles of water like marathon volunteers.

We were belly-crawling across the grass for the second time when Margot and Katherine popped through the edge of the crowd.

"We have something for you," Margot said, glancing around sneakily to locate Frank.

Lindsey, her hair still wet and stringy from the pool and her face streaked with dirt and sweat, looked up from the ground. "He's taking a call from Darius," she said, "so if it's against any of his numerous rules, get to it."

"We can do that," Katherine said, and a semicircle of vampires surrounded her to face us as we wormed our way across the ground. "We thought a little night music might do the trick."

Katherine sang a note to test her pitch, which was as perfect as a well-tuned grand piano. She winked, and with no more ado than that, Katherine and the rest of her vampire glee club began to sing the Beatles' "Black Bird."

The grounds fell completely silent, every vampire quiet as her voice rang, clear and strong, across the night.

Weeks and weeks of Frank's abusive behavior had taken its toll on the House. When Ethan had been Master, Cadogan House had been more than a structure; it had been a home. I hoped Malik could make it that way again, but as Frank had made clear, his goal was to break Cadogan House down, brick by brick, vampire by vampire.

But as I lay on my stomach on cold, dewy grass, I couldn't have felt any closer to those vampires. Tears began to stream down my face, and I wasn't the only one moved. There were tear tracks on Lindsey's face, and Kelley was biting her lip to hold them back.

When the ensemble reached the bridge, the rest of the hundred vampires on the lawn joined her, their voices a chorus against idiocy. Their voices a chorus for the House, and for us, and for all that Ethan had tried to create.

For the family he'd wanted to make of us.

Magic lifted and rose, peppering my arms with goose bumps, and I sent a silent prayer of "thanks" into the universe. Frank may be an asshole, but he'd managed to bring us together even after Ethan's death had pulled us apart.

The chorus had only just finished the song when Frank emerged through the crowd again. The vampires rustled nervously while he pushed his hands into his pockets and surveyed us with obvious disdain.

"I'm not sure concerts are within the spirit of the rules. This is a testing procedure, not a block party."

Malik, who also stood at the edge of the crowd, his hands behind his back, turned to regard him. "It may not be within the spirit of your rules," he said, "but neither is it against their letter. And that, as you have reminded us, is what's important. The rules."

Frank stared at Malik for a moment . . . but he didn't argue. Maybe he could learn to pick his battles after all.

Alas, I was wrong again. Having tested our agility, strength, and stamina, Frank decided to test them all again.

He led us to the far back corner of the House grounds, where four wooden posts the width of telephone poles had been pounded into the ground. They were four feet tall and maybe ten inches in diameter.

"Juliet, Kelley, Lindsey, Merit," he said, pointing to the poles in succession. "Stand atop your pole."

We all looked at him for a second, probably all thinking the same thing: *I'm sorry; you want me to stand on a pole?*

"That wasn't a request," he said in the prickly tone of a leader so inadequate he had to bully people to follow his orders.

We all shared a glance, but without a better option—other than losing our positions in the House—we obeyed.

I hopped up onto the post and windmilled my arms to keep from falling over again. On shaky knees and ankles, arms outstretched, I slowly stood up, then cast a glance back at Frank.

"This volley tests your endurance, your strength, your balance," he said.

"What do we do exactly?" Juliet asked.

"You stand there," Frank said, "until you can't stand there anymore."

"The sun will be rising soon," Lindsey pointed out.

"And you will stand there until you can't stand there anymore," Frank repeated.

I looked at Malik. He nodded at me, an acknowledgment of our struggle, and a promise to intervene should the need arise. I closed my eyes in anticipation of the coming drama and wished for the strength to deal with it.

And so, with three hours to go until dawn, we stood on posts in the middle of Hyde Park, and we waited for the sun to rise.

For nearly three hours, we stood on our posts—vampires being used as pawns in a political game that had nothing to do with us. It was unfair, sure, but certainly not the first time people had been used and manipulated to meet some political goal. Wasn't that the mechanism of virtually every dictator and demagogue in history?

To use the people to accomplish some presumably important political end?

Three hours ago there'd been four of us. Now we were down to two. Kelley had stumbled and fallen from her pole as darkness began to give way to dawn and exhaustion had finally overtaken her. Lindsey, tired and dehydrated, had gotten a cramp and had crumpled to the ground.

The test, whatever its purpose, was down to me and Juliet.

We stood in silence, she of the elfish frame and delicate features. Me with the fortuitous balance of a former ballerina, but still stiff and aching. Juliet had thrown on tennis shoes for the racing portions of the test, but I was still barefoot, and I could hardly feel my feet, the cramps having long since given way to a buzzing numbness. Every other muscle in my body ached from the effort of balancing myself in that spot, and I knew I'd be sore when this task was done.

The eastern sky was beginning to turn a searing shade of orange. The vampires who'd stayed outdoors with us hunched into bits of shade that would protect them from the rising sun.

We had no such option.

Frank walked into the backyard, a pretentiously delicate mug in his hand. He'd popped in and out of the House to check in on us, presumably to ensure we hadn't fallen off the posts or taken disqualifying breaks. I had no respect for a proctor who couldn't bother to keep vigil over the exams he'd decided were crucial for the House.

Malik, on the other hand, stood in front of us, his back to the east, arms crossed over his chest. He looked obviously tired, his eyes swollen with exhaustion, but he'd stayed with us. He'd watched over us. It was like a promise from father to children that even if he couldn't face the trials for us, he'd unwaveringly support us while we went through them.

This man was a Master of vampires.

He watched Frank suspiciously as he crossed the yard. "The sun is rising," Malik said. "If there's a point to this test, you should reach it now."

"Of course there's a point," Frank responded. "This is an endurance test. The endurance isn't merely standing on the pole; that's not exactly a complicated task. The endurance is standing on the pole in the sun."

Juliet and I exchanged a nervous glance. "But that will kill us," she said.

We were partially protected by the trees at the back of the yard, but as the sun rose, the rays of light would shift across the lawn, moving ever closer to where we stood . . . And Juliet was closer to those rays than I was.

"This is ridiculous," I said, and could hear the hysteria in my voice. "She's closer than I am. The sun will burn her before it ever reaches me."

"That was the luck of the draw," Frank said. "She drew the position she finds herself in. There is no one to blame for that."

But that simply wasn't true. Frank had directed us to our poles.

"I cannot believe the GP would condone such a thing," Malik said. "Not to any vampires who've taken oaths to their House, who've sworn to protect it."

Frank tilted his head at Malik. "You don't think facing the sun is an important skill for a vampire? You don't think it's a situation they may encounter?"

"God willing," Malik said, eyes narrowing, "should they ever face it, it would be at the hands of an enemy, not an organization that exists to protect them."

And that, I thought, encapsulated perfectly what I'd seen of the GP. It might have been established all those years ago to protect vampires, to organize Houses, and to provide order, but from what I'd seen of Darius West and this monster, it was only now concerned with proving a political point.

Maybe it was time to reconsider my involvement in the Red Guard. Maybe, now that Ethan was gone and Malik was under the gun, it was time to think about taking a step to protect all vampires, not just those in the House.

As the sun breached the horizon and light crossed the yard, the case in favor of RG membership grew stronger.

The ray of sunlight lengthened, deepened, reaching Juliet's post and crawling up the side. Horrified, I watched as the tips of her tennis shoes began to glow bright red.

"Juliet? Are you okay?"

Tears began to stream down her face, but she clenched her jaw and maintained her position in stoic silence. She must have been in tremendous pain, and still she stood atop her post, refusing to submit.

Her hunger also seemed to take its toll; her eyes silvered and her fangs extended, the predator awoken by pain, hunger, and exhaustion.

I looked back at Frank, who was sipping from his mug, completely unmoved by her agony. "You have to call a stop to this. Can't you see she's in pain?"

He just arched an arrogant eyebrow.

"Fine. If you won't do something, then I will. I'll resign from the test." I made a move to hop down from the post, but his words stopped me cold.

"Maintain your position, Merit. Maintain your position on that post, or your position as Sentinel will be revoked immediately. And the same goes for Juliet. If you cannot respect the importance of the common good over any individual vampire, neither of you deserve your positions."

A sob echoed from Juliet's corner of the lawn as I gaped at Frank. "You can't unmake me Sentinel. Ethan gave me that position. Only Malik can make that call."

"Oh, but I can," Frank said. "It's my responsibility to get this House in order. A vampire who voluntarily withdraws from the testing—who refuses to hold herself to the standards of her brothers and sisters in arms—is not a vampire who has the best interests of the House foremost in mind."

I looked over at Juliet, who was shaking ferociously at the pain, her hands wrapped around her waist as she sobbed.

"Juliet, get down from there!"

"I c-c-can't," she stuttered out. "I can't not be a guard. It's all I've known. This House is my life."

She wouldn't have much of one left if I didn't act. The punishment was unfair, but it was more unfair for Juliet to suffer doubly— the burns of the rising sun and the loss of her position in the House.

For as long as I was able to do it—even if only a few more minutes—my job was to protect the House and its vampires. If I could so easy dismiss the value of her life, I shouldn't have been Sentinel anyway.

It was an easy call, but that didn't mean the repercussions would be easy to bear. Ethan had named me Sentinel. Ethan had Commended me into the House and thrown me into the position. And while I may not have been ready to accept it at the time, it was my position now. Mine to have. Mine to protect.

And just as with my Cadogan medal, mine to forfeit.

I found Malik's face in the crowd, and when he nodded at me, I raised my hands in the air. "I forfeit," I said. "I forfeit. Juliet wins. Get her down!"

There was a mad rush to Juliet's pole. Luc reached up and grabbed her and carried her into the House, followed by a stream of vampires seeking the cover of shade. The sun was rising, and my faculties were deserting me. I was shaking with exhaustion, but I managed to hop down without falling into the nearing ray of light—only to face Frank, who stood before me with a gleeful expression on his face.

"There are simpler ways to get me to resign," I told him, and enjoyed seeing the smile wiped from his face. He'd been the one who'd ensured I was on the safest pole, that I'd have to forfeit in order to protect someone else from being burned. I guess it was a compliment that he thought I'd sacrifice myself . . . and that he thought me dangerous enough that he'd rather leave the House without a Sentinel than leave me in that position.

"I don't know what you're talking about."

"I doubt that," I said, "but that's between you and your conscience." I hurried toward Malik, who now stood in the doorway of the House, ensuring everyone made it inside safely.

Frank was the last one inside, and he made it in just as the sun filled the backyard with light. Thankfully, the House's shutters were already down.

I stood inside the cool, quiet of the kitchen for a moment with my eyes closed, savoring the darkness.

When I opened my eyes, Malik was the only vampire in sight.

"I'm sorry," I told him. "It may not have been the right thing to do for the House—to forfeit my position—but I couldn't just stand there and let her take it."

"It was the only right thing to do," he assured. "That said, with Cabot here . . ."

He didn't need to finish the point. I couldn't stand Sentinel as long as Frank—and the GP—had control of the House.

Oh, how things had changed. In a few short months, Ethan had lost his life and a new Master had been installed. And summarily replaced. The Ombud's office had been dismantled. I'd been stripped of my identity as a Sentinel.

But just as there'd been no choice those months ago when Ethan had named me to the position in the first place, there was no choice now but to accept the change and deal with it with as much grace as possible.

Even if I acted alone, I would act with bravery. A Sentinel in heart and mind, even if not officially.

I nodded. "I understand."

"Ethan would have been proud of you today, Merit. I am proud of you today, as are the other vampires of this House. You played Cabot's game the only respectable way it could have been played, even if the outcome was predetermined."

"The result's the same, though. The House is left without a Sentinel."

Malik smiled slyly. "The forfeit extended only to your current position. You cannot stand Sentinel, at least not for the time being. But he placed no restrictions on your service as a guard."

Although exhaustion was beginning to wear me down, I managed a smile. "Very creative, Liege."

"I have my moments."

I hobbled back to my room, nearly wiped unconscious by the sun, and into the cool, crisp sheets and comforting dark that awaited me there. I wasn't too exhausted to cry when my head hit the pillow, pent up rage and frustration and grief escaping now that I'd managed to finish the testing.

Grief, because in the matter of an evening I'd lost my connections to Ethan and the House: the bond that we'd shared when he named me Sentinel and the medal I'd worn as a symbol of my oaths.

I'd still stand guard for the House, and there was no denying the importance of that role. But it felt like another little bit of Ethan had been torn away.

And that hurt as much as anything else.

CHAPTER SIXTEEN

A HOUSE DIVIDED

I woke up from a thankfully dreamless sleep in the same dark mood I'd been in when I'd fallen unconscious some hours ago. I considered playing sick and hiding in bed under the covers all day, but that wasn't going to solve my problems or the city's.

When I was up and showered, I also considered calling Mallory. I had no doubt she was stressed about exams, but I wasn't sure if letting her hermit while she studied was the best thing to do. On the other hand, she specifically told me not to bother her until she was done with exams.

That still stung.

Sure, it wasn't the first time we'd had a disagreement. There'd been a boy she dated who I'd thought was obnoxious, and she tended to give my parents more credit than I did. We'd grown apart when I'd been made a vampire and hadn't adjusted gracefully to my new life. Her apprenticeship training in Schaumburg hadn't done much for our social schedule.

But we'd always managed to get through. I could only hope

this time was no different, that even with magic and exams between us, we'd manage to find each other again.

After tossing the phone in my hands for a few minutes, I decided not to call. If she really needed space, I'd give it to her. God knows she'd have done the same thing for me.

But while she could avoid me, Catcher couldn't. I dialed up his cell phone and caught him in the car.

"On the way to your grandfather's house," he said.

"Still officing unofficially?"

"Unless we hear something different from the city, which seems extraordinarily unlikely, 'unofficial' is our permanent gig. Unfortunately," he added as a horn honked in the background, "traffic to your grandfather's is much worse than to the office. It takes me twice as long to get there."

"Isn't there an El stop by his house?"

"I prefer my car," he flatly said. "What's happening at Cadogan House tonight?"

"Well, due to unfortunate events, I'm no longer standing Sentinel." I filled him in on Frank's quality testing and my forced failure.

"Classy," he said. "Makes Darius West look like a total peach."

"I wouldn't go quite that far, but you've got something there. Have you had a chance to talk to Simon?"

"I have. He's as mystified as we are. He says he's heard nothing about the *Maleficium* and that it's safe and sound in Nebraska. Out of an abundance of caution, the Order's established a committee to look into things, and they're on their way. He also thinks Tate's bluffing, and he put some stock into your lemon and sugar theory. He says the new 'forensic magic' recognizes trace magical evidence like odor."

Catcher's tone screamed "sarcastic," but there was also a hint of "jealous" in there. Catcher hadn't been a member of the Order for some time, so it stood to reason he wouldn't be up to date on all the latest information and techniques. He clearly had unresolved issues about the Order. Maybe buried beneath his irritation that Mallory was learning about magic from Simon was a little magical jealousy.

"How long until Mal's done with exams?"

"Couple of days, but the schedule is fluid. Simon's apparently trying to keep her on her toes. Listen, I'm just pulling into the driveway. I'll call you if there's news."

"Appreciate it," I said, and he hung up. I had no doubt I'd hear from him again. If I'd learned anything in my months as a vampire, it was that drama was in unlimited supply.

I found a stack of library books outside my door again, all referencing unexplained historical events. The librarian seemed to think Amelia Earhart's disappearance and the Bermuda Triangle were related to our sky and water problems. I was sitting on the floor, waist-deep in magical conspiracy theories, when my phone rang.

Saved by the bell, I thought, and pulled it out. When I saw Jonah's number on the screen, I popped it open.

"Hi," I carefully said, not sure of his mood since we hadn't spoken since the kiss—and nervous that he was calling to relay another crisis. I really could use a break.

"What are you doing?" he asked.

"Reading. What are you doing?"

"I'm at Benson's. Get your ass down here and buy me a drink."

Benson's was the Grey House bar, located across the street from Wrigley Field.

"I'm not going to buy you a drink."

"I'm pretty sure I remember you owing me a drink. Especially after you totally denied me when I poured out my heart to you."

I couldn't help but smile, and appreciated that he'd broken the ice. "I don't recall it happening that way."

"Then you would be incorrect."

"I'm pretty sure you're hallucinating," I said, but glanced down at the books and decided I couldn't read any more crazy theories tonight. I needed a change of scenery, even if that change started with my buying an apologetic round for my partner.

"I'll be there in five," I told him, then flipped the phone closed and slid it back into my pocket. I grabbed my jacket, gave Kelley a heads-up, and headed out.

Benson's was housed in a narrow building that faced the back of Wrigley Field. Stadium seats had been installed on the roof so Cubs fans without tickets could get a view of the action from the even-cheaper seats. The narrow bar was also crammed with as many tables as the owners could fit. This was prime Cubs' rooting territory, after all, and folks who couldn't fit into Wrigley still wanted to be as close to the action as possible. The bar could get stuffy on game days, but there was definitely something to be said for squeezing into a bar with close friends (and total strangers) to root for the Cubbies. Benson's even had a signature Cubs-related drink—a shot layered with blue and red booze. It tasted like cough syrup, but we drank it for the color—not the taste.

Benson's was filled with Cubs memorabilia, and although the Cubs' season had been over for some time, the bar was still packed tonight. Where better to spend the end of the world than with your closest friends and your favorite liquor? Since humans weren't aware the bar was affiliated with Grey House, or vampires generally, the clientele was a mix of humans, vampires, and probably some supernaturals I didn't even know existed.

I waded through bodies until I caught a glimpse of Jonah standing in a back corner. He wore a short-sleeved V-neck T-shirt over jeans and a couple days' worth of stubble. It would have been a lie to deny that he was handsome, and when he looked up to watch me walk across the bar, I could have imagined—in another time and place—approaching him in a bar for an altogether different reason.

"Hey," he said when I reached him. "You managed not to get captured by malcontents. Well done."

There was an irritatingly attractive twinkle in his eye, but since he'd had a good attitude about the kiss, I decided to let him keep it. "Ha ha," I said. "And yes. I did manage not to get captured by malcontents."

Jonah gestured to the man beside him, who was a little shorter than Jonah and had a crop of platinum blond hair. "Merit, Jack," he said. "Jack is a House guard. We've been friends for years. Jack, Merit."

Jack, whose bright blue eyes were lined in kohl, looked me over. "You are—exactly what I expected," he said, in a voice that sang faintly of the South.

I smiled hesitantly. "Thank you, I think?"

"It's totally a compliment. You're adorable, and I love the bangs."

There was something completely disarming about Jack. His smile was huge, and he gave the impression he didn't bother saying things he didn't mean, which made the compliment that much more meaningful.

But I wasn't sure how I felt about the fact he knew what I looked like. Had Jonah been talking about me?

"Thank you," I said. "I hope I didn't interrupt anything?"

"We were talking about double swords," Jonah said, then reached into his back pocket for his wallet. "You need a drink?"

"Not yet, thanks. What are double swords?"

"Using two katanas at a time," Jack explained. "I think it's a circus technique. Completely impractical and used only for show and intimidation."

"And I think our friend Jack here is full of shit," Jonah added, "and double katanas are the next big trend in martial arts training."

"I swear to God you are stubborn," Jack said, rolling his eyes. "When was the last time you were engaged in a battle and happened to have two swords handy?"

"I would if they were standard weaponry."

"Exactly my point," Jack said, offering me a wink. I offered back a smile.

"Look," Jonah said, "I'm talking about scope. And on the battlefield, anything goes."

"Including double swords?" I wondered.

"Including double swords, my single-katana-ed friend."

Jack made a sound of doubt, but clinked his bottle of beer good-naturedly against Jonah's. "I suppose if all else fails we can skip the double and triple swords and go right for the quads."

"*Hooah*," they belted out together, and clinked their bottles again.

Guys were just complete mysteries to me, and I stared blankly back at both of them.

"You know about the Four Swords right?" Jonah asked.

I shook my head.

"Can I give you a lecture about being a total noob?"

"I really wish you wouldn't. Educate me, but only if you can do it without editorial commentary."

Jack grinned. "I knew I was going to like you. I knew it."

"Once upon a time," Jonah began, "in a kingdom far, far away, lived a Samurai. He believed that he was destined to travel the world and assist those who needed him. As a Samurai, he traveled with four swords at his side, each one representing one of the four elements in the world—air, fire, earth, and water."

There was a lot of that going around these days.

"The Samurai traveled the world to educate others about swordcraft and eventually landed in Europe."

"This was the Samurai who trained vampires how to fight with katanas," I said, spoiling his punch line.

"It was," Jonah said. "But did you know Scott was the vampire who met the Samurai and introduced the craft to everyone else? And that those same four swords are now hanging in Grey House?"

I looked between Jonah and Jack. "Is that true?"

Jack touched my arm. "That story's true, but don't believe him when he starts in on how he saved all the orphans in Kansas City the time Godzilla ravaged it."

"It was a retirement village and an escaped mountain lion," Jonah corrected. If he was telling the truth, I figured that was dramatic enough.

Jack waved away the correction and checked his watch. "I have to run. If the world's ending, I want to be in the arms of a loved one when it happens. Or at least Paul," he added with a grumble.

"The end of the world would solve the Paul problem," Jonah offered. "So would breaking up with him."

Jack made a dubious sound. "He's already promised to haunt me in hell if it comes down to it. And a breakup would go over just as well."

"Shut up or nut up, Jack."

"I will cut you," Jack said with a smile, pointing a fierce finger in Jonah's face. But his expression dissolved. "See you tomorrow night, hoss. Quarterlies will be on your desk."

"Appreciated," Jonah said.

Jack held out his arms, and then embraced me in a hug. "Lovely to meet you, Merit. Take care of our captain," he whispered, leaving me with a blush.

"Relationship trouble?" I wondered, hoping Jonah hadn't heard that comment, as we watched Jack disappear into the crowd.

"Never-ending drama," Jonah said. "I am, as you might have realized, not a fan of drama. Jack has a much higher tolerance. Paul's tolerance, unfortunately, is even higher."

"Jack seems like a stand-up guy, the drama notwithstanding."

"Jack is loyalty personified," Jonah said. "I appreciate loyalty."

"It's a great character trait."

"I have a sense you haven't seen much of it lately."

The insight was right on—and a little scary for it. "I'm not Sentinel anymore."

He froze. "What?"

I told him about Frank, about the testing, about everything that had gone down the night before.

"I'm a guard now," I admitted, then frowned. "Well, I'm acting as one. I haven't been officially appointed, as far as I'm aware. Either way, I'll be honest—it feels like a demotion."

"I could see that." Then his smile went a little too self-satisfied for my comfort. "As a guard captain, does that make me your superior?"

"It most definitely does not," I said, pointing a finger into his chest. "I need no additional bosses in my hierarchy, thank you very much."

"Just checking. Anyway, I'm sorry Cadogan's going through this crap. If not you, it would have been us or Navarre. The GP's just . . . well, you know my theory on that."

I opened my mouth, then closed it again, debating what to say and how to get out what I needed to get out. I settled on a segue. "Can we talk about something?"

"Is it about my effervescence?"

"It's about the RG."

His eyebrows lifted in interest. "You do know how to get a boy's attention."

I looked away, then back at him again. "I think it's time I take some steps to protect the House. The GP is putting my colleagues, my friends, in danger. It's not right, and if there's something I can do to help, I'll do it. So, I'd like to join the Red Guard."

Jonah was quiet for a moment. "That's the only reason you should say yes. If you'd said yes for any other reason, I'd have said no."

I looked back at him. "Really?"

"It's a twenty-year commitment, the RG, and it's a serious one. We don't want people who join because they have vendettas. We don't want people who join because they hate authority. We want protectors. Guardians. People who recognize injustice in the system and are moved to stop it."

"Those are good reasons."

"They are. And now I know your reasons are similar. I'll need to make a phone call and to pass word up the chain, but for all intents and purposes, you're in." He smiled down at me, and this time there was something more serious in his eyes. Not flirty. Not friendly. *Partnership.*

"We will work together," he said. "It's a close relationship, and has to be a trusting one. Can you trust me?"

I looked at him for a moment, not wanting to give an answer without having given it earnest thought. I considered what I knew of him, and I considered the times he'd already had my back. At a rave in Streeterville, when we'd saved a young human. At Clau-

dia's, when he'd stepped in front of me to keep me out of harm's
way.

He might have had his reservations, but he'd gone all in when
it counted.

"I trust you," I said.

He nodded, and offered his hand. "Then I am deeply honored
to welcome you, Merit, to the Red Guard."

"That's it?" Not that I'd imagined a sash and a parade, but it
seemed worthy of at least a ceremony or a pinning or something.

"We'll put together a more formal ceremony after I advise
Noah. That'll take a little time to arrange. In the meantime . . ."
He wiggled his fingers, waiting for a handshake.

My promise already made, we shook on it.

In doing so, I pledged away my presumed loyalty to the GP.
Frank might have intended to reduce my influence over the
House. In fact, he'd only managed to bring me closer to my fellow
Novitiates and make me fight harder for them.

"This looks cozy."

We both looked behind us, where a tall, dark-haired vampire
stood, arms crossed, barely hidden malice in his expression.

"Hello, Morgan," I said, thinking Paul would probably appreciate his sense of dramatics.

Morgan Greer, Master of Navarre House, was unquestionably
handsome—alluring in a dark, seductive way. His sense of humor
balanced out his rakish good looks, but his immaturity negated
both, in my opinion. By all accounts, he had everything a Master
could wish for—health, looks, money, and power. But he had the
attitude of a sulking, bitter teenager.

Tonight he wore a button-up shirt over snug jeans and boots.
His dark, wavy hair hit his shoulders, and he looked like he hadn't

shaved in a few weeks. His cheeks were supermodel gaunt, which added a sharp edge to his appeal.

I hadn't spoken with him since the deaths of Ethan and Celina; I wasn't sure how he felt about either, but I guessed the emotions would be mixed, at best. And tonight, he was in a position I hadn't seen before—he had a date.

The girl beside him was tall and thin, with long, dark hair and an exotic face. She'd paired dark leggings and an oversized top (undoubtedly from some couture boutique) with five-inch heels and chandelier earrings. She looked like a model on a go-see, and I felt a small pang of jealousy before remembering that I couldn't care less.

His gaze grazed me, then Jonah, landing on me again with obvious disgust. "You don't waste any time, do you?"

Jonah must have felt the quick flash of magic I threw into the air, because he put a warning hand on my arm. I gave his hand a quick pat of reassurance.

"We're working," I said, trying to maintain my composure and not get into a screaming match with an emotionally stunted vampire.

"I'm sure. What's the occasion?"

There was enough snark in his voice that I couldn't tell if he was trying to harass me, or was honestly clueless about events in Chicago.

"Surely you didn't miss the bit about the lake turning black and the sky turning red?"

"That has nothing to do with us."

Ah, so that was his game—willful ignorance. He knew the facts, but he was playing GP pet and pretending it had nothing to do with vampires.

"Just because vampires haven't caused the problems doesn't mean we don't have a role in fixing them."

"Why should we? Why shouldn't we focus on our own Houses?"

Apparently proud of his answer, the girl at his side offered me a cocky eyebrow.

"Because if the city falls," Jonah said, "the Houses fall with it."

"Chicago isn't going to fall," Morgan said.

Jonah stepped forward. "Because the other Houses take up the slack." The implication in his statement was clear—Navarre wasn't doing its part.

Morgan's cheeks flushed. "You have no idea what my House is or isn't doing for this city."

"That's exactly my point," Jonah said. "We have no idea, although there's certainly nothing we can see right now."

"Recall your place, vampire," Morgan bit out. It was the same warning Ethan had offered to Morgan when Morgan got mouthy. Unlike Ethan, Morgan didn't quite carry it off.

"With all due respect, Mr. Greer, I owe my allegiance to Scott and Grey House. If you have concerns about my obedience, you can take it up with him."

Morgan was obviously fuming, sending plumes of irritated magic into the air. But beneath that irritation was something different. A strain of fear, maybe? That would bear a little investigating, but later. One crisis at a time.

Apparently done with the reunion, Morgan turned on his heel and walked away. His girlfriend stayed behind and gave me a none-too-flattering visual evaluation.

"In case there was any question," she said, "you should keep your hands off him."

"Off Morgan?"

She gave me a bitchy head-bop.

"Rest assured, Morgan's not even on my radar. But good luck with him." You'll need it, I thought, the first time he has a bout of jealousy or starts pouting about some perceived slight.

It's not that I thought Morgan was a bad guy, but the boy loved drama.

The date muttered something unflattering. Being the bigger person, I merely smiled back at her. But the fantasy reaction still played out in my mind—the one in which I put her on the floor with only a finger at one of her pressure points and held her there until she apologized for the slight.

Maybe Ethan had been right. Maybe being a vampire was going to wring the humanity right out of me.

After another few seconds of nasty looks, she turned and disappeared into the crowd. Jonah and I stood there for a moment staring after her. This time, instead of waiting for his strike, I played offense.

"We only dated for a few weeks."

He smiled a little. "I know about the bargain," he said. "Noah and Scott were in the crowd."

I'd forgotten about that. Noah and Scott had both been present when Morgan had shown up at Cadogan House, frantic that a Cadogan vampire had threatened Celina. In my first real act as Sentinel, I'd stepped forward and calmed him down at the point of my sword. He'd submitted, but only on the agreement that I allowed him to court me.

I'd given in, and although Morgan could be incredibly charming, he was much too immature to be a contender.

"How is Noah these days?" I wondered. Noah was a guard himself, but I hadn't heard from him since Jonah had become my primary contact. He was also the de facto leader of Chicago's Rogue vampires, those who weren't tied to a particular House.

"Busy. The Rogues always get nervous when the Houses are in trouble. They fear GP retaliation against them, or internment, if that's the way it goes."

"Reason number four to join the RG," I muttered.

Amusement in his eyes, Jonah slid me a glance. "What were one through three?"

"Helping the Houses, having a reliable partner, and those 'Midnight High School' T-shirts. Do I get one of those?"

"Of course. You'll just have to find somewhere private to keep it."

I hadn't considered that—that there would be RG gear, materials, documents I'd need to keep secreted away even within my own room. I'd have to give that some thought.

Jonah rubbed his hands together. "How about a drink now?"

"Yes, please," I agreed, but before I could place an order, I got a very bad vibe. The building vibrated a little. Only for a moment, but I'd have sworn I felt something.

"Did you feel that?"

"Feel what?"

I froze, and after a moment, wondered if I'd imagined it. And as I stood there waiting, I happened to glance at a cup of water on a bar table beside us. The rumbling started deep and low, sending ripples across the water.

"Jonah—"

"I saw that," he said, then paused. "Maybe it's just really big dinosaurs."

"Or really big magic," I finished. "I think we need to get outside."

I could see in his face that he didn't want to believe anything was out there, but he had a duty to perform, so he was willing to take a look. "Let's go."

We scooted through the bodies and tables—the humans and vampires apparently oblivious to the rumblings—and stepped into the cool November air . . .

And saw nothing.

Partygoers walked up and down the street. Traffic was light, but there were a few cars out and about.

"I know I felt something," I said, scanning the street back and forth.

I took another step forward and closed my eyes, letting down some of the defenses I used to keep the mass of information that flooded into a vampire's brain at bay. For a moment, there was nothing . . . Just the typical smells and sounds of a fall night in Chicago. The air smelled of people and food and grease. Dirt from the ballpark. Smoke from the traffic.

My eyes closed, my head tipped back, I felt the rumble again, the ground vibrating dizzyingly beneath me.

"Merit!" Jonah yelled. I opened my eyes just in time to be snatched backward as he wrapped an arm around my waist and pulled me against him.

The asphalt split, a twenty-feet wide mountain of earth erupting into the middle of the street in front of us.

CHAPTER SEVENTEEN

I FEEL THE EARTH MOVE

"What the hell is that?" he asked, as we watched this new mountain burst through the middle of Wrigleyville. The asphalt around it cracked and moved, stopping traffic and turning over cars on the sides of the road. Car alarms and honking horns began to ripple down the sidewalk as chaos erupted, people streaming from the bars to scream at the bubble of earth in front of them.

Both too stunned to move, we stood on the sidewalk, Jonah's arm still around me, staring at it. I risked a glance at the sky, and saw exactly what I'd expected to see.

It was flaming red again, the sky flashing as lightning lit the clouds from within. And I'd bet good money the lakes and rivers were back to black and were sucking in magic.

"This is earth," I said, foreboding collecting heavily in my abdomen. "I talked to Tate. The problems occur when someone mixes good and evil magic and the balance of the elements is thrown off in the process."

"We'll leave aside the fact that you went to see Tate alone

again," Jonah darkly said. "For now. Bigger point—whoever or whatever is responsible for these problems is at it again."

Before I could answer him, the rumbling began again.

"Jonah," I warned, and he released me, scanning the street for the next eruption.

"I feel it," he agreed, and we watched, horrified, as another mountain punched through the sidewalk in the front of a real estate office down the block a bit. Before we could react, a third followed, a couple of blocks down the road.

"They're still coming."

"And they're headed toward Grey House," he frantically said, pulling out his phone. He dialed some number, but then cursed. "I can't get through."

"Go," I told him. "Go back to your House. Take your vampires with you if you think you need help."

When he looked down at me, for the first time, I saw fear in his eyes.

"They'll bury us with this, Merit. They will bury us."

The heavy weight in my stomach didn't disagree, but that's not what he needed to hear right now.

"Work the problem," I told him. "Work the problem in front of you, because that's the only thing you can do. Don't worry about the next one until this one's solved." I squeezed his arm. "Things will get worse. Consider it an inevitability and know that I'll be there to help work the problem when it comes."

For a second, he closed his eyes, relief obvious on his face. Maybe he'd needed a partner for a long time. Maybe Jonah had needed someone to trust, as well.

"I'll be at the House, and I'll make my way back here once I'm confident things are in hand."

I gave him a nod, and he ran back into Benson's to grab troops. I stared back at the destruction in front of me, unsure what to do.

"Oh, my God!" someone screamed. "There's a woman at the top!"

I snapped my head in the direction of the screams. The third eruption down the street had popped up squarely beneath a sedan, and the occupant—a woman I guessed was in her late twenties—had climbed out of the car and was perched atop the mountain of asphalt and soil. That mountain was probably forty feet tall—the height of a four-story building.

Within a split second, her foot slipped, and she was dangling over an edge of cantilevered asphalt with nothing below her but vehicles and street.

I started running.

"I'm coming!" I told her, as a crowd of humans gathered below, hands over mouths, pointing at the sky. "Just hang on!"

While thunder rumbled and lightning flashed, I climbed up the old-fashioned way—hand over hand. And the going wasn't easy. The hill was covered by chunks of broken asphalt over loose dirt and rock, so the entire mountain was slippery. It was impossible to move forward without sliding back a little, and I lost my foothold every few seconds.

The woman screamed again, clearly terrified, so with dirty nails and slipping boots, I kept my eyes on the dirt in front of me and moved, ever so slowly upward, finally mounting the plateau of asphalt.

I kicked my legs over the side, and when I was sure it was stable enough, crawled on hands and knees toward the girl. I could see her fingers—dirty with bleeding nails—on the edge of the asphalt.

"I'm here," I told her. "I'm here." I belly-crawled to the edge and glanced over it. We were forty feet from the ground. Assuming I remembered how to jump safely, the fall wouldn't bother me. But at this height, she'd wouldn't be so lucky.

I found her wrist and grabbed on.

She sobbed and loosened her grip on the asphalt with that hand, which would make It easier for me to pull her up, but gave me the burden of all of her weight. It's not that she was heavy—she was a very petite girl—but we were both dangling over a square of asphalt connected only by our fingers wrapped around sweaty, dirty skin.

"Don't let go," I told her.

Her face reddened with the effort, but she managed a nod. I had the strength to lift her up, but her skin was damp with sweat, and my fingers were slipping. This wasn't working.

"What's your name?"

"Miss—Missy," she stuttered out. "Missy."

"Missy, I need you to do something for me, okay?" I wrapped another hand around her wrist. Her hand slipped another centimeter, and a bolt of lightning lit the sky.

She screamed, and I saw the pulse of fear in her eyes. "Oh, God. Oh, God. Oh, God."

"Missy, listen to me. Missy. Missy!" I repeated her name until she met my gaze again. "I can help you up here, but I need you to help me, too, okay? I need you to give me your other hand."

Her gaze skittered to her ragged fingernails, which were barely gripping the edge of the asphalt. "I can't."

"You can," I assured her. "You absolutely can. And I'm strong enough to grab you and pull you up, but I need your help okay?"

She slipped another centimeter, and as the crowd below us screamed, I fought back my own rising panic.

"On three," I told her. "I want you to give me your left hand. You can do this. I know you can. Okay?"

She shook her head. "I'm not strong enough. I'm not strong enough."

I'm not sure if she slipped or let go, but I reached out and grabbed her hand just as her fingertips lost contact with the black-top. With both wrists in hand, I braced myself and pulled her up and over the ledge.

She immediately wrapped her arms around me. "Oh, God, thank you. Thank you."

"You're welcome," I said, helping her take a seat on the ledge. She embraced me in a hug, tears flowing now, and I let her cry until she'd calmed down enough to let me pull away.

"You did really good," I told her.

"I still have to get down," she sniffed out. "I was only going to get milk. From the store. Just milk. It's the vampires, isn't it? This is their fault?"

My chest went cold, but I pushed down the burst of anger and my urge to argue with her. This was neither the time, nor the place.

I glanced around. Firemen with ladders were moving toward our mountain. They made eye contact with me, and motioned that they'd be up.

I looked around the rest of Wrigleyville, which looked like a disaster area—dunes of dirt and asphalt and cars riddling the street, people bleeding, dust and smoke everywhere.

I looked back at Missy. "There are two firemen on the way to get you down," I said, pointing at them. "Will you be okay here until they get here? I need to get back to work. There might be other people who need help."

"Of course. God, thank you, thank you."

"You're welcome." I carefully stood up again, but looked back at her. "I'm a vampire," I told her. "We didn't cause this, but we're trying to stop it." I smiled kindly. "Okay?"

Her face went a little more pale, but she nodded. "Okay, okay. Sure. Thank you."

"You're welcome." With a final smile, I took the first truly, truly awful step that turned into the oh-my-God-fucking-fantastic jump back to the ground.

I hit the ground in a crouch again, one hand on the ground, and lifted my gaze to stare back into Morgan's. He stood at the edge of the crowd, his clubbing attire still perfectly clean. Apparently, he hadn't bothered to help.

I shook my head ruefully, and hoped he was embarrassed by his inaction. And if he wasn't, if there was some deeper, better reason for his inaction than his refusal to dirty his fancy clothes, I was going to have to investigate that, too. I was going to have to figure out what the hell was going on in Navarre House. But, again, that was a problem for another day.

I stood up and looked around. Morgan might not be willing to act, but Ethan had taught me better. Even if I had to go it alone, I wasn't going to stand by and let someone else do my job for me.

I walked around the hill of dirt and got back to work.

The earth stopped rumbling, but there were dozens of cars overturned or abandoned and innumerable tons of earth in the middle of Wrigleyville. The architectural damage wasn't extensive, but the roads and sidewalks in four blocks of Wrigleyville were beat to hell. And it wasn't the only one; there were pockets of damage in neighborhoods across the city.

Thankfully, I hadn't heard of any fatalities, but the injuries and damage to cars, roads, and property were going to be bad enough for us. I was filthy, cold, and as the scope of the destruction—and the possibility of severe consequences for vampires—became clear, I grew wearier.

This wasn't our fault. There was no evidence vampires had any role in what had gone on in Wrigleyville. But I hadn't been able to stop it, and that weight sat heavily on my shoulders and in my gut.

I'd investigated and interviewed, hypothesized and theorized . . . and I'd come up empty-handed. Tate knew too much for me to dismiss his involvement, even if I wasn't entirely sure what that was. And while I thought Simon was the key to the *Maleficium*, I couldn't get close enough to him to find out.

That was going to have to change.

I needed a little bit of time and space from the chaos, so I walked up the street a few blocks until the sounds and smells of new, damp earth began to fade.

I reached the barricades the CPD had established at the edge of the destruction, and was ruing the fact that my grandfather could no longer show up at these events in an official capacity, when I stopped short.

A few feet away from the barricade, my father stood on the sidewalk beneath a streetlight in dress pants, a button-up shirt, and a MERIT PROPERTIES windbreaker. He was supervising two men who were unloading plastic-wrapped packs of water bottles onto the sidewalk, where a woman I recognized as an admin in my father's office handed them out.

I walked toward them, and waited until the workers left my father alone. "What are you doing here?"

"Public service," he said. "The office is just up the road, and we happened to have the truck ready for a conference at a building in Naperville. We decided it could be put to a better use, so we hurried down here."

The reason might have been legitimate, but I still questioned his motives. I couldn't help it; my father brought out the worst in me. I'd always been a stranger where my family was concerned, and the business with Ethan hadn't helped. My father thought he'd been doing me a favor—gifting me with an immortality I hadn't asked for—but that didn't make it any less of a violation.

He gestured behind me, and I glanced back. Dusty and scraped men and women stood or sat on curbs nearby sipping water.

"This was a nice thought," I said. "But you can't use bridges that were burned a long time ago."

He used a box cutter to slice through the plastic wrap on a new bundle of bottles and passed one over to me. "That's the difference between you and me: I refuse to believe bridges were burned. Every moment is a new opportunity."

I accepted the bottle of water, and let that stand in for any additional thanks. I walked across the street to the curb and sat down, my muscles aching from the work.

I'd taken a single sip when Jonah sat down beside me. He looked as filthy as I did, streaks of mud and dirt on his jeans and T-shirt.

"Everything okay at Grey House?" I asked.

"Yeah. The damage didn't extend that far." He scanned the street, eyes narrowing when he saw the truck. "Did your father suddenly become charitable?"

"Not without an ulterior motive. A suggestion?"

Jonah took the bottle of water from me and took a long drink. "What's that?"

"While you're busy having my back, don't be surprised when family members are there to stab me in it."

"That's what partners are for," he assured. "Well, that, and getting you out of Dodge when things get dicey." He gestured toward some humans on the other side of the street who were beginning to look at us askew. Maybe they recognized us as vampires, maybe they didn't. Either way, they weren't thrilled about the destruction in their neighborhood, and it looked like they were looking for someone to blame.

"We'll go to Grey House," he said, a hand at my elbow to help me up. "We'll convene there and we'll make a plan and we'll get this thing figured out."

"You think it will be that easy?"

"Not even close," he said. "But it's RG rule number one: Make a plan."

I guess a plan was better than nothing.

Scott Grey's vampires were taking shifts assisting in the aftermath of the destruction, and he'd set up food and aid stations in the House's open atrium for any vampires in the vicinity who needed a break. He also gave me a quiet spot to give Catcher a call.

"How are things up north?" he asked.

"Pretty bad," I admitted, and gave him the lay of the land . . . and the magic. "It looks like Claudia was right and we're looking at elemental magic. Water. Air—"

"And now earth," Catcher finished.

"Yeah. I didn't see any hint this time that Tate was involved, but his magical imbalance theory is looking more plausible. And if he's right, that means someone has the *Maleficium*. I want to talk to Simon."

"And your suggestion for getting past Order bitchiness?"

"Remind them the world might be ending? Tell them we think the *Maleficium* is at work. Have my grandfather call them, or tell them the former mayor—who may or may not be some kind of ancient magical being—may or may not be trying to herald in a new era of evil. Tell them whatever you want. But make them understand."

He murmured something about women and hormones, but when he hung up the phone, I decided I'd made my point.

Jonah stepped into the doorway. "Find anything out?"

"That goddamned bureaucracies are killing me this week. Catcher's giving me trouble about setting up a meeting with Simon."

"We could probably try Tate again, too."

I didn't want to do that, but I was running out of options.

I spent a few minutes giving Kelley and Malik an update, and got the text just as I'd finished: SIMON. ONE HOUR. JENKINS SUPPLY CO.

"Jenkins Supply Company?" Jonah asked when I showed him the message. "What's that?"

"I have no clue," I answered, tucking the phone away again. "Let's go find out."

Jenkins Supply Company, it turned out, was a hardware store not far from Hyde Park. Before heading in, we stood outside for a moment just taking in the building. It was a mom and pop store, with a sign above the door in old-fashioned, red cursive letters. There weren't many cars in the lot, but the lights were still on, so we headed inside.

Like most hardware stores, it smelled like rubber and paint and wood. An older man with white hair and square glasses tidied the area near a cash register, and he nodded at us as we entered.

We offered smiles and moved past him into an aisle of cold weather gear—shovels, ice melt, gloves, and snowblowers. All the necessities of a Chicago winter.

There was no immediate sign of Simon, but there was a lingering trail of magic in the store. I motioned to Jonah, and followed it like a bloodhound.

We found Simon and Mallory together in an aisle with small tools—hammers, screwdrivers, that kind of thing. They were loading items into a basket.

Jonah and I exchanged a glance, then made our way down the aisle.

Simon looked up as we walked toward him. He wore a polo

shirt and jeans, and looked completely innocuous. But there was no mistaking the concern in his expression. Was it concern about what was going on—or because he'd been caught?

Mallory also looked worse for wear; exams had clearly taken a toll. She looked tired, and her T-shirt and skinny jeans seemed baggier than usual. I always gained weight during exams—too many late night pizzas and ice cream breaks. She smiled a little at me, then crossed her arms, hiding her hands. She barely made eye contact.

My stomach balled with nerves. Maybe Simon did know something about the *Maleficium*—and she couldn't get away to tell us.

"How bad is it out there?" Simon asked.

"Pretty bad," I said. "The cleanup is going to take a while."

"There were no fatalities, right?"

"None," Jonah confirmed. "Minor injuries and major property damage. What are you doing here?"

"Gathering supplies," he said, then gestured at Mallory. "Exams are pass-fail, and the Order won't allow exams to be suspended. If we stop, she fails. But we were thinking we could use the last exam to help clean up. Move mountains, as it were."

Curious, I peeked into Mallory's basket. It held candles, salt, and a couple of thick construction pencils. Nothing dangerous, at least from what I could tell, and all stuff that looked pretty witchy. The kind of things you might have used to work a spell you found on the Internet.

"We think they're following an elemental pattern," Jonah said. "Water, air, now earth. Do you know what might be causing it?"

"I've been researching," Simon said. "And I know Catcher has, too. I haven't found anything discussing these kinds of problems."

"What about the Order?"

Simon and Mallory shared a glance, and then Simon looked

around worriedly as if he expected someone to burst through the door after him.

"The Order's taken a hard line," Simon said, leaning forward conspiratorially, and there was no mistaking the fear in his eyes. "They think there's old magic involved—magic that existed before the Order was even organized. That's not their territory, and they don't want anything to do with it."

Awesome. Denial was totally going to help me right now. But I pressed forward, the Order be damned. "What about the *Maleficium*?"

"Don't say that aloud," Simon whispered. "That's dangerous stuff. The Order would go ballistic if they even heard the word mentioned."

"Fine," I said. "Call it what you want. Is it possible someone could be using it now to work some kind of magic? That it could be in Chicago?"

"It's under lock and key," he assured me. "It's not even possible."

Jonah frowned at him. "Then how would you explain what's happening?"

"It's not a sorcerer," Simon slowly said, "so it has to be Tate."

I didn't disagree that we were running out of options. I just wasn't convinced Simon wasn't involved. If I'd learned anything over the last few months, it was that things were rarely as simple as they seemed. Simon was too quick with answers, too positive of his facts. The supernatural world was rarely that black or white.

But if he was telling the truth, and he didn't already recognize that principle, there was no hope for him now. So I offered him a vague smile, then checked on Mallory. She finally made eye contact, her gaze challenging, as if she were daring me to accuse her of something. Maybe she wasn't hiding anything. Maybe she was still angry about the phone call we'd had the other day, about my interrupting her studies to accuse sorcerers of being involved in Chicago happenings.

Her eyes shifted to something behind me, and I glanced around.

Catcher walked through the aisle, his stride determined and no love lost in his expression. He glared at me and Simon, and I wasn't sure if he was pissed or just feeling particularly protective.

"What are you doing here?" Mallory asked, obviously puzzled.

"I thought I'd give you a ride home," Catcher said. "You are done for the night, right?" he looked pointedly at Simon, and made it obvious that's where his suspicions lay.

"We're all done," Simon said. "Mal, I'll see you tomorrow night."

"Sure thing," she said with what looked like a half-forced smile. But that didn't deter the near growl of aggression from Catcher's direction. He took her shopping basket in one hand and put his other hand at her back, where he guided her away from Simon and toward the front of the store.

"I think the stress is getting to both of them," Simon said.

"I think that's probably true," I agreed.

"Well, I need to get some things in place for Mallory's work tomorrow. Get in touch if there's anything we can do to help."

"Sure thing," Jonah said, and we watched him walk back down the aisle.

"Is he that naïve?" I asked.

"I'm not sure. And did Catcher just play the jealous boyfriend?"

"He's fighting some emotional demons right now."

We stood there quietly for a moment.

"If it's Tate," Jonah said, "we're going to have to nail him on our own."

My stomach grumbled. "Can I get a red hot before we save the world?"

"Definitely," he said. "You can buy." He walked toward the door. I followed. "Why do I have to buy?"

He pushed open the store's front door, holding it so I could pass through. "Because you're my new partner. It's customary."

"Let's start a new custom," I suggested, stepping back outside. "Dude pays."

"We'll talk in the car."

Somehow, with Armageddon on our minds, we skipped the red hots and the talk. But when the time came, I decided I'd still make him buy.

Jonah drove me back to the House; my car was still in Wrigleyville, but that was going to have to wait a bit. It was probably still chaos over there, and I didn't have time to wrangle with police and traffic.

I found Kelley, Juliet, and Lindsey at the Ops Room conference table, all eyes on the giant screen. Another newscast showed the destruction in Wrigleyville above a caption that blamed it entirely on us. Not exactly surprising, but still hurtful. We'd been the first ones on the scene; we'd been the ones saving humans. Regardless of all that, the registration law had passed, and we were enemies in our own country.

Kelley flipped off the image, and turned back to me. I was still muddy and dirty, and probably didn't look like much. "What did you learn from Simon?"

"The Order thinks this is a Tate issue. Based on our last conversation, Tate thinks this is a *Maleficium* issue. Simon is convinced the *Maleficium* is safe and sound, and Mallory can't stop her exams because the Order doesn't make exceptions." I sat down at the table beside Lindsey. "In other words, I got bubkes."

"No," Lindsey said, putting a hand on my arm. "You just think you have bubkes. The information's out there. You're just not seeing the forest for the trees."

"So let's look at the forest," I said. Catcher had once used a dry erase board to look for a pattern in raves—vampire blood orgies—that were popping up across the city. We had the computer equivalent, so I grabbed a stylus and switched the screen's input to a tablet computer that sat on the conference table.

"Okay," I said, beginning to sketch out what we knew in a timeline that was projected onto the screen. "So far we've seen three of the four elements. Water. Air. Earth."

"That means fire is probably next," Lindsey said, so I added "fire" and circled it.

"Tate says these things are happening because the balance between good and evil has shifted—they aren't in balance anymore, and that's upsetting the rules of the natural world."

"Because someone is using the *Maleficium*?" Kelley asked.

"That was Tate's theory." I scribbled more. "Good and evil were divided. Evil went into the *Maleficium*. Good stayed outside the *Maleficium*."

"Could Tate be using the *Maleficium*?" Juliet asked.

"I'm not even sure how he could, given his surroundings. He's under a pretty tight lock and key. And his room was empty. Catcher showed me a picture."

"Well," Lindsey said, "is there any other way we could tie him to the magic? Do we have any other evidence? Is anything else strange going on?"

"I've been having awful dreams," I sarcastically said.

But then I thought about it . . .

"Merit?" Lindsey quietly asked after a moment.

My heart began to beat wildly, and I looked over at her. "I've been having dreams about Ethan. They started a few weeks ago. But I've had a bunch just this week."

"There's nothing wrong with having dreams about Ethan," Juliet said. "You know, considering what happened."

I shook my head. "They aren't those kinds of dreams. They're big dreams." Realization struck. "And there's always something elemental in them. There's been a storm, and an eclipse, and then he disappeared into ashes."

"Water, sky, earth," Juliet said, paling a bit. "You're dreaming about the things that are happening in the city."

I thought back to dreams, and quickly scribbled them onto the timeline. When that was done, we stared up at the screen.

"You dreamed about them before they happened," Lindsey quietly said. "But what does that mean? That you're a little bit psychic? I mean, that's possible, I guess. I've got mad skills, after all."

I frowned. That was an explanation, but it didn't sing to me.

Carefully, Juliet raised her voice and asked the question. "Could the magic—whoever's doing it and whatever they're trying to accomplish—could it be affecting you separately? Through the dreams, I mean?"

Silence.

"I don't mean to be cruel," Lindsey said, "but Ethan's gone. The stake, the ashes. You saw him take the stake, and you saw them place the ashes into the House vault."

She was right, so I nodded. "I know."

"Wait," Kelley said. "Let's not get ahead of ourselves. So we think the *Maleficium* is tied to the elements. What is that, exactly?"

"Tate said it was a vessel that holds evil," I said. "That's all I know."

She frowned. "And we're talking, what—like an urn? A vase?

Do you remember seeing it anywhere? Maybe in Creeley Creek when you were there?"

I racked my brain, flipping through mental images of the stuff in Tate's former office, but couldn't come up with anything.

But I knew someone who could. I leaned over to the conference phone in the middle of the table and dialed up the librarian.

He answered with his title. "Librarian."

"It's Merit. I have a question for you. What do you know about the *Maleficium*?"

His silence was shockingly stark, and then his voice was surprisingly stern. "How did you learn about the *Maleficium*?"

I glanced up at Kelley, and when she shrugged, continued. "Mayor Tate. I know it's a vessel that holds evil, blah blah blah. Do you have any more information about it? Is it big? Small? A box? An urn?"

"It is none of those things," he said. "The *Maleficium* is a book. A spell book, for which we are the current guardians."

My hands shook on the table from the sudden burst of adrenaline. "What do you mean *we*?"

"We, as in Cadogan House. It was given to Ethan for safekeeping."

"But the sorcerers all think the Order has it. Catcher mentioned something about Nebraska. How could they not know it was in Cadogan House?"

He made a sound of disdain. "If you had a book that held all the evil in the world and explained its use, would you let sorcerers know where it was kept? Would you let the Order—the very people who'd *try* to use it—be its keepers? They help pick the guardians, but they're the last ones who should have possession."

Point made. So, to summarize, the Order didn't have the *Maleficium*. It was safe and sound in Cadogan House.

At least, it was supposed to be.

But if magic that crossed the boundary between good and evil was being worked across the city to reunite good and evil, maybe it wasn't so safe . . .

"As its guardians," I quietly began, "where do we store the *Maleficium*?"

"I shouldn't tell you this, you know. But given what's going on out there . . ." He trailed off, and for a moment I thought he wouldn't confess it. But then he said the words that changed everything.

"The *Maleficium* is in the House vault."

With that news in hand, Kelley called Malik and Luc down to the Ops Room. Frank, unfortunately, decided to tag along. When we were all assembled, Lindsey closed the Ops Room door again.

"Kelley?" Malik asked. "What's going on?"

She looked at me. "This one's all Merit," she said, and gave me the floor. At her nod, I laid it out.

"We know Cadogan House is the current guardian of the *Maleficium*, the book that holds evil."

The room went silent.

Frank blustered a bit about magic and secrets, but I kept my eyes trained on Malik—and I saw the second he decided to tell us the truth.

"We are the guardians," Malik agreed, holding up a hand to silence Frank. "It is always passed from one guardian to another in secrecy. McDonald House had it last. We have it now."

"And it's stored in the vault?" I asked.

After a moment, Malik nodded.

"I think we need to check the vault."

"Because?" Malik asked.

"I understand the events we've seen reflect an imbalance between good and evil," I explained. "Good and evil used to be united. The world as we know it exists now only because good and evil were separated from each other. The world keeps its rules only as long as they remain in balance, opposites of equal force."

"And when they're imbalanced," Luc said, "the natural world goes haywire. Earth. Air. Water."

"Exactly," I said with a nod. "The *Maleficium* tells of the division between good and evil, and identifies the magical doings that, to be accomplished, require crossing the boundary between good and evil. The mixing of good and black magic."

"So you think that if the natural world is unraveling, someone must be using the *Maleficium*," Luc said. "That's an interesting theory, Merit, but there hasn't been anyone in the House since Tate issued the dictate banning humans—just Mr. Cabot and the Cadogan vampires. And none of us would be capable of using it for more than a really effective paperweight."

For a moment, I thought he was right, but my stomach suddenly curled with fear, all breath leaving me. Luc, I realized, was wrong—*absolutely* wrong.

"Merit?" he asked. "Are you all right?"

I looked around the room, my head spinning with horrible possibilities. "There was someone else in the House."

All eyes turned to me.

"Merit?" Malik asked.

I could barely make myself say it. "The week after Ethan's death, Mallory was here. She was granted permission to stay in my room with me."

Silence again.

"Merit," Luc said. "Mallory wouldn't take something from the House."

Wouldn't she?

I thought about our conversations over the last week, about the things I'd seen and the things we'd discussed. About her chapped, shaking hands. Her inability to make eye contact. Her irritability, and her acceptance of dark magic.

Had I been that stupid? That naïve?

I opened my mouth to speak, but paused, considering the implications of what I was about to say. If I was right, my relationship with Mallory would never be the same.

But if I was right, my relationship with Mallory hadn't been the same in two months.

"I think the magic has changed her. I think whatever she's doing for these exams—or whatever she's been doing in her apprenticeship—have changed her." I offered up my evidence, and then got to the most damning part.

"When I visited her earlier in the week, she was perusing a book."

"A sorceress with a book?" Frank dryly asked. "How surprising."

This time, Malik didn't bother hiding his eye roll. "What did the book look like?"

"It was big." I closed my eyes, imagining myself in Mallory's basement beside her table. "Red leather," I said, "with a gold symbol on the cover."

As if I'd just confirmed his worst fear, Malik rubbed his temples with a hand, and then he pulled a square key on a metal chain from beneath his button-up shirt.

"I hope to God that you are wrong," he said. "But we do not survive on hope. We survive on facing our problems square on. Let's check the vault."

"This is unprecedented," Frank said, "and highly inappropriate. The ashes of a Master vampire are contained there. You will *not* open the House vault."

Malik skewered him with a look. "You are a representative of the GP and a guest in this House. But you are not a Master, and you are certainly not Master of *this* House. You may review the protocols and data as you will, and you may test these vampires as the GP sees fit. But you will not, under any circumstances, issue dictates to me. You are not my Master, Mr. Cabot, and I recommend you not forget it."

With that, Malik turned on his heel and headed for the door.

One by one the rest of us followed.

The trip down the basement hallway to the vault had all the levity of a funeral procession. There was a possibility the sanctity of the House had been violated, and by a woman I'd believed was my best friend—and who'd been my virtual sister for years.

Malik slid the key into the vault, then turned it forty-five degrees. The lock disengaged with an audible *click*. He lifted a hand to the door, but paused for a moment before gripping the handle, steadying himself. After a moment, his fingers were on the latch and the door was open.

Malik stood before it, blocking the view inside, and then stepped to the side, his gaze on me.

My heart beating wildly, I looked inside.

Hope and fear simultaneously blossomed.

The *Maleficium* wasn't the only thing missing.

The vault was empty.

◄──►═◄═►═◄──►

CHAPTER EIGHTEEN

WHICH WITCH IS WHICH?

Ten silent minutes later, we'd reconvened in the Ops Room. All except Frank, who'd gone upstairs to make a phone call, undoubtedly to the GP.

The *Maleficium* was gone.

The ashes were gone. No—*Ethan's* ashes were gone.

"How could she have done this?" Luc quietly asked. "Not only to take the *Maleficium*, but to steal the ashes? Such a thing isn't done. It's not right. It's sacrilege."

"It is what it is," Malik calmly said. "However horrendous the act, we shouldn't convict her of the crime without facts. We don't have any evidence she's done it. Most important, why? Why would a burgeoning sorceress do such a thing?"

"I can't tell you why she did it," Lindsey said, turning back from her computer station, her face unusually pale. "But I can confirm that she did it."

We all moved to her computer, where Lindsey had pulled up two segments of security video. "We don't actively monitor the basement camera because it's right beside the Ops Room," she said, "but we record the video. It's motion activated, so it didn't take long to find what we were looking for."

The video was black and white and grainy, but there was no mistaking Mallory Delancey Carmichael, ad exec turned sorceress, taking the *Maleficium* from the vault.

"How did she get the vault open?" I quietly asked.

"Magic," Lindsey said. "I fast-forwarded through that part. It gives me the willies."

"She only has the book," Malik pointed out, but Lindsey shook her head.

"No, she only has the book this *trip*. She takes the ashes four days later. Runs the same play both times—the same magic, I mean."

"Why the delay?" Malik wondered. "Why take the risk? Why not take them both at the same time?"

In the silence, I'd been piecing together the quilt of my experiences with Mallory and Tate over the last few days—what I'd learned from Tate about magic, and what I'd seen of Mallory.

The finished product wasn't looking good.

"Because she didn't know she wanted the ashes," I quietly said, then glanced at Malik. "She probably learned about the *Maleficium* while working with Simon. She'd used black magic before. Maybe using it made her curious."

"That only explains the book," Luc said.

But I shook my head. "When I visited Tate, he listed some spells that might require the mixing of magic we've seen this week. One of them," I said, "is making a familiar."

"A familiar?" Luc asked.

"A kind of magical assistant," I said. "They help sorcerers funnel the magic they have to wield. A familiar gives them extra capacity, like an external magical hard drive."

"That's a frightening benefit," Luc said. "But I'm confused—you think Tate's making a familiar?"

"Not Tate," I said, nerves and stomach rattling. "I think Mallory might be. She's used black magic before, and she's created a familiar before. A cat. But it's not right—there's something wrong about it. She gave me an excuse, but now . . . I don't know. And she's mentioned she wished there were more of her to help work the magic."

The room was quiet, everyone considering what I'd said.

"A sorceress is being tested this week," I continued. "A sorceress who understands how to make a familiar, at least on a small scale, and who's stolen a book of magic that can help her do more than just dabble in black magic. Ethan's ashes are gone, and now the city is falling apart because good and black magic are being mixed."

"That's a far-fetched idea," Kelley said. "Attempting to revive a vampire to make them a familiar."

"Unfortunately," Malik said, "it's not entirely far-fetched." He looked at me. "Do you know why there are no sorcerers in Chicago, Merit?"

I shook my head.

"It is an anachronism from the days when relationships between vampires and sorcerers were more strained than they are today. If things have progressed the way you suggest, it is not the first time sorcerers have made such an attempt."

The room went silent, all eyes on Malik.

"The making of a familiar requires the application of powerful magic to something—or someone—who the sorcerer desires to make a familiar. The capacity to make that kind of magic is rare, and the capacity of the familiar depends upon their power."

"So a vampire can hold more magic than a cat," I offered.

Malik nodded. "And a Master vampire can hold more power than a still-pink Initiate. The last time a sorcerer tried to make a vampire into a familiar, a Navarre House vampire was kidnapped. She was discovered later in the sorcerer's lair, a mindless, slathering thing."

I shuddered involuntarily.

"The sorcerer exerts a measure of control over the familiar," Malik said. "They become service animals, in effect. Mindless, without free will."

Even as a part of me was thrilled by the idea that Ethan could return at all, hope curdled at the thought that Mallory was attempting to turn him into a mind-controlled zombie. I suddenly had a little less sympathy for her stress—and a lot more sympathy for the cat.

"The sorceress was identified, and she was dealt with by Navarre House. And when that was done, vampires forbade the Order from working in Chicago."

That explained why the Order hadn't wanted Catcher to visit Chicago, and why they'd kicked him out when he insisted. It also said a lot about Ethan—that he'd been willing to take Catcher in upon his arrival despite what sorcerers had once done.

"If a sorcerer tried this before," Luc asked, "why didn't we see the same kind of effects? The natural disasters?"

"We did," Malik assuredly said. "We saw the Great Fire."

The Great Fire of 1871 had destroyed huge swaths of the city.

"The Order argued it was a coincidence," Malik said, "but having seen what we've seen this week, there's a strong argument they were equally in denial then."

"But you're talking about turning a living vampire into a familiar. Ethan is gone," Luc quietly said. "There is nothing left of him but ash. How could she make that happen?"

"If he was human, she probably couldn't," Malik said. "But vampires are different than humans. Genetically. Physiologically. The ties that bind the soul are different—which is why the body simply turns to ash."

"This is real," Luc said after a moment of silence, crossing himself. It was an odd move for a vampire, but there was no doubting the sincerity in his expression.

Malik stood up and pushed back his chair. "I'm going to alert the Order to the possibility that a sorceress is attempting to create a familiar, and has done so using the ashes of a Master vampire. I will also alert them that she may be using the *Maleficium* to do so, and that her attempts may completely disrupt the order of the natural world. Does that sum it up?"

Guilt heavy on my shoulders, I nodded.

He looked at me. "I know that she is practically your family. But this is a crime the GP will not let go unpunished."

I nodded my understanding, and hoped I wouldn't have to be the instrument of her destruction.

I waited in the darkened cafeteria for a phone call. I hadn't been able to reach Jonah or Catcher, and I'd left frantic messages for both of them.

And now . . . I was waiting.

Of course I had to stop her. I had to keep her from finishing whatever magic she was attempting to work. I had to keep the city safe, and I had no doubt that life as a mindless familiar under Mallory's control wasn't a life Ethan would want. He was too independent to be under the thumb of anyone, let alone a woman so focused on achieving a magical end she was willing to destroy Chicago to do it.

How had Catcher missed this? Why hadn't he seen what she

was doing, what she was becoming? Why hadn't he stopped her before it got this far . . . before I had to be the one to clean it up?

I put my elbows on the table and my forehead in my hands, and I rued my luck. It was a catch-22, and I was the one who had to pull the trigger.

My phone rang, and I glanced over at the screen.

But it wasn't Jonah or Catcher.

It was Mallory.

With shaking fingers, I opened the phone. "Hello?"

"I'm behind the House. Meet me outside. Alone."

I shut the phone again, but not before texting Jonah to let him know what I was doing. I tucked the phone into my pocket, then walked to the fence, pushed through a bare spot in the shrubbery, and scaled it. This time, my landing was more graceful, even if a half-crazed, pissed-off sorceress was the only one there to see it.

She stood in front of Catcher's car, a hipster sedan. The blue of her hair seemed to have faded even more since I'd seen her earlier; it was now nearly completely blond. Her eyes were bloodshot, and her hands were chapped and shaking. She looked like an addict in the middle of a wicked craving.

Maybe she was.

My temper rising, I had to remind myself that she was the same person, blue hair or blond, black magic or good.

Mallory pushed off the car and walked forward, carrying an oily breeze of magic with her. I stood my ground. I'd expected at this moment to feel fear or regret, but neither was at the top of the list. Most of all, I was pissed that she'd invaded my home, stolen precious things, and determined to use them for her own narcissistic purposes.

"What have you done?"

"Are you accusing me of something, vampire?"

"I trusted you. I asked you to stay with me when he died because I needed you there. You violated that trust twice over."

"I don't know what you're talking about."

"Bullshit. You stole things from us, Mallory. From me. Where's the *Maleficium*, and where are his ashes?"

"Gone."

My knees shook, and I had to lock them to keep myself upright. "So you could make him a familiar?"

She looked away, but I saw the guilt in her eyes. And that's when I knew this was the real deal, and she'd done it knowing full well what she'd gotten into.

"Black magic isn't what we thought it was," she said.

"There's not an excuse in the world you can make to me right now."

"It's unfair!" she screamed into the night. "Do you think it's right that there's this entire body of magic that I'm not supposed to use? That I'm not supposed to access? Do you know how that feels? Wrong, Merit! It feels *wrong* to funnel magic that's only half right. That's only half made. Good and evil should be together. And if this is a way to do it, then by God it's what I'll do. I cannot live like this."

"You very well can fucking live like this, just like every other sorcerer in history. You do not come into my House and steal a book of evil, and *then* steal the ashes of my Master and try to turn him into your servant!"

"But it would bring him back to you."

I stopped cold, biting my lip to stop tears from falling. "I don't want him back. Not like that. It will *not* be him. And not if I have to lose you to it, Mallory. You are my sister in every way that counts."

She made a snort. "You traded me in for him, and you know it."

"Not any more than you traded me in for Catcher." I softened my voice. "Neither one of us traded the other in. We grew up, and we grew to love others. But I don't want him, not like that. And he wouldn't want it, either." I watched her for a moment, truly wondering if that was the reason why she'd done the things she had. As much as I loved her, I wasn't sure.

"You didn't do this for me," I said.

"Bullshit," she threw out, but the word lacked force. Ethan was a pawn in the game, an excuse for her to dabble in black magic. Maybe Simon was stupid enough, naïve enough, that he honestly didn't know what she'd been doing. Maybe he hadn't known he'd poisoned his star pupil on black magic, and like a junkie needing a hit, she'd do anything to get a little more, the consequences be damned.

"You did this for you." I recalled what she'd said about black magic, about people misunderstanding it. "You tasted black magic and you liked it. Not at first, maybe, but eventually you decided that you liked it. Ethan might have been a handy side benefit, but he's an excuse. Your excuse for tearing the city apart."

"What would you know about it? About the forces inside me? I know the origin stories. Magic separated—good from evil—like twins forced apart." She yanked at her T-shirt. "I can feel them, Merit, and they need to be back together."

She closed her eyes and raised her hands, and magic began to flow in a great circle around us. I could feel it spinning at my back like a centrifuge, the motion pulling me back against it.

"Mallory, stop whatever you're doing. You are killing Chicago."

"The harm is temporary," she said.

Watching her there, perform magic that felt greasy, uncomfortable, *evil*, I knew the repercussions would be anything but temporary.

"This will fix things," she said.

"This will destroy things," I corrected.

But as the magic surrounded us in a tighter and tighter spiral—the centrifugal force pushing the air from my lungs—she shook her head.

"I am tired of worrying about what everyone else wants. You. Catcher. Simon. I was not responsible for the separation of good and evil. But I will be responsible for closing the loop. Stop being so goddamned shortsighted."

I tried my final strategy. "Mallory, I've been dreaming about Ethan. You've been hurting him. And if you finish this spell, if you set the city on fire, it will be me and the rest of the Houses that pay for it."

She smiled a little sadly. "Honey, by then, I'll be long gone."

She lifted her arms, and the magic squeezed into a knot. My vision dimmed at the edges, and then went dark completely.

For the second time in a year, my best friend in the world knocked me out cold.

I sat up just in time to see Jonah running toward me. I rubbed the back of my head, sore from where I'd fallen to the ground, but relieved that I'd been out only long enough for him to get here.

That meant I might still have a chance.

He crouched in front of me, panic in his eyes. "What happened?"

"She confessed. She stole the *Maleficium* and Ethan's ashes to try and bring him back as a familiar. She thinks I want that—but mostly she's obsessed with black magic. She's addicted to it, and she thinks completing the spell will help bring good and evil back into balance."

He helped me to my feet.

"She worked magic on me, knocked me out." I looked over at him. "She's made up her mind to go through with it. We have to find her, and we have to stop her. If she completes the magic . . ."

I didn't finish the prediction; saying it aloud wasn't going to make the choice any easier.

"Do you have any idea where she's gone?"

I racked my brain, but couldn't come up with anything. The only places I knew she'd visited recently were her house in Wicker Park and the hardware store. She trained somewhere in Schaumburg and at Catcher's gym in the River North neighborhood, but neither seemed like likely spots for her to perform big magic.

But if I couldn't find Mallory, maybe I could find the book . . .

I pulled out my cell phone and dialed the librarian.

"The *Maleficium* is gone," I told him, without introduction. "Mallory Carmichael stole it from the vault when she was staying at the House with me. I don't suppose you've got a way to track it?"

Mallory would not have been pleased at the slew of words that erupted through the phone—or the unflattering comments about the ethical propensities of sorceresses. But once he'd gotten that out of his system, he got down to business.

"One does not guard the *Maleficium* without a contingency plan," he said, and I heard rustling on the other side of the phone.

I breathed a sigh of relief. "Do you have a tracking spell or something?"

"You could say that. I slipped a GPS chip into the spine. I didn't mention that to the Order, of course, as they would have crucified me for damaging the book, but that is neither here nor there. This is *exactly* why I did it. Let me pull up the location."

While he worked the tech, I glanced up at the sky. Midnight blue was beginning to tint a sickly shade of red. I didn't doubt the water had darkened, and mountains were moving somewhere in the city.

She'd already started.

"Found it," he said. "It's nearby, and not moving."

"This is a big city. 'Nearby' isn't going to help me."

"Hold on, I'm narrowing." He paused. "The Midway!" he finally exclaimed. "It's in the Midway."

I thanked him, hung up, and pointed down the road. "She's at the Midway. I'm going there now. Find Luc and Malik and Catcher—tell them what's going on."

"I don't want you to face her alone."

I looked back at him and smiled ruefully. "Sixty-seventh rule of the Red Guard—trust your partner."

"That's actually rule number two."

"Even better," I said, faking a smile.

Jonah's jaw clenched, but he relented. "Then find her. Stop her. By whatever means necessary."

That's exactly what I was afraid of.

I jogged four blocks down the street, and then stopped in the middle of it, mouth agape.

The entire Midway Plaisance was on fire. Not with the orange and gold flames of a basic, secular fire, but with flames of translucent blue that reached toward the sky with pointy, clawlike curls. However they looked, their effect was the same as regular fire: The trees on the edge of the Midway had begun to crackle and spark from the heat.

The sky above had gone fully scarlet, an angry pulsing red, bloody like an open wound, and unlike anything I had seen before. Lightning flashed across it, raising goose bumps along my arms.

Beneath me, I felt a dull tremor. Mountains were undoubtedly springing up somewhere. As Mallory worked her magic every element was spinning wildly out of balance.

Fire trucks screamed down the street, sirens blaring. They parked on the edge of the Midway and immediately began shooting water cannons at the blaze; little good they did. The flames roared like a tornado, updrafts of heat that pushed across the park, hotter and harsher as the fire grew.

I found Mallory in front of the Masaryk statue, a pile of books and materials at her feet. The largest item—the *Maleficium*—was open and glowing, the text swirling on the page. Her blond hair whipped around her face in the hot wind thrown off by the fire.

She seemed oblivious to the danger she was creating, so I had little doubt she'd destroy the city if she could. I just wasn't entirely sure what to do about it. I had no sword and no dagger. Maybe I could get close enough to knock her out or at least disrupt the magic, although I doubted she'd let me get that close. But until the cavalry arrived, I had to try.

There was no way I was going to walk between her and the fire, so I ran around the statue and approached her from behind. When I was close enough to see the chipping, matte blue paint on her fingernails, I called out her name.

She glanced back with little evident concern, mumbling words as she spelled her magic. "Little busy here, Merit."

"Mallory, you have to stop this!" I yelled over the roar of the flames. The earth beneath my feet was shaking now, and I stumbled forward. "Can't you see what you're doing to the city?"

A tree popped, cracked, and fell forward, and the inferno rushed toward it, engulfing it in flames. It wouldn't be long before the tree line was breached completely and the fire spilled onto the streets.

"You'll kill us all!"

"Not when the spell is done," she called back. "You'll see. The world will feel so much better when good and evil are joined again. The world will be *whole*."

Her hands were shaking as she dipped them into jars of powders and sprinkled the contents above the open pages of the *Maleficium*. I scanned the detritus of her magic, but saw no sign of the urn that had held Ethan's ashes.

They were gone, maybe used to trigger some previous part of the spell. And when we stopped the spell—*if* we could stop the spell—I wouldn't even have his ashes as a memory.

"Please, Mallory, *stop*."

She kept right on working, but another voice stopped me cold.

"I knew vampires were at the heart of this!"

I glanced back. McKetrick was moving toward us, a big gun in his hands, pointed at me. "Why don't you step away from that girl, Merit?"

"That girl is attempting to destroy the city," I warned him, but he rolled his eyes. Mallory had been blinded by her addiction to black magic. McKetrick was blinded by his ignorance, his unwavering confidence that vampires were to blame for every ill in Chicago.

"It looks to me like she's trying to stop it," he said.

"You couldn't be more wrong," I told him. "You're an ignorant fool."

"I got the registration law passed."

"Because you lied and failed to mention you attacked me on a public street. You fight things that mean no harm to you and are completely blind to the real threats."

Lightning crashed into one of the trees on the other side of the Midway, splitting it in half and sending it crashing down into the flames.

Mallory was still murmuring spell words, and the flames were growing higher by the second.

Yes, he could have used the gun. And yes, an aspen sliver to the heart would probably have done me in. But I was tired of McKetrick, and I didn't have time for his shenanigans right now.

"You are helping her do this," I said, not really concerned that I was outing sorcerers. They were totally on my shit list.

"Liar," he muttered. And hand shaking with fury, he pulled the trigger.

The gun backfired, the barrel exploding, sending wood and metal shrapnel through the air. I instantaneously ducked, and still felt the shock of pain as shrapnel caught me in the back.

But I was still alive.

I looked up. McKetrick was alive, as well, but he hadn't been so lucky. His face was dotted with blood spots from shrapnel hits, and his right hand was a mess of blood and bone. He lay on his back, blinking up at the crimson sky, his hand pressed to his chest.

It probably said unflattering things about me that I had trouble gathering up any sympathy, but McKetrick would undoubtedly blame his injuries on us anyway.

A bolt of lightning struck a light pole nearby, drawing my attention back to the unfolding magical drama. The flames were taller than the trees now, their fingers licking up toward the red sky, which was now covered by a haze of blue smoke.

"Mallory!" I called out, stepping toward the plinth again. "You have got to stop this."

She lifted her hands into the air, and I could feel the magic gathering and swirling again.

"Why should I stop? So you can gloat about how you nailed the screwed-up little sorceress? No, thank you."

"This isn't about you and me!" I yelled full-out over the roar and crackle of fire and the swirling wind. "It's about Chicago. It's about your new obsession with black magic."

"You don't have a clue, Merit. Keep living in your tidy little vampire dorm. You're oblivious to the world around you—to the energy and the magic. But that's not my fault."

Catcher emerged through the smoke on the other side of the plinth. "Mallory! Stop this!"

"No!" she yelled out. "You will not interrupt me!"

"I'm sorry," he said, "but I can't let you do this."

"If you stop me now, you'll kill Ethan." She pointed at me. "Tell her that, Catcher. Tell her that you'll keep me from bringing him back."

But he kept walking closer and closer toward her. "If you bring him back, it won't be him. He'll be a zombie, Mallory, and you know that. I know why you're doing this. I know how good it feels, and how bad it feels, all at the same time. But you can learn to control it, I swear to God you can."

"I don't want to control it," she said. "I want to *own* it. All of it. I want to feel *better*."

But Catcher persisted. "Simon was an awful tutor, and I'm sorry I didn't recognize it. I'm sorry I didn't see how dangerous his stupidity was. More sorry than you'll ever know. I didn't know you were going through this. I just thought you were pulling away from me. I thought he was turning you away from me. This is *my* fault, Mallory." Tears streamed down his face. "My fault."

"You know nothing," she spat out, and hefted up the *Maleficium*. "No one understands this—how important it is."

"It's not that important," Catcher calmly said. "You're just high on it. On the power. On the potential. But it's false, Mallory. That sense that you have in your chest?" He beat a fist against his heart. "It's false. Doing evil won't make the world a better place. It won't make that feeling go away. It will only make it stronger, and you'll have driven away everyone you love."

He raised his other hand, and I could feel the pulse of magic as he prepared to whip something toward her.

"You can't stop this," she said evilly. "You can't affect my magic."

"No, I can't," he said with resignation. "But I can affect you." Magic began to glow and swirl in his palm as he prepared to strike.

Realizing that she'd have to face him down, she changed up her strategy again. "But that will hurt me," she said, her voice more like a child now than a woman of twenty-eight. "Please don't do that."

"If you're telling the truth, then I pray it will only hurt for a moment," he said. He lobbed his hand at her; a diamond-sized glint of light flew in her direction, growing into a giant blue orb.

As if in slow motion, it flew through the air past me. But Mallory dropped the book and batted away the orb. With an explosion of light and rock, it hit the statue and knocked a chunk out of the knight's shoulder.

"I hate you!" she screamed at him, and while I had no doubt the sentiment was just magic and exhaustion talking, the pain in Catcher's face was clear.

"You'll get over it," he said, and threw another orb at her. This one landed, and struck Mallory square in the chest. She flew backward and hit the ground.

All that magic she'd created, all that energy she'd gathered together, was suddenly released. With a freezing cold rush, Catcher's orb exploded, expanded, and spread into a blue plane of light that flew across the Midway with the roar of a 747, extinguishing the flames as it moved.

Extinguishing the spell as it moved.

Extinguishing hope as it moved.

For a moment, there was mostly silence. Smoke rose from the charred grass and singed trees in the Midway, and crackles of leftover magic sparked across the ground like miniature lightning. The haze lifted, and the red in the sky spread and dissolved, a few stars peeking through the haze of smoke. The outer edges of the park still glowed with cinders, but the firemen would be able to make headway now.

It was over.

Mallory was unconscious, her prophecy having come true. She'd been bested by Catcher, the White City at risk no more.

And Ethan was gone for good.

I shook my head to keep the tears inside, refusing to give in to grief. She'd have created a monster, and there was no point in grieving for something that never should have existed in the first place. I'd rather have memories and grief than a perversion of who he was. I'd just have to get back to living the life I had accepted was mine.

"I can do this," I whispered, the tears falling down my cheeks. I stood up, looking over at Catcher and Mallory. He was winding glowing strands of magic around her unconscious body as if to bind her when she awoke. Magical restraints, maybe. I didn't know what the Order would do to her now, but I couldn't imagine it was going to be nice.

I felt pressure at my elbow and glanced around. Jonah stood behind me, gaze scanning my face. "You're bleeding again."

"I'm fine. Just a little shrapnel. McKetrick's gun exploded—he's over there."

Jonah nodded. "I'll make sure the cops find him. Are you okay? I mean, aside from the bleeding?"

"I think so—" I began, but was interrupted by the crackle of a particularly loud bit of residual energy. I ducked a little as it flashed across the park before petering out and sending a prickle of magic through the air.

"Merit," Jonah quietly said. "Look."

I glanced up.

A dark figure moved through the blue haze across the Midway, approaching us. The hair at the back of my neck stood on end.

"Get back," Catcher said, moving toward us. "That thing is walking evil. The spell was interrupted, which means that's the remainder of magic."

But I held out a hand. "Wait," I said, the word falling from my lips even as I began moving toward the figure.

I was compelled forward. Without explanation, every atom in my body was intent on moving to meet whatever was emerging from the fog of falling ash. That move could have been deadly, but I didn't care. I kept walking. And when the fog cleared, brilliant green eyes stared back at me.

Tears sprang to my eyes.

My knees suddenly trembling, I ran toward him.

＋·＋ ⊫◆⊨ ＋·＋

CHAPTER NINETEEN

PHOENIX RISING

He wore the same clothes he'd had on when he'd been staked—dress pants, his House medal, a white button-up shirt, a tear in the fabric in the spot above his heart. Eyes wide, he drank in the sight of me.

I reached him, and we stared at each other for a moment, both afraid, perhaps, of what might come—and what had been.

"I saw the stake," Ethan said. "I watched Celina throw the stake and felt it hit me."

"She killed you," I said. "Mallory . . . She worked magic to bring you back as a familiar. Catcher interrupted the spell. He thought it would create a monster, but you're—you don't seem like a monster."

"I don't feel like a monster," he softly said. "I dreamed of you. I dreamed of you often. There was a storm. An eclipse."

"You dissolved into sand," I added, as his eyes widened in surprise. "I had the same dreams."

Still frowning, he raised a hand to my face, as if unsure whether I was real. "Is this a dream?"

"I don't think so."

He smiled a little, and my heart tripped at the sight of it. It had been so long since I'd seen that teasing smile. I couldn't help the new flood of tears, or the sob that escaped me.

He was here. He was alive. And most important, he seemed to be his own person, not some mindless servant, some black magic familiar of Mallory's. I didn't know what I'd done to deserve a chance at it, but he'd come back, and the gratitude—and shock—was nearly overwhelming.

"I don't know what to say," I told him.

"Then don't," he said, embracing me again. "Be still."

A cool breeze crossed the Midway, and I closed my eyes, just for a moment, trying to take his advice, trying to slow the overwhelming beat of my heart. As I stood there, I'd have sworn I caught the scents of lemon and sugar in the air again.

But then Ethan shuddered. I looked up at him, and his eyes were glazed, his skin suddenly pale.

"Merit," he said, gripping my arms fiercely, his legs suddenly shaking with the effort of standing. I wrapped an arm around his waist.

"Ethan? Are you all right?"

Before he could answer, he collapsed.

Luc and Kelley arrived at the Midway to inspect the damage, their joy at seeing Ethan muted by their fear—*our* fear—for his condition. Once assured Mallory was being cared for, the *Maleficium* was back in safe hands, and Jonah had control of McKetrick, we focused on getting Ethan back to Cadogan.

The trip was surreal—escorting my evidently resurrected vampire lover and Master back to his House. Luc led us back through a gate in the fence I hadn't known existed. We hustled through the back of the House and up the back staircase into Ethan's suite.

Luc placed him on the bed and stepped away while Kelley, apparently having been trained in medicine in some former lifetime, looked him over.

Maybe having seen the fear and exhaustion in my face, Luc moved over to me. "You okay?"

I lifted my shoulders. "I don't know what I am. Is he going to be all right?"

"Hell, Merit, I'm not really sure what he is or why he's here. What happened out there?"

I filled him in on what I'd seen of Catcher and Mallory's magic before he'd arrived. "Is Ethan her familiar? Will she be able to control him?"

"I don't know," Luc quietly said. "If Catcher interrupted the spell, I'm not sure why he's here at all."

"I've been having dreams about him—prophetic dreams about him and the elemental magic—since she took the ashes. Maybe he's been coming back, bit by bit, since then."

"So Catcher's magic finished the resurrection, but kept him from being completely mindless? That's certainly a possibility, but it's not my area of expertise. Hell, I doubt Catcher even knows."

The unknowing, the risk Ethan would be at the beck and call of a girl so addicted to black magic she was willing to throw away her friends—and her city—pushed me over the edge. Fear and panic bubbled to the surface, and I looked away, tears suddenly streaming down my face.

I moved to the nearest chair and sat down, then covered my hands in my face, sobbing from the toll of the emotional roller coaster of Mallory and Ethan—and at the possibilities that I'd already lost Mallory . . . and that I'd have to endure losing Ethan all over again.

I don't know how long I'd cried when I heard rustling, soft but certainly there, from across the room. Slowly, I uncovered my eyes and looked up. Ethan was propped up on the bed. He looked obviously weak, his eyes barely open. And as in my dreams, he said my name. But this was no dream.

I wiped away tears and hurried to the side of the bed beside Kelley. "Are you all right?"

"I'm fine. Tired." He swallowed. "I need blood, I think."

I looked back at Kelley. "Is that an effect of the . . . whatever this is?"

"Possibly. Luc, can you check the second-floor kitchen? Grab some blood?"

Luc immediately went to the door of Ethan's apartments, but came back two minutes later empty-handed, muttering a few choice words about Frank. The second-floor refrigerator was apparently empty of blood. As were the first- and third-floor fridges.

"Long story short, hoss, we're out of blood at the moment."

Ethan sat up a little. "I'm sorry? The House is out of blood? Why would Malik let that happen?"

"I'm going to re-stress the 'long story' bit. It also happens drinking from vampires is currently against the rules of Cadogan House, but I'm pretty sure we'll go to bat for you on this one." He winged up his eyebrows. "Although you may need to impose upon a Novitiate for nourishment."

Now my cheeks were flaming red, but the suggested intimacy— the possibility that my Master needed to take blood from me— didn't seem to faze Ethan.

Luc and Kelley silently slipped out the door.

Suddenly as anxious as a girl on a first date, I sat down on the edge of the bed. This was *so* strange. He'd been gone. And now he was back. I was so glad to see him I thought my chest might burst with it, but it was still surreal.

"Nervous, Sentinel?"

I nodded.

Ethan tilted his head, splaying his golden hair against the pillow behind him. "Don't be. It is the most natural thing a vampire can do." He took my hand and gazed down at my wrist, then rubbed his thumb over the pulse that throbbed just beneath my skin. The sensation sent flutters of warmth through me, but not just of desire. He gazed beyond my wrist as if staring at the blood and life that ran beneath it, his emerald eyes silvering as the hunger for blood hit him.

I'd never given blood to anyone before. I'd taken it from Ethan, but that was the extent of it. Eight months ago, could I possibly have imagined this would be my first experience? That I would be sitting here, with Ethan, in his apartment, ready to offer up a wrist?

He pressed his lips to my pulse, and my eyes drifted shut, my body now humming with predatory interest, my own fangs descending. *"Ethan."*

He made a faint sound of masculine satisfaction, and I shivered when he kissed my wrist again.

"Be still," he said, his lips against my skin. "Be still."

It had been a night for tears. For losing a friend, hopefully only temporarily, to magical addiction. For my own reunion with Ethan. But whatever those emotions, they paled in comparison to the reunion shared by Ethan and Malik.

When Ethan was fed and I'd advised Luc, Malik made his trip upstairs, his eyes as wide as saucers. He looked between me and a stronger-looking Ethan—still resting on the bed—trying to figure out the magic or trick at work. It took him a few minutes to even attempt words.

They'd known each other for a century. It stood to reason the reunion would be meaningful.

And when the reunion was done, as if nothing had passed between them, it didn't take them long to get down to politics.

"The GP sent a receiver," Malik said.

"They didn't waste much time," Ethan muttered. "Who did they select?"

"Franklin Cabot."

"From Cabot House? Good lord." Ethan grimaced. "That man is a worm. Victor would be better off if he met a stake of his own. How bad has it been?"

Malik glanced at me, as if checking in before burdening Ethan with too much bad news. But I knew Ethan well enough to presume he wouldn't want to be coddled. I gave Malik a nod.

"I'll give you the short list," Malik said. "He put the House on blood rations. He revoked the right to drink in the House. He has limited their right of assembly. He revoked Merit's status as Sentinel and sent her to see Claudia. He subjected the guards to a sunlight endurance test."

Ethan's eyes widened in disbelief. "I am at a loss."

"He is incompetent," Malik said. "Out of respect for the House and the GP I gave him room to conduct his investigation. But he has gone too far." Malik cleared his throat. "I heard him on the telephone a few hours ago advising Darius that Cadogan vampires had been in league with a sorceress to destroy the city. I had planned to address the issues with him before the Midway occurred, but now that you're back . . ."

Silence, as Ethan considered. My shoulders tense, I waited for a response, expecting a blowup of temper or carefully modulated fury.

"Screw them," Ethan finally said.

After a moment of utter shock, I enjoyed my second biggest smile all night. Malik's wasn't much smaller.

"I'm sorry," I said, "did you just say 'screw them'?"

Ethan smiled grimly. "It's a new dawn, so to speak. I don't give the GP a lot of credit, but they're smart enough to recognize incompetence when they see it." He looked fixedly at Malik. "And if they don't, they defeat their very purpose for existence."

He hadn't exactly used the word "revolution," but it lurked there—the possibility that Cadogan House could exist without the GP.

Maybe my RG membership wouldn't freak him out as much as I'd thought.

Not that I had any plans to tell him.

"You seem . . . somewhat changed," Malik carefully said.

"I'm on my third life," Ethan said. "And in this one, I may be at the beck and call of a sorceress with an addiction to black magic. It tends to put the GP's irrationality into perspective."

"And control of the House?" Malik wondered.

"The GP will never allow me to retake the House until they're assured Mallory doesn't have control. And while I understand the House isn't exactly fond of the GP right now, I couldn't disagree with that position. It's too risky. The House should remain in your very apt Mastery until you're confident I'm acting of my own free will."

My beeper buzzed with an alert: There was a meeting in the ballroom. Clearly the Master(s) of the House hadn't scheduled it, because they were both here. Curiosity piqued—and since they'd moved right into discussing historical applications of the vampiric line of succession—I politely excused myself and walked downstairs to the second-floor ballroom.

One of the doors was propped open, so I followed the crowd of vampires inside and sidled up beside Lindsey and Kelley, whom I found in the back of the room.

Frank stood on the platform in the front of the ballroom, waxing poetic about the evils of Cadogan House and the lack of restraint of its vampires. "Cadogan House is on an unsustainable course," he said. "Taking too much interest in human affairs. Attempting to solve problems that are outside its purview and authority. That course cannot continue, and I cannot in good faith recommend to the Presidium the continuation of the status quo."

He paused as if for dramatic effect while the vampires looked nervously around, the pepper of tense magic rising in the room. They shuffled nervously, waiting for Frank's verdict.

"There is too much doubt in this House. Doubt about its position within the umbrella of the Greenwich Presidium. Doubt about its loyalties. You have taken oaths to your House. Unfortunately, those oaths have been sublimated by the Masters of this House. Therefore, tonight, you'll each of you take a new oath. You'll recall that you exist through our generosity, and you will swear fealty to the Greenwich Presidium."

The room went silent, the magic peaking with an electric spark that felt strong enough to illuminate the room.

"He cannot be serious," Lindsey whispered, expression aghast as she stared at the podium.

"I think it only appropriate that the captain of our guards, she who is tasked with protecting the House from all enemies, dead or alive, take the first oath."

The wave of turning heads divided, splitting to create a gap that put Kelley directly in Frank's line of sight. He beckoned her forward with a hand.

"Kelley, captain of this House, come forward and swear your fealty."

She looked at me with doubt in her eyes, clearly unsure what to do. I sympathized. If she refused to go forward, she'd undoubtedly catch hell. Sure, Malik and Ethan were in the building, but they were two floors away, and she was surrounded by vampires who'd be honor bound to obey whatever dictate Frank laid out.

On the other hand—swear an oath to the GP? Was this guy crazy?

There was no good option, no right choice, I thought, except to create as little new drama as possible. So I reached out and squeezed her hand, and gave her the same confident nod she'd given me on the lawn.

She took a moment to compose herself, then walked slowly forward through the gap of vampires. Some looked at her with obvious sympathy; some looked like they expected more from their captain than kowtowing to the dictates of a GP figurehead.

She reached the dais at the front of the room, which was Frank's signal to wax poetic again.

"Kelley, captain of this House," he said again. "Swear your oath to the Greenwich Presidium."

"I have sworn oaths to Cadogan House," she said, her voice ringing clearly through the ballroom. "I am already bound."

I felt a surge of relief from the crowd, but the pulse of magic from the front of the room was much less friendly.

"Then rebuke your oaths to Cadogan House."

"I will not rebuke my oaths," Kelley said. "I did not make them lightly, and I will not rebuke them so you can make a better report to the GP."

A vein in his neck pulsed with fury. "You will swear your loyalty to the GP," he gritted out, "or you will regret it from here 'til eternity."

The doors burst open. "Like hell she will."

All heads turned back to the doorway. Malik stood there, fury in his eyes, his arm around Ethan's waist as he helped him into the room. A complete hush fell over the crowd, just before the room erupted in noise and sound and joyful tears. Vampires rushed toward the door, and Malik gave them a moment to welcome their fallen hero.

I took the opportunity to look back at Frank and savor the shocked expression on his face. That expression, after the grief he'd put this House through, almost made it worthwhile.

And then Malik called the vampires to order again.

"Quiet," he said, and the room silenced immediately. "For your information, Mr. Cabot, the vampires of this House take oaths to the House and its vampires, not the GP."

Frank composed himself and offered him a dubious look. "And by whose authority do you challenge mine?"

Malik gave back a look that was just as imperious. "By the authority instilled in Cadogan House and its Master by the Greenwich Presidium."

Frank looked from Malik to Ethan. "A Masterdom that appears to be in some state of disarray."

Ethan cleared his throat. "Malik Washington is Master of this House. He was duly Invested by the GP upon my death, such as it was. He will remain in that position until I am Invested again."

In other words, Malik was Master of the House, and Ethan wouldn't challenge his position.

The crowd rustled with anticipation.

"The vampires in this House," Malik said, "including the captain of its guards, have proven their worth time and time again. Tonight, we saw their willingness to head immediately into battle, the danger to them notwithstanding, to protect this House. They are brave and honorable. And in response, you accuse them of disloyalty and demand new oaths? I seriously doubt the GP would condone such behaviors. You are hereby ordered to leave this House, Mr. Cabot."

"You have no power to order me out."

Malik arched a very Ethan-like eyebrow at Frank. "I have power to remove any forces that are disruptive to this House, and Ethan is in agreement with me. No one would argue that you fall well within that category. You have ten minutes to remove your belongings."

"I will report you to the GP."

"I'm sure you will," Malik said. "You may report that our House is well in order, that it is home to brave and true vampires. Oh— and you can also advise them that Merit has been reappointed Sentinel."

He smiled a bit evilly, and I had to bite back my own wide grin.

"Take that back to the GP, Mr. Cabot. And should the urge arise, feel free to tell them to fuck off."

With Frank expunged from the House, the rest of the vampires surrounded Ethan with joyous celebration. As if energized by their affection, he managed to stand on his own again.

When the vampires quieted, Malik put a hand on his shoulder. "This House is yours, by blood and by bone, and you are welcome in its walls at any hour."

Ethan had once said something similar to me, assuring me that I was a member of his House "by blood and by bone." Maybe it was one of the phrases vampires used, part of the collective vocabulary, the communal memory, of a people bound together by the need for assimilation.

"When the time is right," Malik said, "I will hand the torch back to you. In the meantime, the city will undoubtedly have questions. I've no doubt the mayor will be pounding on the door soon enough."

"Quite possibly," Ethan said, and then took my hand and grinned at Malik. "But if you don't mind, I plan to use the last bit of the evening to full advantage."

I felt my cheeks warm, but I was in good company; even Luc blushed at that one.

With Malik's assurance that Ethan's apartments were his to use, we returned to his room, hand in hand.

We'd barely closed the door before his mouth was on mine, hungry and insistent. Passion flared and spiraled around us with the magnitude of ancient magicks.

I didn't argue with him. I kissed him back with everything I had, devoured him with every tool in my arsenal, and moved in and around him as love ensnared us.

After a moment he pulled back, his own breathing labored; he opened his eyes and captured my cheeks in his hands. "I haven't forgotten where we left things, Sentinel, nor do I plan to forget it."

"You've been gone a long time."

"Only to you. To me, there was only a vague dream of darkness . . . and occasionally your voice. You kept me bound to earth, and I called your name to do the same for you."

I'm sure I paled a bit at that confession. The emotion of his being back was still new, still raw, still untested. I was thrilled that he was back, but the emotion was so unexpected I was afraid to trust it.

He tipped up my chin and forced me to meet his gaze. "Is there someone else?"

"No. But for two months, there was no you, either."

We were silent for a moment while he searched my gaze. "There was a time," he finally said, "when I would have acknowledged your reticence and given you time and space to reach your own decision."

He tipped my head down again and slid his fingers to the back of my neck, sending shivers down my spine. Then he lowered his lips to my ear.

"This is not that time, Merit."

And then his mouth was on mine, and he took my breath away again. He kissed me like a man possessed, like a man with nothing more on his mind but the taste and feel of me.

Like a man returned to life.

"I have been given a third chance at life, even if the circumstances are somewhat disconcerting. You are mine, and we both know it."

He kissed me again, and as I began to believe that he was really, truly back, I felt as possessive of him as I'd ever felt about anything, sure in the bone-deep knowledge that he was *mine*, and regardless of the circumstance, I intended to keep it that way.

After another long moment, he ended the kiss and wrapped his arms around me.

When the sun rose, we were nestled together, two bodies pressed together for warmth, for love, in gratefulness for miracles that probably shouldn't have been.

It was the best night's sleep I'd ever had.

W e awoke with our bodies intertwined, the phone beside Ethan's bed ringing loudly. I crawled across his very naked body and picked up the receiver.

"Yes?" I asked.

Catcher's voice was frantic. "She woke up. She overpowered the guards, and she left."

I sat up and shook Ethan's leg to wake him. "Slow down. What do you mean she overpowered the Order?"

Alarm in his eyes, Ethan sat up beside me, his legs wrapped in a sheet. He pushed the hair from his face.

"They removed the restraints so they could check her out. She managed to convince them that she was feeling better, that she knew she'd done wrong. As soon as they were off, she knocked out the guard. He's banged up pretty badly. She knocked out two others on the way out. They called a few minutes ago."

"Do you know where she went?"

"A temporary guardian left this morning to drive the *Maleficium* to Nebraska. There are rooms in the Order's silo that are impermeable to magic. The plan is to keep it there until a permanent guardian is appointed."

"The Order is supposed to guard the book of evil? That's a horrible idea."

"The Order's just providing the space. The temp is in charge of it until it goes to its new home."

"That's where she'll go. She wants to finish her task," I quietly said. "Combining good and evil together. She thinks it's necessary, that it will help the world."

"They won't let me look for her," Catcher said. "The Order doesn't want me involved. And if she's truly using black magic, they're afraid to allow sorcerers to get mixed up in it."

Honestly, I didn't disagree with the sentiment.

"I considered secreting her away," he confessed.

"She can't run from this," I said. "If she's become addicted to black magic, she needs to deal with it, not pretend it doesn't exist."

"I failed her. I should have known. I thought . . . I thought Simon was trying to turn her against me because of the Order. I thought that's why she was acting so strangely. I was blind. Blinded by my own fear."

"You knew when the rest of us knew," I said. "And you're the one who saved her and the rest of the city tonight. Never forget that."

He was quiet for a moment. "Do you remember when I told you that you had something of mine—something you had to protect?"

Tears immediately sprang to my eyes. "I remember."

"This is the time," he said. "I need you to protect it."

"Then that's what I'll do. I'll find her, Catcher, and I'll bring her back to you, safe and sound." The promise made, I hung up the phone and glanced over at Ethan, worry in my heart.

"So," he said, tucking a strand of hair behind my ear. "When do we leave?"

An hour later, we met in the foyer of Cadogan House, each of us carrying a duffel bag and a sheathed sword. Helen had replaced my Cadogan medal, and a thoughtful someone had collected my car from Wrigleyville. That didn't sway Ethan, though, who insisted we drive his convertible Mercedes to find Mallory. And really, who was I to argue?

Ethan's hair was tied at the nape of his neck, and he wore the SAVE OUR NAME T-shirt—an homage to Wrigley Field—that he'd once let me wear.

"You ready?" he asked.

I nodded.

Vampires began to funnel into the foyer, now cleared of Frank's rules, Malik in the lead. He stepped up to Ethan and me and stretched out a hand. He shook Ethan's, and then mine.

Luc, Lindsey, and Juliet stepped behind Malik, and Ethan's gaze moved to each in turn, then back to Malik. "You have enough coverage to protect the House?"

Malik nodded. "Kelley is confirming temporary replacements as we speak. And in the meantime, we are here if you need us. And when you return."

"Thank you," Ethan said, and after another round of hugs and tears, for the last time in God knew how long, we walked out of Cadogan House together, with a map and a plan.

Unfortunately, I barely made it three feet without stopping short.

Jonah stood at the gate, hands in his pockets, expression blank but for the solemn eyes that shifted between me and Ethan. My heart skipped a beat, anticipation building as I wondered why he was here . . . and what he would say.

We met him at the gate, Ethan's expression shifting between me and Jonah.

"On behalf of Grey House," Jonah said, "welcome back to Chicago." He glanced between me and Ethan. "You're going to find Mallory."

"We are," I said, and we stood there awkwardly for a moment. Time to see how far that trust extended. "Ethan, could you excuse us for a moment?"

"Of course," he said, but raised my hand to his lips and pressed a kiss there before moving toward the Mercedes.

"I suppose you've gotten your partner back," Jonah said.

"I agreed to join the RG," I quietly reminded him. "And I don't take that lightly."

Jonah looked at me for a long time, and I could read the deliberation in his eyes: Was I committed now that Ethan was back?

He must have found merit in my honesty, as he finally nodded. And then he spoke his piece: "We have moved in and out of each others' lives. Twice now, we've crossed each others' paths—for you, both as a human and a vampire. Relationships have been built on less."

I rolled my eyes. "And Ethan would end you for suggesting it."

He smiled. "Ethan would appreciate a man who knows what he wants—as long as I don't interfere. And I don't plan on doing that. You and I are partners. I know where the lines are, Merit, and I can respect them. I have no interest in breaking up a relationship."

I made my good-byes and walked back to where Ethan was loading our bags into the car. I expected suspicion and vitriol in his mood and tone. I did not expect to see the smile on his face.

"Your partner while I was away?" he asked.

I nodded, still unsure of my steps.

"You can relax," he said with a canny grin, then tweaked my chin. "I trust you." And then he tossed something in the air. Instinctively, I reached out and caught it, then glanced down at my open palm—and back up at him.

He smiled cannily. "Omaha's a long drive. You can take the first shift." True to his word, he opened the passenger side door and climbed inside.

I was going to have to learn this man all over again.

I guess all journeys begin with a single step . . . or an $80,000 convertible Mercedes. God willing, it would move fast enough, and we could find Mallory in time.

They were gathered around a conference table in a high-rise, eight men and women, no one under the age of sixty-five, all of them wealthy beyond measure. And they were here, in the middle of Manhattan, to decide my fate.

I was not quite sixteen and only one month out of my sophomore year of high school. My parents, philosophy professors, had been offered a two-year-long academic sabbatical at a university in Munich, Germany. That's right—two years out of the country, which only really mattered because they'd decided I'd be better off staying in the United States.

They'd passed along that little nugget one Saturday in June. I'd been preparing to head to my best friend Ashley's house when my parents came into my room and sat down on my bed.

"Lily," Mom said, "we need to talk."

I don't think I'm ruining the surprise by pointing out that nothing good happens when someone starts a speech like that.

My first thought was that something horrible had happened to Ashley. Turned out she was fine; the trauma hit a little closer to home. My parents told me they'd been accepted into the sabbatical program, and that the chance to work in Germany for two years was an amazing opportunity for them.

Then they got quiet and exchanged one of those long, meaningful looks that really didn't bode well for me. They said they didn't want to drag me to Germany with them, that they'd be busy while they were there, and that they wanted me to stay in an American school to have the best chance of going to a great college here. So they'd decided that while they were away, I'd be staying in the States.

I was equal parts bummed and thrilled. Bummed, of course, because they'd be an ocean away while I passed all the big milestones—SAT prep, college visits, prom, completing my vinyl collection of every Smashing Pumpkins track ever released.

Thrilled, because I figured I'd get to stay with Ashley and her parents.

Unfortunately, I was only right about the first part.

My parents had decided it would be best for me to finish high school in Chicago, in a boarding school stuck in the middle of high-rise buildings and concrete—not in Sagamore, my hometown in Upstate New York; not in our tree-lined neighborhood, with my friends and the people and places I knew.

I protested with every argument I could think of.

Flash forward two weeks and 240 miles to the conference table where I sat in a button-up cardigan and pencil skirt I'd never have worn under normal circumstances, the members of the Board of Trustees of St. Sophia's School for Girls staring back at me. They interviewed every girl who wanted to walk their hallowed halls—after all, heaven forbid they let in a girl who didn't meet their standards. But that they had traveled to New York to see me seemed a little out of the ordinary.

"I hope you're aware," said one of them, a silver-haired man with tiny round glasses, "that St. Sophia's is a famed academic institution. The school itself has a long and storied history in Chicago, and the Ivy Leagues recruit from its halls."

A woman with a pile of hair atop her head looked at me and said slowly, as if talking to a child, "You'll have any secondary institution in this country or beyond at your feet, Lily, if you're accepted at St. Sophia's. If you become a St. Sophia's girl."

Okay, but what if I didn't want to be a St. Sophia's girl? What if I wanted to stay home in Sagamore with my friends, not a thousand miles away in some freezing Midwestern city, surrounded by private-school girls who dressed the same, talked the same, bragged about their money?

I didn't want to be a St. Sophia's girl. I wanted to be me, Lily Parker, of the dark hair and eyeliner and fabulous fashion sense.

The powers that be of St. Sophia's were apparently less hesitant. Two weeks after the interview, I got the letter in the mail.

"Congratulations," it said. "We are pleased to inform you that the members of the board of trustees have voted favorably regarding your admission to St. Sophia's School for Girls."

I was less than pleased, but short of running away, which wasn't my style, I was out of options. So two months later, my parents and I trekked to Albany International.

Mom had booked us on the same airline, so we sat in the concourse together, with me between the two of them. Mom wore a shirt and trim trousers, her long dark hair in a low ponytail. My father wore a button-up shirt and khakis, his auburn hair waving over the glasses on his nose. They were heading to JFK to connect to their international flight; I was heading to O'Hare.

We sat silently until they called my plane. Too nervous for tears, I stood and put on my messenger bag. My parents stood, as well, and my mom reached out to put a hand on my cheek. "We love you, Lil. You know that? And that this is what's best?"

I most certainly didn't know this was best. And the weird thing was, I wasn't sure even she believed it, considering how nervous she sounded when she said it. Looking back, I think they both had doubts about the whole thing. They didn't actually say that, of course, but their body language told a different story. When they first told me about their plan, my dad kept touching my mom's knee—not romantically or anything, but like he needed reassurance, like he needed to remind himself that she was there and that things were going to be okay. It made me wonder. I mean, they were headed to Germany for a two-year research sabbatical they'd spent months applying for, but despite what they'd said about the great "opportunity," they didn't seem thrilled about going.

The whole thing was very, very strange.

Anyway, my mom's throwing out, "It's for the best," at the airport wasn't a new thing. She and dad had both been repeating that phrase over the last few weeks like a mantra. I didn't know that it was for the best, but I didn't want a bratty comment to be the last thing I said to them, so I nodded at my mom and faked a smile, and let my dad pull me into a rib-breaking hug.

"You can call us anytime," he said. "Anytime, day or night. Or e-mail. Or text us." He pressed a kiss to the top of my head. "You're our light, Lils," he whispered. "Our light."

I wasn't sure whether I loved him more, or hated him a little, for caring so much and still sending me away.

We said our good-byes, and I traversed the concourse and took my seat on the plane, with a credit card for emergencies in my wallet, a duffel bag bearing my name in the belly of the jet, and my palm pressed to the window as New York fell behind me.

Good-bye, "New York State of Mind."

Pete Wentz said it best in his song title: "Chicago Is So Two Years Ago."

Two hours and a tiny bag of peanuts later, I was in the 312, greeted by a wind that was fierce and much too cold for an afternoon in early September, Windy City or not. My knee-length skirt, part of my new St. Sophia's uniform, didn't help much against the chill.

I glanced back at the black-and-white cab that had dropped me off in front of the school's enclave on East Erie. The driver pulled away from the curb and merged into traffic, leaving me there on the sidewalk, giant duffel bag in my hands, messenger bag across my shoulder, and downtown Chicago around me.

What stood before me, I thought as I gazed up at St. Sophia's School for Girls, wasn't exactly welcoming.

The board members had told me that St. Sophia's had been a convent in its former life, but it could have just as easily been the setting for a gothic horror movie. Dismal gray stone. Lots of tall, skinny windows, and one giant round one in the middle. Fanged, grinning gargoyles perched at each corner of the steep roof.

I tilted my head as I surveyed the statues. Was it weird that nuns had been guarded by tiny stone monsters? And were they supposed to keep people out . . . or in?

Rising over the main building were the symbols of St. Sophia's—two prickly towers of that same gray stone. Supposedly, some of Chicago's leading ladies wore silver rings inscribed with an outline of the towers, proof that they'd been St. Sophia's girls.

Three months after my parents' revelation, I still had no desire to be a St. Sophia's girl. Besides, if you squinted, the building looked like a pointy-eared monster.

I gnawed the inside of my lip and scanned the other few equally gothic buildings that made up the small campus, all but hidden from the rest of Chicago by a stone wall. A royal blue flag that bore the St. Sophia's crest (complete with tower) rippled in the wind above the arched front door. A Rolls-Royce was parked on the curved driveway below.

This wasn't my kind of place. This wasn't Sagamore. It was far from my school and my neighborhood, far from my favorite vintage clothing store and favorite coffeehouse.

Worse, given the Rolls, I guessed these weren't my kind of people. Well, they *used* to not be my kind of people. If my parents could afford to send me here, we apparently had money I hadn't known about.

"This sucks," I muttered, just in time for the heavy double doors in the middle of the tower to open. A woman—tall, thin, dressed in a no-nonsense suit and sensible heels—stepped into the doorway.

We looked at each other for a moment. Then she moved to the side, holding one of the doors open with her hand.

I guessed that was my cue. Adjusting my messenger bag and duffel, I made my way up the sidewalk.

"Lily Parker?" she asked, one eyebrow arched questioningly, when I got to the stone stairs that lay before the door.

I nodded.

She lifted her gaze and surveyed the school grounds, like an eagle scanning for prey. "Come inside."

I walked up the steps and into the building, the wind ruffling my hair as the giant doors were closed behind me.

The woman moved through the main building quickly, efficiently, and, most noticeably, silently. I didn't get so much as a hello, much less a warm welcome to Chicago. She hadn't spoken a word since she'd beckoned me to follow her.

And follow her I did, through lots of slick limestone corridors lit by tiny flickering bulbs in old-fashioned wall sconces. The floor and walls were made of the same pale limestone, the ceiling overhead a grid of thick wooden beams, gold symbols painted in the spaces between them. A bee. The flowerlike shape of a fleur-de-lis.

We turned one corner, then another, until we entered a corridor lined with columns. The ceiling changed, rising above us in a series of pointed arches outlined in curved wooden beams, the spaces between them painted the same blue as St. Sophia's flag. Gold stars dotted the blue.

It was impressive—or at least expensive.

I followed her to the end of the hallway, which terminated in a wooden door. A name, MARCELINE D. FOLEY, was written in gold letters in the middle of it.

When she opened the door and stepped inside the office, I assumed she was Marceline D. Foley. I stepped inside behind her.

The room was darkish, a heavy fragrance drifting up from a small oil burner on a side table. A gigantic, circular stained glass window was on the wall opposite the door, and a massive oak desk sat in front of the window.

"Close the door," she said. I dropped my duffel bag to the floor, then did as she'd directed. When I turned around again, she was seated behind the desk, manicured hands clasped before her, her gaze on me.

"I am Marceline Foley, the headmistress of this school," she said. "You've been sent to us for your education, your personal growth, and your development into a young lady. You will become a St. Sophia's girl. As a junior, you will spend two years at this institution. I expect you to use that time wisely—to study, to learn, to network, and to prepare yourself for academically challenging studies at a well-respected university.

"You will have classes from eight twenty a.m. until three twenty p.m., Monday through Friday. You will have dinner at precisely five o'clock and study hall from seven p.m. until nine p.m., Sunday through Thursday. Lights-out at ten o'clock. You will remain on the school grounds during the week, although you may take your exercise off the grounds during your lunch breaks, assuming you do not leave the grounds alone and that you stay near campus. Curfew is promptly at nine p.m. on Friday and Saturday nights. Do you have any questions?"

I shook my head, which was a fib. I had tons of questions, actually, but not the sort I thought she'd appreciate, especially since her PR skills left a lot to be desired. She made St. Sophia's sound less like boarding school and more like prison. Then again, the PR was lost on me, anyway. It's not like I was there by choice.

"Good." Foley pulled open a tiny drawer on the right-hand side of her desk. Out of it she lifted an antique gold skeleton key—the skinny kind with prongs at the end—that was strung from a royal blue ribbon.

"Your room key," she said, and extended her hand. I lifted the ribbon from her palm, wrapping my fingers around the slender bar of metal. "Your books are already in your room. You've been assigned a laptop, which is in your room, as well."

She frowned, then glanced up at me. "This is likely not how you imagined your junior and senior years of high school would be, Ms. Parker. But you will find that you have been bestowed an incredible gift. This is one of the finest high schools in the nation. Being an alumna of St. Sophia's will open doors for you educationally and socially. Your membership in this institution will connect you to a network of women whose influence is international in scope."

I nodded, mostly about that first part. Of course I'd imagined my junior and senior years differently. I'd imagined being at home, with my friends, with my parents. But she hadn't actually asked me how I felt about being shipped off to Chicago, so I didn't elaborate.

"I'll show you to your room," she said, rising from her chair and moving toward the door.

I picked up my bag again and followed her.

St. Sophia's looked pretty much the same on the walk to my room as it had on the way to Foley's office—one stone corridor after another. The building was immaculately clean, but kind of empty. Sterile. It was also quieter than I would have expected a high school to be, certainly quieter than the high school I'd left behind. But for the click of Foley's heels on the shining stone floors, the place was graveyard silent. And there was no sign of the usual high school stuff. No trophy cases, no class photos, no lockers, no pep rally posters. Most important, still no sign of students. There were supposed to be two hundred of us. So far, it looked like I was the only St. Sophia's girl in residence.

The corridor suddenly opened into a giant circular space with a domed ceiling, a labyrinth set into the tile on the floor beneath it. This was a serious place. A place for contemplation. A place where nuns once walked quietly, gravely, through the hallways.

And then she pushed open another set of double doors.

The hallway opened into a long room lit by enormous metal chandeliers and the blazing color of dozens of stained glass windows. The walls that weren't covered by windows were lined with books, and the floor was filled by rows and rows of tables.

At the tables sat teenagers. Lots and lots of teenagers, all in stuff that made up the St. Sophia's uniform: navy plaid skirt and some kind of top in the same navy: sweater; hooded sweatshirt; sweater-vest.

They looked like an all-girl army of plaid.

Books and notebooks were spread on the tables before them, laptop computers open and buzzing. Classes didn't start until tomorrow, and these girls were already studying. The trustees were right—these people were serious about their studies.

"Your classmates," Foley quietly said.

She walked through the aisle that split the room into two halves, and I followed behind her, my shoulder beginning to ache under the weight of the duffel bag. Girls watched as I walked past them, heads lifting from books (and notebooks and laptops) to check me out as I passed. I caught the eyes of two of them.

The first was a blonde with wavy hair that cascaded around her shoulders, a black patent leather headband tucked behind her ears. She arched an eyebrow at me as I passed, and two other brunettes at the table leaned toward her to whisper. To gossip. I made a prediction pretty quickly that she was the leader of that pack.

The second girl, who sat with three other plaid cadets a few tables down, was definitely not a member of the blonde's pack. Her hair was also blond, but for the darker ends of her short bob. She wore black nail polish and a small silver ring on one side of her nose.

Given what I'd seen so far, I was surprised Foley let her get away with that, but I liked it.

She lifted her head as I walked by, her green eyes on my browns as I passed.

She smiled. I smiled back.

"This way," Foley ordered. I hustled to follow.

We walked down the aisle to the other end of the room, then into another corridor. A few more turns and a narrow flight of limestone stairs later, Foley stopped beside a wooden door. She bobbed her head at the key around my neck. "Your suite," she said. "Your bedroom is the first on the right. You have three suitemates, and you'll share the common room. Classes begin promptly at eight twenty tomorrow morning. Your schedule is with your books. I understand you have some interest in the arts?"

"I like to draw," I said. "Sometimes paint."

"Yes, the board forwarded some of the slides of your work. It lends itself to the fantastic—imaginary worlds and unrealistic creatures—but you seem to have some skill. We've placed you in our arts track. You'll start studio classes within the next few weeks, once our instructor has settled in. It is expected that you will devote as much time to your craft as you do to your studies." Apparently having concluded her instructions, she gave me an up-and-down appraisal. "Any questions?"

She'd done it again. She said, "Any questions?" but it sounded a lot more like "I don't have time for nonsense right now."

"No, thank you," I said, and Foley bobbed her head.

"Very good." With that, she turned on her heel and walked away, her footsteps echoing through the hallway.

I waited until she was gone, then slipped the key into the lock and turned the knob. The door opened into a small circular space—the common room. There were a couch and coffee table in front of a small fireplace, a cello propped against the opposite wall, and four doors leading, I assumed, to the bedrooms.

I walked to the door on the far right and slipped the skeleton key from my neck, then into the lock. When the tumblers clicked, I pushed open the door and flipped on the light.

It was small—a tiny but tidy space with one small window and a twin-sized bed. The bed was covered by a royal blue bedspread embroidered with an imprint of the St. Sophia's tower. Across from the bed was a wooden bureau, atop which sat a two-foot-high stack of books, a pile of papers, a silver laptop, and an alarm clock. A narrow wooden door led to a closet.

I closed the door to the suite behind me, then dropped my bag onto the bed. The room had a few pieces of furniture in it and the school supplies, but otherwise, it was empty. But for the few things I'd been able to fit into the duffel, nothing here would remind me of home.

My heart sank at the thought. My parents had actually sent me away to boarding school. They chose Munich and researching some musty philosopher over art competitions and honors society dinners, the kind of stuff they usually loved to brag about.

I sat down next to my duffel, pulled the cell phone from the front pocket of my gray and yellow messenger bag, flipped it open, and checked the time. It was nearly five o'clock in Chicago and would have been midnight in Munich, although they were probably halfway over the Atlantic right now. I wanted to call them, to hear their voices, but since that wasn't an option, I pulled up my mom's cell number and clicked out a text message: @ SCHOOL IN ROOM. It wasn't much, but they'd know I'd arrived safely and, I assumed, would call when they could.

When I flipped the phone closed again, I stared at it for a minute, tears pricking at my eyes. I tried to keep them from spilling over, to keep from crying in the middle of my first hour at St. Sophia's, the first hour into my new life.

They spilled over anyway. I didn't want to be here. Not at this school, not in Chicago. If I didn't think they'd just ship me right back again, I'd have used the credit card my mom gave me for emergencies, charged a ticket, and hopped a plane back to New York.

"This sucks," I said, swiping carefully at my overflowing tears, trying to avoid smearing the black eyeliner around my eyes.

A knock sounded at the door, which opened. I glanced up.

"Are you planning your escape?" asked the girl with the nose ring and black nail polish who stood in my doorway.

Chloe Neill was born and raised in the South, but now makes her home in the Midwest—just close enough to Cadogan House and St. Sophia's to keep an eye on things. When not transcribing Merit's and Lily's adventures, she bakes, works, and scours the Internet for good recipes and great graphic design. Chloe also maintains her sanity by spending time with her boys—her favorite landscape photographer and their dogs, Baxter and Scout. (Both she and the photographer understand the dogs are in charge.) Visit her on the Web at www.chloeneill.com.